## Praise for *Eternal*

"I absolutely loved this page-turning novel. The writing is superb, and the historical research is outstanding. *Eternal* is an important book about the Holocaust and fascist Italy, and tells a story that needs to be told. As a Holocaust educator and a Child Refugee Survivor of the Holocaust, I strongly recommend everyone read this book."

—Dr. Miriam Klein Kassenoff, Director, The Holocaust Teacher Institute,
University of Miami

"*Eternal* brings to vivid life the drama and tragedy of a dark chapter in history."

—Dr. Stanislao Pugliese, Fulbright Scholar, Distinguished Professor in
Italian and Italian-American Studies at Hofstra University

"What Elena Ferrante did with her Neapolitan Quartet, Scottoline does for war-time Rome: brings it to life as the city is ripped apart by men in power and barely held together by the courage and decency of those who stand against them. *Eternal* is a must read."

—Lorenzo Carcaterra, author of *Three Dreamers*

"At its heart, *Eternal* is a beautiful, heartbreaking, yet ultimately uplifting love story. Meticulously researched, this riveting World War II-era novel explores what happens when beautiful Elisabetta must choose between lifelong best friends Sandro and Marco. As they get caught up in the madness that overtakes Italy when it becomes a satellite of Hitler and the Third Reich, each must make a gut-wrenching choice that determines the course of the rest of their lives. Action-packed and haunting, *Eternal* will stay with you for a long time after you finish reading it. I loved this book!"

—Karen Robards, author of *The Black Swan of Paris*

"Lisa Scottoline is a magnificent storyteller. *Eternal* is a triangular story of first love, told against the backdrop of WWII in Rome, that is both terrifying and magical; three young people at one of the worst times in history are filled with love, hate, fear, rage, and at the end, survival and hope. *Eternal* is brilliantly written. Scottoline hits new heights in this spellbinding tale of decades-old family secrets and rips apart the fragility of first loves. I was pulled in from the first page by the lives of Scottoline's characters as they tried to make their way through events beyond their control in this richly detailed story that makes you feel like you're right alongside them."

—Andrew Mayne, author of *The Girl Beneath the Sea*

"This nuanced take on WWII Italy offers a variety of perspectives, but at its heart, this is a love story, with heroes lost being warmly remembered and love conquering all. . . . Best-selling crime writer Scottoline successfully changes course in a coming-of-age WWII love story that will entrance fans and newcomers alike."

—*Booklist*

"Scottoline's admirable foray into historical fiction . . . expertly brings historical events to life. Fans of WWII fiction will be drawn to this immersive, emotional novel."

—*Publishers Weekly*

"Quite a change from Scottoline's bestselling contemporary thrillers: an ambitious, deeply researched historical account of three Roman families caught in the meltdown of fascist Italy . . . Heartfelt."

—*Kirkus Reviews*

"A powerfully moving story of loss, loyalty, family, and love."

—*Woman's World*

"*Eternal* offers us hope. Somehow love really can save the day—romantic love, brotherhood, spiritual love, love for a good nation and the democratic process. May the scholarship and literary invention of this extraordinary novel find a home in the hearts of readers everywhere."

—Bookreporter.com

# ETERNAL

## Lisa Scottoline

G. P. PUTNAM'S SONS
NEW YORK

**PUTNAM**
—EST. 1838—

G. P. PUTNAM'S SONS
*Publishers Since 1838*
An imprint of Penguin Random House LLC
penguinrandomhouse.com

Front matter map reprinted from *Muirhead's Northern Italy 1927 Blue Guide*,
courtesy of Touring Club Italiano.
Image on title page and part openers by Shutterstock

The Library of Congress has catalogued the
G. P. Putnam's Sons hardcover edition as follows:

Names: Scottoline, Lisa, author.
Title: Eternal / Lisa Scottoline.
Description: New York: G. P. Putnam's Sons, [2021]
Identifiers: LCCN 2020053286 (print) | LCCN 2020053287 (ebook) |
ISBN 9780525539766 (hardcover) | ISBN 9780525539773 (epub)
Classification: LCC PS3569.C725 E79 2021 (print) |
LCC PS3569.C725 (ebook) | DDC 813/.54—dc23
LC record available at https://lccn.loc.gov/2020053286
LC ebook record available at https://lccn.loc.gov/2020053287

First G. P. Putnam's Sons hardcover edition / March 2021
First G. P. Putnam's Sons international edition / March 2021
First G. P. Putnam's Sons trade paperback edition / February 2022
G. P. Putnam's Sons trade paperback edition ISBN: 9780525539797

Printed in the United States of America
1st Printing

Book design by Lorie Pagnozzi

*For my wonderful daughter, Francesca, with all my love*

Pal. Massimi
17
Pal. Vidoni
V. d. Sudario
S. Andrea d. Valle
S. M. d. Grotta
Pio
E m a n u
V. Arco d. Ciambella
d. Pigna
v. del Gesù
pza Grazioli
Pal. Grazi
S. Franc. d. Stimmate
Pal. Altieri
V. del Ple
14
16
e l e
pza d. Gesù
Gesù
S. M
Teatro Argentina
S. Nicola de' Cesar.
V. d. Barbieri
Pal. Bolognetti
V. d. Botteghe Oscure
V. Florida
SS. Carlo ni Catinari
P. di S. Anna
Piazza Arenula
V. Arenula
Pal. Cactani
Pal. Mattei
S. Cater. d. Funari
Margana
Ponte di età
Fte. Specchi
Pal. Santacroce
18
Pta. Cairoli
V. de' Falegnami
V. d. Plauto
pza Costaguti
pza Mattei
V. de' Funari
V. d. Delfini
pza Campitelli
Min. di Giust.
e Aff. di Culto
olette
Via Arenula
Via S.
Pal. Cenci
V. Cenci
Bart.
V. Progresso
Ghetto
V. Catalana
Via Portico d'Ottavia
Vecchio
Sinagoga
S. Maria in Campit
S. Angelo in P.
Portico Ottavia
Vallati
Lungotevere d. Cenci
Teatro di Marcello
Pal. Orsini
pza 15
Montanara
Ponte Garibaldi
Ospedale Fatebenefr.
13
Ponte Fabricio
Lungot. d. Pierleoni
S. Nicola in Carc.
V. Bocc
Isola Tiberina
16
S. Bartolomeo
S.
anzio
19
L. d. Anguillara
Piazza Sonnino
Ponte Cestio
Casa di Cres
S. Agata
Torre d. Anguillara
Lungot. d. Anguillara
Lungot. d. Alberteschi
S. Criso-gono
Lungaretta
pza in Piscinula
Via d. Salumi
Pte. Rotto
Coorte d. Vigili
V. de' Genres.
18
Pte. Palatino
Cloaca Massima
Bocc

## DRAMATIS PERSONAE

**THE D'ORFEO FAMILY,
OF TRASTEVERE**

Ludovico, father

Serafina, mother

Elisabetta, daughter

Rico and Gnocchi, willful cats

**THE SIMONE FAMILY,
OF THE GHETTO**

Massimo, father

Gemma, mother

Rosa, daughter

Alessandro "Sandro," son

Cornelia Rossi, nanny and
housekeeper

David Jacobs, Rosa's boyfriend

**THE TERRIZZI FAMILY,
OF TIBER ISLAND**

Giuseppe "Beppe," father

Maria, mother

Emedio, firstborn son and priest

Aldo, middle son

Marco, youngest son

**OTHER CHARACTERS**

Giuseppina "Nonna" Servano,
matriarch and owner of Casa
Servano

Paolo, her son

Sofia, his wife

Commendatore Buonacorso,
Fascist officer

Comandante Spada, retiring
Fascist officer

Carmine Vecchio, Fascist thug

Stefano Pretianni, Fascist thug

Rolf Stratten, Nazi aide-de-camp

Professor Tullio Levi-Civita,
mathematician

Ugo Foà, President of the Jewish
Community of Rome

Dante Almansi, President of the
Union of Italian Jewish
Communities

Lieutenant Colonel Herbert
Kappler, highest-ranking officer of
the Schutzstaffel, or SS, in Rome

Baron Ernst von Weizsäcker,
German Ambassador to the Vatican

*Omnia vincit amor.*

Love conquers all things.

—VIRGIL

❧

# Elisabetta

May 1957

---

Elisabetta had kept the secret for thirteen years, but it was time to tell her son who his father was. She had been waiting until he was old enough, but she didn't want to delay any longer. He deserved to know the truth, and she had never been comfortable concealing it from him. The secret had grown harder to keep over time, like a bag of groceries carried the first block, then the second, but by the third must be set down.

She stood at the kitchen sink, finishing her coffee, and the apartment was quiet and still, as her son was out playing soccer. She prepared herself for the conversation, realizing she would have to relive the worst days of her life and even of her country's history, since her youth had encompassed the *ventennio*, the twenty years of Mussolini's rule and a war that had turned Italy topsy-turvy, during which good had become bad and bad had become powerful.

Tears filmed Elisabetta's eyes, but she blinked them away. She hoped she could make her son understand why she hadn't told him. The revelation would shock him, as he suspected nothing, resembling her so strongly that it was as if his father's biology expressed itself in his personality, rather than his facial features.

Her gaze strayed to the window over the sink. She eyed a view ingrained in her memory, from Trastevere to Vatican City, a palimpsest unique to Rome, which had been adding to itself since the beginning of Western civilization, layer upon layer of travertine marble, brick arches, medieval turrets with crenellations, and the red-tiled roofs of houses with façades of amber and ochre. Church domes dotted the timeless scene, interspersed with palm trees, cypresses, and umbrella pines. Soaring above them all was Saint Peter's Basilica, its iconic dome gilded by the Italian sun.

Elisabetta withdrew from her reverie and set her coffee cup in the sink. Her son would be home any minute. The kitchen filled with the aroma of lasagna, his favorite meal. She had made it because he was going to hear a difficult story, but one he needed to know. One she needed to tell.

She heard the front door open, and he entered the apartment, dropping his soccer ball. She braced herself. *"Ciao, amore!"*

"Mamma, are we having lasagna?"

"Yes! Come in the kitchen, would you?"

# PART ONE

Let everyone, then, have the right
to tell his story in his own way.

—Ignazio Silone, *Fontamara* (1933)

The One remains, the many change and pass;
Heaven's light forever shines, Earth's shadows fly;
Life, like a dome of many-colour'd glass,
Stains the white radiance of Eternity,
Until Death tramples it to fragments.—Die,
If thou wouldst be with that which thou dost seek!
Follow where all is fled!—Rome's azure sky,
Flowers, ruins, statues, music, words, are weak
The glory they transfuse with fitting truth to speak.

—Percy Bysshe Shelley, "Adonais" (1821)

❧

## CHAPTER ONE

# Elisabetta

May 1937

E lisabetta made up her mind. Marco Terrizzi would be her first kiss. She watched him doing bicycle tricks by the river, riding on his back tire, his head thrown back in laughter, his teeth white against his tanned face. His thick, dark hair shone with pomade in the sun, and his legs were knotted with muscles inside the baggy shorts of his uniform. He rode with joy and athleticism, achieving a masculine grace. Marco Terrizzi had *sprezzatura*, a rare and effortless charm that made him irresistible.

Elisabetta couldn't take her eyes from him, and neither could the others. They had grown up together, but somewhere along the line, he had gone from boyhood to manhood, from Marco to *Marco*. That he was terribly handsome there could be no doubt. He had large, walnut-brown eyes, a strong nose, a square jaw, and a broad neck marked by a prominent Adam's apple. He was the most popular boy in their class, and everything about him seemed more vivid than everyone else. Even now, the sun drenched him in gold, as if Nature herself gilded him.

Elisabetta wondered what it would be like to kiss him. She guessed it would be exciting, even delicious, like biting into a ripe tomato and letting its juices run down her chin. She had never kissed a boy, though she was already fifteen years old, and at night she practiced kissing on her pillow. Her tabbycat, Rico, with whom she slept, had grown accustomed to her routine, as cats endure the silliness of young girls.

Elisabetta had no idea how to make Marco think of her as more than a friend. She usually achieved what she set her mind to, getting good grades and such, but this was different. She was too blunt to flirt. She lacked feminine wiles. She had been a *maschiaccio*, a tomboy, when she was little, which was how she had grown close with Marco. She was trying to become more womanly, but she still didn't wear a brassiere. Her mother said she didn't need one, but the other girls made fun of her, talking behind their hands.

"Elisabetta, help, I'll drown!" Marco raced toward the river, and she was about to call to him, but stopped herself. She had read in a female advice column that denying men the attention they craved drove them mad with desire, so she ignored him, while the other girls responded.

"Marco, no!" Livia called back.

"Marco, be careful!" Angela gasped.

The boys waited to see if calamity befell Marco, but he cranked the handlebars, veering away from the river's edge. They laughed and returned to their textbooks, spread out on the grass. They were doing homework, having come from their Balilla meeting, the party's compulsory youth group. They all wore their uniforms, the boys in their black shirts and gray shorts, and the girls in white muslin shirts and black skirts.

This quiet spot on the riverbank, just north of the Ponte Palatino, had become a hangout of her classmates after school, though Elisabetta typically sat with Marco or Sandro, apart from the other girls. Somehow she had missed her chance to become their girlfriend, and it was too late now, for they rebuffed her overtures. Perhaps they had judged her as preferring the boys, which wasn't true, and she would have loved to have had a good girlfriend. Whatever the reason, Angela and the other girls kept her at a distance, and she tried not to let it bother her.

"Look, Betta!" Marco called again, using her childhood nickname.

"Use my proper name!" Elisabetta called back, from behind her newspaper. She did prefer her full name, as she hoped to become a journalist someday. She practiced her byline at night, too. *By Elisabetta D'Orfeo.*

"Elisabetta!" Marco rode over, sliding to a stop on the grass. "Hop on my handlebars. Let's go for a ride."

"No, I'm reading." Elisabetta hid her smile behind the newspaper.

Angela rose, brushing grass from her skirt. "Marco, I'll go, take me!"

"Okay!" Marco extended his hand, Angela clambered onto his handlebars, and the two rode off together.

Elisabetta lowered her newspaper, wondering if the female advice column had been wrong. If she wanted Marco, she would have to attract him another way. She sensed she was pretty enough, now that she had grown into her features, according to her mother. Her large, round eyes were greenish-brown, and her shoulder-length hair was a rich brunette, wavy and abundant. Her nose was strong, but proportional to her prominent cheekbones, and her lips were full. Her problem was her *bocca grande*, big mouth, which proved a disadvantage when it came to boys, her Latin teacher, and that old bitch at the newsstand.

Elisabetta leaned back on her elbows, breathing in the odors of the Tiber, its water a milky jade with wavelets topped with ivory foam. Swallows skimmed the surface for a drink, cicadas rasped, and dragonflies droned. Pink oleander bushes, umbrella pines, and palm trees lined the riverbank, and the natural oasis was shielded from the hustle-bustle of the city by gray stone walls.

Elisabetta's gaze found the Ponte Rotto in the middle of the river, a bizarre sight. Centuries ago, the stone bridge had connected the riverbanks, but time had reduced it to only a single arch rising from the water, leading nowhere. Romans called it the broken bridge, but she thought that it was a survivor, standing despite the elements and the Tiber itself, which sent blackish-green vines up its sides, as if trying to pull it underwater.

Beyond the Ponte Rotto was Tiber Island, the only island in the river, barely large enough to contain the Basilica di San Bartolomeo all'Isola with its faded-brick belfry, the Church of San Giovanni Calibita, and the hospital, Ospedale Fatebenefratelli, with its rows of green-shuttered windows. Across from the hospital was Bar GiroSport, which Marco's family owned and lived above. Elisabetta lived only a few blocks away from him in Trastevere, the bohemian neighborhood that she and her father loved. Unfortunately, her mother had ceased loving anything.

It was then that Elisabetta spotted Sandro Simone striding toward her and the others. Sandro was her other best friend, and Marco's, too, as the three of them had been a trio since childhood. Sandro walked with his characteristically lanky stride, and his light brown curls blew back from his long, lean face. He was handsome in his own way, his features more refined than Marco's and his build like a sharpened pencil, slim but strong, the way a wire cable supports a modern bridge.

"*Ciao*, Elisabetta!" Sandro reached her, smiling and taking off his fez. He wiped the sweat from his brow, slid off his backpack, and sat down. His eyes, a brilliant azure color with long eyelashes like awnings, narrowed against the sunlight. His nose was long and aquiline, and his lips finely etched into his face. Sandro lived on the east side of the river in the Jewish quarter, called the Ghetto, and throughout their childhood, Elisabetta, Sandro, and Marco had traveled back and forth on an axis from Trastevere to Tiber Island and the Ghetto, riding bikes, playing soccer, and generally acting as if Rome were their private playground.

"*Ciao*, Sandro." Elisabetta smiled, happy to see him.

"I stopped to get us a snack. Have one." Sandro produced a paper bag from his backpack and opened its top, releasing the delicious aroma of *supplì*, rice croquettes with tomato sauce and mozzarella.

"*Grazie!*" Elisabetta picked up a *supplì* and took a bite. The breading was light, the tomato sauce perfectly salty, and the mozzarella hot enough to melt on her tongue.

"Where's Marco? I brought some for him, too."

"Off with Angela."

"Too bad." Sandro chewed a *supplì* and glanced at her newspaper. "What are you reading?"

"Nothing." Elisabetta used to love reading the newspaper, but her favorite columnists were gone, and she suspected they had been fired. Benito Mussolini and the Fascists had been in power for fifteen years, and censorship had become the order of the day. "All the articles are the same, about how great the government is, or they reproduce ridiculous posters like this one."

"Let me see." Sandro wiped his hands on a napkin.

"Here." Elisabetta showed him a picture of an Italian peasant woman in traditional dress, holding babies in each arm. She read him the caption. " 'The ideal Fascist woman is to bear children, knit, and sew, while men work or go to war.' It's propaganda, not news, and anyway, not all women are the same."

"Of course they aren't. The newspaper isn't always right."

"No, it's not." Elisabetta thought of the female advice column. Marco and Angela still weren't back.

"Don't let it bother you."

"But it does." Elisabetta disagreed with the Fascists, though she didn't discuss it with anyone other than Sandro and Marco. Those who spoke against the government could be arrested and sent into *confino*, exile, far from their homes. Informers abounded in Rome, even in Trastevere, and though Elisabetta's family wasn't committed to any particular political party, as artists they were congenitally leftist.

"You don't like being told what to do."

"Who does? Do you?"

"No, but I don't take it so much to heart as you." Sandro leaned over. "Guess what, I have amazing news. I was accepted to an internship with Professor Levi-Civita at La Sapienza."

"*Davvero?*" Elisabetta asked, astonished. "You, a high school student? At the university?"

"Yes, it will be an independent study." Sandro beamed with pride.

"Congratulations!" Elisabetta felt delighted for him. He was a mathematical prodigy, and his preternatural talent had been plain since primary school, so she shouldn't have been surprised that he would be at La Sapienza, the city campus of the University of Rome. "And this professor is the one you always talk about, right? Levi-Civita?"

"Yes, and I can't wait to meet him. He's one of the greatest mathematicians of our time. He developed tensor calculus, which Einstein used in his theory of relativity. In fact, he just got back from seeing him in America."

"How wonderful. How did this come about, anyway? For you?"

"Professoressa Longhi recommended me, and I've been waiting to hear. I just stopped by the hospital to tell my mother."

"She must be so proud." Elisabetta admired Sandro's mother, who was one of the few female doctors she had ever heard of, an obstetrician at Ospedale Fatebenefratelli.

"She was, but she was surprised I hadn't told her I was being considered."

"I am, too. Why didn't you tell us?" Elisabetta meant her and Marco.

"I didn't want you to know if I failed."

"Oh, Sandro." Elisabetta felt a rush of affection for him. "You never fail, and Levi-Civita is lucky to have you. You'll be a famous mathematician someday."

Sandro grinned. "And you'll be a famous journalist."

"Ha!" Elisabetta didn't know what Marco would become, but dismissed the thought.

"How can you read in the sunlight?" Sandro squinted at her newspaper. "It's so bright."

"It is, I know."

"Allow me." Sandro slid the newspaper page from her hand and stood up.

"No, give me that back." Elisabetta rose, reaching, but Sandro turned away, doing something with the newspaper.

"It's only the obituaries."

"I like the obituaries." Elisabetta always read the obituaries, as each one was a wonderful life story, except for the endings.

"*Ecco.*" Sandro held out a hat of folded newspaper, then popped it on her head. "This will keep the sun from your eyes."

"*Grazie.*" Elisabetta smiled, delighted, and all of a sudden, Sandro kissed her. She found herself kissing him back, tasting warm tomato sauce on his lips until he pulled away, smiling down at her, with a new shine in his eyes that confused her. She had just decided that Marco would be her first kiss.

"Sandro, why did you do that?" Elisabetta glanced around, wondering if the others had seen. Her classmates were bent over their homework, and though Marco was approaching with Angela on his handlebars, he was too far away.

Sandro grinned. "Isn't it obvious why?"

"But you never kissed me before."

"I never kissed anybody before."

Elisabetta felt touched. "So why me? Why now?"

Sandro laughed. "Who asks such questions? Only you!"

"But I thought we were just friends."

"Are we? I—" Sandro started to say, but Marco interrupted them, shouting from a distance.

"*Ciao*, Sandro!"

"*Ciao*, Marco!" Sandro called back, waving.

Elisabetta blinked, and the moment between her and Sandro vanished, so quickly that she wondered if it had happened at all.

CHAPTER TWO

# Marco
### May 1937

M arco pedaled home from the river on the Lungotevere dei Pierleoni, the wide boulevard that ran along its east side. The sun had dipped behind the trees, shooting burnished rays through the city, which had come to boisterous life as the workday ended. Cars honked, drivers cursed, and exhaust fogged the air. The sidewalks thronged with people, and businessmen hustled to catch trams.

Marco accelerated, preoccupied with Elisabetta. He was in love with her, but she treated him as a pal, the way she always did. She hadn't even cared when he had taken Angela on his bike. He felt stumped, which never happened to him with girls. He could have his pick, but he wanted Elisabetta. She was beautiful, which was reason enough alone, but he loved her passion, her strength, her *fire*. She had thoughts about everything, and though her intelligence was superior, she treated him as if he were equally intelligent. Marco would stop at nothing to win her over. He was love's captive.

He flashed on seeing Sandro by the river today, standing oddly close to her, as if they had been having a great discussion or even sharing a secret. Anxiety gnawed at Marco, and he experienced a flicker of envy at the bond that Sandro and Elisabetta shared, for they were always talking about books or the like. But Marco knew that Sandro and Elisabetta were only friends, and Sandro had no female experience whatsoever.

Marco turned onto the Ponte Fabricio, his tires bobbling on the worn travertine. The footbridge was the oldest in Rome, walled on both sides— and since it connected to Tiber Island, it was essentially the street on which he lived. He dodged businessmen and veered smoothly around a cat that darted in front of him. He reached the top of the gentle span and saw that his father, Beppe, wasn't standing outside his family's bar, Bar GiroSport, as he usually did. It meant that Marco was late to dinner.

He sped to the foot of the bridge, passed the bar, and steered around to its side entrance on Piazza San Bartolomeo all'Isola. He jumped off his bicycle, slid it into the rack, then flew inside the crowded bar. He scooted upstairs, dropped his backpack, and entered a kitchen so small that one pot of boiling water could fill it with steam. On the wall hung framed photos of his father in the Giro d'Italia and a calendar featuring Learco Guerra, the great Italian bicycle racer. A small shelf held a framed photo of Pope Pius XI, a crucifix of dried palm, and a plaster statue of the Virgin. Marco's mother worshipped Christ; his father worshipped cycling.

"*Ciao*, everyone!" Marco kissed his two older brothers, Emedio and Aldo, then his father, as they were sitting down at the table.

"Marco!" Emedio smiled, looking like a younger version of their father. Both had curly, dark brown hair, a prominent forehead, and thick brows over coal-dark eyes, wide-set above broad noses and flat mouths. Marco's father still had the muscular build of a professional cyclist, his skin perennially tanned and his upper lip scarred from a wolf attack in the mountainous farming region of Abruzzo, where he had grown up. The story was that Marco's father, only ten years old at the time, had been watching the family's sheep when the wolf had struck, but the boy had wrestled the animal to the ground, then chased it away. No one who knew Beppe Terrizzi doubted the veracity of the story.

"*Ehi, fratello.*" Aldo smiled in his tight-lipped way, self-conscious due to his teeth, which were crooked in front. He took after the Castelicchi side, with a quieter temperament, eyes set close together, and a characteristic cleft in the chin. Aldo was the shortest of the Terrizzi sons, but he loved cycling and still had on his sweaty white jersey and bike shorts. If their mother wished he would change for dinner, she would never say so. Everyone knew who ran the household, and it wasn't her.

"Mamma, that looks delicious. *Brava*." Marco kissed her as she was la-dling *pomodoro* sauce with whitish chunks of crabmeat onto a platter of spaghetti for the first course. Bright orangey claws stuck through the red-dish pulp, their pincers jagged, and the uniquely fishy tomato aroma made him salivate.

"*Ciao*." His mother smiled up at him, her small, light brown eyes warm. Steam billowed from the sink, curling the dark tendrils that had escaped her long braid, and she had a flat nose, a broad smile, and the honest, open face of a country girl. Marco's parents were *contadini*, of peasant families, and they had grown up in houses shared with goats and chickens. They had married and moved to Rome, where his father had parlayed his cycling celebrity into Bar GiroSport. The café was frequented by hospital employ-ees, locals, and cycling fans, called *tifosi*, for they were as crazy as those afflicted with typhus.

"Just sit, son." His father motioned from at the head of the table.

"Here, boys." His mother set the platter of spaghetti near Marco's father, served him first, then the rest. They prayed over the meal, and everyone ate quickly except for Marco, who savored every bite while his father quizzed Aldo about his training times. Emedio stayed out of the line of fire, having escaped a cycling career by entering the priesthood. Marco could never make such a sacrifice, as he had a duty to the female population. And someday, to Elisabetta.

His mother turned to Emedio, who worked at the Office of the Holy See. "What news? Anything?"

"Did you hear about the German encyclical on Palm Sunday?"

"No, what is it?"

"*Mit Brennender Sorge*. It means 'With Burning Anxiety' in German. The Pope issued an encyclical that was distributed to almost thirty thou-sand German churches, a direct message to German Catholics." Emedio leaned over. "Cardinal Pacelli assisted in its composition, but I tell you that confidentially."

His mother drew her index finger across her lips like a zipper, and her eyes twinkled. To her, Vatican gossip was the best gossip.

"The encyclical was read by German parish priests to their congrega-tions, with no prior notice to anyone. Can you imagine, all those churches, and no one let it slip out? It was printed and distributed in complete secrecy."

"Why in secrecy?" His mother frowned. "It's the word of Our Holy Father."

"It was reiterating his teaching that German Catholics should follow God, not Hitler. As a result, Hitler sent the Gestapo to arrest those who had printed and distributed the encyclical."

"How terrible!"

His father shot Emedio a look. "No politics at the table."

Emedio fell silent, and their mother pursed her lips. His father was a Fascist of the First Hour, meaning he had joined in 1919, even before the March on Rome in 1922, when the King appointed Mussolini to be Prime Minister. Traditional by nature, his father believed that the party would be good for small business owners, as well as bring law and order to Italy.

His father cleared his throat. "Now, as I was saying, this will be a significant year for the Giro, and I know who will win the pink jersey. I predict Bartali will repeat his victory."

Aldo nodded. "I agree, though I'm putting a side bet on Bini. And Olmo, who was so fast in the Milan–San Remo."

"No, wrong." His father sipped some wine. "The Milan–San Remo is child's play. And Del Cancia won, anyway. You'll lose your money, Aldo."

"No matter who wins, he shouldn't wear the pink jersey. Think of it. Pink?" Aldo chuckled, and Marco had heard this before. Mussolini had declared that pink was an effeminate color, confusing Fascists and *tifosi* alike.

His father scoffed. "The color of the jersey isn't the point. The achievement is all. Right, Marco?"

"Yes, Papa."

"Marco, you know, I was at the window tonight, watching you when you turned onto the bridge. You were late for dinner."

"I'm sorry, Papa."

"That's not my point." His father rested his bulky forearms on the table, his gaze newly intense. "You rode very well. You held your line. You even picked up speed. You surprised me."

Marco didn't interrupt, feeling a knot in his stomach.

"I saw what happened with the cat, too. It ran into your path, but you didn't lose a split second. It's time for you to train in earnest. Imagine what you can do with my regimen, son. You could wear the *maglia rosa* someday. You could win the Giro, the premier race in all of Italy. You could take your place in cycling history."

"Papa, I'm not that good," Marco said, since it was the last thing he wanted.

"I think you can be. It's in your blood."

Aldo frowned. "Papa, what about me? I'm training hard."

Their father turned to Aldo. "I've told you, you're not building the muscle you should. You're not getting any faster. You must not be working hard enough."

"I'm trying."

"Keep at it, then. Prove me wrong. Two are better than one, anyway. You can train together." His father's head swiveled back to Marco. "Son, tonight you begin. Understand?"

"Yes, Papa," Marco answered, having no choice in the matter.

## CHAPTER THREE

# Sandro

### May 1937

Later, Sandro sat alone at the dining room table. The night air wafted through the window, and the crystal chandelier shed a gentle light on his notebook. His family had just had dinner, and he was supposed to be working, but his head was full of Elisabetta. He didn't understand how to think about anything else while you were in love. He marveled that people did so, every day. He had never *felt* anything so intensely in his life. His intellect enabled him to think so much, but perhaps until now he had felt too little.

He couldn't stop thinking about when he'd kissed her, by the river. The thrilling closeness of her body, nearer to him than ever before. He loved everything about her, especially the way she regarded him. As his intellectual abilities had come to the fore, everyone treated him differently, whether for good or ill; the teachers adored him, but his classmates thought him odd. Elisabetta did neither. She had liked him from the beginning, for who he was inside, and so he could be himself with her.

Sandro's gaze strayed out the window. The Simones lived in one of the houses lining the elegant Piazza Mattei, on the Ghetto's north side. Their apartment was on the third floor, catercorner to the refined Palazzo Costaguti, and he could see his neighbors through their windows. Giovanni Rotoli was doing homework at the table, and on the floor below him the Nardunos, an older couple, were sharing the newspaper. The Ghetto was typically quiet at night, and the only sound was the water bubbling in the Fontana delle Tartarughe below, the fountain of the turtles.

Sandro loved living in the Ghetto, which was the oldest living Jewish community in Western Civilization. The Community was established nearly two thousand years ago, when Jerusalem had fallen to the Emperor Titus, who had sacked the Temple and brought Jews back to Rome as slaves. The conquest was commemorated in the grand Arch of Titus in the Roman Forum, which Gentiles viewed as a majestic arch but many Jews considered a symbolic yoke. In 1555, the Ghetto was created, and Pope Paul IV had ordered that walls be built surrounding the neighborhood, with doors that were locked at night and guards on patrol, for which the Community had to pay. There were thousands of Jews in Rome at the time, and they were compelled to wear yellow badges and forced to live in the Ghetto, packed into about a hundred and thirty homes on a handful of city blocks that encompassed less than three hectares, or seven acres. It was considered the least desirable neighborhood in Rome, situated on low-lying ground that flooded every winter from the Tiber, bringing malaria and other diseases. Its streets were narrow and dark, permitting little light or circulation of air. Churches were built at its entrances, and Jews were forced to listen to sermons pressuring them to convert.

The Ghetto walls were torn down in 1888, after Rome had been absorbed into the new nation of Italy in 1870, and Jews were permitted to come and go. The Ghetto was cleaned and an embankment built around the Tiber to prevent flooding. A beautiful synagogue, the Tempio Maggiore, was consecrated in 1904, with its square dome that distinguished it from the hundreds of churches with round ones. Some said that the synagogue was designed to be the tallest building in Rome, since Saint Peter's Basilica was technically in Vatican City, and it became the spiritual home of the Community. Many Roman Jews still lived in the Ghetto, although those with means had moved away. Sandro's house had been in his father's family for generations, so the Simones would never dream of leaving, though they were far better off than their neighbors.

Sandro's thoughts were interrupted by bickering from the kitchen, where his sister, Rosa, and his mother had begun fussing. His father, Massimo, was in his study, and Sandro heard him close his door. Rosa, an interpreter at the British embassy, could argue in five languages. Suddenly his sister burst from the kitchen, smoothing her hair into its dark, glossy twist. She was a beauty, with quick brown eyes, a straight nose, and lips that looked full, especially when she wore lipstick. She was ten years older than Sandro and always dressed stylishly, tonight in a blue suit with a tiny belt.

Rosa's disconcerted gaze found Sandro at the table. "She drives me crazy!"

"What's the matter?"

"I want to go to London." Rosa came over and sat down. "I got the time off, and I'm spending my own money, but she says I can't go. I'm an adult and I can make my own decisions."

"If you're an adult, why ask permission?"

Rosa hesitated. "If I go, she'll get mad."

"She'll get over it. You always forgive each other."

"Maybe you're right."

"I know I am."

Rosa eyed his notebook. "What are you working on? Would I understand?"

"No." Sandro wondered if Rosa might have advice for him about Elisabetta. "To tell you the truth, I'm not getting much done. I'm in love."

"You're too young to be in love."

"You're too old to ask permission."

Rosa laughed. "But you look so serious. You don't seem happy about it."

"What's more serious than love?" Sandro didn't add that Elisabetta was a girl to be taken seriously. He doubted his sister would understand, as her hobby was cynicism.

"Okay, who are you in love with?"

"Elisabetta." Sandro loved saying her name.

"You pal around with her and Marco like you're the Three Musketeers. You treat her like one of the boys." Rosa looked at him like he was crazy. "Do you think women like that, *genius*?"

Sandro didn't think anyone was a genius about women, except Marco. "So what are you saying? Do you have some advice?"

"Of course." Rosa shifted closer. "Start by telling her you like her hair or her dress, and that she looks pretty. That will lay the foundation, and she'll be more inclined to you. Don't say it all at once. Spread it over a few days. Give love time to work."

"You make it sound like magic."

"It is, in a way. And bring her a gift. What does she like?"

"Newspapers."

"I meant something romantic, like flowers."

"Books are romantic. She likes to read."

Rosa rolled her eyes. "Fine, a book. Then, after you have done those things, tell her you love her and kiss her."

Sandro hadn't realized he was supposed to bring gifts, *then* kiss her. Evidently there were steps like a mathematical proof, and he had done them out of order. He felt stupid, a sensation he disliked. "What if she sees me only as a friend?"

"Be optimistic. Your feelings grew. Maybe hers did, too."

"What if she likes somebody else?"

Rosa smiled warmly. "That's not possible. Who's better than you?"

"Marco."

"Oh no." Rosa's smile faded. "Does Marco like her, too?"

"Marco's better, isn't he?"

Rosa burst into laughter. "No, I was kidding!"

"Really?"

"Really."

Sandro didn't believe her, but he didn't ask again.

## CHAPTER FOUR

# Marco

### May 1937

The night was cool, and Marco rode far behind his brother Aldo, who was turning onto the Lungotevere Aventino. Traffic congested the boulevard, and Marco didn't know why his brother was riding ahead of him. They had grown up training in the conventional method, taking turns in each other's draft to save energy. Marco's breath grew ragged, and his thighs burned. If it was hurting him, it had to be killing Aldo.

Marco put on a burst of speed and caught up with him. "Aldo, slow down!"

"No!" Aldo pedaled like a madman. Sweat slaked his face and drenched his jersey.

"What's wrong with you? Stop!"

"Leave me alone!" Aldo accelerated, and so did Marco. They were flying, one brother beside the other, blood racing blood. Marco clamped a hand on Aldo's forearm, and both bikes wobbled crazily, but Marco was the stronger rider and he kept his grip on Aldo, forcing him to slow. The traffic zoomed past them as the two bikes skidded to a rough stop, side by side.

"What's the *matter*?" Marco shouted, angry. He hunched over, panting, and his mouth tasted of exhaust fumes.

"I don't want to ride with you!" Aldo's eyes flashed with anger in the headlights.

"Because Papa said to? It's not my fault! I don't want to race!"

"Everybody knows that but him!"

"So don't blame me!"

Aldo exhaled heavily. "Marco, listen, I didn't want to tell you this, but I don't really train at night. I only pretend to. That's why I'm not getting any faster."

"What do you mean?" Marco felt dumbfounded.

"I go elsewhere, and you're ruining it. I can't ride with you at night."

"What are you talking about? Where do you go?"

Aldo hesitated. "I have a woman."

"You, Mr. Shy Guy?" Marco burst into astonished laughter. "*Bravo*, Aldo! You've been lonely too long, brother!"

Aldo didn't brighten. "She's married."

"Married?" Marco repeated, worried. Aldo had had his heart broken before, as he was too reserved a fellow to press his suit, and his only loves had gone unrequited. As a result, he could be naïve when it came to the opposite sex, and there were plenty of husbands with jealous hearts.

"Don't tell. It would kill Mamma and Papa."

"Agreed." Marco nodded, knowing their mother. There weren't enough novenas in the world.

"How long have you been seeing her?"

"About six months. I met her by chance, on the street. Her husband works the night shift, so this is the only time she can see me."

"You love her?"

"Deeply. It pains me not to be with her all the time, but I can't *not* love her."

Marco felt the same way about Elisabetta. She had been a part of his life for all of his life, and if he had to pinpoint the moment he had fallen in love with her, it had been when he was only eleven. She had tumbled into his arms while they were playing soccer, and the unexpected warmth of her touch had raced through his body like an electrical charge.

Aldo shifted onto his bicycle seat. "I'm going to see her. Meet me at the bridge at ten thirty. We'll ride home together, with no one the wiser. Goodbye."

"Goodbye." Marco felt a mixture of pride and concern, watching Aldo until he lost sight of his white jersey.

## CHAPTER FIVE

# Aldo
### May 1937

Aldo left Marco and raced down Via dei Cerchi, surprised that he had convinced his younger brother of the story. He was a bad liar because he had never had anything to lie about, until now. He had known that Marco would accept the story because romantic love motivated his younger brother. But Aldo was his own man, and though he had been unlucky with women, he believed that love came in many forms. Love of God, love of country. There was more to him than anyone in his family knew. He was charting his own course in life, and the stakes were getting higher for him, in ways he could never have imagined. He was past the point of no return.

He lowered his shoulders and pedaled southward, toward the quiet outskirts of the city. Traffic diminished, and trees and grass appeared, then became abundant. The night grew darker, since there were no streetlights and little ambient light, and sweat cooled on his forehead. He breathed in a deep lungful of air, and it smelled like grass, hay, and manure. He sailed past the Circo Massimo, deserted at this hour, and maintained his speed past the ruins of Terme di Caracalla, hulking shadows in the dark.

He reached the Via Appia Antica, the most ancient route of this ancient city. There was less traffic, but nevertheless it was perilous to cycle here, for he had to keep his tires from wedging between the cobblestones and the road was narrow, made for pedestrians, horses, and even chariots. Tree limbs grew overhead, and he struggled to see in the darkness. In time there were no lights at all, and no houses or buildings. If it hadn't been for the moonlight, Aldo wouldn't have been able to see where he was going.

His jersey was soaked, his thighs burned, and his heart pumped hard. He kept his pace even though the wind blew stronger here, and the elevation was higher. He reached a vast, open pasture near a quarry for *pozzolana*, volcanic rock, and raced across a dirt road in a pasture. He spied an over-grown ravine marked by a lone tree, which was the appointed spot.

He pedaled there, jumped off his bicycle, and slid the flashlight from the pack under his seat, then turned it on. He moved the vines aside and exposed the other bicycles that lay camouflaged on the ground. He left his bicycle with them and covered it with underbrush, an excessive precaution in this rural area, but he could take no chances. He walked thirty paces south, light-ing the way to a spot where more vines had been used as a cover. He moved them aside, revealing a tunnel barely big enough to accommodate him.

He crouched into a racer's tuck and scrambled into the tunnel, then cov-ered the entrance behind him. He used his flashlight to light the way, and the tunnel was earthen on all sides, connecting to the ancient catacombs of the early Christians, an underground cemetery containing hundreds of thousands of graves, a veritable *necropolis*, city of the dead. Some of the entrances were known, but some weren't, which made the catacombs the perfect meeting place.

Aldo scrambled downward in the tunnel, descending lower and lower. He reached the bottom of the crypt and found himself in a narrow hallway with a packed floor. The air was coldest here, chilling his skin in the damp jersey, and he made the Sign of the Cross on his chest, out of respect for this sacred place. The walls on both sides contained *loculi*, rectangular niches in tiers excavated into the *tufo*, a grayish-red volcanic rock. They were stacked from floor to ceiling, a hallway lined with the remains of the early Christians, which had been wrapped in sheets, closed behind the *loculus*, and then sealed inside the tomb with lime. Here and there he spot-ted the shorter graves of children.

Aldo hurried ahead through a bone-cold maze. He was taking his life in his hands, coming here. At nineteen, he was old enough to follow his heart, even if it led him down a dark tunnel. He had joined a cell of fervent anti-Fascists opposing the regime, and as such, had become an enemy of the state. Informers abounded, and Mussolini's secret police, OVRA, were known to arrest, torture, and kill anti-Fascists with impunity.

Aldo had tried to be the son his father wanted, a cyclist and a Fascist, but he had doubts about the party from its earliest days. When he was younger, walking with his father on an errand, they had seen a cobbler beaten in the street for making a joke about a Blackshirt. His father had said the man was one of the "thuggish element" in the party, but the crime had made Aldo wonder whether thugs were the exception, or the rule.

He had noticed that the textbooks changed in school, publishing only propaganda, and Mussolini had made radios inexpensive so that his speeches could be heard everywhere. The party exalted ultra-patriotic pride in Rome, *Romanità*, and in Italy, *Italianità*, but that troubled Aldo, too. He didn't believe that one race was superior to others, but rather that all men were children of God, beloved in His eyes. Aldo shared his mother's deep faith, so he was appalled to see the Fascists follow Mussolini as if he were Christ himself, calling him Il Duce and replacing the Ten Commandments with the ten Decalogues. No mortal could erase God from Aldo's heart, and soul. He had witnessed Mussolini's rise, feeling daily more oppressed, his heart had grown heavy, and he felt as if he was living life with his head down, until he realized he had to stand up and fight for the country he loved.

He kept going, and as he got closer to the others, he heard their voices echoing, inflected with a mixture of dialects, for they came from all over Rome and its outskirts. They had been meeting for about six months, but they changed their meeting places in case they were being surveilled.

Aldo's step quickened, driven by purpose, and he hurried toward the light at the end of the hallway.

CHAPTER SIX

❧

# Elisabetta

### June 1937

———

The morning sun peeked through the shutters, but Elisabetta was already awake, cuddling her tabbycat, Rico. His face was perfectly proportional, with not too long a nose, Tiber-green eyes, and a mouth that occasionally revealed a tooth, as evidence of his ferocity. An excellent mouser, Rico would occasionally bite her, albeit without malice. Otherwise he accepted the affection she showered on him, since he regarded himself as the most important thing in her world, and perhaps all of Italy.

Elisabetta got out of bed and slid off her nightgown, pausing to gauge the growth of her breasts, cupping them as if her hands were scales. They felt nice and soft, and they were heavier, which satisfied her. She remembered when they had first appeared on her chest, feeling like olives under her skin, but they had grown to apricots, then lemons, and finally tangerines. Surely they were fruity enough to justify a brassiere.

She dressed in her uniform, then opened the shutters, breathing in the natural perfume of the star jasmine climbing up the wall. Her window overlooked the back of their house, which offered a view of small gardens stuffed with potted plants, flowers, and herbs. She loved flowers and wanted a garden when she grew up, so Rico could chew the parsley plants.

The sky was clear, and the sun rose over the east bank of the river, above the Ghetto. Elisabetta knew Sandro would be waking up, too, and she wondered if he was thinking of her, after that kiss. Oddly, nothing had seemed different between them since then. Marco had been his usual self, too, but showing more interest in Angela than her. Elisabetta wondered if boys were worth the trouble.

She left the bedroom and hurried into the kitchen with Rico at her heels, his tail held like an exclamation mark, as all cats have punctuation in their repertoire. He jumped to the table while she went to the refrigerator, which they had come into after the old man upstairs had died. She found a sardine tin and forked some fish onto a plate, mashing the oily gray flesh and flimsy bones.

She started the coffee brewing, got *fette biscottate*, twice-baked bread, and put them on plates. She ate while Rico purred and chewed, sounding like clothes on a washboard. The coffee began to percolate, and she turned off the stove and poured some for her mother and father.

"Mamma, coffee!" Elisabetta called out, and her mother came hurrying into the kitchen, off to teach singing. Her mother, Serafina, had a heart-shaped face with remarkable light blue eyes, an unusually fine nose, high cheekbones, and a small mouth. Her caramel-brown curls had been combed into a loose topknot, and her filmy dress clung to the lovely curves of her body. She had the stunning beauty of the artists' model she had once been, which was how she had met Elisabetta's father, posing for his painting class. She still carried herself as a woman aware of her effect on men, though lately she worried about getting wrinkles, spending hours with a cold rag to the corners of her mouth, hoping to forestall them. And her unhappiness at their home life was palpable, as if it had become a member of the family.

"Good morning." Elisabetta handed her mother her coffee.

Her mother drank it, squinting. "Oh, that's hot."

"Mamma, I really think I need a brassiere. Can we—"

"No, I told you, you don't need one. Stop asking me. When I was your age, my breasts were twice your size."

Elisabetta's face burned. Her mother's breasts were grapefruits, but that wasn't the point. "Still, mine are big enough."

"I said no. You're too young. Brassieres are for women, not girls."

"I'm the only girl in my class who doesn't have one."

"You can't be." Her mother scoffed, setting down her coffee.

"I am. I see through their shirts, and they see through mine. They tease me."

"Ignore them. You don't need them. Women are jealous creatures." Her mother picked up a *fetta biscottata* and went to the chair for her purse, but Elisabetta went after her.

"Mamma, please, I'm old enough. You don't even have to buy it for me. I bet I can sew one myself, if you let me keep my pay. The sewing teacher says that cotton costs—"

"*Basta*. I'm late." Her mother opened the door and left, closing it behind her.

Elisabetta shook off her disappointment, picked up her father's coffee and *fetta biscottata*, and went to the living room, where he was sleeping on the couch. His face was long and slender, unshaven, his shaggy hair a dark brown. An empty wine bottle rested in his misshapen fingers, which had healed improperly after a bicycle accident when Elisabetta was an infant. The injury had ended his painting career and started his drinking career. His vibrant watercolors of Trastevere covered the walls of their apartment, capturing the neighborhood's charm as well as its mystery, with its tiny alleyways that disappeared into darkness. It was almost inconceivable to Elisabetta that her father had painted them, given his current condition, but they showed her the colors that illuminated his soul.

"Papa, good morning, wake up." Elisabetta set the breakfast down on a side table.

"Oh, my head hurts." Her father opened his eyes, a bloodshot brown, and he broke into a smile. "Such a pretty one you are. I love you so much, my darling."

"I love you, too." Elisabetta meant it, even though her mother called her father an *ubriacone*, a drunk. Her parents used to quarrel, but even that had stopped and her mother had withdrawn from him. Elisabetta understood her mother's unhappiness, but didn't share it. Her father had tried many times to stop drinking, and he hated himself for his failing. She couldn't blame him when he blamed himself so harshly, and she knew that he loved her. Wine made one speak the truth, and her father's words to her were always tender.

Her father stroked her cheek. "My darling little Betta, are you happy? Are you?"

"I am, Papa. Here, have some coffee." Elisabetta helped him bring the cup to his lips.

"Delicious." Her father shifted upward on the sofa. "That helps my headache. What would I do without my girl? Your heart, it's as fierce as a lion. Mark my words, that's what matters in life."

"I'm sure." Elisabetta smiled, for she had heard this many times.

"Tell me, have you gotten the newspaper yet? What's that thug up to now? Parades and marches? Guns and knives? Those idiots follow him like sheep! But *he* is the wolf!"

"Shh, Papa." Elisabetta worried that passersby would hear, since their apartment was on the ground floor and the window was open.

"Is it a nice day? Perhaps I'll paint *al fresco*." Her father closed his eyes again. "I'll paint something wonderful, I just know it. I feel the tingling in my fingers. How they itch for the brush."

"You rest." Elisabetta had heard this before, too. Sometimes she wondered if he said it for her benefit, or if he even knew that he hadn't painted in years. She kissed his grizzled cheek, then rose with the empty wine bottle. "I have to go to school. Bye, now."

"Of course, goodbye, my darling girl, my special light, I love you so much."

"I love you, too, Papa."

"Fetch me a bottle before you go, will you, my dear?"

CHAPTER SEVEN

# Marco

June 1937

Marco watched dustmotes swirl in a shaft of sunlight, while his classmates were getting their essays from their backpacks. The classroom was stifling, small, and devoid of decoration other than the Italian flag, a large wooden crucifix, and portraits of King Vittorio Emanuele III and Il Duce. A sign bore the party credo, CREDERE, OBBEDIRE, COMBATTERE—Believe, Obey, Fight. There were thirty other students in his class, including Elisabetta and Sandro, all dressed in their uniforms.

Their teacher, Professoressa Longhi, was an older woman with thick glasses and gray hair in a bun, thick-waisted in her dark dress, which sported the tricolor emblem. She motioned for them to sing *"Giovinezza,"* the party anthem, and the class rose halfheartedly, weary of the routine this late in the school year. She didn't reprimand them, and Marco suspected she had joined the party only to keep her job, as he had noticed her rolling her eyes at their textbooks from time to time. The standard joke was that some teachers joined the PNF, the Partito Nazionale Fascista, but others joined *Per Necessità Famigliare*, only to support their family. Secretly he felt the same way, a Fascist because of his father, and it was the only way he knew. At heart, he believed in love, not politics.

Marco began to sing with his classmates, loudly to make Elisabetta laugh:

> "Your warriors' valor,
> Your pioneers' virtue,
> Alighieri's vision,
> Today shines in every heart."

Marco turned around to see if Elisabetta was laughing, but instead she was looking at Sandro, whose desk was near the front. Her face bore a curious expression, one that Marco hadn't seen before, and he had seen all of her expressions. She lifted her right eyebrow when she listened, she frowned when she read the newspaper, and she wrinkled the bridge of her nose when she laughed hard. She could even look dreamy-eyed, like when she watched the screen at the movies. Oddly, she was looking that way now, at Sandro.

Marco felt bewildered, remembering the afternoon that he had seen Sandro and Elisabetta standing close at the river. What if something had happened between them? Were they becoming more than friends? Neither of them had told him so, but then he hadn't told either of them about his own feelings. Marco couldn't imagine competing with Sandro for Elisabetta, and it was inconceivable that any girl, even she, would come between them.

"Class, please take your seats," Professoressa Longhi said after the song ended. "Let's get started. Take out your essays."

Marco sat down, retrieved his essay from his backpack, and hid his paper so no one would see his handwriting. His letters were large and deformed, as if written by a much younger student. His teachers thought he was sloppy or careless, but the truth was worse. Writing and reading were a struggle for him, even at his age. His classmates could read with ease, even aloud, but every time he looked at a page, the words appeared to him as a collection of nonsensical squiggles and he had to figure out their meaning from the context, or from what the teachers said. He didn't recognize any of the words except for the ones that reoccurred, like Mussolini, and Marco had begun to fear that he was simply born stupid, which shamed him. His grades were falling, and last year, one of his teachers had summoned his mother, telling her that he had to study harder. His mother had nagged him and prayed to Saint Thomas Aquinas and Saint Joseph of Cupertino, but Marco knew he would have been better off with Saint Jude, Patron Saint of Lost Causes.

"Okay, class, let's begin. Who would like to read his essay aloud?"

Marco raised his hand, according to one of the stratagems he had devised to hide his deficiency. He would volunteer to read, instead of waiting to be called upon, so he could control when he spoke. Then he would pretend to read his essay aloud, making his eyes move back and forth like the others did, but he would simply be speaking about the subject of the assignment. Marco had an excellent recall, able to remember everything the teacher had said, so he had learned the information, and he loved attention, so he was an entertaining speaker. None of his classmates had guessed his secret, so far. But every day, he worried that the king of the class would become its buffoon.

Last night's homework had been to write an essay entitled "Mussolini's Greatness from My Unique Viewpoint," and Professoressa Longhi had explained the assignment was to be a personal essay, rather than the generic treatise that filled the new textbooks, showing Il Duce commanding vast crowds, firing a gun, harvesting wheat bare-chested, piloting an airplane in goggles, leaping over obstacles on horseback, swimming, hiking, and even playing with a lion cub.

"Marco," said Professoressa Longhi, "come read your essay. Sandro, you'll read yours next, after Marco."

Marco rose and walked to the front of class, then Professoressa Longhi cocked her head, as if she had a second thought. "Marco, why don't we do something different this time? Why don't we switch? You read Sandro's essay, and, Sandro, you read Marco's."

"No, wait," Marco said, his mouth going dry, but it was too late, as Sandro was coming to the front of the class.

"Marco, here." Sandro handed Marco his essay. "Let me have your essay."

"I wrote it in a hurry, that's why it's messy." Marco handed Sandro his essay.

"It's perfect, written with passion and vigor." Sandro smiled, and Marco realized that Sandro was covering for him.

Professoressa Longhi motioned from her desk. "Marco, please begin. Read us Sandro's essay."

"Okay." Marco stared at Sandro's assignment, stricken. He recognized a few words, but he couldn't begin to read the essay, which was written in his best friend's neat handwriting. Marco's heart began to pound, and he swallowed hard. He glanced up to see Elisabetta looking at him with a sweet and expectant smile. He couldn't bear her reaction if she found out that he couldn't even read. She loved newspapers and books, and she would never fall in love with him then. She would pity him, and he would be humiliated in front of her.

"Marco?" Sandro said, all of a sudden. "I'll read your essay first, if that's okay with you."

"Sure." Marco nodded, his cheeks aflame.

Sandro cleared his throat. " 'As everyone knows, my interest is cycling, and I see Mussolini in that way. Like a cyclist who must keep his balance, no matter the terrain, our leader guides Italy . . .' "

Marco listened with astonishment, and Sandro managed to decipher some of Marco's horrible handwriting and made up the rest as he went along, inventing insights about cycling and Mussolini that Marco himself would have thought of. Only a friend who knew him so well could accomplish such a feat, and the class listened to the end, then clapped.

Professoressa Longhi nodded. "Marco, that essay was fascinating! Now, Marco, would you read Sandro's?"

"Certainly." Marco realized he could make it up, too. " 'Benito Mussolini excels in literature, but particularly, in regard to mathematics. Mathematics requires logical adherence to rules, much like Fascism itself . . .' "

Marco continued, moving his eyes back and forth, and Sandro nodded as if Marco were reading exactly what he had written. Marco finished the essay and bowed with a flourish, and everyone clapped again.

"*Bravi*, boys!" Professoressa Longhi beamed. "Sandro, that is the most thoughtful analysis I have ever heard!"

The boys walked side by side back to their desks.

Elisabetta smiled at them both, and Marco sat down, reassured. He must have been mistaken, and nothing must have happened between her and Sandro that day by the river.

## CHAPTER EIGHT

# Sandro

### June 1937

---

S andro sighed, sitting next to his mother. Night had fallen outside the window, and the dinner table had been set with their best china, silverware, and crystal glasses. His sister had met a new beau in London and was bringing him to dinner tonight, but they were late, and so was Sandro's father, Massimo. His mother was annoyed, for as she always said, tardiness was allowable only in babies born past their due date.

His mother, Gemma, was an elegant woman, dressed tonight in a sheath of gray linen with a pearl necklace and matching earrings. She wore her graying hair back in a chic twist, and her eyes were bluish-gray behind her steely glasses, which perched on her long nose. Her face was long, too, but in a refined way, with a neck like a Modigliani painting. She was weary after a long day at the hospital, and Sandro was proud of having a mother who was also a doctor, though the neighbors talked behind their hands about her, for not being at home like a proper mother.

The aroma of fried conch and roasted potatoes wafted in from the kitchen, where their housekeeper, Cornelia Rossi, was preparing the meal. "Mamma, can't we eat?" Sandro asked, his stomach growling.

"Of course not. We'll wait for the others."

"Dottoressa, I can't keep the first course warm any longer." Cornelia, a heavyset widow in her sixties with a cheerful temperament, entered the dining room with a platter. She had been Sandro's nanny, but had stayed on as a housekeeper, and he loved her like a second mother. Her hooded eyes were dark, her nose wide, and her smile omnipresent.

"I understand, thanks." Sandro's mother shook her head. "We'll watch it get cold."

Cornelia set the platter on the table. "*Buon appetito*. Sandro, I made *olive all'Ascolana*."

"Thank you!" Sandro said. Cornelia was from Ascoli Piceno, and her specialty was its signature dish, breaded olives stuffed with lamb, beef, cheese, vegetables, and seasoning. "Mamma, please, may I start?"

"Just one."

Sandro popped a fried olive into his mouth, and it exploded with taste on his tongue. The breading was thin, golden brown, and crunchy, and the meat filling had a warm, spicy sweetness. "Delicious, Cornelia."

"Yes, *grazie*." Sandro's mother reached for an olive.

"You're welcome." Cornelia smiled, then left the room.

Gemma turned to Sandro. "So, how was school today?"

"Fine, and I picked up a new assignment from Enzo, Levi-Civita's graduate assistant."

"Good." His mother chewed thoughtfully. "Are you enjoying the work?"

"Yes, but it's difficult."

"You can do it." His mother smiled. "Have you met Levi-Civita yet?"

"No. He's always busy in his office."

"Maybe you should introduce yourself. I'm sure he'd love to meet such a brilliant young man."

Sandro chuckled. "Levi-Civita once found an error that Einstein had made in his calculations, in his *Entwurf* paper. Do you really think he would love to meet a fairly able student from a local *liceo*?"

His mother laughed. "You could be the next Levi-Civita. Did you ever think of that?"

"Perhaps, in my dreams." Sandro wasn't kidding, for he had dreamed as much.

"You must believe in yourself. Levi-Civita chose you, didn't he?"

"He also chose a slew of students from all over the world."

"Still, I'm proud of you." His mother touched his arm. "I know you think I'm nagging you, but don't mistake me. I urge you forward not for your own personal ambition, but for something more important. God has given you a magnificent gift in your intellectual abilities, and He did so for a reason. That reason is for you to discover, and pursue."

Sandro blinked in surprise, having never heard his mother speak that way, and he knew all of her lectures. He had no immediate response, but the conversation was interrupted by the opening of the apartment door, and it was Sandro's father. Massimo Simone was older than most of the fathers of Sandro's classmates, and his hair, sparsely black with silvery strands, looked windblown. He was of such a short stature that he had been called Minimo in school, so he had sought refuge in his studies, which had led to his profession as a tax lawyer. Sandro's father always told the story to show that one could turn disadvantage to advantage.

*"Buona sera, sposa e giovanotto."* His father took off his hat, his dark eyes lively behind his bifocals. "Sorry I'm late, but the meeting at the synagogue ran long." His father came over and kissed his mother. "Guess who's the new general counsel to the Board?"

"Not you, is it?" his mother asked, with indulgent disapproval.

"Yes, the very same. Perhaps I'll make something of myself yet." His father sat down, with a wink.

"But you're already so busy, Massimo."

"Perhaps, but this is important, and I'm needed."

"That's wonderful, Papa." Sandro felt happy for his father. The Jewish Community of Rome was governed by a Board of fifteen men called Councilors, who were also responsible for administering its affairs, paying bills, and taking census information. His father had been advising them unofficially on legal matters, spending more and more time at the synagogue, so it was nice to have his role acknowledged, even though Sandro's mother was probably right about his schedule.

The door opened again, and at last Rosa entered on the arm of a tall redheaded man with bright blue eyes, a nice smile, and freckles. He wore a dark suit of English tailoring, and Rosa seemed in high spirits, in a black dress she saved for fancy occasions. "Mamma, Papa," she said, "sorry we're late! Everyone, this is David Jacobs. He just started at the embassy."

"Welcome to our home, David." His father rose and shook the young man's hand.

"Signor Simone, thank you for having me." David turned to Sandro's mother with a well-mannered nod. "Dottoressa Simone, thank you, too."

"Welcome, and please, sit down. May I serve? The meal's getting cold." Sandro's mother shot Rosa a look, but Rosa was oblivious, pulling out a chair for David. Sandro thought he had a kind manner, though his Italian sounded schooled, which could be forgiven. They both took their seats, and Rosa winked at Sandro. He was delighted to see the shine in her eyes, but felt a touch regretful. He hadn't mustered the courage to give Elisabetta a gift, having lost any momentum he had gained since their kiss at the river.

His father said a prayer over the meal and raised a glass of wine. "Rosa, tonight is a special occasion. Not only do we have a guest at the table, but I've been elected to the Board. Let's toast to Italy's good fortune, under me and Mussolini."

Rosa laughed. "*Bravo*, Papa!"

"*That's* a surprise," David blurted out.

Sandro's father blinked, and Rosa shot David a warning glance. Silence followed, and they sipped their wine in momentary awkwardness. Sandro's mother began serving everyone, but David turned to Sandro's father.

"Signor Simone, my apologies. My comment didn't sound the way I intended. What I meant was, I'm surprised that you can be Jewish and so ardently Fascist."

"Thank you for your apology, but it's unnecessary." Sandro's father smiled pleasantly. "As for your confusion, many Jewish families are proud Fascists. As a statistical matter, Jews join the party in the same proportion as Gentiles."

David pursed his lips. "My surprise is due to the blatant anti-Semitism of Adolf Hitler, in Germany. Doesn't that concern you, as a Jew?"

"Yes, but National Socialism has nothing to do with us. We're Italian Fascists, and there's no anti-Semitism in Italian Fascism. Il Duce was in power for a long time before Hitler even appeared on the scene, not the other way around. Hitler imitates Mussolini, not vice versa."

"Yet Hitler is Chancellor of Germany."

Rosa shifted in her chair, and Sandro wondered if she was trying to kick David under the table, like she used to do to him when he was little.

His father cleared his throat. "But that's beside the point. Germany is Germany, and Italy is Italy. We defeated the Germans in the Great War. I myself served as an army officer, in the Twenty-Ninth Piedmont Infantry, and many Jewish veterans belong to our party. We wanted a strong leader, and the economy has grown under Mussolini. He simplified our byzantine tax laws, and my practice is more robust than ever. I represent many small businessmen, and all of them are doing better." His father picked up his fork. "One prominent Jewish banker, Ettore Ovazza, encourages more Jews to become Fascists. I may travel to Turin to see him, in my newfound capacity."

His mother interjected, "Really, Massimo? When?"

David frowned. "Signor Simone, the question isn't how you view yourself, but how others view you."

Rosa shifted again in her chair, and this time Sandro spotted David wince.

His father cocked his head. "I can tell you, our fellow Italians view us as Italian Jews, which we are. The Simone family is among the most Roman of Romans, and our family's ancestors came to Rome not only before Christ, but before the destruction of the Temple." His father rested his forearms on the table. "Jews have completely assimilated here, as shown by the rate of intermarriage, about fifty percent. A former Prime Minister, Luigi Luzzatti, was Jewish, and so was a former Mayor of Rome, Ernesto Nathan. I could go on and on, listing prominent Jewish citizens and leaders."

Sandro had heard this speech before. His father kept a running tally of successful Jews, as if keeping score for the home team.

"I agree with my husband," his mother interjected.

"Thank you, dear." His father flashed his little smile. "A rare victory."

Everyone laughed, lightening the mood, and his mother sipped her wine. "David, I never experience antipathy at the hospital, though it's associated with the Church. My colleagues feel the same way."

His father added, "And Mussolini is no anti-Semite. He has a Jewish mistress."

"Massimo, please." His mother glanced at Sandro, who already knew what a mistress was, but his father continued.

"He lives with her and her daughter. Ovazza told me so, he knows Mussolini personally, isn't that something?"

His mother rolled her eyes. "You're still not going to Turin. You don't have the time."

David nodded. "Then I stand corrected. As a Jew, I never underestimate anti-Semitism—"

"David, on to brighter topics," Rosa interrupted him. "Why don't you tell my parents about your family in Gloucestershire? I'm sure they would love to hear!"

## CHAPTER NINE

# Elisabetta

### July 1937

Aafter school, Elisabetta changed into her blue-and-white checked dress for her waitressing job, and Rico watched from the bed, his eyes narrow with resentment. She hadn't had time to give him attention, as she had to finish her housework and make dinner for her father, who had taken to bed.

"I'm sorry, Rico." Elisabetta scratched him, but he didn't forgive her enough to purr. She left the bedroom just as her mother came home with her friend Giulia Martorano, whom Elisabetta adored. Giulia was as warm and exuberant as her mother was chilly and sour, and Elisabetta always wondered why Giulia remained friends with her mother, who treated her badly, tolerating her rather than enjoying her company. Giulia had big brown eyes, plump cheeks, and an oversized smile, with a face framed by glossy black curls. Her clothes were from a palette that only an art teacher would wear successfully; a blouse of pink and red flowers paired with a voluminous emerald-green skirt and a long necklace of *millefiori* beads.

Elisabetta met them in the kitchen. "*Ciao*, Mamma, Giulia."

"*Ciao*." Her mother looked typically lovely in a white pique dress that showed her figure to advantage, and she set down her purse with a heavy sigh. Elisabetta knew that her mother wanted to be asked what was wrong and she was about to do just that, when Giulia swept her up in a hug.

"How's my girl?" Giulia kissed her, and Elisabetta kissed her back.

"I'm good, *grazie*."

Giulia beamed. "You're more beautiful every day, and I loved the essay you wrote. Your mother gave it to me to read."

"Oh, how nice!" Elisabetta relished the praise. Last week, she had written an essay entitled "On the Necessity of Cats," hoping to submit it to a newspaper and get an internship. She had gotten the idea from Sandro and wanted to try, even though she had never written anything outside of school, except for various letters to the editor, which the newspapers didn't publish. She had wanted to write on a weightier subject such as the rights of women, but she had noticed that the few female journalists wrote only about domestic life, household tips, or beauty advice. Besides, cats mattered, at least to her.

"I had no idea you were such a good writer, dear. Your essay was very clever, and your authorial voice is original."

"You're not saying that because you know me, are you?"

"Not at all." Giulia patted her arm.

"Do you think it's good enough to be published?"

"Absolutely. They might even pay you."

"That doesn't matter to me. I would be proud—"

"It should matter." Elisabetta's mother interrupted her from the chair, where she sat rubbing her feet. "We need money. Be practical."

"I am, Mamma."

"No, you're not. You're wasting your time in school."

Elisabetta didn't want to fight about school again. She loved learning and wanted to stay until graduation.

"You'll never be a journalist, Elisabetta. They don't hire girls. Anyway, it doesn't pay like waitressing."

"But I don't want to waitress my whole life, and money isn't everything."

"That's your good-for-nothing father talking."

Elisabetta flushed, ashamed when her mother disparaged her father, especially in front of someone else. Her mother resented that her father didn't support their family, even though Elisabetta worked harder than her mother. It was her own waitressing money, not her mother's singing lessons, that paid the rent. But her mother had wanted to become an opera singer, and losing the chance had embittered her.

Giulia smoothed over the awkward moment, fishing in her purse and handing Elisabetta the essay. "Here we go. Good luck. Just don't offer it to *Il Tevere* or *Il Popolo*. Fascists don't care about a woman's point of view. Or cats."

"Thank you." Elisabetta turned to her mother. "Mamma, what did you think of it?"

"I didn't read it. I told you I was too busy. Did you feed your father?"

"Yes, he's in bed."

"Of course." Her mother sighed heavily again. "Don't you have to get to the restaurant?"

"Oh yes." Elisabetta picked up her purse and put the article inside. "I'd better go. Goodbye."

Her mother nodded, still rubbing her feet.

"Goodbye, dear." Giulia kissed Elisabetta's cheek. "I hope to see you again soon."

"Me, too." Elisabetta left the house, brightening as she stepped outside, since it was impossible to stay glum walking through Trastevere. She loved her neighborhood, with its small houses and pretty pastel façades, and each home unique, with a wrought-iron balcony that had ivy dripping down, or a little shrine to the Virgin embedded in a façade, or a window strung with festive, colored lights. It felt freer here than in Rome proper, and because the buildings were fewer stories, more sky showed. Twilight was a wash of transparent blue with the stars shimmering behind, waiting for their chance to shine.

Elisabetta passed the Basilica di Santa Maria in Trastevere, its graceful arches lighted, illuminating its lovely cornice and gilded mosaics. Taller buildings ringed the cobblestone piazza, and couples held hands or sat kissing on the steps of the fountain. Everyone socialized in the evening during the *passeggiata*, showing off their most presentable clothes. Girls promenaded in hopes of being seen, and boys did their best to oblige.

Elisabetta thought about Marco and Sandro when she kissed her pillow, but after experiencing the real kiss with Sandro, even her vivid imagination couldn't transform the dryness of the cotton fabric into the remarkable warmth and softness of a boy's mouth. But Sandro hadn't tried to kiss her again, and Marco had been monopolized by Angela and the other girls, all of whom flirted with him. Meanwhile the teasing about Elisabetta's not having a brassiere had intensified, and Angela had started calling her *Centesimi*, copper pennies, claiming that her nipples showed through her shirt. Now Elisabetta held her books or schoolbag against her chest at all times.

She took a left, winding her way through the narrow streets, approaching the restaurant, Casa Servano. The place wasn't much to look at from the outside, an old converted house with an ugly door of brown wood set in a façade of cracked gray stucco, and only a single window. Neither a sign nor a menu was posted, and no one frequented Casa Servano except locals, who knew it served the best homemade pasta in Rome. Since working here, Elisabetta had learned why.

She reached the restaurant and let herself into the dining room, which was empty because they weren't open yet. The ground floor of the house fit only ten tables and on the right, a bar with stools. The ceiling was of embossed tin, and the white stucco walls were adorned with photographs of the Servano family, who had owned the place for generations. At the center of every photo was Nonna Servano, the *matriarca*.

"*Ciao*, Elisabetta." Paolo, Nonna's son, smiled from the bar, where he was drying wineglasses. He was short and skinny, balding even in his forties, but of a genial manner that served him well as manager and bartender.

"*Ciao*, Paolo! Well, what kind of mood is she in, good or bad?"

"Good. So I say *agnolotti*."

"I say *tortellini*." Their game was to guess which type of pasta Nonna would be making that night. In a good mood, she would make *pasta ripiena*, which were stuffed pastas like *ravioli*, *tortellini*, and *caramelle*, as festive as a gift wrapped with fresh dough. In a bad mood, she would make easy types like *spaghetti*, *bigoli*, and *tagliatelle*. Customers who were lucky enough to get a table at Casa Servano ate whichever pasta Nonna had made, for as she often said, *Only the pilot flies the airplane.*

Elisabetta reached the kitchen and pushed open the swinging door, greeted by delicious aromas. Paolo's wife, Sofia, labored over a cauldron, slow-cooking thick tomato sauce with meat, seasoned fresh basil, bay leaves, onion, and garlic. Paolo's cousin Vito was sautéing garlic, cousin Nino was filleting branzino, and second cousin Giovanni was scooping hot marrow from a bone. Steam billowed from a massive pot of boiling water, and sinuses were always clear in the kitchen.

Elisabetta greeted them and went to the pantry, where Nonna Servano sat making pasta in a high-backed chair at a wooden table, her presence so regal that she transformed a stockroom into a throne room. Her tiny head was shaped like a quail's egg, and her fine white hair was pulled back smoothly into a bun. Her steel-rimmed glasses perched on a beak-like nose, and cataracts had begun to impinge on her dark irises. Wrinkles draped her cheeks and radiated from her thin lips, drawn tight as a rubber band in concentration, as she worked. She wore a traditional black dress, a gold necklace with a filigreed crucifix, and earrings of coral drops that stretched her earlobes. Nonna was frail, but hardly weak, and she measured only 149 centimeters, but didn't appear small. She looked older than her sixty-seven years, but age hadn't diminished her faculties. On the contrary, she claimed that it had sharpened them, and nobody dared tell her different.

"*Ciao*, Nonna. What type of pasta are you making?" Elisabetta kissed her on her cheeks, which felt as soft as sifted flour.

"*Cappelletti*. Sit down, girl. You make me nervous, standing like a lamppost."

Elisabetta sat down. So Nonna was in a good mood, but neither Elisabetta nor Paolo had guessed correctly. Atop the wooden table, on a thin dusting of flour, lay flat sheets of dough, yellow with egg yolks, and one of the sheets had been scored into squares with a knife, which rested next to a floured wooden rolling pin, long enough to serve as a cudgel. A mound of pungent ricotta rested in the center of each square, waiting to be formed into shape by Nonna's fingers, still nimble despite her arthritis, perhaps from this very task.

"*Guarda,*" Nonna said. Watch. Nonna picked up the square of dough and folded it into a triangle. "Make sure the edges don't match. Leave a little at the bottom, then press them together and make the seal." She pushed gently on the dough with her fingertips, leaving the faintest prints. "You see?"

"Yes." Elisabetta had learned from watching Nonna that there were many different types of pasta, and sauces. Pulpy marinara sauce was served with shorter types, which were usually factory-made. *Fatto a mano*, homemade pasta, was never served with *aglio e olio*, oil and garlic, as the pasta absorbed too much oil. Lighter tomato sauces and *brodo*, broth, were best for ridged *cavatelli* and *radiatori*, as they trapped the sauce, and a little went a long way.

"Now, I fold." Nonna picked up the triangle by one of its corners on the long side, then picked up the other end with her left hand. Holding it between her thumb and forefinger, and with the triangle facing toward her, she slipped her right index finger around the back of the triangle and pushed the bottom upward. In one expert action, she brought the two corners together, pinching them, forming a perfectly round circle of filled pasta with a tiny triangle at the top, looking like a little cap, a *cappelletto*.

"Nonna, that's the way I fold napkins, isn't it?" Elisabetta flashed on Sandro, making her a hat from her newspaper by the Tiber.

"No, not at all. You weren't paying attention. I can't stop working to explain everything. The pasta will get hard." Nonna picked up another square. "I have something important to discuss with you. I have done you a great favor. I've asked a very special guest to dine with us."

"Who?"

"Your future."

"What do you mean?" Elisabetta had grown accustomed to such mystic pronouncements, as if Nonna were the *strega*, witch, of Casa Servano.

"Moro Gualeschi, a name you will undoubtedly recognize."

"Of course I do!" Elisabetta adored Gualeschi, whom she read every day. "He writes for the leftist papers. How do you know him?"

"I know everyone. Rather, everyone knows me." Nonna kept folding pasta. "Leftists, rightists, centrists, no matter. Politics comes and goes. You know what abides?"

"Love?"

"No, pasta. I say *sapore*, *sapere*, to taste is to know. One cannot know me without tasting my pasta. One cannot know Trastevere without tasting our pasta. Likewise, Gualeschi prefers stuffed pasta, so I know he is a man of appetite, one who savors life. I had considered making *cappellacci dei briganti* tonight for him."

"Why?"

"*Cappellacci dei briganti* is a hat with a wide brim that flips up, like the *briganti* used to wear after the Unification. I didn't make it because Gualeschi wouldn't have gotten the joke. Communists lack humor." Nonna folded another piece of pasta with her floured fingertips, and the yellow *cappelletti* lined up in front of her, awaiting her command.

In the next moment, the door swung open and Paolo popped his head into the kitchen. "Mamma," he said, "he's here."

Elisabetta jumped up. "Gualeschi is out there *now*? May I meet him?"

"You must."

"Thank you!" Elisabetta squealed.

"Don't embarrass me." Nonna's hooded gaze shifted sideways. "By the way, you need a brassiere."

Elisabetta reddened. "I'm trying—"

"*Ascolta*, I told Gualeschi that you wrote an article, and he agreed to read it."

"My article? How did you know about my article?"

"You never shut up about it. Do you think I'm deaf? Send it to him."

"I have it with me, in my purse."

"Then show it to him."

"Do you really think I should?"

"I just said you should." Nonna dusted flour from her fingertips. "I told him you're a magnificent writer."

"But you haven't read it. What if it's no good?"

"Have you *read* what they print?" Nonna pinched another *cappelletto*. "I told him to hire you immediately. People are always wondering what young people think. Mistakenly, in my view, but there you have it." She brushed flour from knobby fingers. "Go meet him. Don't go on and on like you do. Get to the point. You're too talkative."

"Thank you, thank you!" Elisabetta retrieved her article and headed for the kitchen door. "Wait, what does he look like?"

"Like a *rigatone*."

Elisabetta hurried off, pushed through the kitchen door, and glanced around. Several tables were occupied with couples, but seated alone near the door was a dark-haired man with heavy glasses, who was short and wide. A *rigatone*, indeed.

She beelined for Gualeschi's table. Her heart beat harder, and she realized that she could be taking the first step toward writing for a real newspaper. She wondered if she would look back on this day and tell this as a funny story, sitting at a table with her fellow journalists. If Sandro could have a brilliant future, then perhaps so could she.

Starting right this minute.

She reached Gualeschi's table. "Signor Gualeschi, my name is Elisabetta

D'Orfeo, and I admire your writing very much. I read you every day, and your article yesterday was especially interesting." She remembered Nonna's advice not to talk too much. "I'm sorry, I talk a lot, I know. It's just that I have so many thoughts."

"You can never go wrong praising a writer for his writing." Gualeschi blinked with amusement behind his glasses.

"But everyone must praise you, all the time."

"Not enough for my satisfaction, or with sufficient specificity. My mother thinks my apartment is too big, but I fill it with my ego." Gualeschi chuckled. "In any event, thank you for your kind praise. I understand you've written a piece for submission. You may send it to my attention at the newspaper."

"I have it with me, in fact." Elisabetta held out her essay, and Gualeschi accepted it with a smile.

"Excellent. I will read it during my meal, and we can discuss it afterward, if you have a spare moment."

"I would like that very much."

Suddenly the door of the restaurant burst open and slammed back against the wall, rattling the framed photographs. Standing in the doorway was Elisabetta's father, so drunk that he had to brace his hand on the wall to keep from falling over.

"Papa." Elisabetta's face flamed. Gualeschi grimaced, recoiling, as her father lurched toward her.

"Betta, my darling, look at you! I came to see if you had a few *lire* for me. Do you?"

Elisabetta felt mortified in front of Gualeschi. "Papa, no, please."

"I only need enough for a glass of red, or perhaps you can offer me one, on the house?" Her father looked around, stumbling, and the diners turned to watch. Her father tripped, and Elisabetta opened her arms just as he fell into them, a dead weight that knocked her off balance.

"Oh no!" Elisabetta struggled to stay upright, and Gualeschi leapt to his feet and took her father's arm.

"Allow me," the journalist said, dropping the essay.

"My Betta is so pretty, so smart, and I love her so, she's my darling angel." Her father mumbled, oblivious, then he started to cough.

Elisabetta realized what was going to happen.

In the next moment, her father vomited on her and Gualeschi.

And on her essay, which lay forgotten on the floor.

## CHAPTER TEN

# Marco

July 1937

M arco rode on Lungotevere Aventino under a dark sky, after Aldo had departed to see his secret girlfriend. The full moon was as round as a bicycle wheel, and lamps shone along the length of the Tiber. A fishy breeze blew off the water, and its rushing sounds soothed him.

He spotted a *gelateria* and headed toward it, then dismounted and went inside. A few people were in line, and the brightly lit place smelled of chilled fruit, sugar, and fresh cream. A glistening aluminum display case dominated the shop, and behind it two pretty girls scooped *gelato*.

Marco looked over the mounds of green *pistacchio*, rich brown *cioccolato*, and the happy yellow of *ananas*, or pineapple. Each had a handwritten sign that he couldn't read, but he didn't need to, and he could never decide which flavor. His current favorite was *nocciola*, hazelnut, and before that, his favorite had been *fiordilatte*, made from cream. Elisabetta loved *cioccolato* in a cone and she never changed.

"May we help you?" the shopgirls asked in unison, when Marco reached the counter.

"Yes, I can't decide which."

"Take your choice." The shopgirl smiled slyly. "We're both off at eleven."

The other shopgirl flushed. "Teresa!"

"That's a very generous offer." Marco smiled, but he wasn't tempted. He took this as a sign of maturity, or perhaps he had lost his mind due to his utter celibacy. Nevertheless he made his ice-cream choice in Elisabetta's honor. "I'll take two scoops of *cioccolato*, in a cone."

*Gelato* in hand, Marco paid and left. He licked his dessert, which tasted creamy and sweet, then he hopped on his bicycle, steering with one hand. The *gelato* began melting, so he looked for a place to stop. He found himself in the *centro storico*, the oldest part of the city, near the Roman Forum on Via dell'Impero, which was being expanded to showcase the ruins, under Mussolini's plan. The area was under excavation, avoided by most of the traffic, which meant it would be quiet, so he rode in that direction.

He reached a wooden fence that was more a suggestion than a barrier, like most in the city. He got off his bike, draped it against the fence, then climbed through an opening and looked for a place to sit down. The excavation site was a gigantic hole shaped like a square and shored on all sides by retaining walls of wooden planks. At the bottom of the hole was a floor of gray-white marble, glimmering in the moonlight.

Marco stood and ate as his eyes adjusted to the darkness. He had ridden through this district many times, but it had never been excavated before, and it intrigued him. He noticed a rope strung across railroad ties serving as a staircase to the bottom, so he finished his *gelato*, went over, and descended. The rich smell of earth filled his nose, and the air cooled as he went deeper. The sounds of the city receded into the distance, as the walls cocooned the site in silence.

Marco neared the bottom, where the marble floor seemed to collect and reflect the moonlight, creating a spectral haze that hovered like the ghosts of the ancients. He marveled at the phenomenon, and the hairs stood up on the back of his neck when he reached the bottom, standing in the soft glow of light all around him.

He walked along the floor, amid massive sections of columns that lay on their sides, some with florets carved into the marble and others with fragments of lettering. He ran his hand along their gritty surface and scanned the broken sections. Marco couldn't read Latin any better than Italian, but for the first time, it didn't bother him. He wedged his finger into one of the letters to measure its depth, and the marble came up to his first knuckle.

He withdrew his hand, overcome with awe. He had always known that there was a subterranean Rome, a city underneath the city itself, having learned as much in school and encountered random artifacts all over the city. But being here tonight made it real to him in a way it had never been before. He finally understood its meaning and felt his spirits soar. His ancestors had chiseled these letters, carved these columns, and constructed this magnificence. He couldn't read as well as his classmates, but now he knew he possessed native intelligence, as he was descended from these ancients.

He was a son of Lazio. Of Roma. And he stood tall, bathing in the moonglow, for a very long time.

**CHAPTER ELEVEN**

# Aldo

July 1937

---

Across town, Aldo hurried down the frigid hallway of the catacomb and reached a *cubiculo*, a small room containing a family crypt. There, the anti-Fascists sat on the floor around a few lighted candles, bottles of Chianti, and loaves of rustic bread. The men were of all ages, shapes, and sizes, but each face wore a similarly tense expression. Each man knew he was running a lethal risk in being here, so much so that for security reasons, they didn't reveal their true identities even to each other, but used *nomi di battaglia*, battle nicknames. The names were based on their appearance or demeanor, such as Bug Eyes, Chubby Cheeks, Broken Tooth, Apple Eater, and Pipe Smoker, or less obvious ones like Speaks French and the Tsar.

Aldo was called Signor Silenzio, and their leader went by Uno, self-appointed and self-named. Aldo didn't know anything about him, but surmised from Uno's demeanor and vocabulary that he was an intellectual of privileged background. Uno was tall and lean, with thoughtful brown eyes behind his horn-rimmed glasses, and his fine nose was set in a smooth face, with high cheekbones and small lips. His Italian was without dialect, though its inflection sometimes sounded Milanese to Aldo, who had heard a similar inflection from Milanese customers at the bar. It made Aldo feel geographically inferior to Uno, for snobs often said that Rome was only a Mediterranean city, but Milan was a European city.

"*Ciao*, Signor Silenzio." Uno rose quickly, shaking his hand. The rest of the men joined in, greeting Aldo.

"Here, Signor Silenzio." Uno's wife, whom they called Silvia, smiled and passed him a bottle of wine. She was the only female in the anti-Fascist cell, and Aldo felt shy around her, as with most women, especially because she was pretty. She had on a purple frock of a fine cut, and her bright blue eyes and straight blond hair evinced a northern Italian heritage. Aldo assumed she was Milanese, too, but she said little and Uno did all the talking.

"*Grazie*." Aldo sat down on the cold, hard floor of the crypt.

Uno remained standing, his face barely illuminated by the candlelight below and his shadow elongated on the crypt wall. "Now that we're all here, I will begin by saying that this is our most important meeting yet. As you know, so far we have engaged only in acts of sabotage against the regime, printing and distributing leaflets to convince others of the merits of our cause, or damaging cars, supplies, and other equipment. However, I have come to regard these as vandalism and mischief, not amounting to anything. I have been making new plans. Tonight, I wish to announce them."

"Yes, it was mischief at best!" Loud Mouth shouted, and Bug Eyes and the Tsar exchanged significant glances, then nodded. Aldo wasn't sure he agreed with Uno, since he had distributed leaflets, and even that had unnerved him. He had risked arrest if caught, and his father would have killed him.

Uno paused. "Men, we are about to strengthen our resistance. We are ready to intensify our efforts. It is time to take the next step, one that executes our goal to free Italy from the tyranny of Fascism. I have decided to call it Operation First Strike."

The men looked grave and shifted forward, and Aldo detected a dangerous undercurrent among them, one that he had been worried about for some time. He was the newest member of the cell, having been recruited by Broken Tooth after a chance meeting on the street, but he had begun to realize that Uno and many others were more militant in their views. Aldo took a swig of Chianti, hoping to allay his anxiety.

Uno straightened. "Now, I propose that we intensify our efforts. We know that the *fascio*, the local office of the Fascist party, is under the command of Comandante Spada. I have reason to believe that Spada has decided to retire, and there is talk of a retirement party for him. It is tentatively scheduled to be held at the Bella Donna restaurant around the corner from the Palazzo Braschi headquarters."

Excitement ripped through the men, and Loud Mouth shouted, "How do you know all of this, Uno? Is the information reliable?"

"Yes, it is," Uno answered, then frowned. "But I cannot divulge how I have learned it, for your own safety. Now, as I was saying, all of the top party brass will be at the retirement party, presenting us with an opportunity that we must seize. I propose we attack that night and take them all down at once."

*"Bravo!"* Loud Mouth cheered, and the others erupted in agreement, a collective release of pressure, like a steam valve.

Aldo didn't join them, and his gut clenched. Operation First Strike required murder, plain and simple. Murder was a mortal sin. He had never done anything remotely violent. He didn't want to, and he didn't know if he could. He took another swig of wine, but it didn't help.

Uno quieted them, his expression darkening. "I know it seems like a long time from now, but it will take that much to prepare Operation First Strike. There are twenty-one of us, and by then I hope we will grow in number. We are more than up to the challenge, and I will reveal the details of my plan in due course. We will assign tasks, drill with weapons, and rehearse every particular. We will do everything possible to succeed and guard our own safety. Our goal is victory without the loss of even a single man. Do you agree, men?"

"Agree!" Loud Mouth shouted again, and everyone but Aldo joined in.

Uno nodded, smiling. "It gladdens my heart to hear you say so. I fault no man who does not want to go forward. We welcome differing views, unlike our enemies. Men, is there any one who disagrees? If so, please so state, and we will discuss it in a rational manner."

"We all agree!" Loud Mouth hollered, and the others shouted their agreement and pumped their fists, stirring the air so much that the flames wiggled atop the candles.

Uno raised a finger. "Excellent, but I want to hear from each of you individually. Unanimity is important, for tonight we form a sacred pact. Loud Mouth, do you agree?"

"Yes! I say yes!"

"Good. Bug Eyes?" Uno turned to Bug Eyes, who answered yes, then Uno went around the circle asking each man, and each agreed.

Aldo grew more and more nervous as his turn came closer. Murder was against everything he had been taught, and he feared for his eternal soul. He had been an altar boy, and his brother Emedio was a priest. Aldo believed in his faith with all his heart, and he went to Mass every morning with his mother. He couldn't imagine killing a human being.

Uno eyed him. "Signor Silenzio? Do you agree?"

Aldo hesitated. "Uno, this is a significant escalation for us, don't you think?"

"Yes, but do you disagree?"

"Well, uh, I was caught unawares. I'm trying to decide."

"Kindly tell us your thinking." Uno smiled, and Aldo became aware that everyone was turning to him, so he suppressed his jitters and spoke his mind.

"Uno, I believe in our cause, but I am a man of faith. Murder is a mortal sin. It's against the commandment 'Thou shalt not kill.' I love God and follow His word."

Uno blinked, and the men recoiled, frowning.

Loud Mouth hissed, "Coward."

Uno's head snapped to Loud Mouth, and he scowled at him. "No name-calling. Let the man speak."

Loud Mouth scowled back.

"I'm not a coward," Aldo said, grateful that the leader would defend him. "But distributing pamphlets is one thing, and murder quite another."

The men stiffened, and Aldo sensed his words were giving them pause.

Uno nodded thoughtfully. "Signor Silenzio, I respect your religious beliefs, as we all do, for we are faithful, too. Yet the Church teaches that killing is not a sin if necessitated in a just war. That is exactly what we are engaged in, a just war against Fascism." Uno kept his tone soft, not argumentative, and he eyed the men in the circle, addressing them, too. "Every day, Mussolini and his regime oppress our fellow citizens and lead our beloved country farther down the path to war. Yet his wars are not just, are they? Ethiopia was not a just war. Worse, we all know that he used poison mustard gas on those poor souls, and that is an atrocity. His goal is the death and destruction of anyone who doesn't follow him."

The men nodded, but didn't interrupt Uno.

"Consider the countless lives we will save, and the human losses we will prevent if we undertake Operation First Strike. The local *fascio* supports the party in our city. Palazzo Braschi is arguably the most important local party office in the country. Can you imagine what good we will do if we cut the head off of this snake? Could there be a war more just?"

Aldo mulled it over, torn. His brain told him that Uno might be correct, but his faith told him that murder was the most grievous of sins. He wished he could pray over the matter, and contemplate. He had never been so confused, and he didn't like being the odd man out, the only one arguing with Uno. The other anti-Fascists were narrowing their eyes at him, even Broken Tooth. Aldo felt their judgment and he feared they would think him disloyal, so he succumbed to the pressure of the moment. This was neither the time nor place for a crisis of conscience.

"Uno, okay, then, I see it your way," Aldo managed to say.

"I have persuaded you of the correctness of our cause?"

"Yes, absolutely."

Uno beamed. "Then we move, as one."

"*Bravo!*" Everyone cheered, their faces alive with animation and their fists pumping again.

Uno raised an index finger, silencing them. "Now we may begin. Our first step is to obtain sufficient weapons. I have located a source of pistols in Orvieto, but I will not divulge the details. They have guns and are willing to sell. We have the money, and I will set up the meeting in the months to come."

Another ripple of excitement went through the men, but Aldo felt the situation slipping out of control. He never should have agreed. He still couldn't imagine aiming a gun at the chest of a fellow human being. Ironically, it was the Fascist youth group, the Balilla, that had taught him to use a gun. He was a terrible shot.

Uno continued, "I will deliver the money when it's safe to do so. However, I cannot obtain the guns at the same time. If I was apprehended, the Fascists would have the proof of guns for money, an illegal transaction. So we must divide the transaction in two steps. The money goes separately from the guns."

"Good thinking, Uno." Loud Mouth nodded. Aldo wondered how much the guns cost and where Uno was getting the money, but nobody asked.

"So, men, after I have delivered the money, we need someone to travel to Orvieto and pick up the guns." Uno scanned the men, and though his face was in shadow, the candlelight flickered on his fine spectacles. "Whoever does so will be carrying weapons. If you are caught, you will be arrested. And you can't travel by train to Orvieto because the police watch for us. It would be best to go by bicycle. It's quite a distance, so we need an athlete, a cyclist. Who will ride for us?"

The men began looking at each other, then all of the faces turned to Aldo.

Uno turned to Aldo last, then smiled in a newly fraternal way. "Signor Silenzio, you come to our meetings in cycling clothes, and you have the best bicycle. You are young and very fit. Are you, perchance, an amateur cyclist?"

"Yes." Aldo's heart pounded so hard that he couldn't hear himself speak. He had gotten himself into a terrible position. He sensed he had to prove his loyalty after his earlier objection, and Uno's argument in favor nagged at him. Their cause was undeniably just.

"Signor Silenzio, when the time comes, will you pick up the guns?"

Aldo's mouth went dry, and his thoughts raced. Maybe this was like a war, a just war. Maybe it *was* time to act. Maybe he needed to step up, like the other men. He had joined them for love of country. He had to be brave enough to fight, as his father had in the Great War. After all, Aldo was a son of Lazio. Of Roma.

"Yes, I volunteer," he answered, after a moment. "For Italy."

## CHAPTER TWELVE

# Elisabetta

July 1937

Elisabetta headed through the Piazza di Santa Maria in Trastevere with her father leaning on her, her dress spattered with vomit. She felt heartsick to remember the disgust on Gualeschi's face, and knew she would never work for the newspaper, now. She despaired of the opportunity she had lost, and she felt ashamed that everyone at the restaurant knew about her father.

She had never felt so angry at him, but at the same time she felt guilt for her anger. People filled the piazza, enjoying the summer night, and they looked over, talking behind their hands. She spotted some of her classmates and averted her face, hoping they didn't see her. Thank God Marco and Sandro weren't around. She would have been mortified for them to see her this way.

Elisabetta and her father left the piazza and joined the throng in the street, where people flowed in and out of shops or sat at tables outside restaurants. Diners turned away when she and her father struggled past. She spotted her house on the corner, with its lemon-yellow façade and wisteria bower over the front door, next to a brass light fixture. It was so picturesque that tourists would often photograph it, and tonight a group was posing in front of her door.

Elisabetta approached with her father, and the tourists turned to watch them, pointing and chattering. She couldn't understand what they were saying, but she could guess. She tugged her father to their front door, where she fumbled with the doorknob, helped him inside the entrance hall, and closed the door.

She got him to their apartment door, then eased him slowly to the floor. He sat with his back against the wall, falling asleep. He would be too heavy for her to move without her mother's help. She unlocked the door and entered the apartment, but the kitchen was empty, so her mother must have gone to bed. Rico rose from the windowsill in a crouch, his tail curling into a question mark.

"Mamma, I need help with Papa!" Elisabetta went to the bedroom, and her mother appeared in the threshold wearing her best dark dress, fully made-up.

"Why are you home so early?"

"Papa came to the restaurant." Elisabetta noticed a suitcase on the bed. "Are you going somewhere?"

"Yes." Her mother turned away and picked up the suitcase. "I'm leaving."

"What?" Elisabetta asked, confused. "Where?"

"That's not your concern." Her mother stiffened, averting her eyes. "I have to go. I can't stay here anymore."

"What are you talking about? Where are you going?" Elisabetta spotted her mother's gramophone in its polished wooden case, sitting by the bed. It was her mother's most prized possession.

"I'm leaving."

"Leaving what? Home? For *good*?" Elisabetta shook her head in disbelief. "But you can't!"

"I have to. I have one last chance and I'm taking it." Her mother picked up the suitcase and the gramophone, then walked into the kitchen.

"What do you mean?" Elisabetta hurried after her, stricken. "Where are you going?"

"I've given your father my best years. I'm done. Finished." Her mother grabbed her purse and kept going. "If you're smart, you'll learn from my mistake. Marry well."

"Mamma!" Elisabetta caught her mother's arm, but her mother wrenched it away, almost dropping the gramophone.

"Elisabetta, let me go."

"But you can't just go!"

"Yes, I can. My mind is made up." Her mother glanced down at her father with contempt.

"He's your husband!"

"I've done enough for him."

"But what about me?" Anguished tears filled Elisabetta's eyes. "You can't leave *me*."

"I'm sorry, but I have to. You can take care of yourself. You're a young woman now. You told me that."

"What? When?" Elisabetta wracked her brain, her thoughts in tumult. What did her mother mean? Was it the brassiere? Was she leaving because of the brassiere?

"Goodbye." Her mother turned away and hustled through the entrance hall, but Elisabetta dogged her step, grabbed her arm again, and turned her around to face her.

"Mamma, don't you love me?"

"Yes."

"But not enough to stay?"

Her mother's gaze hardened, and her lips seemed to seal.

Elisabetta burst into tears. She released her grip. Her arm dropped to her side. Her mother turned her back and left, without another word.

### CHAPTER THIRTEEN

# Marco

### 25 July 1937

----

Marco and Aldo worked behind the counter on a banner day at Bar GiroSport, which was packed with regulars, Sandro and his father, Massimo, minor party officials, and *tifosi*. The last stage of the Tour de France was just ending, and the radio played the finish. Everyone listened, holding his breath, and the announcer shouted that Roger Lapebie, a Frenchman, crossed the finish line first, winning the race. The Italian rider Mario Vicini came in second.

Marco and everyone else erupted into profanities. *"Dio, no!" "Non possibile!" "Mamma mia!"*

The customers slumped into their seats and stared into their wine.

"Beppe, how did this happen?" one man shouted to Marco's father. "It was Bartali's to win! We were robbed, were we not?"

"Absolutely!" His father scowled, standing among the tables. "First, Bartali should have won. He won the Giro last year. It was his race, everybody agrees. But after stage eight, his injury became too much for him. He struggled, but could not maintain his lead. That was the end for Bartali, but it *wasn't* the end for Italy, was it?"

"No, no, it wasn't the end!" "A new hero emerges, Mario Vicini!" "His first Tour, never even in the Giro, correct, Beppe?"

*"Esatto!"* Marco's father nodded. "Imagine Mario Vicini, from Emilia-Romagna, enters the Tour de France, not affiliated with any team. He proves his worth, stage after stage. He finishes *second* in the general classification." His father raised his glass. "A toast to Vicini!"

*"A Vicini!"* everyone shouted, toasting.

His father nodded. "Vicini should have won, and Lapebie cheated during the mountain stages."

"Yes, Lapebie cheated!" "I heard that spectators pushed him up the hills!" "I heard that, too! The judges penalized him for it!" "But Lapebie said he didn't want them to do it! They did it on their own volition!"

"Allow me to clarify this issue, legally," Massimo interjected, from his seat next to Sandro. "Lapebie got help from the sidelines. As a lawyer, I will tell you that it was illegal, and Lapebie should have been disqualified."

"An excellent point, Signor Simone!" said a party official at the same table, whom Marco had never seen here before.

"Lapebie was a victim as well!" somebody called out. "I heard they sawed his handlebars!"

But everyone else chorused in disapproval, telling the customer he was not only wrong but disloyal, maybe even a traitor. The customer shouted back, others joined the hollering, and Marco sensed the mood turning volatile, as alcohol and defeat made a bad marriage.

Marco raised a glass of red wine. "Everyone, I propose a toast! To Italy!"

"To Italy!" Everybody joined in, raising his glass.

Marco kept talking. "Friends, Italy wasn't robbed today, not to my mind! We have so many treasures here, especially in Rome! Treasures that no one can ever take from us!"

"*Bravo*, Marco!" Massimo called to him, and Sandro grinned.

Marco warmed to his topic, even though Aldo looked at him like he was crazy. "After all, who cares who wins the Tour de France? It's not the Giro d'Italia! We're not French, we're Italian!"

The customers burst into joyful chatter. "Yes, we have our own race!" "The Giro is more difficult—and more fair!" "Italians don't cheat! We have heart!"

"Yes, and we have so many treasures in this amazing city!" Marco thought of the ancient sights he had seen when he rode at night. "We walk by them every day, but how often do we really see them? Do we really appreciate them?"

Agreement rumbled from the room.

Marco gestured to the open door. "For example, right outside this bar stands the Ponte Fabricio. A footbridge built by the ancient Romans, still in use! We inherited it as a legacy from ancient times, even before Christ himself! Such a wonder is our birthright!"

The customers nodded and cheered.

"And Trajan's Column, rising into the sky! Have you ever really examined its figurines? They tell a story! Someone *carved* those figures! Do you know who? Romans! *We Romans!*" Marco bubbled over, feeding on the enthusiasm of the customers. "What about the Coliseum, the greatest arena in all the world! Have you noticed the perfection of its design? Like a big bowl of Roman sky!"

"That's true!"

"Marco has grown into a brilliant young man!"

"And a patriot!"

"An excellent cyclist, too, I hear!"

Marco beamed. "Here is my point, everybody! Our city was here before the rest of the world! We were first about what matters! Not a silly bicycle race, but Western Civilization!"

Everybody clapped, even Aldo.

Marco acknowledged the applause, then caught sight of his father motioning to him from the back of the room, his expression grim. Marco threaded his way through the customers, then entered the hallway, where his father took him into the stockroom, closing the door.

"Marco, you're making fun of a bicycle race? Calling it silly? That's our stock in trade!" His father smacked him on the side of the head. "I finished twentieth in the Giro d'Italia, need I remind you? It was the proudest day of my life!"

"Papa!" Marco felt stung. "I was only trying to help!"

Suddenly the door opened, and Massimo stood smiling in the threshold, gesturing to the party official who was standing next to him. "Beppe, excuse me. Allow me to introduce Commendatore Buonacorso, who is the commander of the local *fascio*. He wanted to meet you."

"*Piacere*, Commendatore Buonacorso," his father said, extending a hand.

"*Piacere*, Beppe. Please, call me Romano." Buonacorso shook his father's hand, flashing a politician's smile. His eyes were small and brown-black, his pencil mustache shiny with oil, and his nose unfortunately bulbous. He was of average height, reasonably fit, and impeccably groomed, with the creases of his uniform pressed into sharpness.

"Romano, to what do I owe the pleasure of this introduction?"

"Your son Marco is an impressive young man. May I speak with you both?"

## CHAPTER FOURTEEN

# Sandro

### August 1937

---

Sandro could barely wait for Professor Levi-Civita's lecture to start. The lecture hall was the largest at La Sapienza, filled with university administrators, professors, and staff from the mathematics and physics departments, even in the summertime. He was proud to be sitting with Enzo and the graduate students. Everything was so much more grown-up than high school, and he was among the most brilliant mathematicians and physicists of his time. For once, Sandro wasn't at all the smartest person in the room, and the notion electrified him. He had so much more to learn, and they could teach him. Someday, he would make a contribution of his own to Italian mathematics. He realized that his mother had been right in that regard, and he knew now what she had meant. God had given him his gift for a reason. Maybe the reason was to give to his country.

Professor Levi-Civita appeared from the side of the stage and walked to the lectern, and the audience burst into applause. Sandro was charmed by Levi-Civita's demeanor and appearance, having seen the great mathematician only once or twice in person. Levi-Civita smiled modestly, then adjusted the microphone downward, since he was of remarkably short stature, perhaps 152 centimeters. He had thinning silvery hair, his face was a small oval, and his eyes twinkled behind his round glasses. He wore an old-fashioned suit with wide lapels, light pinstripes, a stand-up collar, and a silk ascot.

Levi-Civita began to speak, his voice calm and soft, so that the audience had to lean forward, and Sandro listened, spellbound. He could barely understand in some places, but his attention remained riveted on the professor, and he didn't take notes because he preferred to concentrate. In time, Levi-Civita rolled over a blackboard and began to scribble calculations as he spoke. Sandro's mind engaged like never before, so galvanized during the entire lecture that he felt dazed when it ended and Professor Levi-Civita bowed in an old-fashioned way.

Sandro leapt to his feet and clapped, and the audience gave Levi-Civita a standing ovation that lasted for fifteen minutes, then the faculty and dignitaries surged toward the stage. Students began to file out, flooding the aisles toward the exits, but Sandro was in no hurry, wanting to stay in the room, soaking in the experience for as long as possible.

"Sandro, this way." Enzo touched his arm.

"Okay," Sandro said reluctantly, and he followed Enzo to a side entrance, then heard someone say:

"I'll be damned if I'll clap for a dirty Jew."

Sandro stopped. He turned around to see who would say such a thing, but the crowd was moving. Two students who looked old enough to be graduate level stood closest to him, and he sensed they were the likeliest culprits. "What did you just say?" he asked them.

"Nothing," the one answered, with apparent nonchalance.

The other shrugged.

"Someone just called Professor Levi-Civita 'a dirty Jew.'" The insult curdled on Sandro's tongue. His anger emboldened him, even though he was younger than they. "Was it you?"

The graduate student shook his head. "We didn't say anything."

"Sandro, let it go." Enzo tugged him forward.

"No." Sandro kept an eye on the graduate students. "If you didn't say it, did you hear it? You must have."

"We didn't hear anything, either." The students hurried to the left, and Sandro's sense of fairness prevented him from accusing them further, as he couldn't be sure. He scanned the scholarly, well-dressed audience, appalled that one of them could have uttered the slur. If Sandro had ever wondered what an anti-Semite looked like, he realized that they looked like everybody else.

"Come on." Enzo ushered him out of the auditorium, and they reached the entrance hall, where students flowed around them, leaving the building.

Sandro couldn't let it go. "Enzo, didn't you hear that?"

Enzo checked his watch. "I have to get home, and you need to pick up your next assignment."

"Doesn't it surprise you?"

Enzo shrugged. "Not these days. Anyway the professor considers himself an agnostic, and his wife is Catholic."

"So? That's not the point." Sandro had never thought about whether Levi-Civita was Jewish. He guessed now that the professor was Jewish, from his name.

"Here, let's talk privately." Enzo took Sandro by the arm and led him to the side wall. "It's his politics."

"The professor's? Who even knows his politics?"

"University professors were required to sign a loyalty oath to Fascism, six years ago. If they didn't, they were fired." Enzo kept his voice low. "Only twelve out of twelve hundred refused to sign. Vito Volterra, the elder, was one of them. Volterra was a member of Parliament, a Socialist, so of course he couldn't have signed. As a result, he was fired."

"What does that have to do with Levi-Civita?"

"It's rumored that he wrote the university a letter arguing that mathematics wasn't political, and he didn't feel it was necessary to declare his political beliefs. I heard it caused quite a stir, and ultimately he signed the oath only because he didn't want to be fired."

"But he's right. Politics has nothing to do with mathematics. The obvious conclusion is that he's agnostic in religion and politics. It's a consistent position."

"Nevertheless, there's a suspicion that he leans left, and his history is against him. People know that way back in 1925, he signed Benedetto Croce's letter protesting Fascism, which was published in the newspaper."

"So?" Sandro knew about the infamous letter from his father, who disapproved. "Hundreds of university professors, journalists, and artists signed that letter. It's not like Levi-Civita was the only one."

"I'm just telling you that Fascists don't admire the professor as much as you and I do."

Sandro had no idea what to say, given that he himself was a Fascist. "But what does it have to do with his being Jewish, anyway?"

"Most Jews are anti-Fascist, aren't they?"

"No, not all," Sandro shot back, then hesitated. He had been about to reveal that he was Jewish and a Fascist, but stopped himself. He didn't know if Enzo was a Fascist, but he assumed Enzo was. He also assumed that Enzo was Gentile, since Enzo hadn't reacted to the slur. Sandro assumed there were other Jewish students and professors in the Mathematics Department, but he had never given it any thought. Suddenly he could see how politics and religion could get bollixed up, despite their lack of logical connection.

"I have to go. Your next assignment is in my mailbox. See you later." Enzo hurried out the front door.

Sandro returned to the hallway and turned left into the mailroom, which was a small square room lined floor to ceiling with wooden mailboxes. Each one had a little glass window and the faculty member's name on a placard. He opened Enzo's mailbox, retrieved the envelope with his assignment, and tucked it in his backpack. He was just about to leave the mailroom when he stopped himself.

Sandro scanned the placards on the mailboxes, reading the faculty names, and found the one he was looking for. He took out his notebook and pencil from his backpack, tore off a page, and wrote:

*Professor Levi-Civita,*

*It may be presumptuous of me to write to you, but I felt compelled to do so. I attended your lecture and I am inspired by you and your love of mathematics. You are a true genius and obviously a kind and admirable gentleman. It is an honor to work for you, even in my humble capacity, as I am merely a high-school student who reports to Enzo Vigorito. I remain your dedicated servant,*

*Alessandro Simone*

Sandro folded up the note, put it in the mailbox, and left.

## CHAPTER FIFTEEN

# Marco

August 1937

T he summer sun was hot, making the thick black fabric of Marco's shirt feel itchy and heavy, but he had to wear his Balilla uniform for his interview at the *fascio*, the local Fascist party. That day in the stockroom at the bar, Commendatore Buonacorso had asked him to apply for a job as his assistant, and Marco's father had leapt at the chance that his son would work for the party. Marco was intrigued by the job, even though he knew he would only be a *portaborse*, a briefcase carrier. He wasn't political at heart, so he wasn't particularly interested in serving Fascism, but he knew the job had to pay better than working in the bar.

Marco hustled through a bustling Piazza Navona to Palazzo Braschi, the *fascio* headquarters, which was housed in what used to be the majestic villa of the aristocratic Braschi family. The grand palazzo anchored the south side of the piazza, and it soared several stories high, with a lovely façade of large gray stones and on the bottom, narrow, amber-hued bricks. Its vaulted entrance was a courtyard marked by graceful arches in the front and back, large enough to fit old-fashioned horse-drawn carriages.

Marco had never been inside and approached the entrance, flanked by armed guards, with some trepidation. He and the guards exchanged Fascist salutes, then he went ahead to another pair of guards that flanked a glass-doored entrance and exchanged more salutes. The guards took his name, led him to a desk where he checked in, then told him to go upstairs to the topmost floor. He found himself vaguely intimidated as he ascended a magnificent staircase of gray marble, and each landing was inlaid with black marble triangles framed by warm gold-colored marble. He almost tripped looking up at the massive dome of a ceiling, decorated with large florets; at its top was an oculus, a circular eye to the sky, which seemed to be watching him.

He reached the top floor and approached another reception desk, located in a small room with a floor of multicolored marble and a ceiling covered with friezes of lions, angels, and Roman gods and goddesses. Finally he was shown into a large office, which was dominated by a polished, carved desk covered with stacks of neat papers. Commendatore Buonacorso stood up behind the desk, and flanking him were two other officers, one younger and one old.

"Duce," Marco said, saluting.

Buonacorso saluted and approached him, extending a hand in his dark uniform, with his quicksilver smile. "At ease, Terrizzi. Please meet the other officers." He gestured. "On your left is Comandante Spada, and on your right, Comandante Terranova. Gentlemen, this is young Marco Terrizzi."

"Terrizzi," Comandante Spada said stiffly. He was bald with a deeply lined face, gray eyebrows that needed trimming, and short gray hair that stood up like a brush. His demeanor was cranky, and his back was curved like a cooked prawn.

"Welcome, Terrizzi." Comandante Terranova extended a hand, which Marco shook. He had large eyes that were a light brown, with a strong nose, full lips, and thick curly brown hair. His build was beefy, straining the buttons of his uniform, and his manner relaxed and benign, with an easy smile despite uneven front teeth.

"Please, Marco, sit down." Buonacorso gestured to the fancy chairs across from the desk.

"Thank you." Marco sat down, and so did Buonacorso and the others.

Buonacorso nodded. "Marco, I've been telling these gentlemen about the pride you feel in being Roman, as you expressed at your father's bar. In addition, we have spoken with Captain Finestra of your Balilla unit, and he reports that you are extremely popular among your peers, and remarkably athletic. Does working for us interest you, Marco?"

"Yes, of course." Marco felt honored simply that Buonacorso would speak to him in such a respectful way.

"That is, if you are qualified, Terrizzi," Spada interjected, scowling. "I have had many, many aides in my time here. None has performed to my standards. Even those who do well in Balilla don't take our doctrine as seriously as they should. You must know some of those."

"Yes." Marco *was* one of those, having joked his way through most of their paramilitary drills.

Buonacorso nodded. "As Comandante Spada points out, not everybody is up to snuff. I have no idea why we don't attract more young men like you. Do you have any thoughts in that regard?"

Marco knew how he felt inside. "I think that we're required to learn Fascist doctrine in school, so sometimes students consider it merely another assignment."

"A good point. I'm sure that your father has inspired you, hasn't he?"

"Yes," Marco answered, though his father talked about cycling more than politics.

Spada interjected again, "This is platitudinous. Let's see how much you really know, Terrizzi. Do you know the Decalogue?"

"I do."

Spada folded his arms. "Recite it then."

Marco didn't hesitate. The Decalogue of the Young Fascist was a set of ten Fascist precepts modeled on the Ten Commandments, and he had memorized them from hearing them so many times, in school and at Balilla meetings. He began: " 'Number One. God and Fatherland. All other affections, all other duties come afterward. Number Two. He who is not ready to give body and soul to the Fatherland and to serve Il Duce without question does not deserve to wear the Black Shirt, as Fascism shuns lukewarm faith and half measures. Number Three . . .' " Marco continued until he had finished a perfect recitation.

Buonacorso smiled. *"Bravo."*

Terranova nodded. "I agree."

But Spada only narrowed his hooded eyes. "Hmph! Do those words mean anything to you, boy? Or are they merely something you regurgitate?"

"They mean everything to me." Marco knew what they wanted to hear, and he realized that he could read people, even if he couldn't read books. "I know how much Fascism has done for Italy, and in particular the interest it shows in young people like me. I think it's important to understand that not everybody has a father like I do, one who will take the time to teach them, mold their mind, and build their character."

Buonacorso nodded. "That's quite right."

Spada leaned over, frowning. "So what's your point, boy?"

Marco swallowed hard. "My point is, Fascism can act as a father to such boys, so they grow into good Fascists. Our party can teach those boys how Fascism will build a stronger Italy, in the way that Il Duce is a father to our country."

Buonacorso beamed. "Marco, I told them you were a remarkable young man, and you have proved it. Hasn't he, gentlemen?"

"I agree." Terranova grinned.

"Perhaps." Spada curled his upper lip. "It's up to you, Romano. He won't be working for me, anyway. I'm on my way out."

Buonacorso turned to Marco. "You have the job, son."

"Thank you, so much." Marco felt his chest expand, as if he had gotten good grades, for a change.

"You will come every day until school starts, then in the afternoons. You will run errands and the like, and accompany me as my assistant."

"That sounds wonderful." Marco sensed that a whole new world was opening up to him, one that mattered more than school. One in which he could succeed.

"Of course, you will be paid."

"Thank you!" Marco said with newfound pride, and they shook hands all around, sealing the deal.

## CHAPTER SIXTEEN

# Elisabetta
### September 1937

———

Elisabetta was getting dressed for the first day of school, turning this way and that in front of the mirror, eyeing her reflection in her dark skirt and brand-new brassiere. It was proving a disappointment. It had pretty scalloping at the top, but the cups were shaped like cones in a geometry textbook. She couldn't fill them all the way to the pointed tops, so they crumpled like little frowns. The saleswoman had assured her that the fit was correct, so Elisabetta could only conclude that her breasts were incorrect. She wished she had someone to ask about such matters, but her mother had never come home.

"Rico, what do you think?" she asked, and Rico eyed her with mute sympathy.

Elisabetta returned to her reflection and considered stuffing the cups with socks, but that would only worsen matters. She put on the white shirt of her Balilla uniform and buttoned it up, noting with relief that the outline of the brassiere showed underneath, as if proof of its purchase. The brassiere's stiff white cotton was thick enough to mask her nipples, so maybe the other girls would shut their mouths. She finished dressing, fed Rico and her father, and kissed them both goodbye.

She picked up her rucksack, left the apartment, and stepped into the sunshine on the busy, noisy street full of businessmen and excited students in their uniforms, making a shifting pattern of black and white. The breeze carried the mild snap of autumn, which invigorated her, and she looked forward to school, her classes, and seeing Marco and Sandro with more regularity. They had seen each other off and on through the summer, but nothing had happened between the three of them, except in her imagination. It seemed ages ago that Sandro had kissed her, and she wondered if romance always came in fits and starts. She hoped her new brassiere would change things.

She made her way along streets full of pink and white oleander blossoming in clay pots, and verdant canopies of ivy bowed with the weight of new growth. The warm gold, orange, and pink stucco of the houses revealed patches of brick underneath, which made them even more charming to her. The grocery and cheese shop were opening for the day, their metal shutters rolling up with a clatter. A newsboy dropped papers outside the tobacconist's with a *thump*. Elisabetta didn't buy a newspaper and she hadn't written anything since the debacle with Gualeschi, who had never returned to the restaurant. Nonna had let the matter drop, and Paolo regarded her with pitying eyes, which made her feel worse.

In time, she reached the *liceo*, a nondescript box of gray stucco surrounded by a low stone wall, set off on a cobblestone *largo*, a small piazza. Students filled the *largo*, chattering away before the first bell.

"Elisabetta," Marco called from behind her, and she turned to see him riding up on his bicycle. He jumped off grinning, as handsome as ever in his black uniform, though he seemed to have grown stronger. His hair glistened darkly with brilliantine, and his tan had deepened, which made his smile even more dazzling.

"*Ciao!*"

Marco kissed her on both cheeks, smelling of pomade, and Elisabetta felt her senses come alive. Marco grinned over her shoulder. "And look, here's our Sandro! *Ciao*, brother!"

"*Ciao, amici!*" Sandro dismounted from his bicycle and turned to Elisabetta, kissing her on both cheeks.

Unlike Marco, Sandro smelled of hard soap, and she couldn't decide which scent appealed to her more. Sandro's face had grown longer and leaner, emphasizing his intelligent blue eyes, and his shoulders had broadened, filling out his uniform.

"Hey," said Sandro, "let's get together after school, by the river."

Marco nodded. "Great idea. Elisabetta, do you have to work?"

"Not until later," Elisabetta answered happily. "I'll be there."

Sandro touched her shoulder. "I'll bring you *supplì*, like last time. Do you remember that day?"

"Yes," Elisabetta answered, surprised.

"What day?" Marco asked, but Sandro didn't reply, and just then the bell rang for the start of school. The question lingered unanswered as the three friends were swept into the building.

A fter school, Elisabetta settled into the soft grass of the riverbank, at the spot where her classmates always gathered. Nothing had changed about the place, and the Ponte Rotto stood where it had for centuries, with the Tiber flowing jade green around the surviving arch of the bridge. Her Latin textbook lay open in front of her, but she wasn't getting her homework done, and the page was too bright to read in the sun. She wished for a paper hat, but she had no newspaper and Sandro wasn't here yet, anyway.

Meanwhile Marco was showing off on his bicycle for Angela, and Elisabetta sensed he was trying to make her jealous. If so, it was working, and she felt lost without her female advice column. The other boys played ball, and the girls gossiped in their group, still not including her. But they didn't tease her, so that was progress.

Elisabetta spotted Sandro hurrying toward her, with a brown paper bag. It looked as if it contained *supplì*, but she didn't want to get her hopes up. She was coming to understand that she placed too much significance on matters that boys didn't think twice about, which was leading to a generalized restlessness about romance. She tried to put it from her mind.

"*Ciao!*" she called to him, as he got closer.

"I brought *supplì*," Sandro said, sitting down beside her. He opened the bag, took out *supplì* wrapped in wax paper, and handed her one with a napkin.

"Thank you." Elisabetta accepted the *supplì*, its breading warm in her fingertips. She felt happy, but tried not to feel too happy. She took a bite of *supplì*, which tasted cheesy and filling.

Meanwhile Sandro chewed his *supplì*, which left olive oil shining on his lips, and she found herself noticing his mouth anew. She wondered if he would kiss her again, as he was sitting undeniably close, his hip touching hers, which sent a thrill through her body, though she tried to make normal conversation.

"So, are you enjoying La Sapienza?"

Sandro shrugged. "I do my assignments and hand them in, but no one gets back to me to tell me if I'm doing well or badly."

"I know what you mean. The restaurant is the same way."

Sandro chewed his *supplì*. "These are so delicious. Is it possible that food can make you feel good?"

"Of course."

"That is, food and excellent company." Sandro grinned down at her.

"That's just how I feel." Still she tried not to get excited.

"Where's your paper?" Sandro cocked his head. "I miss your views on the news of the day."

"No more newspapers. It's all propaganda and it makes me too angry."

Elisabetta had been too embarrassed to tell him about her essay and Gualeschi. "I'm reading only books these days. Mostly Grazia Deledda, she's a wonderful author."

"I've heard of her, but haven't read her. What does she write about?"

"Families and love. People say they're women's books, but I don't agree."

"Nor do I. I'm interested in such things."

"I'm learning so much from reading her." Elisabetta warmed to the topic, since Sandro loved to read, too. "Sadly, she passed away recently, and her last book, *Cosima*, was published after her death. She won the Nobel Prize in Literature, did you know that? She was the first Italian woman to win."

"And you'll be the second?"

"Ha!" Elisabetta flushed.

He shrugged again. "You should write a novel. I bet you can do it."

"Do you think so? Isn't that too much to hope for?"

"Not at all." Sandro grinned. "You can write anything you want to. I have faith in you. What do your parents say?"

Elisabetta hesitated. "Um, well, my father would say I should try, and my mother, well, she left this summer. She said she wasn't happy and she didn't want to stay."

"Oh no." Sandro's face fell, and he touched her shoulder. "I'm so sorry, what happened? Did your parents have a fight?"

"No, not really, she just said she had to go." Elisabetta didn't want to explain to him about her father's drinking, as it was shame upon shame. She doubted Sandro would understand, since his family was so respectable, with a father who was a lawyer and a mother who was a doctor, and nobody a drunk. Elisabetta had come to understand that her family was lower class, something she hadn't completely realized before her mother's departure.

"When will she come back?"

"I don't think she will."

Sandro frowned in a sympathetic way. "I'm sure she will."

"No, she won't." Elisabetta could tell from his guileless expression that he couldn't conceive of a mother leaving her own family, because his mother never would.

"How do you know?"

Elisabetta realized how she knew, and it broke her heart all over again. "She took her gramophone, and that was what she loved the most in the world."

"So how are you getting along?" Sandro asked, nonplussed.

"Fine," Elisabetta answered, feeling a deep pain inside her chest. She hadn't realized how upset she was until this very moment, and she found herself flashing on her mother walking out the door, as if it were happening right now. Tears filmed her eyes, but she blinked them away.

"Hey, watch out!" Marco rode over on his bicycle, spraying gravel. His grin vanished when he saw Elisabetta upset. "Betta, what's wrong?"

Elisabetta wiped her eyes, as this wasn't the way she had imagined this day to go, at all.

Sandro answered for her. "Her mother left over the summer."

"No!" Marco's eyes flared with outrage, and his heavy eyebrows flew upward. "What kind of mother . . . That's a disgrace!"

Elisabetta cringed. "Let's not talk about it."

"You shouldn't shed a tear over her, not one single tear!" Marco leaned over, took Elisabetta by the arm, and lifted her to her feet. "Come on, you're coming with me! Get on the handlebars! You need cheering up!"

"No, Marco." Sandro rose and took Elisabetta's other arm, holding her back. "She's upset, and this isn't the time."

"Marco, I'm afraid to sit on the handlebars." Elisabetta was pulled in opposite directions by Sandro and Marco, but not in the way she had hoped.

"*Boh!*" Marco waved them off. "Sandro, we need to lighten her mood! Elisabetta, if you're afraid of the handlebars, take the seat! I won't take no for an answer!" He lifted Elisabetta, put her onto the seat, and before she or Sandro could stop him, he had jumped on the pedals and was riding off with her. "Put your arms around me!"

"Marco, go slow." Elisabetta's hands reached around his waist as they lurched away.

"Tighter!" Marco pedaled faster, and they picked up speed, racing along the river. "Here we go, into the sky!"

Elisabetta held on tighter, holding Marco from behind. The sudden intimacy made her giddy, and she found herself feeling lighter and freer, with the wind flying through her hair. A burden lifted from her shoulders, one she hadn't realized she had been carrying, and it felt good to let it go. They sped beside the water with the trees whizzing past and the birds flying around and the sun overhead. She experienced what it was like not to feel ashamed but to simply live her life, or better yet, the life of every other young girl, who came from respectable families and had properly shaped breasts.

"I've been dying to get you on this bicycle!" Marco called out, laughing, and Elisabetta flushed with happiness.

She glanced backward to see Sandro in the distance, shading his eyes with his hand. She felt a pang at leaving him behind, but at the same time let herself be spirited away by Marco, by his emotion, and by hers.

CHAPTER SEVENTEEN

# Marco

September 1937

The crowd mobbed the Termini train station, music blared from bands, and flags and banners flew. Mussolini was due to arrive in Rome at any moment, having spent the week with Hitler in Berlin. Rallies, parades, and speeches had been scheduled all over the city to celebrate his return. Only dignitaries, officials, and topmost military brass from Palazzo Venezia, the head of national government, and the *fascio* were authorized to be inside the station, to welcome Mussolini as soon as he disembarked. Each man expected to get a glimpse of Il Duce, except for Marco, who was attending to Comandante Spada at the very back of the crowd, with Commendatore Buonacorso and Comandante Terranova.

"Here you go, sir." Marco took the cap off the bottle and poured water in a glass for Spada, who had decided that he was thirsty. Marco had found himself indentured to the old man, as Spada's list of needs never ended and Buonacorso's were relatively few. Spada tried Marco's patience at every turn, demanding his espresso blazing hot, his tea medium cool, and his *biscotti* warm from the morning bake.

Spada squinted at the bottle. "Boy, is this water sparkling, as I asked?"

"Yes, sir, it's sparkling." Marco hoisted the bottle to show him, but Spada only frowned.

"You can't expect me to see that label in this light? With my eyes."

"Sorry, sir."

"You know sparkling improves my digestion."

"Yes, sir." Marco masked his repugnance, since after Spada drank his sparkling water, he customarily emitted a fetid belch.

"Hurry up, boy. I can barely swallow, I'm so parched."

"Here we go." Marco handed the glass to the old man, who took it but didn't drink.

"Are you sure this glass is clean, boy? I loathe a dusty glass."

"Yes, I'm sure."

"Dust is the last thing I need in my throat right now."

"I understand, sir. The glass has no dust inside."

"Did you wipe it out first?"

"Yes, of course," Marco said, but it was a lie. Spada finally sipped some water, and Marco consoled himself with the knowledge that the old man was set to retire. Marco was counting the days until then, and the *fascio* planned to throw Spada a retirement party at a local restaurant. Marco looked forward to celebrating all night.

Buonacorso turned to Terranova. "I think Il Duce's trip was a stunning success, don't you? The newspaper accounts were favorable, and the photos even better."

"I quite agree," Terranova answered, smiling.

"I don't." Spada sniffed, holding his water glass. "I'll never like the Germans, and they'll never like us. They regard us as inferiors. I don't trust them."

Buonacorso dismissed him with a wave. "But it was almost a weeklong visit, Spada. That's unprecedented. Parades, tours, and the big speech in the Olympic Stadium. A million spectators, despite the rain. Il Duce spoke in German, isn't that incredible?"

"Yet they mocked his accent, those bastards. Instead of yelling Il Duce, they yelled *Il Dusche*. It means 'shower' in German, and it was raining." Spada sneered. "How I abhor the German language! All that clacking gives me a headache. Thank God I don't hear as well as I used to."

"Don't be so contrary, Spada. Be open-minded."

"Too late. The National Socialists imitate everything we do. The youth group, the propaganda ministry, we did it all first. They ape us. It's been that way from the beginning. Hitler copied the March on Rome for his feckless Beer Hall Putsch, and all he did was get thrown in jail. They stole the ancient Roman salute from us, too, for their *Sieg Heil*."

"And we're stealing the goose step from them, calling it the *passo romano*." Buonacorso chuckled. "Anyway Il Duce is far too clever for Hitler. Il Duce has more strength in his little finger than Hitler has in his whole body. Il Duce's aggression in Ethiopia is the reason we won that war. He'll use the Nazis to serve our purposes, you'll see."

"Let's hope so," Spada shot back, and Marco mentally filed it away. Working here, he learned so much about the party, met important officials, and memorized every name, fact, and figure. He had even managed to hide his inability to read when he had been asked to organize a file system for the *fascio*'s bills. He couldn't read the bills or vendors' names, but he could match them by color and appearance. He was never tasked with taking notes, as his boss employed a secretary for such purposes, a redhead who wasn't nearly as pretty as Elisabetta.

Marco wished he could get Elisabetta off his mind, but he couldn't. He had been enticing her by jealousy, when he should have been more straightforward. He kept expecting her to throw herself at him, like Angela and the other girls did, but that wasn't happening. Perhaps he needed to be more aggressive, like Il Duce with Ethiopia, and press his suit like a campaign, in war.

He wouldn't win her if he didn't try harder.

It was time to start.

## CHAPTER EIGHTEEN

# Aldo
### October 1937

Aldo concealed his anguish, as he sat with his back against the frigid wall of the crypt. He could barely listen while Uno and the others talked away, discussing the particulars of Operation First Strike. Aldo had done nothing the past few months but worry about the attack on Spada's retirement party, for, in a horrifying turn of events, Marco had gotten a job at the *fascio* working for the top brass, which put him directly in harm's way.

Aldo had been trying to figure out what to do, but he hadn't come up with any answers. He tossed and turned, night after night. Some days he could barely keep down a meal, and he lost weight and muscle mass. His father told him to eat more liver, his mother worried that he was ill, and Marco thought he was lovesick, still believing he had a secret love affair. Meanwhile every night at dinner, his brother regaled his family with funny stories about the cranky Spada and others at the *fascio*, which made Aldo more and more fearful. He had tried to convince Marco to quit the job, saying that it was boring to be a *portaborse*, but that hadn't worked. Marco liked the salary, and Aldo sensed that his brother's self-esteem was growing in his new job, in alarming ways.

Aldo hated that his political beliefs were diametrically opposed to those of his younger brother, in addition to his father, but that was the least of his concerns, with Marco's very life endangered by Operation First Strike. Aldo prayed every morning at Mass for God to show him a way out of the situation, or send him a sign, but so far nothing had appeared.

Aldo considered his options, but there were none. He couldn't reveal to Marco that he himself was an anti-Fascist, for fear of compromising his brother. Nor could he quit the anti-Fascists, for then he'd be unable to learn the details of Operation First Strike. The more he knew, the better he could protect Marco when the time came. The anti-Fascists had no idea of his inner conflict, for none of them knew the others' real names or identities, so they didn't know that his brother worked at the *fascio*.

"Everybody, quiet down," Uno was saying. "We remain on our countdown to Operation First Strike at Spada's retirement party. I have made progress since we last met. I can now announce to you that I have already delivered the money to buy the guns. So we've accomplished our first step."

The thought made Aldo sick to his stomach. He was a step closer to his ride to Orvieto. He had pledged to pick up the guns that could kill his own brother. He felt his face drain of blood, and he knew he must look like a ghost in the crypt. He didn't think anyone noticed, for they generally didn't notice him, and they were so excited about Uno's announcement.

Only Loud Mouth shouted, "What if they cheat us?"

"We will not be cheated, I promise you that. I know our cohorts in Orvieto personally, and I vouch for them. Now, as for timing, we had to wait through September because of Mussolini's trip to Berlin. As you know, because he took the train from Rome, the route was protected by army, OVRA, and Blackshirts. It was too dangerous to send Signor Silenzio north to Orvieto."

The anti-Fascists responded: "Mussolini only did it for the propaganda!" "There were more pictures than people!"

Uno shook his head. "True. Mussolini's visit was a stage show, but it increases instability. Danger grows on the world scene, with the agreement between the Germans and the Japanese against the Russians."

"*Vaffanculo!*" someone yelled profanely.

Uno chuckled. "I agree, friend. However, men, I have made another decision. Even though Mussolini has returned, I believe that we should nevertheless delay in sending Signor Silenzio for our guns."

Aldo sent up a prayer of thanks, wondering if this was the sign from God that he had been waiting for. The delay would give him more time to think of a way out of the situation, and he felt a temporary reprieve. He plastered a disappointed expression on his face, not to arouse suspicion and to match the disapproval of the men around him.

"Why wait?" Loud Mouth shouted, and others joined in: "What's the holdup?" "We need our weapons! We need time to train and drill with them! My shooting is rusty!"

Uno pursed his lips. "Put matters in perspective, and in context. Mussolini has signed the agreement, and Italy is officially allied with Germany. Mussolini and Hitler are setting themselves up as defenders of Western values against the threat of the Soviets. We know better."

"They're the threat!" hollered the Tsar. "Not Bolshevism!"

Uno nodded. "Brothers, we need the situation to cool down before Signor Silenzio can travel." Uno turned his spectacled gaze to Aldo. "Signor Silenzio, I know you're ready to go, but I would never risk your safety unduly. Do you understand my reasoning?"

"Yes, Uno," Aldo called to him, masking his relief. "I agree with you. It's better to be prudent now, to ensure our success later."

"Exactly." Uno frowned. "By the way, you look like you've been losing weight. Stay strong, we're counting on you."

Uno turned to the others. "Now, as far as Spada's retirement party, I have further information. The party is an official function, so no family members of the brass will be in attendance, not even Spada's. I regard this as good news, and you will, too. We don't want the blood of wives or children on our hands. They are off-limits."

"Good, good!" the men chimed in. "We're not animals, like they are!"

Aldo masked his reaction. Family members were off-limits for others, but not for him. If the attack went as planned, he would be an accomplice to his own brother's murder. He could never allow that to happen.

Uno continued, "I have it on good authority that Spada is a widower, and his only daughter is estranged from him. From what I understand, the old codger is even more selfish than most Fascists."

The men chuckled, and Aldo knew exactly how selfish Spada was, from his brother's stories.

Loud Mouth snorted. "Then he deserves what's coming to him! They all do! Every one of them will get their just deserts!"

Aldo shuddered. He had one last hope, so he forced himself to ask. "Uno, which officers do you expect will be there?"

"All of them, as Spada is the grayest of heads. They're a top-heavy organization, so there are plenty of bosses. Buonacorso, Terranova, DeNovo, and Medaglio will be there, for sure. Buonacorso is our main target, as he's the rising star, set to replace Spada. He's the future of the *fascio*."

The information confirmed Aldo's worst fears, though he didn't let his expression betray him. If Buonacorso would be there, so would Marco. Aldo was running out of time. Somehow he had to make sure Marco came to no harm. He could only pray Marco would quit before then. Aldo would keep trying to convince him.

Uno straightened. "Events have taken a dangerous turn. We must proceed with the utmost caution. Forces are arraying against us, so we must array against them! Men, unite!"

"Unite! Unite! Unite!" everyone chanted, stamping their feet.

Aldo joined in, hiding his despair.

CHAPTER NINETEEN

# Sandro

December 1937

Sandro had never been to a Fascist rally at night, and the magnitude of the spectacle astounded him. It was rumored that almost a hundred thousand people flooded Piazza Venezia, and darkness cloaked the crowd except for a spotlight sweeping back and forth. Armed Blackshirts stood in formation, like dark shadows with white sashes, and soldiers played drums, waved banners, and hoisted Fascist flags.

Men, women, and children filled every available space in front of the buildings, standing on fences and hanging on the pedestals of lampposts. They swarmed the gigantic Vittoriano, the illuminated monument to Vittorio Emanuele II, made of white Brescian marble, and Palazzo Venezia, a stately medieval edifice that was the seat of the Italian government. Mussolini himself was about to speak from the palazzo's majestic balcony, announcing Italy's withdrawal from the League of Nations. His father believed that the decision was justified, given that the League had levied unfair sanctions on Italy for the Ethiopian war.

Everybody waited shoulder to shoulder in their heavy coats, chanting "Duce! Duce! Duce!" The many voices shouting in unison thundered in Sandro's ears, and he chanted with them, growing excited. He had come to the piazza with his father and some higher-ups from the Board, but he had lost sight of them. Marco was at the rally, too, with his boss and the other brass from the *fascio*, but Sandro didn't see him, either.

Suddenly Mussolini stepped into a spotlight on the balcony, and Sandro felt a jolt of electricity course throughout his system. He could barely see Il Duce from this distance, but he knew Mussolini's features as well as his own, from textbooks, newspapers, newsreels, posters, money, and the tribute coins that his father collected, in glassine envelopes. Il Duce's features were nothing short of theatrical; a fierce, dark gaze under a prominent brow, expressive eyebrows, a strong nose, a large, bold mouth, and the iconic chin, with a jawline as pugnacious as a bulldog's.

The crowd chanted louder, pumped banners and flags, and waved caps and fezzes. Sandro felt caught up in the enthusiasm until Il Duce silenced them, beginning his speech.

"Blackshirts!" Mussolini bellowed, his voice amplified through loudspeakers. "The historic decision which the Grand Council has acclaimed and which you have welcomed with your very enthusiastic cheering could no longer be put off! For many long years we have tried to offer to the world the spectacle of unheard patience! We have not forgotten and will never forget the shameful attempt at economic strangulation of the Italian people perpetrated at Geneva!"

The crowd roared in collective outrage, and Sandro shouted with them.

Mussolini raised his hands. "And one would have thought that at a certain moment the League of Nations would have made a gesture of reparation! It did not do this! It did not want to do this! The good intentions of some governments were drowned as soon as their delegates came into contact with that deadly environment that is the Geneva Sanhedrin, maneuvered by dark occult forces hostile to Italy and to our revolution!"

Sandro deflated, for the word *Sanhedrin* meant a Jewish tribunal in Jerusalem. He had never heard Il Duce say such a thing before, suggesting that Jews were a hostile force. Sandro eyed the shouting mob in the darkness, and no one but him was reacting to the reference. Each gaze remained riveted to the balcony, idolizing Il Duce.

Mussolini raised his hands, spreading them. "Under such conditions, our presence in the halls of Geneva was no longer possible! It offended our doctrine, our style, our temperament as soldiers! The hour was approaching when it was necessary to choose in this dilemma! Either in or out. In?"

"*No!*" the crowd shouted, but now Sandro didn't join them.

Mussolini asked, "Out?"

"*Sì!*" the crowd roared, and Sandro looked around at the faces in the gloom, each one contorted with an angry sort of joy, their lips drawn back to expose their teeth, like snarling dogs.

Mussolini continued his speech, but Sandro was seeing Il Duce and the crowd with new eyes. He flashed on Levi-Civita's lecture, when someone had called the professor a "dirty Jew," with venom in his voice. Sandro had never felt that his Jewishness set him apart from his fellow Italians, but he wondered if he had been wrong.

Mussolini was finishing his speech, but Sandro had lost enthusiasm. Everyone around him was shouting, enraged and defiant, a massive display of collective might, power, and emotion that used to appeal to him. He sensed an undercurrent of danger, that the same feverish mob could be turned against him.

"Papa!" Sandro shouted, though he knew the crowd would drown out his voice. He searched the heads for his father's, but couldn't find him. Home was only a twenty-minute walk. He turned away from Palazzo Venezia, wedged his way back through the throng, and headed off.

After the rally, Sandro sat at the dining room table, his papers spread out in front of him. He was supposed to be working, but he was worried about his father. Sandro didn't know if Rosa had gone, but he worried about her, too. His mother was at the hospital, and Cornelia had gone home.

The window was closed against the cold, but Sandro looked outside to see people flooding Piazza Mattei, heading home after the rally. Some were

Ghetto residents, others were passing through, and rowdy Blackshirts were stumbling along in groups, drinking from bottles of wine.

Sandro heard talking in the staircase, his father's voice and Rosa's. He turned to the door, and they entered the apartment, arguing.

"Rosa, listen to me. You don't have all the answers." His father took off his hat and coat, but Rosa left her red wool coat on.

"Papa, I know what I'm talking about. How can I convince you?"

"Convince him of what?" Sandro stood up. "Rosa, were you at Piazza Venezia, too?"

"Yes." Rosa's lovely eyes flared with anger. "I went with David and my friend Olinda Miller from the embassy. It was appalling."

"No, it wasn't." His father scoffed. "Must you be so *melodrammatica*, dear?"

Sandro crossed to them. "I thought it was unsettling, too. What Mussolini said about the Geneva Sanhedrin, right?"

"Yes," Rosa shot back, "but also the entire speech. Italy is a pariah since we attacked Ethiopia, so much so that the League of Nations sanctioned us, and Mussolini's solution is to withdraw? What's next, we withdraw from the civilized world? And we're fighting to destroy democracy in Spain!"

His father frowned. "Rosa, you're too influenced by that Brit of yours. Please remind him that Lord Chamberlain has a bond with Mussolini and Hitler."

"Not everyone at the embassy agrees with Chamberlain, and David thinks appeasement is the wrong approach."

Sandro interjected, "Papa, I'm concerned, too."

"Don't worry." His father's expression softened. "You parse words too carefully. You simply can't do that with Il Duce's speeches. He spoke with great emotionality, as is typical of him. No one can convince me that Il Duce is an anti-Semite. He isn't. He's going home to a Jewish mistress."

Rosa looked pained. "You're making excuses for him. You're more loyal to him than he is to you. To us."

"No. He's loyal to the Jewish community, to patriots, to veterans—and I am all of those things. He's been a strong leader all this time, since 1922."

"Papa, look forward, not back. Look where we're going. I've heard a rumor that Hitler's coming to Rome, next spring."

"So?"

"So that's not good. You're not listening to me, and I've been telling you and Mamma for months. It's time."

"Time for what?" Sandro interjected, confused. "What are you talking about, Rosa?"

"Don't answer." Sandro's father held up his hand, silencing her. "There's no need to worry your brother."

Rosa faced Sandro. "Sandro, you're old enough to know. I've told Papa and Mamma, I am coming to believe we should emigrate."

"*Emigrate?*" Sandro repeated, incredulous. "You mean leave Italy? Leave Rome?"

"See?" His father threw up his arms. "Now you're getting your brother upset over nothing."

"This is our home." Sandro thought of Elisabetta, Marco, La Sapienza, Levi-Civita. His life was here in Rome and always had been.

Rosa looked at him directly. "David believes there's a real threat to Jews who stay here. He's not alone in this. Jews are leaving Germany and Poland, immigrating to the United Kingdom, Switzerland, the United States, even to Palestine. There's an organization that helps." Her eyes filmed, and Sandro felt an awful realization dawn on him.

"Are *you* leaving Rome, Rosa?"

Rosa nodded. "It's going to take months, maybe even a year to finalize, but David thinks he can get me a job with a relief agency in London. He can get you to London, too, and Mamma and Papa. I've been trying to persuade them to go. They have to decide now."

Sandro realized this had been happening behind his back. "This is crazy. I don't want to go, and I don't want you to leave us. We're your family."

"I know that, that's why I'm trying to persuade—"

His father interrupted. "Rosa, your mother and I don't need our children to tell us what to do. Fascism will not become anti-Semitic. Jewish refugees are fleeing to Italy from everywhere else, seeking safety. Why would they do that if it wasn't safe here?"

"They're making the same mistake you are, Papa."

"No, you're overreacting. Influenced by David. We live here. We're Romans, for generations upon generations."

Rosa shook her head. "You can't let history hold you back."

"History doesn't hold me back. It holds me *up*. It gives me strength, like my country and my religion. All of these things are of a piece. They're part of me, of our family, too."

"Papa, you're so frustrating." Rosa turned away, picked up her purse, and headed for the door. "I'm going to David's. I'll be back later."

"Rosa, wait!" Sandro ran to the door, raced out into the hallway, and hurried down the staircase after her. "Can't we talk about it some more?"

"Later!" Rosa hit the landing and flew out the front door.

Sandro reached the front floor, ran outside, and found himself in Piazza Mattei amid a cadre of drunken Blackshirts, their laughter raucous. They swarmed the lovely turtle fountain, its lighting illuminating their faces from below, exaggerating the shadows on their features like masks at Carnevale.

Sandro searched for Rosa, but an inebriated Blackshirt jostled him, then one of them began urinating into the fountain.

Sandro spun around, reeling. His sister was leaving Rome, his family was breaking up, and his country was losing her mind.

He turned and fled inside the house.

CHAPTER TWENTY

# Elisabetta

January 1938

The dinner shift at Casa Servano was in full swing, and Elisabetta left the kitchen with a carafe of red wine, served the couple at a table against the near wall, and scanned the dining room. Her gaze stopped at a table across the room, where, to her surprise, Sandro was sitting. He spotted her at the same moment, breaking into a smile, and she felt a surge of happiness. She had no idea what he was doing here, but he was unusually dressed up in a nice blue sweater with a jacket, a loose dark scarf, and slacks, like a real university student.

Elisabetta crossed to him. "Sandro, what are you doing here?"

"I'm hungry." Sandro beamed up at her.

"Really?" Elisabetta asked, feigning suspicion.

"Well, I wanted to see you alone, and since you work so much, I came here." Sandro took a gift wrapped in silvery paper from his backpack and presented it to her. "I brought you a present."

"How sweet! What for?"

"To make you happy. Need there be another reason?"

"Oh, Sandro," Elisabetta said, feeling a little thrill. She unwrapped the paper, delighted to find a copy of the novel *Cosima*, by Grazia Deledda. "Oh my, it's just what I wanted!"

"I know, you said so. Now turn to page thirty-seven."

Elisabetta flipped to the page and wedged inside was a flyer from the Literature Department at La Sapienza, which she read quickly. "What's this? A notice about a lecture on Deledda?"

"I thought we could go together."

*"Davvero?"* Elisabetta asked, her heart soaring. Sandro was asking her on her first real date. "That would be wonderful."

Sandro's grin widened, but Elisabetta became distracted by shouting coming from the street, which sounded as if someone was calling her name. She tensed, fearing it was her father again, and diners were turning to the noise. The older couple at the table by the window was looking outside, and Paolo hustled to them.

Elisabetta went to the window to see a sight so romantic it could have been in an old-fashioned movie. Marco was standing in the street in his dark uniform, holding a bouquet of red roses. She could see him clearly in the streetlight, and he met her eye, smiled his dazzling smile, then dropped to one knee as in a proper, traditional serenade. He burst into "Chitarra Romana," a popular love song about a young woman of Trastevere:

> Under a mantle of stars
> beautiful Rome appears to me

Elisabetta gasped, dumbfounded. Marco sang well and with sincerity, not like when he clowned around in school, and she couldn't help but think he had rehearsed. She had never dreamed that he, or any boy, would serenade her, but the timing was terrible. She'd spent months wondering whether either boy could view her in intimate terms, and they had both shown their hand on the very same night.

Excitement rippled through the restaurant, and the diners made comments to each other: "What a handsome young man!" "He's singing to the waitress!" "Why didn't you ever serenade me, dear?"

Outside, passersby stopped to watch Marco, who threw his arms open and crooned the next verse at the top of his lungs, leaving Elisabetta flushed with happiness—but also confusion. She had just agreed to a date with Sandro, but here was Marco, making a grandly romantic gesture.

Out of the corner of her eye, Elisabetta saw Sandro leave his table and join the customers behind her, just as Marco was ending his serenade. He strolled to the restaurant with his bouquet, and when he opened the door, the customers burst into applause. Marco acknowledged them with a brief nod, but his gaze focused only on Elisabetta.

"Wine on the house!" Paolo called out, caught up in the moment, and the customers cheered, heading back to their tables.

Marco strode to her, his dark eyes shining. He bowed and presented her with the red roses. "These are for you."

"Thank you." Elisabetta accepted the roses, flustered and moved, breathing in their sweet fragrance.

Sandro stepped beside her, chuckling. "That was quite a show, friend."

Marco burst into laughter. "*Ehi*, what are you doing here?"

Sandro shrugged, smiling. "Your singing wasn't terrible."

"Thank you." Marco bowed again. "Elisabetta, I would like to take you to dinner, on a proper date. Would you like to go with me, the next night you have off from work?"

"Oh my!" Elisabetta blurted out, caught betwixt and between. The two boys were smiling as if they thought it was funny, but she felt completely awkward, holding Sandro's book and Marco's bouquet. The only thing worse than having neither boy interested in her was having both of them interested in her. It struck her that romance with either Marco or Sandro wasn't without risk. If one of them broke her heart, or she broke one of theirs, she would lose their friendship. She was inevitably going to lose one of them, and choose one of them. Or might she somehow lose both? She hadn't anticipated that the situation would be so complicated.

Sandro chuckled again. "Marco, she can go out with you after she goes out with me."

"Or before," Marco shot back.

Sandro shrugged. "Either way, a girl has to eat."

"Yes, okay, Marco," Elisabetta answered, confused.

Meanwhile, Paolo motioned to her, meaning she had to get back to work, and Elisabetta turned to Marco and Sandro.

"Thanks so much, both of you. I have to go."

After Marco and Sandro had left, Elisabetta fled the kitchen, and Nonna motioned her into the pantry, where she sat making the final batch of pasta, her knobby fingers dusted with flour. Tonight they had served *spaghetti alla chitarra*, which was made on a *chitarra*, a pasta guitar, a set of fine gauge wires strung across a wooden frame. The dough was black with squid ink and dusted with flour. Only connoisseurs loved squid-ink pasta, but only connoisseurs ate at Casa Servano.

"Yes, Nonna?" Elisabetta asked, coming over.

"What just happened in my restaurant? Two boys came courting you?" Nonna draped a flat sheet of dough over the *chitarra* wires. "Sit down."

Elisabetta obeyed. "I'm sorry, I didn't know they were coming, I had no idea—"

"Do you like these boys?"

"Yes, I like them, I know them both very well, and they're both wonderful. One is more serious minded and one is more adventurous, and—"

"Please, enough. Why must you talk so much?"

"I'm sorry." Elisabetta tried to calm down, but she couldn't. "I can't decide which to choose."

"What does your mother say?"

Elisabetta hesitated. She had been too embarrassed to tell Nonna about her mother, especially since that awful night with her father. "Well, uh, she's gone. She left."

"What?" Nonna looked up, her frown fierce behind her glasses. "Your mother *left* you? Elisabetta, why didn't you tell me?"

Elisabetta had no immediate reply. "I'm fine. My father's home."

Nonna sniffed. "How are you doing?"

"Let's not talk about it now."

"But why would you keep that from me? Don't you know I can help?" Nonna pursed her lips, making the wrinkles pucker more. "Then you need my advice about these boys, don't you? Don't choose either. See both of them."

"I can't. They're best friends."

"So?" Nonna rolled the inky dough with a wooden rolling pin, pressing it against the wire.

"We're good friends, all three of us."

"Again, so?" Nonna rolled the pin on the dough until it was cut by the wires, then dropped in strands onto the bottom of the wooden frame. "You're unmarried, aren't you? Why act married when you're not?"

"But I don't want to hurt either one of them."

"Elisabetta, mark my words." Nonna's hooded eyes met hers. "It's not like in my day. I was sixteen when I married. Fortunately for me, my husband understood I was my own woman. Our marriage worked for that reason. Stay your own woman. Preserve your independence. Mentally." She pointed to her temple, leaving a faint fingerprint in flour. "Take your life in your hands, like dough. Form it the way you want it to be. Choose a boy only when you're ready. Not a minute before."

"How do I choose between them?"

"Your heart already knows which love is true, and it will tell you its secret when you are ready to listen." Nonna lifted the wire frame off the *chitarra*, revealing perfect squid-ink pasta lying in the bottom wooden tray.

"Really?"

"Do you doubt me?" Nonna separated the black strands of spaghetti with her curved fingernail. "Now. Tell me about these two boys, and please, don't go on and on. Compose your thoughts, then speak."

"The one who came with the book is Sandro, and he's very nice and very smart. We have wonderful talks, and he's a good listener."

"*That*, you need." Nonna snorted. "Does he come from a good family?"

"Yes."

"Last name?"

"Simone."

"His mother is the female doctor?"

"Yes."

"Very nice. What about the other one, who thinks he's Enrico Caruso?"

Elisabetta smiled. "Marco. His father owns the bar on Tiber Island."

"Bar GiroSport? His father is Beppe Terrizzi?"

Elisabetta detected a chill in Nonna's mood. "What's the matter?"

"Terrizzi's not for you."

"Why?"

"Elisabetta," Nonna said with a rare sharpness. "Just mark my words. And get back to work."

CHAPTER TWENTY-ONE

# Marco

January 1938

Marco left Casa Servano with Sandro, falling into stride as they walked through Trastevere. It was a cold night, but bars and restaurants were busy, and the street was full of families, couples, and tourists. Marco didn't know what to say, given that both he and Sandro had evidently begun to court Elisabetta, on the very same evening. It made him uncomfortable, and Sandro hadn't said a word to him about his intentions.

In fairness, Marco hadn't told Sandro, either, so he was in no position to blame him. Obviously, the situation needed to be sorted.

"Well." Marco shrugged. "I didn't expect to see you there."

"I didn't expect to see *you* there." Sandro laughed, and Marco joined him. Humor seemed to release the pressure between them, and Marco felt like himself again.

Sandro looked over. "So, I gather our feelings for Elisabetta have grown."

Marco nodded. "We both have excellent taste."

"If poor timing."

Marco noticed Sandro was better dressed than usual. "For once, you bathed."

Sandro smiled. "Yes."

"And a fancy scarf?"

"They wear them at La Sapienza."

"I assumed. Very nice."

"Thank you. But I didn't sing, like you. A serenade, of all things!"

"I know, I'm more direct these days. Unfortunately, I didn't have a guitar. I should have, since the song is about a guitar."

"Yes, but you brought flowers. That was a good move."

"Ah, but you gave her a book. She loves books." Marco flushed, knowing he couldn't compete on that level with Sandro. Marco was curious about the book, but didn't want to ask. "So are you wooing Elisabetta now? Is that what I'm to understand?"

"Yes, and you are, too? Albeit off-key?"

"How dare you." Marco chuckled. "I sang beautifully."

Sandro nodded. "Just like an alley cat."

Marco recoiled in mock offense. "I sing with gusto."

"You do everything with gusto."

"Exactly! That's what's so great about me!" Marco threw up his hands, exulting comically, then turned abruptly serious. "But what are we going to do, brother? We're best friends—and we want the same girl."

"What's there to do?" Sandro shrugged.

"It's obvious." Marco shot him a sly look. "You need to move along. Elisabetta is taken."

Sandro chuckled. "Sorry, but no. My heart is set on her."

"You really can't court another, Sandro?"

"I'm not interested in another. Only Elisabetta."

"Since when?"

Sandro shrugged.

Marco asked, "Did you kiss her by the river that day?"

"Yes, and she kissed me back." Sandro winked. "Come on, what about you, Marco? Why don't you court another? You can have your pick. Angela is crazy about you. They all are. They *swoon*."

"Elisabetta's the one I want. I suggest you step aside before further embarrassment."

Sandro's eyes widened theatrically. "Me?"

"Yes, sacrifice yourself on the altar of love. That would be so like you." Marco clapped. "*Bravo*, noble Sandro!"

"Do *you* want to be the one to tell her that we made her decision for her?"

"An excellent point."

They walked along, quiet for a moment until Sandro spoke. "Our friendship is strong enough to withstand a test, don't you think?"

Marco thought it over, for it was a serious question. "Absolutely," he answered, after a moment.

"I don't mind a friendly competition, do you?"

"No. If I have to compete for Elisabetta, so be it. You're worthy of her. If it isn't to be me, I'd want it to be you."

"I feel the same way. May the better man win." Sandro extended his hand, and Marco shook it firmly, then grinned.

"You know she'll choose me. How could she not?"

"Incredible." Sandro chuckled. "I was just thinking the same thing. About me."

Marco smiled. "You know, we have so much in common, we should be friends."

"Agree!" Sandro threw an arm around him, and they walked home together.

## CHAPTER TWENTY-TWO

# Elisabetta
### January 1938

Elisabetta waited for Marco, checking her reflection in a window. She looked pretty enough, in her dark blue cloth coat and one of her best dresses, paired with brown pumps that had looked worn until she had wiped them with a damp cloth. She had on reddish lipstick borrowed from Paolo's wife, Sophia, which made her feel grown-up. She had curled her hair and even used some French perfume that her mother had left behind, called Habanita. The scent made her a little sad, but she dismissed that from her mind.

Piazza Navona was alive with a nighttime crowd, bigger than any in Trastevere. Elisabetta never came to Rome proper and had forgotten how busy, exciting, and cosmopolitan life was on this side of the Tiber. The women wore fashionable felt hats with long feathers, and the men had suits so well-tailored they looked as if they had been born in them. She overheard an array of languages, a reminder that her hometown was a world-famous capital, and she wondered if she could ever live on this side of the river, among the upper class. She would need a better coat and shoes, to be sure. She would have to mold her life like dough, as Nonna had told her, but Elisabetta didn't know if that was realistic. She couldn't afford to quit waitressing, so she didn't know how she could afford to be anything but a waitress.

"Elisabetta!" Marco strode toward her in his black uniform, so handsome that other girls looked at him as he passed by.

*"Buona sera!"* Elisabetta called back, and her heart gave a little thump.

"You look stunning!" Marco reached her, drawing her to him and kissing her on both cheeks, closer than usual. She caught a whiff of a spicy cologne he must have put on.

"Thank you."

"Isn't this great?" Marco threw open his arms, as if Piazza Navona belonged to him. "I love it here."

"Oh, it's very exciting. I've never seen so many fur stoles."

"How many were there?"

"Fourteen."

Marco smiled. "You really counted?"

"Yes."

Marco chuckled. "Let me show you Palazzo Braschi, then we can go to dinner."

Marco took her hand as if it was the most natural thing in the world. They walked together to the palazzo, which looked elegant, its stone façade a warm amber and its tall windows aglow from within. Uniformed guards with long guns flanked the graceful arch of the entrance, vaguely incongruous in this courtly setting.

"Can you imagine living here? A noble family did, but now it's our headquarters. You'll be amazed when you see inside."

"Are you sure it's okay, at this hour?"

"Don't worry, you're with me." Marco saluted the two guards. "Giuseppe, Tino, meet Elisabetta. Isn't she beautiful?"

"*Certo*," the first guard answered, saluting back, and the second one said, "You're a lucky man."

"That, I know." Marco swept Elisabetta past them into an impressive hall, with a lovely glass entrance and two more uniformed guards who saluted Marco, and he returned the greeting. "Gentlemen, meet my beautiful Elisabetta. You can look, but don't touch."

"*Buona sera*, Elisabetta!" said one guard, and the other gave Marco a playful shove.

Marco shoved him back. "Out of my way, I'm taking my girl to the top floor."

"*Ma dai!*" The second guard snorted. "If you're trying to impress her, take her to dinner, not the office."

"Are you kidding, old man?" Marco shot back. "Your last date was in ancient Rome. You took her to the Coliseum!"

They all laughed, and Marco led her to a grand marble staircase. They ascended, and he pointed out the carved statuary on each landing, the fine detail of the marble molding, and the beautiful florets in the large dome ceiling, with its inky oculus onto the dark night.

"Isn't this such a lovely place?"

"Yes, but are we allowed to go up?"

"I told you, yes, absolutely. The bosses have left for the day." They reached the top floor, and Marco led her to a large anteroom on the right, where Elisabetta took in gleaming floors of parquet marble, painted friezes, and vaulted ceilings, though in her view, the Fascist flags and myriad photos of Mussolini detracted from its elegance. She had never been inside such a large villa, and she couldn't imagine that the entire place had once belonged to a single family.

"*Ciao*, Marco!" A guard saluted from beside an office with a graceful arch as its entrance.

"*Ciao*, Benedetto. Please, meet the beautiful Elisabetta! I'm showing her Buonacorso's office."

The guard opened the door for them with a flourish. "Go right ahead, Commendatore Terrizzi!"

"Finally, the respect I deserve!" Marco chuckled, leading Elisabetta inside a large office with a massive desk of carved mahogany, flanked by the Italian flag. Oil landscapes in gilded frames lined the plaster walls between bronze sconces, and ornate murals of the countryside covered the coffered ceiling. On the far side were portraits of King Vittorio Emanuele III and Mussolini, hung between floor-to-ceiling doors with glass panes.

Elisabetta heard the door close behind them with a solid metallic sound. They were alone together. "Did you plan this?" she asked.

"Of course, I'm not an amateur." His expression grew serious, and Elisabetta wondered if he was about to kiss her, but in the next minute he led her to the desk.

"You have to sit in my boss's chair." Marco pulled out the desk chair, which had shiny red leather cushions. "Here, sit and pretend you're Commendatore Buonacorso."

Elisabetta sat down at the glistening desk of polished wood, which was completely clear except for two telephones, a fancy enameled pen set, and a golden clock.

"Give me an order, as my boss." Marco sat opposite her, pretending to take notes on an imaginary pad. "I'm ready to obey."

Elisabetta giggled. "Okay. How about, Behave yourself."

"No, never." Marco pretended to throw his pad in the air, then jumped from the chair, came around the desk, and took her by the hand to the glass-paneled doors, which he opened into a balcony that wrapped around the outside of the building, overlooking Piazza Navona. "Follow me."

"Marco, really?" Elisabetta balked on the threshold. The balcony had a tiled floor and a wide balustrade of white marble, but it was so high up.

"Don't be worried. The view from here is amazing. See?" Marco led her onto the balcony, and Elisabetta walked carefully to the balustrade and looked over its top. The people in the piazza below were small silhouettes around the three beautiful fountains, their green water aglow with decorative lights. The Egyptian obelisk rose in the center of the piazza, and the lamps shining up from its base brought out its bas-relief carvings. Magnificent four- and five-story buildings lined the piazza, each with restaurants on the first floor and outdoor seating areas. To her left was the massive Sant'Agnese in Agone church, with its ornate dome and flanking spires, glowing white as the moon in the dark night. Elisabetta felt as if Rome lay at her very feet.

"Isn't it lovely?" Marco leaned forward and rested his forearms on the balustrade.

"It really is," Elisabetta answered, breathless, either because of Marco or the experience he was giving her, she wasn't sure, and it might not have mattered.

"I'm glad you're here, *cara*." Marco touched her arm, smiling up at her, and she could see in his handsome face the little boy he had been as well as the young man he had become, as he had been in front of her, all this time.

On impulse Elisabetta leaned over and kissed him, realizing too late that she wasn't sure how to initiate a kiss. She simply put her mouth on Marco's, and his mouth felt suddenly like her own, warm and soft and slightly open, so that she could inhale his very breath. She felt transported, to where she didn't know, and again, it didn't seem to matter, but it left her dizzy, then Marco came alive. He took her in his arms and kissed her with experience she could feel, as she knew he was no virgin, and the knowledge thrilled her. She followed his lead, kissing him back, and she felt an excitement she never had before, kissing this handsome man in this beautiful place somewhere above the magical, crazy, chaotic city that had given birth to them both.

"Trust me?" Marco murmured, releasing her from their embrace, and Elisabetta felt woozy, which she guessed must be something that happened with kissing.

"Yes, why?"

"Watch me." Marco climbed onto the balustrade, then rose to a stand on top.

"Marco, no!" Elisabetta gasped, though Marco had been climbing things since they were children. There had been no fence he hadn't wanted to scale, no low-hanging limb he hadn't jumped up to tap. The top of the balustrade was wide enough to fit his feet side by side, but not much wider. He could fall to Piazza Navona if he wobbled, for nothing was behind him but the darkness of night, and above, the stars.

But Marco was smiling, the curve of his cheekbone illuminated by the ambient light. He held out his hand, his fingers extended. "Come up with me."

"No, it's dangerous!"

"Please?"

"No, I can't."

"It's wide enough. You don't even have to balance. I do it all the time."

"You do? What does your boss say?"

"I don't do it when he's around, of course. Come on, climb up."

"What does it feel like?" Elisabetta asked, stepping closer to him. Part of her wanted to experience the feeling, and part of her wanted to forget the whole thing or maybe kiss again.

"You have to find out for yourself." Marco kept his hand open to her, and Elisabetta thought back to that day when he had put her on his bicycle seat and spirited her off. This time was more respectful of her wishes, and Elisabetta felt herself responding, and she put her hand in Marco's.

"Now put your other hand on the railing, climb on, and rise slowly."

"You make it sound easy." Elisabetta felt her heart start to pound, but she didn't know if she was happy, terrified, or both.

"It is, and you can do this. You can do anything." Marco seemed preternaturally calm. "You're the bravest girl I know. Nothing stops you."

"Marco . . ." Elisabetta didn't know how to finish the sentence, and before she could use her better judgment, she placed her free hand on the railing, felt its solid stone beneath her palm, and climbed up into a crouch.

"*Brava*. Look at me and rise to a stand. Don't look down. Look at my eyes."

Elisabetta looked up at Marco, who was looking down at her, holding on to her fingertips. His eyes were so dark and warm, like heated coals, and she rose slowly, seeing the curve of his smile. She felt herself smile back as she reached a standing position, and they looked into each other's eyes, holding fingertips lightly, balancing together on the balustrade high above Piazza Navona.

"What does it feel like, *cara*?" Marco asked her.

"I don't know." Elisabetta's heart filled with so many emotions she couldn't parse them, especially not this far above the ground.

"I'll tell you what it feels like, to me."

"What?"

"Love," Marco answered, kissing her.

CHAPTER TWENTY-THREE

# Elisabetta

February 1938

Elisabetta sat next to Sandro and waited for the Deledda lecture to begin. She felt entirely out of place at La Sapienza, among the professors and university students that packed the lecture hall, which had a vaulted ceiling like a church. She had worn the same coat, dress, shoes, and perfume as she had with Marco, and Sofia had given her the tube of red lipstick. Still she was one of the few women present, and the others looked like female professors, with black-framed reading glasses, amber lorgnettes, and accordion briefcases. One graded typed papers using a red pencil, and another read a thick novel; all of them seemed so well educated that Elisabetta felt her heart sink, wondering if this was the closest she would ever come to a college education.

"Everything all right?" Sandro asked, looking over.

"It's intimidating."

"Just relax." Sandro placed his hand atop hers. A calm came over her at his touch, and she realized that it was a very nice thing to have him rest his hand over hers, like a roof over her head.

A hush came over the audience as Professor Oreste Lucci, thin and be-spectacled in a dark suit, strode to the lectern. "Ladies and Gentlemen, thank you. The subject of our lecture is our Grazia Deledda, who won the Nobel Prize in Literature and passed away before the publication of *Cosima*. Though we have lost Deledda, we have this wonderful, complex, and even troubling read."

Elisabetta perked up, for she had loved *Cosima*, surprised to find that it was almost autobiographical.

Dr. Lucci continued, "The literary scholarship on *Cosima* has yet to be written, since its publication is so recent. My preference tonight is not to focus on the plot of the novel, in which a girl finds her voice to become a celebrated novelist. After all, this pedestrian plotline is not what makes this novel special."

Elisabetta blinked. She didn't think the plotline was pedestrian. It was exactly what had made the novel speak to her.

"Instead I would like to focus on the troubled family at the core of *Cosima*." Professor Lucci adjusted his glasses. "Cosima is ruled by her broth-ers, the tyrannical Andrea and the alcoholic Santus. The novel illustrates that most modern of maladies and shows how it destroys the family, disfig-ures it beyond recognition."

Elisabetta stiffened, thinking of her father.

"Deledda shows us how Santus's drinking taints Cosima's life, and al-though the doctor says alcoholism is a disease, I find Santus to be selfish. His love for his family is dubious, at best. He cares only for himself."

Elisabetta felt her chest tighten. She didn't think her father was selfish and she knew he loved her. She thought of her mother, not loving her enough to stay.

"Recall the scene in which Santus experiences delirium tremens. He's pale and shaking uncontrollably, his eyes 'wide with a metallic sheen.' He imagines killers hide under the bed. He thinks the walls swarm with snakes. This description is groundbreaking in its realism."

Elisabetta remembered the scene, having been horrified at its accuracy. Her father had tried to quit drinking many times, and she had held him while he shook, hallucinating demons, evil spirits, and Fascists coming to kill him. One night, he had raved so loudly that she had feared he was losing his sanity. The memory brought tears to her eyes, even now.

She jumped out of her seat and made her way down the row. She heard Sandro behind her but she kept going. Heads turned as she reached the aisle, but she hurried out of the auditorium. She ran through the entrance hall and pounded through the doors, finally reaching the steps outside. She hurried down the staircase, taking in gulps of the night air.

"Elisabetta, what's the matter?" Sandro came running up behind her, putting an arm around her.

"I'm—sorry—I couldn't stay." Elisabetta wiped her eyes. "I hope I didn't embarrass you."

"Not at all, what is it? Here, let's go sit down." Sandro guided her to a sitting area out of the path of travel, with hedges on either side.

Elisabetta tried to compose herself as they sat down on a bench, and Sandro rubbed her back.

"What upset you? Was it me?"

"No, not you, it's nothing." Elisabetta didn't want to trouble him with her drunken father or her runaway mother.

"I know, the book is upsetting in some parts. Is that it? I felt the same way. I had to set it down after the scene the professor described."

"You read *Cosima*?"

"Of course. I knew we were going to the lecture. We couldn't talk about it if I hadn't read it, and I wanted to read what you were reading."

"That was so thoughtful of you." Elisabetta wiped her eyes again, recovering her composure.

"I imagined myself as Antonino, the brilliant and handsome young man that Cosima falls in love with." Sandro smiled. "Though Cosima says he is too involved with his 'eternal studies.' When I read that, I thought, 'Oh no, is that what Elisabetta thinks of me?'"

"No!" Elisabetta smiled back. "I don't think that of you. Antonino is smart, and I understand why Cosima was attracted to him."

"That's good." Sandro reached for her hand. "I knew you would like the novel. Remember when she says she likes the 'magic' of words?"

"Yes." Elisabetta remembered that part, which had struck a chord. She marveled that Sandro knew her so well, and a wave of affection for him swept over her. Her hand was warm in his, and she wasn't inclined to move it away.

"And what about when Deledda says Cosima has an Amazon instinct in her? You have that, too. That strength. You always have. So what bothered you, what made you upset? Something about Santus?" Sandro's expression softened. "Is it because of your father?"

"You know about him?" Elisabetta felt mortified. Her face warmed, and tears came to her eyes again. She should have figured he would know about her father.

"Elisabetta, listen." Sandro held her close. "You mustn't feel bad about your father. I don't think Santus was selfish, as the professor said."

"You think the professor was wrong?"

"Well, I disagree with him. I can read the book for myself, and you can read the book for yourself, too. We can interpret it how we wish. I thought Deledda's portrait rang more true to life."

"I did, too. Deledda said that Santus was 'at heart good and mild' and that he was 'the first to be mortally unhappy about his vice.' That's how my father is, exactly." Elisabetta realized it was the first time she had spoken about her father, to anyone. "He feels terrible for drinking so much, and I *know* he loves me."

"I'm sure he does, too." Sandro gave her hand another squeeze. "So let's not go back inside the lecture hall. I've learned enough for one night."

"Okay," Elisabetta answered, relieved. "But what did you learn?"

"*Beh*, I always preferred mathematics to literature, since mathematics is absolute and literature is subjective." Sandro looked away, up at the stars.

"I used to believe that subjectivity was a bad thing, until tonight. But now, I think it's a good thing."

"How so?" Elisabetta rested her head on his shoulder, feeling the warmth of his neck and the vibration in his throat as he spoke. She loved the sound of his voice, which had a softness and sibilance unique to him. She didn't know if it was possible to prefer one voice to all others, but her ears attuned to Sandro's like music.

"The fact that the interpretation of the novel is subjective leaves room for the reader to enter the analysis. It offers a space for the reader to think for himself, thereby leaving open the possibility of a higher, more universal truth. I didn't learn that from the professor, I learned it from you."

"No, that can't be true."

"I wouldn't lie to you, ever. I love talking to you."

"I love talking to you, too." Elisabetta snuggled against him, wishing she could stay here forever, cozy on a bench, the two of them talking under a spray of white stars in a black sky. Sandro had become a part of this world, a vast campus of lecture halls, libraries, and classrooms she would never see, professors she would never meet, and textbooks she would never open, but when she was with him, she felt like she fit in.

"Nothing about our families matters." Sandro shifted to look down at her, a frown buckling his forehead. "It only matters who we are. They're the past, and we're the future."

Elisabetta blinked, her heart lifting.

"You and I have our own lives, and we can make whatever life we want. And someday we can make one together, if you want." Sandro met her eye evenly, and his smile turned serious. "I know we've been friends, but I've fallen in love with you."

"You have?" Elisabetta asked, her breath taken away.

Sandro kissed her softly, and Elisabetta felt the warmth of his mouth on hers, just as she had that day by the river. She realized that Sandro kissed differently from Marco, more slowly and perhaps less expertly, but when she kissed Sandro back, she could feel what he was thinking, as if the two of them were communicating, having a conversation without speech.

Elisabetta loved the feeling, understanding that all kisses weren't the same but each one unique to the man, and she could feel Sandro answering her question in his kiss, affirming that he had fallen in love with her, and the notion filled her with happiness, just as it had with Marco, who had told her above Piazza Navona.

Elisabetta didn't know if she loved Sandro, Marco, or both, so she let herself feel what she was feeling, hoping that someday, her heart would tell her its secret.

Until then, there was kissing.

CHAPTER TWENTY-FOUR

# Marco
March 1938

Marco passed under the bower over Elisabetta's front door and entered the entrance hall of her house. She had said she would be home, so he thought he would drop by and surprise her with a bouquet of roses. He knocked on the door to her apartment, which was opened by her father. Ludovico D'Orfeo blinked sleepily as if he had just been awakened, naked to the waist in droopy pants. His hair was greasy and his beard untrimmed. Marco had never seen much of him, though he had always suspected the man had a drinking problem.

"Marco!" Her father glowered at him, unsteady on his feet. "What do you want?"

"*Buona sera*, Signor D'Orfeo. Excuse me for disturbing—"

"Flowers? What for?"

Marco could smell the wine wafting off the man. "They're for Elisabetta. Is she—"

"No, she's not here!" Her father exploded, enraged. He snatched the bouquet from Marco and threw the flowers to the floor, where some broke, their petals scattering.

"Signor D'Orfeo, what are you doing?"

"Are you fucking my daughter?"

"Sir, no!" Marco recoiled, shocked.

"Don't lie to me! Are you?"

"No, I swear to you!"

"Then why bring her flowers?"

"I love her."

"No! No, no, no!" her father shouted, practically spitting. "You do *not* love Elisabetta! You may *not* love her! I will not allow it! Never!"

"Why do you say this, sir?" Marco had no idea why the man didn't like him. "I assure you, my intentions are honorable."

"Don't talk to me about honor! Terrizzis have no honor! Your father fucked my wife, did you know that?"

Marco gasped. It was impossible, as his parents barely knew Elisabetta's. He had no idea why her father would say such an awful thing.

"Yes, believe it, your father fucked my wife! Everybody knows it but you and my daughter! The great Beppe Terrizzi is not the honest man he pretends to be! I may be a drunk, but I'm an honest man! Not a scoundrel!"

"That's not . . . possible," Marco stammered, hushed.

"Oh yes, it is! Your father, he ruined my wife! She was never the same! She took one lover after the next! It was the beginning of the end for me! For my family!"

Marco edged away. "My father would never be unfaithful to my mother."

"Terrizzis ruined my wife, but you will not ruin my daughter! Get out of my house! Go! Don't you dare tell Elisabetta or I'll throttle you with my own hands!" Her father showed his gnarled hands to Marco. "They still work! Don't doubt it! Never see her again!"

Marco turned and flew out the door.

## PART TWO

Rome is the city of echoes, the city of illusions,
and the city of longing.

—Giotto di Bondone

Rome is our point of departure and reference.
It is our symbol or, if you wish, our myth.
We dream of a Roman Italy, that is to say wise, strong,
disciplined, and imperial. Much of that which was the
immortal spirit of Rome rises again in Fascism:
the Fasces are Roman; our organization of combat is
Roman; our pride and our courage is Roman:
*Civis Romanus sum.*

—Benito Mussolini, April 22, 1922,
*Opera Omnia* 18, 160–61

## CHAPTER TWENTY-FIVE

# Marco
### March 1938

Marco pedaled away from Elisabetta's house in a frenzy. Sweat poured from his body, and he accelerated past cars as if he had taken leave of his senses. It couldn't be true that his father had been unfaithful with Elisabetta's mother. Marco was riding north to the Borgo District, just outside the Vatican walls, where his brother Emedio lived. The oldest son, Emedio had always been his mother's confidant, having the most mature and responsible temperament of the Terrizzi boys. They all thought that he had been born a priest, rather than called to it in later life, and Marco was betting that Emedio would know the truth.

His mind reeled, frantic for explanations. What Elisabetta's father had said must have been a drunkard's ravings. Delusions afflicted men who drank, Marco knew from the regulars at the bar. They consumed glass after glass, even in the morning, sometimes ordering two at a time. It had to be that Elisabetta's father had an addled, wine-soaked brain, because Marco knew that his father was an honest man, a moral man, and his hero. He admired his father for so many reasons, for becoming one of the best cyclists in the country, serving so bravely on the Isonzo front, making a success of himself, and providing a business for their entire family.

Marco's legs churned at top speed, and his thoughts raced. He knew that his parents had a loving relationship, he had seen as much. He would catch them stealing kisses or see his father squeeze his mother's bottom. He could feel the earthy heat between them and he even heard them at night, making love. They worked as partners, his father in the front of the bar and his mother in the kitchen, supporting each other in every way. He had always thought that theirs was the kind of marriage he would have with Elisabetta.

Marco sped into Emedio's neighborhood, which was lined with well-maintained houses and leafy trees. Priests in black cassocks and nuns in black or blue habits walked in groups along the pavement, for the district attracted Vatican employees and clergy. Twilight fell softly, bringing with it a quiet peace, though Marco felt anything but.

He zoomed down Via Bonifacio VIII and saw that the lights were on in Emedio's front window. He tore through the intersection to Emedio's apartment, where he jumped off his bike and hollered at the window. In the next moment, his brother stuck his head out, leaning on the sill with a smile.

"I'll be right down," Emedio called down. "I was just going out."

"Hurry!" Marco tried to compose himself, but it was impossible, and as soon as Emedio appeared in the front door, he launched into a feverish account of the story, telling every detail before they'd even moved from the doorstep. Emedio listened, his expression typically attentive, and when Marco was finished, he looked directly into his brother's large, dark eyes, which were so much like their father's.

"Emedio, it can't be true, can it?"

"Brother, you need to calm down."

"You have to tell me it's not true!"

"Relax." Emedio tried to place his hands on Marco's arms, but Marco broke his grasp.

"Emedio!"

"Let's walk and talk, then. I need cigarettes, and I'd rather my neighbors not hear more than they already have." Emedio started walking, and Marco fell in step beside him, rolling his bicycle at his side.

"Well?"

"It's true."

Marco felt it as a blow to the chest. He stopped in his tracks. "I don't believe it. How do you know?"

"Mamma told me."

Marco felt a wave of sympathy for his mother. "How did she find out?"

"She caught them in bed."

"No!" Marco gasped, appalled. He had so many questions. "When did this happen? How did they even know each other?"

"Let's walk, Marco." Emedio resumed walking, his head down and his hands clasped behind his back. The hem of his black cassock popped forward with every footstep. "It happened when you were a baby, but I don't know more. She didn't want to talk about it, and I didn't want to press her."

"I can't believe this." Marco raked his hand through his hair. He walked beside his brother, but had never felt so alone. "Does Papa know that you know?"

"No, and we've never spoken of it. I've gone from being his son to his moral compass. She told me years ago, saying they had both put it behind them."

"Does Aldo know?"

"No, and don't tell him. Mamma wants it that way. It's in the past."

"Why didn't you tell me?"

"For the same reason, and I knew you would have an emotional reaction."

Marco boiled over. "It's normal, don't you think?"

"Yes, but it's unpredictable. Anyway, you were younger then."

"But Papa sets himself above us! He acts as if he's perfect, without faults!"

"And now you know better, so you have to accept that." Emedio looked over, his eyes frank. "You're not naïve. You know that married men stray."

"But not our father! Cheating on our *mother*!" Marco shook his fist. "I should tell him I know! I should throw it in his face!"

"Please don't." Emedio grimaced, as they walked under a tree. "You'll only hurt Mamma. Let it lie."

Marco sensed that Emedio was right. "But how could Mamma get over such a thing? Why did she forgive him?"

"Her faith."

"Is faith the answer to everything?" Marco shot back, reflexively.

"Yes, exactly," Emedio answered, amused. "What have I devoted my life to? Faith is the answer to everything. Faith in God, in love, in forgiveness."

"*Basta!*" Marco threw up his hand. "Why don't you feel angry on her behalf? Father Terrizzi, is there no limit for a father, who pretends to be a wonderful family man? Who pretends to be a good Fascist, who reveres law and order?"

"Our Father is in heaven. My mortal father runs a bar. He's a human being who makes mistakes. And Fascism is no guarantee of moral rectitude. On the contrary."

"Oh, that's right." Marco fumed. "I forgot you hate us now."

"I don't hate anybody." Emedio turned onto Via di Porta Cavalleggeri, a main thoroughfare lined with offices and shops. "Mussolini may think war is strength, but I know different. Every Christian does." He gestured at Saint Peter's Basilica. "Look, isn't that the most beautiful sight?"

Marco looked up at the lighted dome of Saint Peter's, emanating a warm ivory glow against a darkening sky, under a moon as white and round as a Communion wafer. On any other night, he would have found the sight comforting, but not tonight. Tonight, nothing helped.

"Marco, I worship the Prince of Peace, so I'm no Fascist."

"And I worship the Prince of War?"

"Let's not discuss politics when I need a cigarette." Emedio pursed his lips. "So what about Elisabetta?"

"What about her? She doesn't know about Papa and her mother, and I'm not going to tell her, if that's what you mean."

"That's not what I meant. I meant, you're not going to keep seeing her, are you?"

"Yes."

Emedio stopped. "You can't, Marco. You can be friends with her, but no more."

Marco stopped, too. "But I love her."

Emedio frowned. "Can you imagine Elisabetta at our table for Sunday lunch? How do you think Mamma would feel, serving the daughter of her husband's mistress? Think of Papa, too. Mamma says Elisabetta reminds him of her mother. It's not tenable."

"Papa deserves what he gets!" Marco's gut wrenched. "I love her, and we've been friends forever."

"But now that you know the truth, you can't be together."

"I can't give her up." Marco knew it was true, even though he understood Emedio's objection. "And why did they let us be friends, anyway? Why allow it?"

"You were classmates, and it couldn't be helped. They thought if they intervened, you'd only want each other more." Emedio's tone softened. "Look, you're young. You can have any girl you want. You can't tell me she matters that much to you."

"She does."

"How far has it gone?"

"You ask me that, brother?" Marco felt offended. "It hasn't gone that far."

"You? Wait for a woman?" Emedio lifted a dark eyebrow. "I don't believe you."

Marco's mood worsened. "I have every right to be with Elisabetta."

"It's not about what you can do, but what you *should* do. Give her up."

"I won't. You know, Sandro wants her, too. You can root against me. Does that make you feel better?"

Emedio's forehead eased. "Let Sandro have her. He'd be good for her."

"*I'd* be good for her! Why do you think I'm not?" Marco stiffened. "You still see me as your baby brother, but you need to take another look. I work for the party now, and they respect me. I know all the top people at Palazzo Braschi. I'm moving up."

Emedio pursed his lips. "Forgive me if I don't salute."

"Watch your step, now." Marco regretted the words as soon as they had left his lips.

Emedio frowned. "That was your dark side talking."

"I don't have a dark side."

"Everybody does. You're losing God's voice, working at the *fascio*."

Marco didn't want to hear any more. He began rolling his bicycle away. "Goodbye."

"Marco, wait!"

But Marco leapt onto his bicycle and pedaled off. He picked up speed, not caring where he was going. Everything he had known about his family was false. His world had been shattered, and he didn't know whom to believe in, if he couldn't believe in his father.

## CHAPTER TWENTY-SIX

# Sandro
### April 1938

---

Sandro opened the door to find his family getting ready for their seder, as it was first night of Passover. He had come from La Sapienza with wonderful news, happy to be able to share it on a special night, with Rosa home. The dining room table was set with their best linens, china, glasses, and silver, and his mother was positioning a vase of flowers as a centerpiece. A Vivaldi violin concerto played softly on the radio.

"Happy Passover, Sandro!" said his father as he straightened his tie in the mirror.

Rosa and David also greeted him, setting wine on the sideboard.

"Happy Passover, everybody!" Sandro hung his backpack on the coatrack, then kissed his father and sister, who was dressed up in a suit of dark blue that set off the glossy russet of her hair. She had on makeup and floral perfume, which she had been wearing more of.

"You smell better than usual," Sandro said, teasing her.

"You smell worse," Rosa shot back, with a smile.

"Sandro, good to see you." David shook his hand, and Sandro liked him, though his brown tweed suit was more stuffy than any Roman would wear, especially in the springtime.

Sandro's mother embraced him, dressed up in a gray suit with her pearl necklace and pearl-drop earrings, and her hair was swept into its chic silvery twist. Cornelia entered the dining room carrying a silver platter of *haroset*, a purée of dates, raisins, oranges, and figs—a traditional part to the Passover meal, served to represent the bricks and mortar used by Jewish slaves.

"That looks delicious, Cornelia!"

Cornelia received his compliment with a nod. "We're having *matzah lasagna* and *pesce in carpione*, the way you like."

"Wonderful! Everybody, gather around now, I have something to show you." Sandro extracted the envelope from his jacket pocket, flushed with happiness. "It's a letter from Professor Levi-Civita. I wrote to him, and he responded. Look."

"Let's see that." His father hurried over, and his mother, sister, David, and Cornelia clustered around him.

Sandro read the letter aloud. "'Dear Alessandro, Thank you for your note. I have seen your work, and it is superb. You show great promise for the future of Italian mathematics. I would like to offer you a job reporting directly to me upon your graduation from *liceo*. I hope to meet you as soon as my schedule allows, and I shall remain in touch. Best regards, Levi-Civita.'"

His father patted Sandro's back. "Congratulations! How exciting, son! You're on your way!"

"How wonderful!" His mother clasped her hands together in delight. "I'm so proud of you, Sandro! I told you!"

"Brilliant!" David said, smiling.

"*Bravissimo!*" Cornelia beamed.

Rosa snorted. "But do we have to call you Mr. Future-of-Italian-Mathematics now?"

"Ha!" Sandro grinned, returning the letter to his breast pocket. "Try *Dr.* Future-of-Italian-Mathematics!"

They all laughed, especially his mother. "Sandro," she said, "your father's new clients, the Ferraras, are coming tonight. Do you mind if we tell them about your job offer?"

"Can anybody stop you?" Sandro answered, and they all laughed again.

"The Ferraras will be so impressed. They're bringing their daughter, Rachele. She's your age and an excellent student, so you have that in common."

"Son, I've seen her picture." His father winked behind his glasses. "She's a real beauty."

Sandro realized that his parents were playing matchmaker. He hated to disappoint them, but he couldn't go along. "Mamma, Papa, I don't want to meet a girl."

"Don't be shy," his mother said, with an encouraging smile. "You're old enough and very eligible, with a brilliant future ahead of you."

His father nodded. "She's right, Sandro. We never wanted your abilities, as prodigious as they are, to prevent you from having a normal life. You work hard, but it's time to socialize with the opposite sex. You're entitled to have a family, someday."

Sandro hesitated. "But I'm already seeing someone. Elisabetta."

His father frowned. "D'Orfeo?"

His mother blinked. "But she's an old friend. We mean a girl you could be interested in romantically."

His father nodded. "Rachele's father has a ceramic factory that's doing quite well. They live in the suburbs and they're a lovely family."

Sandro felt his chest tighten. He wanted to please his parents, but this time he couldn't. "I'm sorry, but I'm not interested in anyone except Elisabetta."

His mother's smile began to fade. "When did this come to pass?"

"Sandro, we had no idea," his father added, disconcerted. "I always thought you and Elisabetta were just friends."

"We've grown into more. My feelings for her—"

"But she's not Jewish," his father interrupted, matter-of-factly.

"Right." His mother nodded, her pearl earrings swinging. "Sandro, you can't become serious with a Gentile girl."

"Why can't I?" Sandro asked, causing an immediate reaction. His father recoiled, and his mother pursed her lips. Rosa remained silent, and David looked down. The holiday mood vanished, and Cornelia fled to the kitchen. Vivaldi's violins continued to play, soothing no one.

"Sandro, this can't be." His father's eyebrows sloped unhappily downward. "Judaism is important to us. You were properly raised in our faith. You feel the same way, don't you?"

Sandro hadn't given Elisabetta's religion much thought until this moment. He had been focused on trying to win her heart. "Well, of course, my Jewishness is important to me."

"Then why weren't you looking for a Jewish girl?" his mother interjected, frowning.

"I wasn't looking for any girl at all. What happened was that one day, actually, it happened on the day that I got the internship with Levi-Civita, I was with Elisabetta at the river and it dawned on me that I had feelings for her. I knew because when I got the good news about the professor, she was the one I wanted to tell, after I told you, Mamma."

His mother's frown remained in place. "But can't you have feelings for a Jewish girl?"

"I suppose so, but that's not what happened. It doesn't matter to me whether Elisabetta is Gentile or Jewish. She's Elisabetta, and that's all that matters. The rest will sort itself."

"When?" his father shot back.

"How?" his mother added.

"I don't know," Sandro answered, pained. "All I know is that I've fallen in love with her."

"You *what*?" His father's eyes flared.

"You *do*?" His mother gasped. "You *love* her? You can't!"

Rosa intervened, touching their father's arm. "Papa, there's no reason to make an issue of this now. It's not as if Sandro's going to marry the first girl he's serious about."

"I disagree," his father snapped. "You know Sandro. He's a serious young man. How many girls do you think he'll court before he settles down?"

His mother lifted an eyebrow. "Rosa, did you not hear what your brother just said? What if he marries Elisabetta?"

Sandro was grateful for Rosa's attempt to help, but it only worsened matters. The talk of marriage was getting ahead of him, but he couldn't say that he *didn't* want to marry Elisabetta.

His father faced him. "Son, if you marry Elisabetta, your children won't be Jewish unless she converts. Is she willing to convert?"

Sandro's mouth went dry. "I don't know, we haven't discussed it yet and—"

"Your children must be Jewish. Your mother and I want Jewish grand-children. You know how important our lineage is, too. Our family has history here. We *are* history here."

Rosa turned to their father. "But, Papa, Elisabetta is a lovely girl, and plenty of Jews intermarry. You made that point the first time we had dinner with David, remember?"

His father recoiled. "I was speaking in the abstract, not with respect to my own son."

Sandro felt bewildered. His father was always so rational, but this didn't stand to reason. "Why should the result be different? It shouldn't turn on whether it's me."

"We Jews shouldn't intermarry more often than we do. Our numbers are small enough." His father pursed his lips. "Son, we forbid you to see Elisabetta."

His mother straightened. "Your father's right. You can be friends with her, but we won't allow more than that."

Sandro caught Rosa's eye, and they exchanged glances. He wondered if she remembered what he had told her once, that asking permission was inconsistent with adulthood. "Mamma, Papa, I'm sorry to upset you, but I'll continue to see Elisabetta."

Suddenly the sound of chatter came from the stairwell outside the apartment, and they all turned to the door in dismay.

"Happy Passover!" a voice called out, over the sound of knocking. "It's the Ferraras!"

CHAPTER TWENTY-SEVEN

# Marco
April 1938

Marco sat in the office waiting for the school principal, Preside Livorno. The two older secretaries, Edda and Natalina, sat at their desks, typing so rapidly on their black Olivettis that the keystrokes sounded like a fusillade. The waiting area contained the same old wooden furniture, stacks of files, and cluttered bulletin boards as every other room in school, and the same Italian flags and framed photographs of King Vittorio Emanuele III and Mussolini. Sunlight struggled to make its way through the dirty windows, and the air smelled of cigarette smoke.

Marco fidgeted in the smooth wood of the chair. The King, Mussolini, and Preside Livorno put him in mind of his father, whom he had not been able to look in the eye since learning about his infidelity. It left him unhappy and unmoored, tied to nothing and admiring even less. He felt essentially fatherless, leaderless, and try as he might to make sense of the revelation, he couldn't. It didn't help that he couldn't discuss it with anyone, as he was angry at Emedio, forbidden to tell Aldo, and too embarrassed to tell Sandro.

The bell ran loudly, signaling the end of the school day. The building erupted with the talking, laughter, and shouting of hundreds of students, so loud that it came through the walls of the office. Marco glanced out the door, which had a window in its upper half, and a horde of students piled into the hallway to leave school. Suddenly he spotted Elisabetta walking down the hallway with Sandro.

Marco salt bolt upright, newly impatient. He didn't want to give them a chance to be alone together, as at school, he and Sandro were constantly jockeying for her time. Elisabetta had started working in the afternoons, like Marco at the *fascio* and Sandro at La Sapienza, so their carefree days at the riverbank were no more.

Preside Livorno emerged from his office, holding a cigarette with falling ash. "Marco—"

"Sir! I'm ready, let's meet." Marco jumped up, hurried into the office, and sat down in a chair in front of the principal's desk, which was covered with piles of papers, school records, notebooks, and an overflowing ashtray. Behind the desk was a thick shelf that held books and photos of Preside Livorno's family with a brown-and-white pony. Smoke fogged the air.

Preside Livorno closed the door and crushed out his cigarette as he eased into his seat. White hair billowed on either side of his head, and heavy glasses perched atop his hawkish nose, magnifying his dark, hooded eyes. He was old and thin, lost in a worn gabardine suit with a tricolor lapel emblem.

"Preside Livorno, I hope this won't take long." Marco wanted to catch up with Elisabetta and Sandro. "I'm late for work."

"What work is that?" Preside Livorno asked, his voice raspy.

"I work after school at the *fascio*. I serve as assistant to Commendatore Buonacorso."

"Commendatore Whoever will have to wait." Preside Livorno linked his arthritic hands on top of a thick manila file. "Marco, I have reviewed your academic records and I am concerned. Your grades have been declining for a long time. The consensus among your teachers is that you have not applied yourself. Your assignments are sloppy and not proofread."

Marco had heard this many times before and didn't know how many times he could hear it again.

"Importantly, many of your teachers have noted that your ability to read lags far behind your class. In reviewing some of your recent assignments, I have doubts about whether, in fact, you can read."

Marco's chest tightened. He felt exposed, caught. His face went hot with shame.

"These matters should have been addressed a while ago, but I cannot speak to what happened before my time. I believe previous reports have incorrectly analyzed the problem. In my opinion, there may be some physiological explanation, so I have drafted a letter for you to take home to your parents." Preside Livorno opened the manila folder, pulled out a piece of paper, and passed it over the desk.

"Why do you want me to give that to my parents?" Marco glanced at the letter, but couldn't possibly read it, which made him wonder if it was some sort of test.

"It requires their signature. I would like them to consent to your seeing a neurologist, for an evaluation."

"A neurologist?" Marco asked, aghast. He hadn't thought he could feel worse than he already did about school, but evidently, that was possible. "Isn't that a brain doctor?"

"Well, yes, in a sense—"

"There's nothing wrong with my brain. I may not be as smart as the others, but my brain is *normal*."

"You misunderstand me." Preside Livorno pushed up his heavy glasses, flustered. "I'm not saying there's something wrong with your brain. On the contrary, many of your teachers remark that your memory is excellent, you solve problems effectively, and your wits are quick. The neurologist I propose has expertise in a relatively new field, that of educational disabilities—"

"Just because somebody can't read doesn't mean there's something wrong with his *brain*." Marco jumped to his feet, mortified. "I can ride faster than anybody I know, but there's nothing wrong with the legs of people who ride slower, is there?"

"No, no, that's not what I'm saying."

"But it is! On the one hand, I'm quick-witted, but on the other, my brain is disabled. Which is it? How can I solve problems effectively with an abnormal brain?"

"Marco, sit down and allow me to explain. I fear that you cannot succeed in school unless you—"

"No!" Marco slung his backpack over his shoulder. "I do an excellent job at the *fascio*. I organized the entire filing system for our bills. I handle reports every day. I'm entrusted with confidential communications. I'm the youngest assistant at Palazzo Braschi. No one else from school even has that job, did you know that?"

"Marco, I'm sure—"

"And don't think I didn't notice your attitude toward my boss." Marco found his emotional footing, in anger. "You're lucky I don't tell Commendatore Buonacorso all about you. You betray your government with that disrespectful talk, sir."

Preside Livorno blanched, which emboldened Marco. On the spot, he made a decision.

"Keep your letter, sir. Don't dare send it to my parents. They'll find it as insulting as I do. I'm finished with school. I quit."

"What?" Preside Livorno's eyes rounded in alarm.

Marco headed to the door, just as Preside Livorno rose from his chair.

"Son, you don't mean this—"

"Goodbye." Marco left the office and hurried to the exit. He joined the stragglers leaving school, his heart pounding with adrenaline. He had never been so embarrassed. He thanked God that nobody else had heard what Preside Livorno had said to him. He fleetingly wondered if the secretaries knew, then realized one of them must have typed the letter.

Tears came to his eyes, but he blinked them away. He suppressed his emotions and scanned the schoolyard for Elisabetta and Sandro. Sandro's bicycle was gone, and Elisabetta always walked to school, so Marco took a guess that Sandro was walking her to the restaurant.

Marco dashed to his bicycle, jumped on, and pedaled from school. He realized it was the last time he would ever do so, and he tried to look on the bright side. He no longer had to worry that Elisabetta, Sandro, or any of his classmates would figure out that he could barely read. He no longer had to develop strategies to pretend. All of the games were over, and he looked forward to the future. He was free.

He rode through Trastevere and spotted Elisabetta and Sandro a block ahead, talking in front of the cheese shop. Marco was about to call to them, but a sudden realization stopped him. Now that he had quit school, he would lose the opportunity to see Elisabetta every day. Sandro would automatically gain ground with her.

Marco pedaled toward them, his mind racing. "Elisabetta, Sandro!"

Sandro turned with a smile, and so did Elisabetta. She was stunning in a fresh yellow dress, looking like sunshine itself, standing next to a tall clay pot of pink, white, and yellow snapdragons.

"What kept you with Preside Livorno?" she asked, tilting her head.

Marco slowed his bike and managed a grin, to save face. "Guess what, I quit school."

"*What?*" Elisabetta's lovely eyes flared. "You mean, for good?"

Sandro frowned. "Are you sure? Why? How did this come about?"

Marco dismounted, his smile in place. "He summoned me to the office to talk about my work, and I started telling him how much I enjoyed my job. The more I talked about it, the more I started to realize that I liked it better than school."

Elisabetta blinked. "But that doesn't mean you should quit, does it?"

Sandro nodded. "Right, and we're so close to graduating."

Marco shrugged, but he felt touched. Elisabetta looked worried about him, and Sandro, his best friend and rival for her affection, was genuinely concerned. He felt like embracing them, but had to make light of the matter. "I know, but I don't want to wait until graduation. Quitting now makes sense for me. I make good money at the *fascio*, and if I work longer hours, I can make even more. Work is my future, and why shouldn't my future begin today?"

Elisabetta nodded, sympathetic. "I understand completely. I'm trying to stay until graduation, but that may not work out."

Sandro met his eye. "But, Marco, what will your father say?"

Marco felt anger flame in his chest, at his father. "I'll explain it to him, but honestly, I don't care. I'm growing up and I have to make my own decisions. Do you understand?"

"Absolutely." Sandro's expression darkened. "Lately, I've been thinking along the same lines. We can't always do what our parents say. We have to do what we think is right, no matter what they say. We're adults."

Marco felt validated, if surprised, as Sandro never deviated from his parents. Elisabetta remained silent, and Marco realized she had been an adult for a long time, in that she had to support herself and her drunken father, with no mother at all. His heart went out to her, and he loved her all the more.

Sandro checked his watch. "I'm late, I have to get to work."

"Me, too." Elisabetta nodded.

Marco looked from Elisabetta to Sandro, and back again. Maybe leaving school would help him win her, since he would be able to provide for her sooner than Sandro could. He didn't say so, as he didn't want to hurt Sandro's feelings. It wasn't easy to love the same woman as his best friend.

And Marco had a feeling it was only going to get harder.

## CHAPTER TWENTY-EIGHT

# Elisabetta

### 19 June 1938

Elisabetta hustled from the kitchen with a platter of *fettuccine alla romana*, a pasta with sausage, short ribs, and *pomodoro* sauce. The tray felt hot on her forearm, but she wasn't allowed to hurry at Il Cacciatore, the fanciest restaurant in Trastevere. She had just started working extra shifts here, since Casa Servano and Nonna had helped her get the job, for which Elisabetta was grateful, as the pay was better and she was able to bring home leftovers for her father and Rico.

She crossed the packed dining room, which was served by six other waitresses, a cadre of busboys, and a sommelier. Chatter filled the air, as did the clatter of dishes and silverware, mixing with the aromas of sizzling *braciola*, a house specialty. She would make money today, as Italy had just won the World Cup and Rome was celebrating. Il Cacciatore's food was excellent, though overpriced, and its dining room was decorated to perfection, with the finest white tablecloths and centerpieces of fresh sunflowers. Sunshine poured through its large front windows, bordered outside with wisteria that made a beautiful frame.

"Here's your pasta, sir. *Buon appetito*." Elisabetta served a man at a table with his wife and two young sons.

"Thank you," he said, nodding.

"May I get you anything else?" Elisabetta asked, setting the tray on the sidebar.

"No, thank you," the father answered, and Elisabetta checked her station to see if anybody else needed anything. She spotted a party of six being seated at one of her tables by the window, and in the next moment, she realized that it was Sandro with his parents and another couple—with a pretty daughter about their age. Sandro was smiling at the girl, his handsome face alive with animation, and the girl was smiling back.

Elisabetta's heart sank. He hadn't mentioned anything about the dinner, and he didn't know that she was working here today. It hadn't occurred to her that he would be interested in another girl, but maybe he was. He could have become impatient, waiting for her to decide between him and Marco. But he had said that he loved her, and she had never known him to be anything but true to his word.

Elisabetta stalled, loath to serve them. Sandro sat down next to the daughter, chatting her up. She had rich brown eyes, shiny, dark hair, and a blue dress with a tailored cut. The families had been celebrating the World Cup victory, dressed up in nice clothes, wearing the blue scarves of the Azzurri. As a group, they looked sophisticated, well-heeled, and respectable.

The restaurant manager motioned to Elisabetta, signaling that she serve Sandro's table. She braced herself, took her pad from her apron pocket, and walked over. "Hello, welcome to Il Cacciatore," Elisabetta said, with a professional smile. The Simones were reading their menus, and the father of the other couple, seated at the head of the table, looked up.

"Thank you, we're celebrating Italy's victory! It's back-to-back wins for us! What a day for the Azzurri and the Blackshirts, eh?"

"Yes, what a day." Elisabetta forced a smile. "May I get you some water? Still or sparkling?"

"We'd like a bottle of your finest *prosecco*! We are lucky to live in the time of Meazza!"

"I'll send the sommelier over immediately." Elisabetta glanced at Sandro, whose head was down, reading his menu. Meanwhile Signor Simone and Dottoressa Simone had recognized her, with unhappily surprised expressions.

Signor Simone smiled tightly. "Elisabetta, how nice to see you."

Dottoressa Simone smiled, equally tightly. "Yes, these are our friends, the Ferraras."

Sandro looked up, then burst into a grin. "Elisabetta? I never expected to see you here!"

*Evidently not,* Elisabetta thought. "It's good to see you."

Signor Ferrara looked over. "Oh, Sandro, do you know the waitress?"

Elisabetta held her breath. She didn't know how Sandro would answer. She wished she could flee to the kitchen.

Signor Simone interjected, "Yes, this is Elisabetta D'Orfeo. She's a classmate of Sandro's."

Dottoressa Simone nodded. "Elisabetta grew up with Sandro, a childhood friend."

"Mamma, Papa, that's not quite correct." Sandro turned his attention to Signor Ferrara with a sly smile. "Elisabetta is far more than a childhood playmate. I'm in love with her, and I hope she'll be my girlfriend someday."

Elisabetta laughed, and a surge of happiness raced throughout her body. Sandro was wonderful to stand up for her so publicly, when he could easily have let it pass. She met his shining blue eyes with hers, feeling the strength of the bond between them.

"Elisabetta, allow me to introduce you." Sandro gestured. "You know my parents, and our guests are my father's clients, the Ferraras and their daughter, Rachele."

"It's very nice to meet you," Elisabetta said to the Ferraras.

"Elisabetta, it's very nice to meet you." Signor Ferrara nodded politely.

"Yes, very nice," Signora Ferrara added.

"*Ciao*, Elisabetta." Rachele smiled sweetly.

"*Ciao*," Elisabetta said, sympathetic.

"Glad we cleared that up!" Sandro winked at her.

"The *prosecco* is on me," Elisabetta said, in a newly celebratory mood.

CHAPTER TWENTY-NINE

# Marco

### 14 July 1938

The morning sun streamed through the stone archway at Palazzo Braschi, and Marco picked up the heavy box and carried it inside the entrance hall, sweating from the effort. His wool uniform tortured him in the heat, and he did all the heavy lifting at work, as the youngest and strongest. The bosses were away today, and the guards Giuseppe and Tino were reading the newspaper, their heads bent together and the black tassels of their fezzes falling into their faces.

"Marco, did you see this article?" Giuseppe asked him.

Tino shook his head, reading. "*Madonna*, this is big news!"

"What?" Marco set the box on a stack by the elevator, in a small lobby behind the reception area.

"Look." Giuseppe held up the front page, but Marco averted his eyes, as he couldn't read a word.

"Read it aloud so I can keep working, would you?"

"Okay. It's a letter called the 'Manifesto of the Racial Scientists,' and it's signed by forty-two scientists. In the beginning, it says obvious facts like 'human races exist,' then in paragraph six, it says, 'There exists by now a pure Italian race.'" Giuseppe continued reading aloud. "Then it says there is a 'pure blood kinship that unites today's Italians with the generations that for millennia have populated Italy. This ancient purity of blood is the greatest measure of the Italian nation's nobility.'"

"*È vero.*" Marco picked up another box.

"*Viva l'Italia!*" Tino raised a fist.

Giuseppe continued, "'The conception of racism in Italy must be essentially Italian and with an Aryan Nordic tendency. This doesn't mean, however, that theories of German racism should be introduced unchanged into Italy . . .'"

Tino lifted an eyebrow. "Of course it doesn't. Hitler *wishes* he could be Duce."

Marco set the box on the stack. He didn't like Hitler, though he kept that to himself, especially since the rally in Piazza Venezia. There had been increasing talk of war at work, but nobody knew if Italy would choose Germany's side or Great Britain's. Despite Hitler's visit to Rome, Italy had signed an agreement with Great Britain, in April. Everybody at Palazzo Braschi held his breath to see which way Italy would go, and Marco sensed this country was like Elisabetta, trying to choose between two suitors.

Giuseppe cleared his throat. "Here's the big news. The 'Manifesto of the Racial Scientists' says in paragraph nine, 'Jews do not belong to the Italian race.'"

"What?" Marco didn't understand what he was hearing. He stopped hauling boxes. "You must be reading it wrong. Of course Jews belong to the Italian race. They're Italian Jews."

"Not anymore." Tino lifted an eyebrow. "It says so, right here in the manifesto. This must be the position of the party, as of today. This manifesto wouldn't have been published without approval of the big bosses at Palazzo Venezia."

"But it can't be." Marco recoiled. "Il Duce wouldn't do that. Jews have always been considered Italians. It's never been any other way."

"It's changing, Marco." Tino shot him a warning look. "That's what Giuseppe's trying to tell you."

Giuseppe frowned over the newspaper. "Hold on, I'm almost finished with the article. It says, 'The Jews represent the only population that has never assimilated in Italy because it is racially non-European, completely different from the elements that created Italians.' "

"But that's not true." Marco felt stricken. He knew Sandro would be horrified when he read the newspaper. "Jews are no different from us. They were born in Italy. They're Italians and Europeans. My best friend is Jewish."

"Marco, enough." Tino lowered his voice. "Keep that to yourself from now on, *capisce*?"

"He's right, Marco." Giuseppe looked up, his lips pursed.

"Okay, enough politics." Marco concealed his emotions, out of prudence. "Why don't I go get us some *biscotti*? I know a great bakery. It's a short ride away. What do you say?"

"Great idea!" Tino answered, nodding.

Giuseppe brightened. "I agree."

"I'll get my bicycle," Marco said, taking off.

Marco rode to see Sandro with a dozen anisette *biscotti* in his backpack, having used the errand as an excuse. The Ghetto was a quick ride from Palazzo Braschi, and he hoped he could catch Sandro before he left for La Sapienza. He entered the Ghetto from the north side, closer to Sandro's house. His tires bumped over the cobblestones as he reached Piazza Mattei, where a group of men stood discussing the manifesto, newspapers in hand. He recognized the elderly Signor Narduno and the Ingegnere Rotoli, who were so upset they barely noticed him.

Marco sympathized. It bewildered him to think that with the stroke of a pen, some so-called racial scientists would arbitrarily decide that Italian Jews would no longer be considered Italian. He could only hope that Il Duce would disavow the manifesto in the days to come.

He hopped off his bicycle and looked up at Sandro's house, its well-maintained façade an ochre hue, and its shutters the conventional dark green. It was one of the loveliest homes lining this quiet, refined piazza, which was comfortably shady in summer, and at its center stood the elegant Fontana delle Tartarughe, a fountain that had four turtles perched at the top of its white marble bowl. Water gurgled from its spouts, still fed by an ancient Roman aqueduct, the Acqua Vergine, and its cool spray misted the air.

"Sandro!" Marco called up to the open window, the way he always did, and Sandro's face popped into view.

"I'll be right down!"

Marco leaned his bicycle against the wall, and after a few minutes, Sandro emerged from the house, dressed for La Sapienza in a white shirt and tan pants with leather shoes. They greeted each other warmly, then Marco asked him, "Do you have time to catch up? I sneaked out of work to see you."

"Sure." Sandro gestured him to the fountain, and they sat down on the ledge together, another thing they always did.

"Here, have some *biscotti*." Marco took the box from his backpack and opened it, releasing the fresh scent of baked anise. He handed a *biscotto* to Sandro. "Did you see the manifesto in the newspaper?"

"Yes, it's shocking. Insulting." Sandro frowned, pursing his lips. "I'm Italian, no matter what they say."

"Of course you are." Marco was about to take a *biscotto*, but lost his appetite. It hurt him to see Sandro hurting.

"There's no valid science behind it. It's not fact-based in the least."

"I know, and it doesn't make sense. I can't abide this happening to you and your family, or to anyone in the Ghetto. I have to believe it will be discredited."

Sandro exhaled slowly. "My father thinks it will. He says it's pure propaganda, but I've been worrying that Mussolini is becoming more like Hitler."

"He can't be." Marco felt disgusted by the very notion. "*We* can't be."

"My father says the manifesto doesn't address Fascist Jews. He sees us as an exception."

"But the manifesto didn't say that, did it?"

"No, but my father says it lacks the force of law. You know how he is, he seeks the rational explanation. He likes to put a good face on everything and hope for the best." Sandro shook his head, chewing his *biscotto*.

"So what can we do?"

"Nothing." Sandro looked away, chewing, and Marco felt terrible for him. "It will be discredited. You're Italian, and that's all there is to it."

"It's . . . anti-Semitism." Sandro fell silent, the word dropping between them with a weight of its own. Marco felt its gravity, even though he wasn't Jewish.

"That's exactly right. If I hear anything new about it at work, I'll let you know."

"Thanks." Sandro sighed.

"How's La Sapienza?"

"Wonderful, and challenging. I learn something new every day."

Marco shook his head. "And as for romance, we're at an impasse. Elisabetta still hasn't decided between us."

Sandro chewed his *biscotto*. "We can't push her. She's so busy, with a lot on her shoulders."

"True. I feel sorry for her."

"So do I." Sandro looked over, finishing his *biscotto*. "I think about her all the time."

"So do I." Marco rolled his eyes. "It won't go away. Sometimes I wish it would."

"I feel the same way. I don't concentrate as well as I need to, at work."

"I know what you mean, and when I'm riding at night, I peek in the window of the restaurant, trying to catch a glimpse of her. It's pathetic."

Sandro smiled. "And you still date no one else? No other girl tempts you?"

Marco smiled back. "Not a one. I live like a priest. I'm the second Father Terrizzi."

Sandro laughed. "Look at us, lovesick. Mooning over the same woman."

"*Mah!*" Marco said, frustrated.

"I'd better get going." Sandro rose, swinging his rucksack over his shoulder. "It was good to see you."

"Me, too." Marco stood up, giving Sandro a hug goodbye. It struck him as no longer fun that they were competing for the same woman, and for the first time, Marco realized that no matter which of them Elisabetta chose, he would lose.

For he loved Sandro, too.

## CHAPTER THIRTY

# Elisabetta

### August 1938

———

"Papa, wake up." Elisabetta set her father's coffee next to the couch, then kissed him on the cheek. She could smell that he needed a bath, and he had been wearing the same clothes for days, despite her protestations. He had become terribly thin, and his unshaven face had a yellowish tint, as he had been diagnosed with *cirrosi epatica*, cirrhosis of the liver. The doctor had ordered him to stop drinking, and from that day she had refused to bring him another bottle. Unfortunately, the result had been that he went out drinking at night.

"Papa, I have your coffee." Elisabetta patted his arm.

"Eh?" Her father stirred, and his eyelids fluttered open. His bloodshot gaze found her face, but it was unfocused. "She was beautiful . . . the way she looked . . . her eyes, the perfect blue . . ."

"Papa, wake up." Elisabetta thought he could be sleeping with his eyes open, as if in a waking dream.

"She was innocent and yet . . . wise . . . graceful and beautiful . . . he loved women, the most beautiful women . . ."

"What are you talking about?" Elisabetta began to worry in earnest. Her father was looking at her, but he wasn't seeing her. He never acted this way, even when he woke up drunk.

"Look at her, they're blue . . . knowing, yet innocent . . . and the blue, it's the color of truth itself . . ."

"Papa, wake up." Elisabetta jostled him gently.

"Only Raphael could do it . . . and the *Madonna of the Meadow* . . . masterful . . . the *sfumato*, a perfect example . . ."

Elisabetta realized he was talking about the painter Raphael and *sfumato*, the technique of blurring the shadows in a painting. It was one of his favorite subjects, but she didn't know why he was talking about it now. She felt a bolt of alarm that something was seriously wrong, and just as she had that thought, her father's eyes rolled back in his head, and his head dropped to the side.

"Papa!" Elisabetta shook him, frantic. "Wake up! Wake up!"

"I'm fine," he mumbled, his eyelids fluttering again.

"Should I get Dr. Pastore?"

"No, no." Her father waved her off feebly, but didn't come to full alertness. He had never looked so ill, his pallor having gone from yellow to gray, and Elisabetta made a decision.

"Papa, I'm going to get the doctor. I'll be right back." Elisabetta sprang to her feet and hurried from the room. She didn't want to take any chances, and the doctor's office was only a few blocks away.

She flew out the apartment door, frantic. She ran down the street as fast as she could, her heart in her throat. Men moved out of her way, women gave her a wide berth, and children clung to their mothers' skirts.

Elisabetta realized she looked crazy, but she didn't care. She kept running, and her breath came ragged. The doctor's office was in a small brick house ahead, with pink geraniums in the window boxes. A bicycle veered into her path, but she jumped to the side, hurried to the doctor's, and flung open his door. Two men in the waiting room looked up from their newspapers, startled.

The receptionist at the desk frowned. "What are you—"

"Where's Dr. Pastore?" Elisabetta hustled to her desk. "My father needs help—"

"Sorry, Dr. Pastore is with a patient."

"I can't wait!" Elisabetta ran past her to the examining room at the end of the hall, where she threw open the door to find short, bald, and bespectacled Dr. Pastore with an older man who sat on the examining table, in his clothes.

"Elisabetta?" Dr. Pastore recoiled, disconcerted.

"Dr. Pastore, you have to come!"

"What do you think you're doing?"

"My father woke up and he's not making any sense! You need to come right away!"

"No, you must leave this instant." Dr. Pastore threw up his hands. "Can't you see I'm with someone? You shouldn't be in here."

"But there's something really wrong, I can tell! Please, he can't wait!" Elisabetta grabbed Dr. Pastore's arm, but he wrenched it from her grasp, and his patient shifted away from her on the table.

"Yes, he can. Control yourself. His disease progresses slowly. He'll have spells now and then, as ammonia may be building up in his body, altering his mental status as a result of the decompensated cirrhosis. It's nothing to become alarmed about. Now, please leave."

"You have to come with me! It's an emergency!"

"No, it's not."

"Yes, it is!"

"Go home, and I'll be there at lunchtime. You saw, I have patients waiting."

"No, now!" Elisabetta could feel a nurse materialize behind her.

Dr. Pastore sighed heavily. "Okay. As soon as I'm finished with this patient, I will come. That's the best I can do. Now, leave or I'll have you thrown out."

"Thank you, but hurry!" Elisabetta turned around and flew past the disapproving nurse, then raced from the office and out of the doctor's house. She took a right when she hit the cobblestone street and ran home as fast as she could, pushing open the front door.

"Papa!" Elisabetta bolted through the kitchen and back to the living room, where her father lay on the couch, shifting onto his side. "Papa, the doctor will be here very soon. I want him to look at you."

"I'm fine, Elisabetta." Her father opened his eyes, but to her surprise, they were wet with tears.

"Papa, are you in pain?"

"No, no."

"What is it? Why are you crying?"

"My darling daughter, my little one, I love you."

"I love you, too." Elisabetta could see that his gaze was connecting with her, though his pallor was still strangely gray. She gestured at his coffee, which sat cooling. "Do you want your coffee? Or something to eat?"

"No, I . . . don't feel very well." Her father closed his eyes, and Elisabetta embraced him, holding him close, as if keeping him with her, instinctively acting on an unspoken terror of the worst.

"The doctor will be here right away. You'll be all right."

"Elisabetta, I am so sorry for being such a terrible father. You know that, don't you?"

Elisabetta's throat caught with emotion. "Don't say that. You're a wonderful father."

"No, I'm not, and I need you to forgive me. Tell me that you do."

"What do you mean?" Elisabetta asked, stricken. "Why do you need to hear such a thing?"

"I do, and please tell me you forgive me, my darling. I feel so sick, and I want to go, I need to go, and I need to hear you forgive me. Do you?"

Elisabetta felt tears spring to her eyes, at a moment that she couldn't acknowledge even to herself, in which her father seemed to be asking her permission to leave this earth. "Papa, I can't answer you. I don't want you to go."

"Betta, please tell me you forgive me, and let me go." Her father touched her arm, and Elisabetta began to cry, realizing the awful choice he was giving her and knowing that there was only one answer, even though it was the last thing in the world she wanted, for her father was all she had left.

"Papa, if there is anything to forgive, I forgive you."

His expression changed instantaneously. The frown in his forehead vanished, and his lips curved into a smile that she hadn't seen in years. His eyelids fluttered, and his eyes opened and met her gaze directly, full of a love that she could feel to her very marrow.

"Papa, don't leave me alone."

Her father's serene gaze met her terrified one, and the light in him faded away, until all she saw in his dark irises was her own heartbroken reflection, and she knew that she had released him, even though she couldn't bear that he was gone.

"Papa!" Elisabetta shook him, trying to wake him up, but nothing happened. He lay with his head to the side, his neck drooping as if it were stretched. Every muscle in his face slackened, and his mouth hung open, his jaw unhinged. His left arm flopped over the side of the couch.

Elisabetta burst into anguished tears, and sobs wracked her body. She held him close and felt his soul departing his body, ascending into heaven where he belonged, there to live in a heaven of Raphael-blue.

## CHAPTER THIRTY-ONE

# Elisabetta

### August 1938

---

The afternoon sun beat down, dry and oppressive, and Elisabetta wilted at her father's graveside, while the local priest conducted the service. Verano Cemetery was almost nineteen centuries old, one of the world's most beautiful cemeteries, a suitably artistic setting for him to be laid to rest. Next to his grave was a carved marble statue of an angel in repose, on the headstone of a certain DiGiulio family. She sensed he would have liked that.

His own headstone was small and of gray marble, as she hadn't been able to afford more. The ornate family mausoleums were in another section, but her father was being buried among humbler graves, some of which had large curved headstones bearing enameled portraits of the deceased. In his heyday, her father would have painted far better portraits.

Her head hung, and the black dress fit her poorly, as it was one her mother had left behind. She had been hoping all morning that her mother would magically appear at the church or at the cemetery, having read the notice of her father's death in the newspaper. But that did not happen, and Elisabetta felt silly for holding out such a vain hope.

She had cried all the tears she could cry, having regained her emotional footing since her father's death, busying herself with sending out notices, ordering flowers, and arranging for the Mass with the priest and for the burial with the undertaker. She had used her savings to bury her father, but that hadn't been enough, so the fund for the indigent had contributed and the undertaker had extended her a partial credit, which had been kind.

Marco stood on her right, and Sandro on her left, and she felt touched that both of them had come. Marco had taken the time off from work, somber in his black uniform, and Sandro was in his dark jacket and pants, going in late to La Sapienza. Nonna stood behind them with her son, Paolo, and his wife, Sofia, and the only other mourners were a few slovenly drinking buddies of her father's. She couldn't help but harbor resentment at them for encouraging his drinking, working against her efforts even after his diagnosis.

The priest finished the prayer, everyone blessed themselves, and Elisabetta realized that the time had come to say her final goodbye to her father. Tears blurred her vision, though she maintained her composure and told him how much she loved him, and always would.

"God be with you," the priest said, walking to her as he closed his breviary, and Elisabetta thanked him, grateful that he had agreed to officiate, though they rarely went to Mass.

"Nonna, thank you for coming." Elisabetta embraced her, moved to feel Nonna hug her fiercely in return, her grip surprisingly strong, and when Elisabetta pulled away, Nonna's eyes were glistening.

"You have my sympathy." Nonna wiped wetness from underneath her glasses with her handkerchief.

"And thank you, Paolo and Sofia, too."

Paolo nodded. "Please feel free to take a few days off."

"No, I'm fine. I can come in tomorrow." Elisabetta needed the money, but she didn't want to say so in front of everyone.

"Fine, then." Nonna flattened her lips, and Elisabetta knew that she understood. After Nonna and the Servanos left, Elisabetta crossed to her father's drinking buddies and thanked them for coming, out of respect to her father.

"Elisabetta, we're so sorry." Marco took her arm.

"Yes, we are." Sandro took her other arm.

"Thank you both," Elisabetta said uncomfortably. They were being nice, but competing to console her, which made her feel guilty. "I'll be fine. Don't you have to get to work?"

Marco squeezed her arm gently. "Sadly, I do."

Sandro answered, "I don't, not yet."

Marco glanced at Sandro. "Take care of her, will you? She shouldn't be alone."

"Yes, of course." Sandro nodded, and Marco kissed Elisabetta on the cheek, then left.

Elisabetta sat with Sandro on a bench at the cemetery, under the shade of an umbrella pine. Headstones, monuments, and mausoleums surrounded them, packed tight in rows among white oleander bushes, cypresses, and palm trees. The walkways between the graves were of yellow pebbles, and here and there a small green lizard darted into the sun, then escaped under a bush.

Her tears were finally spent, and she felt numb with grief. Sandro remained companionably silent. Her father's grave was a few rows away, and she couldn't bring herself to leave him just yet. She didn't know how to separate from him. Was she supposed to just walk away?

Elisabetta wiped her face with her handkerchief. "Sorry to make you wait, Sandro. You can go if you need to."

"No, I'm fine."

"He wasn't a perfect father, I know that."

"Few are."

"Yours is," Elisabetta blurted out. "He's a lawyer, an important man. Everyone looks up to him."

"That's true, I'm lucky in him. But he's not perfect." Sandro paused. "What will you do now, on your own? Can I help you? Anything you need . . ."

"No, I have it figured out. I'll move, as rent makes up the most of our—sorry, *my*—monthly expenses, and I only need one bedroom."

"You'll stay in Trastevere, of course."

"Yes. I've been looking around, but so far none of the landlords will allow Rico."

"You can't leave him behind. He's your boy."

"That, he is."

"Maybe someday I'll be your boy, eh? I'll settle for second place, but not third." Sandro smiled, and Elisabetta knew he meant Marco, but she felt awkward again and wanted to change the subject.

"Sandro, why do you say that about your father, that he's not perfect? He's your hero, isn't he?"

"My hero?" Sandro pursed his lips, thinking it over. "No, not really. I love and I admire him, but I can't say he's my hero. I do have one, though."

"The professor then. Levi-Civita."

"No, not him, either."

"Then who?"

"You, Elisabetta. You are my hero."

"Me? I'm a *waitress*." Elisabetta looked up to see if he was kidding, but his expression was sincere.

"You don't see yourself as special, but you are. You do what needs to be done, no matter what. You kept doing after your mother left and you will keep doing after your father. I don't know anyone who does that, but you. Only you."

Elisabetta felt her mouth go dry, not knowing what to say, but she couldn't deny the power of his words, or that they made her feel stronger, even on the worst day of her life.

CHAPTER THIRTY-TWO

# Elisabetta

### August 1938

That night, Elisabetta sat at the kitchen table watching Rico eat, still in her black dress from the funeral. The cat's throaty chewing was the only sound in the empty apartment, and she felt her father's absence, for he had been good company, even if he wasn't sober. She had no one to take care of now, except Rico.

Someone knocked, the sound startling her. She rose, crossed the kitchen, and opened the door, surprised to find Marco there, smiling at her, in uniform. "Marco?"

"Elisabetta, come with me."

"What? Where?"

"Come on! Let's go." Marco took her hand and led her from the apartment, then to the street, which was almost blocked by an elegant black convertible coupe with a gleaming chrome grille, curved sections over each wheel that came to a dramatic point, and more flashy chrome on the sides.

"You know this car?" Elisabetta asked, astonished.

"Yes, it belongs to my boss." Marco strode to the passenger side door, opening it for her with a flourish. "Isn't it beautiful? It's a Lancia Astura, designed by Pinin Farina. Get in, I'll take you for a ride."

"*You* drive?"

"They taught me. It's easy."

"But you have to be twenty-one. You have to have a license. It's against the law."

"Elisabetta, we *are* the law. Now please, get in." Marco gestured at the open passenger door, and she crossed to the car and climbed inside reluctantly, taking in the rich leathery smell of the seats. She had only ever been in a car a few times, as one wasn't necessary in the city. Her gaze marveled at its dashboard and around its mysterious dials and knobs.

"Here we go!" Marco slid inside the driver's seat and closed the door. He started the engine, and the car began motoring through the narrow streets. "My boss loves cars, and this is one of three he owns. I'm in charge of getting them serviced and maintained. They say Il Duce favors the Alfa Romeo, and most of those sedans are used on official business, but this car is a gem. This is the only *convertibile*."

"Does your boss know you have it?"

"He's out of town." Marco beamed as he drove ahead, but Elisabetta felt self-conscious at being so visible, as she had never driven in a *convertibile*. It felt disrespectful on the day she had buried her father, and she hoped the neighbors didn't see.

"Everyone's looking at us."

"They're jealous." Marco shrugged.

"No, they think you're in the government."

"I am." Marco glanced over, his expression soft. "You've had a hard time today and you need a diversion. I'll get us onto the Lungotevere, and we can go fast."

"I don't want to go fast."

"Maybe you just don't know it yet." Marco smiled, and the car picked up speed, turning onto the Lungotevere Sanzio. Her hands flew automatically to her hair, hoping to keep it in place. He joined the line of traffic, stopping at a red light, then turned to her. "It will get more fun now, and you'll love the feel of the wind."

"We won't be able to hear ourselves talk."

"That's true, but there are things you can't do when you're talking." Marco leaned over, giving her a peck on the lips.

Elisabetta shook her head at him. "I should've known."

"But you didn't. You don't know everything, *cara*. I know some things that you don't, and I'll show them to you. Wouldn't that be a wonderful way to live?"

Elisabetta warmed. She hadn't expected to hear words of love in an open car, but Marco could be spontaneous that way. Life with him *was* a sort of adventure, and he lifted her spirits, every time.

The traffic light turned green, and the car leapt forward. They were quickly out of Trastevere, and in no time she found herself enjoying the ride. The big engine rumbled as they traveled southward, and she gave up on her hair, letting it whip around her face in a crazy fashion. She realized that after a heartbreaking day, it felt good to empty her head and whiz past the lights and shadows of the beautiful buildings, ancient ruins, and imposing municipal offices. They zoomed out of the city, and she surrendered to Marco's plan, having none of her own except to survive the day on which she had buried her father.

The buildings gave way to fields, and the odors changed from diesel fumes to fresh air and earthy manure, natural and good. She rested her head back on the cushioned leather seats and looked up at the night sky as they drove through the countryside, so that the environs were as dark as the sky and all around her was a soft blackness.

The car raced into the night, and Elisabetta experienced the sensation that she and Marco were hurtling together through space and time. Tears came to her eyes. She thought of her father and wondered where he was right now, perhaps on his way to heaven, as suspended as she in time and space. She wished she could see him just one more time.

Marco slowed the car and pulled over to the side of the road, but Elisabetta didn't know why. She looked over, expecting to find him grinning, exhilarated from their adventure. Instead she could see in the light from the dashboard that he looked crestfallen, and his large eyes glistened.

"Marco, what's the matter?"

"I'm sorry your father died. I can't imagine how sad you are, but I know you must be worried about so many things, especially money. Is that right?"

"Thank you, but I know what to do."

"Elisabetta, you don't have to do this alone. I love you, and I will help you. I will give you any money you need. Anything to make your life easier."

Elisabetta felt moved. "Marco, I don't need your money."

"I wanted you to know that you never have to do anything alone, ever again. You are no longer alone, as long as I live."

Elisabetta felt her heart respond, as the sentiment comforted her on the very day she felt more alone than ever. She leaned over and kissed him gently on the lips, and he kissed her back, more fully, and she felt lost in his kiss the way she always did with him, as his tenderness swept her away. In the next moment, he released her from his embrace, moving a strand of her hair back.

"Now, it's your turn." Marco got out of the driver's seat, opened her car door, and gestured her out of the car. "Come on, get in the driver's seat."

Elisabetta recoiled. "Marco, are you crazy? I don't know how to drive."

"It's easy. Idiots do it every day."

"Not this idiot."

"Look, this is the perfect place to learn." Marco gestured at the country road, a dark line stretching into the night. "There's no other traffic, and all you have to do is go straight."

"Marco, no."

"Elisabetta, what did I tell you? You can do anything. Come on." Marco hustled to the passenger side and opened the door, where despite her objections, he lifted her bodily from the seat, marched her around to the driver's seat, and closed the door.

"Marco, I can't drive." Elisabetta put her hands on the steering wheel.

"Yes, you can. I'll help you." Marco vaulted inside into the passenger seat and landed with a little grunt, then they both burst into laughter.

"You're crazy!"

"You're not crazy enough. Feel on the floor with your feet. There's a gas pedal on the right and a clutch pedal on the left."

Elisabetta fumbled for the pedals, then placed her feet on them. "Okay."

"*Brava!* Now press your right foot down to feed the car gas, and press up with your left foot to engage the clutch."

"At the same time?"

"Yes, but when I tell you. Right foot down, left foot up. I'll do the rest."

"What's the rest?"

"The gearshift. Don't worry about it."

"Still, it sounds hard."

"Only at first. You'll get the hang of it."

"So do it now?"

"Yes. Now."

Elisabetta pressed one foot down and the other up. The car lurched, bucked, then stopped, the engine screeching as if in agony. "Oh no! Did I break it?"

"No." Marco chuckled. "Try again. Ready? Now."

Elisabetta tried again, but it happened a second time, which left her shaken, if determined. "Again!"

"Okay. Now."

Elisabetta tried again, and though the car stutter-stepped forward and the engine screeched, this time it didn't stop. "Oh, look! Did it work?"

"Keep going, give it more gas!" Marco spoke louder to be heard over the engine.

"No more clutch?"

"Not until I say!"

Elisabetta gave the car gas, squeezed the wheel, and tried to steer straight. The car's headlights shone cones of light in the darkness, and she didn't dare to look left or right, focused on her driving. The car sped up, and the smooth sensation of motion made her smile, then the engine whined at a higher pitch, like a cat with its tail stepped on.

"Clutch again! Now!"

Elisabetta didn't understand. "The clutch is already up!"

"Press down and up! Now!"

Elisabetta did so, and it must have worked because the car jolted forward and they started to go faster. "I did it!" she yelled, excited.

"More gas!"

"Where are we going?"

"Forward!"

"Is it safe?"

"Of course not!"

Elisabetta laughed and gave the car more gas, then even more, pressing the clutch pedal when Marco cued her. They flew down the road, spraying gravel and dirt, and she felt thrilled by the sensation of speed and power at her command.

She began to giggle, racing a big black convertible to a place she didn't know at all. She sensed that was her life now, in that she knew only what was behind her and had no idea what lay ahead. She gave the car more gas, feeling truly in charge, a free woman of Rome, and for all of that, she had Marco to thank.

She raced along, the car shuddering beneath her. Was it possible she had fallen in love with both him and Sandro? And if so, how would she ever choose?

Elisabetta kept driving, into the future.

## CHAPTER THIRTY-THREE

# Sandro

5 September 1938

---

Sandro slid his bicycle into the crowded rack in the schoolyard. It was the first day of school, and all of the students were outside, standing in groups. Usually they'd be chattering, laughing, and fooling around, but they were quiet and seemed unusually subdued. Elisabetta was uppermost in his thoughts. He scanned the crowd for her, but she wasn't here yet.

He spotted his classmates Carlo, Ezio, and Vittorio standing in a circle looking at a piece of paper, and approached them. "*Ciao!*" he said, happy to see them. "How were your summers?"

The three looked up from the sheet of paper, their expressions stunned, and none of them offered a response.

"What's the matter?" Sandro asked, puzzled.

Carlo frowned. "The government passed some 'Race Laws,' whatever that's supposed to be."

"Race Laws?" Sandro asked, puzzled. "What does that mean?"

"We don't understand." Ezio pursed his lips. "It's horrible. It means that the Jews are kicked out of school. The Jewish teachers and the Jewish students, both."

"Are you joking?" Sandro didn't understand. It wasn't funny.

"No, it's not a joke. Preside Livorno is going to speak about it any minute. They gave us all a notice. Here, take a look." Vittorio handed him a sheet of paper. "The first part is about the teachers."

Sandro accepted the paper, and its title was "Measures for the Defense of Race in Fascist Schools." He read the first paragraph:

### ARTICLE I.

The position of teacher in state or state-controlled schools of any order or degree and in the nonstate schools, of which the studies are legally recognized, cannot be granted to people of the Jewish race, even if they won the position through a competitive state examination prior to the present degree; nor can they be granted positions as university assistants, nor can they obtain a university teaching qualification.

Sandro looked up, stricken. "There can't be Jewish teachers anymore? That's crazy! What happens to them?"

Carlo shook his head. "We think they're fired."

Ezio's face fell. "Professoressa Longhi is crying. All the teachers are upset. None of us know what's going on or why."

"Oh no!" Sandro kept reading, horrified:

### ARTICLE 2.

Students of the Jewish race cannot be enrolled in schools of any type or level of which the studies are legally recognized.

Sandro gasped, incredulous. He read the sentence twice. If he hadn't seen it printed in black and white, he never would have believed it was possible. "I don't understand. I'm already enrolled in school. Is this real? This is a law now? I'm not allowed to go?"

"I think so," Carlo muttered. "I don't know why they're doing this. It was never this way. It's wrong to single out the Jews, for no reason."

"This can't be true!" Sandro had a million thoughts at once. "I'm Jewish, so I can't go to school anymore? What do I do? This is my school! I go here! I'm graduating this year! Does this mean I don't graduate? I'm kicked out of my own school?"

"We don't know, either." Vittorio frowned. "I'm so sorry, Sandro. Maybe Preside Livorno will explain. It doesn't make any sense to us."

"My God!" Sandro couldn't believe it was happening. He wanted to go to La Sapienza for undergraduate and graduate degrees in mathematics. He wanted to learn all he could, then teach and publish papers. He wanted to *contribute*, like Professor Levi-Civita. He had goals, but he couldn't achieve a single one if he couldn't graduate from high school. All of a sudden, he had no future at all.

He glanced around in disbelief. His anguished gaze sought out the other Jewish students, though he had to pause before he remembered who was Jewish and who wasn't. It had simply never mattered to him or anyone else at school. He had no idea why it mattered now. He spotted Giulia and Carlotta, whom he knew from synagogue, and tears stained their cheeks as they read the sheet of paper.

He returned his attention to the sheet, trying to collect his thoughts. Ezio and Carlo fell silent, and Sandro read Article 3, which said that Jewish teachers were suspended, and then Article 4, which stated:

### ARTICLE 4.

Those members of scientific, literary, and artistic academies, institutes, and associations who are of the Jewish race will cease to be part of said institutions beginning on October 16, 1938, XVI.

Sandro's mind reeled. Professor Levi-Civita was Jewish, and if Jewish professors could no longer teach, that meant that the professor was suspended, too. It was unthinkable. It was insane. Sandro was supposed to go to La Sapienza after school today. He didn't know if Professor Levi-Civita or if any of the other Jewish professors would be there, or the Jewish students.

Suddenly the students erupted in chatter, turning to face the entrance to the school, and Preside Livorno appeared, with the faculty grouped behind him. His bright white hair blew in the breeze, and his gaze was solemn behind his glasses. He was stooped in his three-piece suit. All of the teachers were distraught, clinging to each other, and many had puffy eyes as if they had been weeping.

"Students!" Preside Livorno motioned. "Please, I need your attention!"

Sandro felt someone touching his arm. He looked over to see Elisabetta. Without a word, she took his hand, looking heartbroken for him.

Preside Livorno gave the Fascist salute, which everyone returned, then he began to speak. "Students, you have already received a copy of this new law, *Regio Decreto* Number 1390. It is a royal decree. I am very sorry to say that according to this law, Jewish students are no longer permitted to attend school here. In addition, Jewish teachers are no longer permitted to teach here."

"Preside Livorno, this is wrong!" Sandro called out, angering. "This law is wrong! You can't do this!"

Other students shouted, "This is unfair!" "Yes, this is wrong!" "Can they do that?" "Why are they doing this?" "This is my school!" "You should refuse to do it, Preside Livorno!"

"Please, settle down." Preside Livorno motioned for silence again. "We were instructed to give no opinion regarding this law, so we will not. We were instructed to see to its enforcement, so we must. We have been informed that Jewish students will be permitted to form their own schools, which they may attend with other Jewish students."

Sandro called out again, "You mean, *make* our own schools? How do we do that, Preside Livorno? This is unjust!"

Preside Livorno's lined face fell. "Sandro, we were told there may be funding to the Jewish community, in that regard. Again, we are very sorry."

"But how do I graduate?" Sandro shot back.

Other students chimed in to echo Sandro's concern.

Preside Livorno's eyes filmed behind his glasses. "My deepest apologies. I'm afraid I can say no more. I have no choice in this matter, under this law."

The bell sounded, signaling that classes were to begin, but no one moved. Sandro froze, unsure whether to stay or go. It was his school, and he had been so excited about the school year. His final one before graduation. His time with Elisabetta.

Preside Livorno called out, "Students, come in, the school day must commence. To all of our Jewish students, we wish you the best of luck in your future endeavors. Everyone else, please enter the building with dispatch."

Sandro glanced over as Carlo, Ezio, Vittorio, and his other classmates headed into the building.

Elisabetta embraced him. "Sandro, I'm so sorry."

"They can't do this, can they?"

"I . . . don't know."

Sandro released her. "Go," he said softly. "You have to go inside."

"No, I want to stay with you."

"Please, go."

"I'm staying with you." Elisabetta took his hand, but Sandro touched her shoulder, easing her off.

"Listen, I'll see you later."

The final bell rang, and Preside Livorno turned to the students. "For those permitted, please come in. We were instructed to keep classes on schedule. We mustn't start later than necessary."

Sandro tried to absorb the shock. "Really, go inside. I want to go to La Sapienza and see what's happening with the professor." He kissed her on the cheek. "I'll see you when I can."

"Of course."

Sandro watched Elisabetta turn reluctantly away, walk to the entrance with the other Gentile students, then glance back at him. He could see how much she was hurting for him, so he put on a brave face and waved goodbye. She climbed the steps into school amid the throng, and the schoolyard emptied of everyone except the Jewish students, Carlotta, Malka, Giulia, and others whose names he didn't know, teary and confused.

The doors to the school closed, and Sandro stood in mute astonishment on the outside, among the other Jewish students. Noise and chatter emanated from the school's open windows, and he knew that everyone would be filing into the classrooms, about to sing *"Giovinezza."* He had sung it every day, too, but today, Fascism had excluded him from his school and everyone he knew, including the girl he loved.

"What do we do now?" Giulia approached, wiping her eyes.

"I don't know, but I have to go." Sandro hurried for his bicycle.

Sandro pedaled through the streets, faster than he ever had before. The morning rush hour was in full swing, and it was all he could do to stay out of the way of cars, trams, and other bicycles. Everyone was hurrying to get to work or school, oblivious to the upheaval in the lives of Rome's Jews. He reached La Sapienza in record time, steered onto the asphalt path that ran through the center of campus, and joined the other students riding bicycles and walking in groups. He passed the new administration building, a massive edifice that had been built under Mussolini, which Sandro was seeing with new eyes. Its monolithic design used to impress him, but today it intimidated him.

He turned onto the path leading to the round, ultra-modern building that housed the Mathematics Department, and a large crowd of students buzzed on the grass in front. He jumped off his bike just in time to see a line of students, devastated and distraught, leaving the math building carrying their belongings.

Sandro felt stricken, witnessing the scene with dismay. Next to him stood a heavyset student, who also looked upset, and Sandro turned to him. "Excuse me, is this because of the new law?"

"Yes, the Jewish students were thrown out this morning. The Jewish professors received letters of dismissal, so they're fired. The course schedule is chaos. Nobody knows what to do. It's shocking."

"What about Levi-Civita? Has he left yet, do you know?"

"Levi-Civita? You have Levi-Civita?" The student's dark eyes lit up with new regard. "I'm Franco Dutolo."

Sandro introduced himself, shaking his hand.

"Which course do you take with Levi-Civita?"

"No course, an independent study."

"I haven't seen him yet, but I just got here. I'm on a waiting list for his seminar, or I was. I transferred from the University of Padua. Levi-Civita taught there for years. Everyone loved him. He takes the students on trips to the Alps." Franco turned and eyed the scene, shaking his head. "This is disgusting. It's bigotry. I never would've thought this could happen, and people are saying it will decimate the math department. Professors Volterra and Castelnuova already left. Believe it or not, some of the students were jeering."

Sandro recoiled, appalled.

"I heard that Professor Enriques tried to get into the library, but they wouldn't let him." Franco's eyes flared in outrage. "They threw him out. One of the finest mathematicians of the century."

"This is terrible." Sandro watched the graduate assistants walk by, some looking numb, many crying.

"Can you imagine, this is happening at universities all over the country. Padua. Bologna. Turin. Ferrara. Milan."

"I have to go inside."

"Don't, they told us not to. They told us to wait outside."

But Sandro wasn't following the rules anymore. He rolled his bicycle to the entrance, made his way through the crowd, and hurried into the building, his heart in his throat. Chaos reigned in the noisy hallway, and students milled everywhere, chattering and crying. Staff hugged each other, and professors wiped away tears.

Sandro took a right turn, heading for Professor Levi-Civita's office, driven to see him one last time, to say goodbye and thank you. He threaded his way through the crowd in the hallway and spotted Enzo standing outside the professor's office.

"Enzo!" Sandro hurried over, but the professor's door stood open and his office was empty.

Enzo's eyes glistened. "You just missed him. I'm so sorry. I knew you would come. I was hoping you would get here in time."

Sandro felt his throat thicken, and all of the emotions he had been suppressing caught up with him. He wanted to break down and cry, not only for himself, but for the professor and everyone else, too.

"I'm so sorry about this . . . *law*." Enzo sniffled. "Obviously, it disgusts me. It's discrimination, and it should be overturned, but I know that doesn't help you now. You were a brilliant student. I learned from you, not the other way around."

"Thank you," Sandro said, swallowing hard, as the kind words brought his sadness to the fore. "How was the professor? Was he upset?"

"Yes, but he held his head high. This is a nightmare. We're losing everybody."

"Where did he go?" Sandro struggled to maintain his composure.

"I don't know. Everybody's in an uproar. No one understands this new law." Enzo rubbed his face. "The rumor is it's going to affect almost a hundred professors across the country. It's so stupid and wrong, and it will only hurt Italy. We're going to lose the best. What's the sense in that?"

Sandro didn't have any answers. He would have to leave La Sapienza right now, never to return. He would never get his chance to work for

Levi-Civita. He would never teach here or contribute to the field of mathematics.

"Are you going to be okay?"

"Does it matter?" Sandro answered matter-of-factly.

<br>

CHAPTER THIRTY-FOUR

# Elisabetta

5 September 1938

<br>

After school, Elisabetta entered the steamy kitchen at Casa Servano and hung up her purse outside the pantry, where Nonna sat at her table. Four chubby lines of soft dough sat dusted with flour, and the old woman's silvery head was bent over them as she cut one line into small sections, leaving a row of small pasta pillows.

Elisabetta assumed Nonna was making *gnocchi*, but Paolo hadn't been at the bar to play the guessing game, and she was in no mood anyway. She had worried about Sandro all day, and school had been awful, with all the students, teachers, and administration upset and angry.

"*Ciao*, Nonna." Elisabetta crossed to kiss Nonna on the cheeks, breathing in her familiar smells of flour and rosewater. "Did you hear what happened today, to the Jews?"

"What do you think, I live in a cave? Mussolini turns on the Jews, bringing Trastevere to tears! Throwing children out of their schools! Teachers out of jobs! The man is a monster, a scourge! Now you!" Nonna glanced up from her work, her mouth pursed tightly. "Sit down."

"Me? And Mussolini?" Elisabetta sat down, bewildered.

"Isn't that my newspaper?" Nonna gestured to yesterday's newspaper, resting on the other chair.

"Yes."

"I'm angry with you."

"Why?"

Nonna pressed her index and middle finger into one of the soft pillows of pasta, made a dimple in the center, then sent it skidding across the flour with a deft backhand of her fingernails. "You wrote on my newspaper?"

Elisabetta had circled some rooms to let. "I suppose so, yes. I'm sorry."

"You're looking for a place to stay?"

"Yes."

"You didn't think to ask me?" Nonna rolled another piece of pasta. "Don't you realize how insulted I am? Didn't you think I'd have a room for you? Don't you know I'm a woman of means? Don't you know I own property? I have a very nice room in one of my buildings. It even has a bathroom."

"For me?"

"Of course for you!" Nonna scowled, exasperated.

Elisabetta didn't understand. It sounded like an offer, if not for Nonna's manner. "Well, thank you, then. How much is the rent?"

Nonna's head snapped up, her hooded eyes flaring behind her spectacles. "Elisabetta, what kind of woman do you think I am?"

Elisabetta felt overwhelmed. "A room, for free? I can't possibly accept such generosity."

"Then I'll fire you. Say goodbye to Casa Servano and me."

"No!" Elisabetta rushed to say, confused.

"You mean 'yes.' What's the matter with you? Can't you say 'yes'?"

"Yes!" Elisabetta answered, grateful to be prompted. It wasn't a conversation, it was a minefield. "Thank you! Where is the room?"

"Via Fiorata 28."

Elisabetta blinked. "That's where you live, isn't it?"

"Yes, I told you, I own it. Don't you listen?" Nonna sent another *gnocchi* flying across the flour. "I am on the ground floor. You will be upstairs, with your very own bathroom."

"Wonderful, thank you!" Elisabetta felt relief wash over her like a warm bath, but Nonna was looking up at her fiercely, with a knife in her hand.

"There is one problem. Your stupid cat."

"How do you know about my cat?" Elisabetta swallowed hard. She would never put Rico on the street. She would rather give up the free room.

"You don't know I see you collecting fish scraps? Or hear you talking about how smart he is? How handsome? How affectionate?"

"May I bring him?"

"Does he spray?"

"No."

Nonna eyed her, deciding. "Then, yes."

Elisabetta hugged her, unable to hold back.

"But if he sprays," said Nonna, "I'll cut off his *gnocchi*."

CHAPTER THIRTY-FIVE

# Sandro

5 September 1938

Rosa!" Sandro looked up from his notebook, happy to see his older sister entering the apartment. She had moved into her own place with some roommates and didn't come home that often. She crossed into the dining room, setting down her purse, and embraced him. She had on her fashionable tan suit, with her hair pulled into its twist, and he caught a fading whiff of her floral perfume.

"I heard what happened at school, Sandro. I'm so sorry."

"Thanks. It happened at La Sapienza, too. Levi-Civita left. I was too late to say goodbye."

"Oh no. You must be so sad."

"I'm trying not to be." Sandro spoke from the heart. "I'm trying to stay on track."

"You can't stay on track when your own government is derailing you." Rosa frowned sympathetically. "Mussolini has turned against us. The manifesto and the Race Laws show he doesn't want Jews in Italy any longer. He's going to make life so hard for us that we leave."

"But why, do you think? Why now, after all this time?"

"It's what David and I have been worried about. Mussolini is choosing to side with Hitler, and if Hitler is against the Jews, so is Mussolini." Rosa touched his arm tenderly. "I know you love Papa, and so do I, but he's missing what I see at the embassy."

Sandro felt torn. "But he knows people in the party and he reads the papers."

"He reads only the Fascist papers, and all of his closest friends are Fascists. They go with Mussolini, no matter what." Rosa squeezed his arm. "Anyway, just because Papa thinks something doesn't mean you have to. Fascism is now our enemy. Jews should leave the party, after today. The Race Laws are the last straw. They threw you out of school. It's outrageous!"

"Papa says it will be temporary."

"He's wrong. Sandro, you have to think for yourself."

"Rosa!" His mother entered the room and kissed Rosa on both cheeks, followed by his father.

"What a nice surprise!" His father held out his arms to embrace Rosa, but Sandro detected the effort in his parents' smiles. All evening, they had been talking privately in his father's study.

Rosa kissed them both. "What a terrible day. I'm horrified."

"As are we," his mother said, her tone controlled. "But your father is already working on solutions. You'll stay and eat, won't you?"

Sandro interjected, "It's my consolation dinner, Rosa. Cornelia promised me something fried."

Rosa chuckled, a happy sound amid the tension. "I'd love to stay."

"Good, sit down, and I'll get another place setting." His mother turned and left for the kitchen.

"Yes, sit down, both of you." His father crossed to the table, picked up his wineglass, poured some, and offered it to Rosa. "How have you been?"

"Fine, until today." Rosa accepted the wine and sat down. "Papa, what about the Race Laws? What is Mamma talking about, solutions?"

"We have to keep our wits and go forward. There is a provision for Jewish schools to be established with government funding."

"But what do you think of the party now? You, of all people, who are so loyal, must have been shocked. It's an about-face, is it not?"

"As I told Sandro, I am shocked by the promulgation of the Race Laws.

However, since then, I've had some time to study the law, confer with members of the Board, and make some calls."

Rosa frowned. "It's horrifying, nothing can change that, Papa."

"The Board is already exploring renting a space in which to hold classes, and members of the Community are volunteering to teach. We certainly have plenty of teachers and professionals who can help us."

"But—" Rosa started to say, but his father raised a hand.

"Jewish teachers who were displaced today have been calling the synagogue, looking for work, and we are making a list to see how many we can hire. I have suggested we take Professoressa Longhi, Sandro's math teacher. Sandro can help teach arithmatic to the younger students. He's always wanted to teach, so perhaps we can look on this as an opportunity."

"An *opportunity*?" Rosa repeated, her disapproval undisguised. His mother reentered the room with the place setting, set a dish and silverware in front of Rosa, then sat down.

"Yes," his father answered firmly. "Obviously, this is a bad situation, but we must make the best of it. There's no reason for Sandro and the others to lose time, as they will still be eligible to take the state examination at the end of the year. If they pass, they will graduate."

"So that's been provided for?"

"Yes. What matters most is that the academic needs of the students are met." His father patted him on the shoulder. "Obviously, this is not a problem only for Sandro's *liceo*. There are early estimates that about six thousand Jewish students are affected, one hundred and seventy secondary school teachers, and a hundred university professors. So we'll adapt and go on. After all, survival is what we Jews do best."

"Well put, dear," his mother said, as Cornelia entered the dining room with a dish of *carciofi alla giudia*, fried artichokes, a Jewish specialty.

Sandro's eyes lit up. "*Bravissima*, Cornelia."

"Just for you." Cornelia smiled as she set down the platter, and the fried artichokes looked delicious. The light breading glistened with olive oil and lemon, and was dotted with coarse flakes of sea salt. His father said a prayer over the food, and Sandro plucked a spear of artichoke, taking a bite.

"Mmm, I'm officially consoled."

"Good." Cornelia patted his shoulder and went back to the kitchen.

Rosa cleared her throat. "I have something to tell everyone, even though this night is already a difficult one. I might as well come out with it. My job at an international relief agency has come through, and everything is in place. I am going to emigrate with David, and it's all set up. I'm sorry to have to tell you tonight, but I'm leaving at the end of the week."

Sandro felt stunned and sad. He had never believed she would go through with it. He didn't know what to say. It felt like a blow, but he would keep that to himself.

"So soon?" His mother's hand flew to her mouth.

His father's lined face fell. "This is sudden, isn't it?"

"Not really," Rosa answered, her tone softer. "I've been waiting for it to come through. I don't want to go without you all, but I'm afraid to stay. I'm afraid for you if you stay."

"We'll be fine," her father said quietly. "We live here. We work here."

"We have to stay, Rosa," her mother added, and Sandro looked down at his plate, stricken. He agreed with his parents, and he certainly didn't want to leave Rome, or Elisabetta. But the turn of events had shaken his confidence in his position.

"Listen to me, one last time." Rosa leaned over. "What worries me is that at some point, you will not be permitted to emigrate. I hear things at the embassy, and I know you'll say that's not official, but it's reliable. Jews all over Europe are fleeing the Nazis. And I know you say Jews are coming to Italy, and you're right, but they'll be in the same terrible position. Those who act quickly have a chance to go. If you delay, it will be only more difficult and more dangerous."

"Dangerous?" His father scoffed.

"Yes, Papa." Rosa pursed her lips. "Other countries are already moving to block refugees. The United States has quotas on Jews and it's raising more restrictions. Their State Department procedures are fraught with delay. Even if you can get a visa, there are regulations about how much money you can leave Italy with, and if it's not enough to support you, nobody will admit you."

His father frowned, and his mother arched an eyebrow, but Rosa wouldn't let them get a word in.

"Nobody wants to take Jews, and even the British are asking applicants to pay thousands of pounds to get a visa to Palestine. If I didn't work at the embassy, it would've been much harder for me. Please come with me to London. This is your last chance."

"No, thank you," his father said, shaking his head. "We've already told you."

"I'm sorry," his mother added.

Sandro felt heartsick, but he could see that his sister was on the verge of tears. He loved her, so he knew what he had to say. "Rosa, I understand why you want to go. You should do what you have to do."

"Thank you." Rosa smiled shakily at him, then returned her attention to their parents. "And there's one more thing you have to know. I got married to David in London last week, so now I'm his wife."

"*What?*" His father's mouth dropped open. "You're married?"

"Rosa?" His mother's eyes rounded behind her glasses. "My goodness! Why didn't you tell us?"

Sandro looked over, astonished, but Rosa was taking their mother's hand.

"Mamma, I didn't tell you because I know how you and Papa felt about me marrying somebody who wasn't Italian. And doesn't that objection seem beside the point, after all that's happened? According to the manifesto, we're no longer Italian because we're Jews. Papa, do you see the absurdity?"

"No." His father folded his arms. "The manifesto is still not the law. No one can deny history. We're Italian Jews. We're Roman."

His mother shook her head, stunned. "You could've told us, Rosa. You could have let us know. We weren't even at your wedding!"

Rosa looked stricken. "I knew you would have tried to talk me out of it, and I didn't want to give you the chance. We had to get married there to improve my chances for immigration."

Sandro understood, though he was sad he hadn't gotten to see her get married, either. He felt happy for Rosa, but remained heartbroken that she was leaving the country. His emotions roiled within him. Everything was going wrong. His father was angry, his mother was reeling, and he couldn't wait until this awful day ended.

His father shook his head. "Rosa, he's not Italian. How could you?"

"We love each other, that's how." Rosa frowned. "He's a wonderful man, and we were married in a Jewish ceremony, with his parents and brother there."

"That doesn't make him Italian!" His father threw up his hands. "We wanted Italian grandchildren."

All of a sudden, Sandro felt the emotions he'd kept inside explode. "Papa, does it matter? First you say I can't see Elisabetta because she's not Jewish. Then you say Rosa can't marry David because he's not Italian."

His father turned to him, wounded. "Your mother and I have wishes for both of you, and we are entitled to that. Where is your respect, son?"

"I respect you, of course." Sandro realized that he had to think for himself, as Rosa had said, so he did. "But can't I disagree with you? Doesn't what happened today demonstrate the fallacy in your logic? People aren't categories, and it's morally wrong to throw me out of my school because I'm Jewish. It hurts people, to no end. It's just plain *wrong*. The government is discriminating against us, so we can't discriminate in return, can we? It's unprincipled."

His mother rose, clutching her napkin, uncharacteristically shaken. Her eyebrows sloped down, and her lower lip trembled. "I hate this fussing. I wanted to see my daughter get married. Now, I can't, and I never will." She held her napkin to her nose as she began to cry, then she turned and hurried from the room, with Rosa at her heels.

It left Sandro and his father alone at the table, and they fell silent, neither speaking to fill the void. Sandro looked down at his plate, trying to sort his emotions. He had to acknowledge a diminishment of respect for his father, whose views simply didn't stand to reason. Sandro never used to have such cross words with him, except for the last conversation about Elisabetta.

Sandro wished they could resolve the issue, so he looked up, but was surprised to find his father sitting stiffly upright in his chair. His father's eyes had filmed behind his glasses, and Sandro experienced a wave of regret. Never before had he seen his father cry.

"Papa?" he said, rising, but his father waved him to stay in his seat.

"When you have children of your own, you'll understand."

## CHAPTER THIRTY-SIX

# Aldo
### October 1938

Bar GiroSport was busy, and Aldo manned the coffee machine at the counter with their older barmaid, Letizia. His father worked in the outside seating area, taking care of customers and shooing away the accordion player and photographer who tried to make money from the tourists. Marco was serving a table of pretty nurses, and Aldo looked on, amused. Marco had always been naturally at ease with women, and Aldo often wished that he had his little brother's charm, but it was unique to him. Aldo loved him too much to be envious.

*"Due caffè ristretti,"* Letizia said, meaning two coffees, short and dense, and Aldo picked up a cup and turned the lever on the tall Victoria Arduino coffee machine, with its gleaming eagle on top.

He brewed the coffee, his thoughts straying where they always did—to the danger presented by the anti-Fascists' plans. Spada's retirement party was getting closer, and Aldo was getting more terrified for Marco. To his growing horror, the anti-Fascists rehearsed the attack at every meeting, pretending that sticks were guns, since he hadn't been dispatched to Orvieto yet. Every morning and night, he prayed to God for guidance, but none had come.

Aldo handed the coffee to Letizia and started brewing another cup, completely preoccupied. He had still been unsuccessful in persuading Marco to quit his job, but had been thinking of an alternative plan. It sounded crazy, but he was considering giving Marco tainted pork on the day of the retirement party, rendering him too sick to go. The only problem was that Marco had an iron stomach, so it would require a lot to get him sick, and Aldo didn't want his little brother to end up in the hospital across the street. Anyway Marco would go to the party unless he was truly, deathly ill because he couldn't wait to celebrate Spada's departure.

Aldo handed Letizia the second coffee, glancing outside. His gaze happened to fall on the blond hair of a woman taking a seat at one of the tables in their outside seating area. He recognized her. It was Silvia, Uno's wife.

Aldo looked down, hiding his face. His heart began to pound. Silvia had no idea that he worked here. If she saw him, she would learn his true identity.

"One coffee, *senza schiuma*," Letizia said, meaning a coffee without the top of foam.

Aldo had to get out of sight. "Letizia, can you cover for me? I have to go to the bathroom."

"Sure," Letizia answered, and Aldo left the counter and was about to hurry into the back, when he realized that he was too late. Silvia had gotten up and was talking with his father, probably asking him where the bathroom was. In the next moment, Silvia entered the bar, making a *bella figura* in a nice blue dress that clung to her lithe form.

Aldo's mouth went dry. He couldn't let her see him. Meanwhile the sight of her turned Marco's head, for his brother never missed a pretty girl. Aldo didn't know what to do. He couldn't let Marco start talking to her. Knowing his little brother, he'd bring up his *fascio* job to impress her, and all would be lost.

Aldo froze. Silvia was walking toward him and Marco. He couldn't avoid her. If he went left or right, she would see him move. He turned his head away as if he were talking to some customers. Out of the corner of his eye, he was aghast to see Silvia looking right at him, and she slowed her step.

Aldo looked over and met her eye, caught. Silvia gazed directly back at him. Strangely, her expression registered no surprise, then she nodded as if sending him a signal. She made her way to the back of the bar and into the narrow hallway, where the stockroom and restrooms were located. Luckily Marco looked away, summoned by a customer.

Aldo followed Silvia, his mind racing. He turned into the hallway, and Silvia was waiting for him.

"I need to talk to you," she said under her breath.

"Okay, in the stockroom." Aldo showed her inside the tiny room under the stairwell, which was lined with groceries. He closed the door quickly and turned on the light. "Silvia, what are you doing here?"

"Uno sent me to see you, Aldo."

Aldo felt shocked. "How do you know my name? Or that I work here?"

"Uno found out because we needed to talk to you. It's urgent."

Aldo recoiled. "But how did he find out?"

"He has ways."

Aldo masked his alarm. "I thought our identities were secret. I thought we trusted each other. We shouldn't spy on each other."

"I agree with you, but you don't understand the risks Uno takes. That's why I came instead of him." Silvia's forehead creased. "Trust me, he has good reasons for how he operates. I won't hide anything more from you, so I'll tell you, he knows that your father is a Fascist of the First Hour."

Aldo thanked God that they didn't know about Marco. He got his bearings. "I'm sure I'm not the only one of our cell to have a father who's a committed Fascist. I'm my own man, and nevertheless loyal to our cause."

"We know that, and that's not why I've come. I'm here to tell you to go to Orvieto tonight."

"Tonight?" Aldo swallowed hard, off balance. "Why tonight? What happened?"

"Something came up, that's all I can say."

Aldo wished he could stall her. The longer he could put off getting the guns, the better. "But I don't know if I'm ready."

"Why not?"

Aldo tried to think of a lie, but he was a terrible liar. "Uh, but tonight is such short notice."

"It couldn't be helped."

"But I have to prepare."

"Prepare what?"

"My bike. I have to get it in order."

"Is it broken? Can't you fix it?"

"No, well, it's not broken, but—"

"Aldo, are you afraid? Is that it?" Silvia's blue eyes sharpened with suspicion. "Is that why you've gotten so thin? Is it from anxiety?"

"Yes," Aldo answered, sensing that the woman was too smart to believe an outright denial. "But I didn't want to admit it in front of the others."

"I knew it. I see things my husband doesn't." Silvia patted his arm. "Be brave. It's dangerous, but not unreasonably so. You said you would go, and you must. My husband shouldn't have to do everything. Do your part. Keep your word."

"Okay." Aldo resigned himself to going, as it didn't bring the date of the retirement party any closer.

"*Bravo.*" Silvia smiled briefly. "Leave after nightfall and be back by morning. Our contact will be waiting for you at a tavern called Piccolo's, on Via del Duomo off the Corso Cavour."

"How will I know him?"

"He goes by Fabio and he'll be wearing a checked cap. He's going to give you a package of six pistols. Ride back to Rome straightaway and place them in a hole in the underbrush near the Terme di Caracalla, where Viale delle Terme di Caracalla intersects Via Antoniniana. Are you familiar?"

"No."

"I just told you the location. You'll find it with ease. If it's not safe for any reason, hide in place or travel the next night. Don't go back to Orvieto looking for our contact. Understand?"

"Yes."

"Good luck. Goodbye." Silvia opened the door to the storeroom and left, and Aldo heaved a sigh. His chest felt too small for his lungs to fill, and he had always had excellent wind. He left the stockroom and entered the bar.

Marco crossed to him with a sly smile. "Aldo, was that *her*?"

Aldo understood the mix-up, which worked to his advantage. "Uh, yes."

"A blonde! What a beauty!"

"Uh, thank you." Aldo realized that he wouldn't be able to ride home with Marco tonight, if he had to go to Orvieto. "She came by to tell me that her husband's going out of town, so I can stay with her the whole night. Will you cover for me with Papa and Mamma?"

"Yes, of course. But what about in the morning, when you're not home?"

Aldo felt nonplussed, but Marco's face lit up.

"I have an idea. I'll tell Papa that you felt good and decided to train until late, like take an endurance ride. Then he and Mamma won't wait up. Just be back before they're up in the morning."

"Great idea," Aldo said, forcing a smile. The irony wasn't lost on him that his little brother was helping him obtain the guns that would be turned against him.

"Now tell me." Marco leaned closer, his eyes glinting. "What happened in the stockroom? Did you give her some, that quick?"

"Marco, no!" Aldo chuckled, though he felt sick to his stomach.

"It can be done, brother. I know, for a fact."

Aldo didn't reply, except to shove him playfully.

Evening darkened into nightfall, and Aldo rode out of Rome and found the back roads heading north. He kept an eye on the traffic around him, making sure he wasn't followed, but he felt safe. His thoughts churned as he went, knowing that each revolution of his wheels brought him closer to something he dreaded. He had to save Marco, and tainted pork seemed like his best alternative.

Over three hours passed on the bike, and Aldo finally reached the medieval town of Orvieto. He rode through its cobblestone streets and found Piccolo's, a shabby bar on a narrow street lined by closed shops. Everything was dark except for the tavern, which shed an elliptical shaft of light onto the sidewalk. Slumping against the wall near the entrance was a man in a checked cap, drinking from a wine bottle. It had to be Fabio, posing as a drunk. On the ground next to Fabio lay a bulky package wrapped in brown paper and twine. The guns.

Aldo slowed his pace, glancing around to make sure he wasn't being watched. The street was deserted, and no one was around. A dog barked in the distance, otherwise there was absolute stillness.

In the next moment, Fabio rose, wobbly, then staggered away, pretending to lean on the wall to steady himself. The wrapped package remained on the ground.

Aldo didn't hesitate. He sped up, leaned over as he rode past, snatched it, and kept going. It was heavy, and he tossed it into the pouch on his handlebars.

Aldo found his heart beating hard, now that he had the pistols. There really was no going back now. He sent up a prayer for forgiveness. He resolved again to find a way to save Marco. Now it was time to get back to Rome.

He scanned the street, and it remained empty, dark, and quiet. He rode down the street, turned around, and steered back the way he came, due south. His eyes swept the streets as he pedaled faster, heading out of town. He left Orvieto and kept going, every muscle tense as he gripped the handlebars.

His thighs began to burn, and he accelerated, barreling into the dark night. The road wound this way and that, with a long ride ahead. The pistols in the pouch clinked against each other, making noise when he hit a bump.

Aldo lowered his upper body to improve his aerodynamics. He made his way through pastures with grazing horses and cows in the darkness. The headlights of a passing car shone on him, but he ignored it. He accelerated, then the car accelerated, but didn't pass him. He didn't understand. He signaled to the car to pass him, but it didn't. It didn't make sense.

Aldo held steady with the car at his heels, over his right shoulder. The big headlights illuminated him. He glanced over his shoulder to see it was a big, dark sedan. He felt a tremor of fright. He told himself to calm down, but it wasn't working. He slowed, but the sedan slowed, too. He sped up, and the sedan sped up. But it still didn't pass him.

Fear bolted through him, powering his fatigued body. The sedan dogged his back tire, toying with him. Aldo pedaled harder, channeling his fear into effort. The sedan sped so close that he could feel heat emanating from its big engine. He heard men laughing. Maybe drinkers, having fun at his expense. There was no one around to help. He was on his own.

The sedan gunned its engine, gaining on him. He couldn't hope to outrun them, but he kept going, his heart hammering from a growing terror. Suddenly a bottle hit his shoulder, and the men burst into raucous laughter.

Aldo gripped the handlebars but didn't fall. His front tire wobbled but he kept control. He tried to think of a way out. There was none. He was on a long stretch of road flanked by fences and farms, with no byway to the left or right. The men in the sedan must know the roads better than he. He was frightened, but prayed they would leave him alone.

Aldo could barely see in the darkness. Ahead the road curved to the right and disappeared. The wind buffeted him broadside, and clouds raced to conceal the moon. He steered around the curve to the right, then saw to his horror that the road was blocked by a line of sedans that were facing him, head-on. Their headlights were switched off.

An ambush.

Aldo braked as hard as he could. The cars switched on their headlights, blasting him with light, blinding him. He slid into a fall. His bicycle vanished from under him. The package of guns flew from the pouch.

Everything happened at once. He fell to the ground, half-rolling and half-skidding off the road. The asphalt tore his jersey off and flayed his skin. An agonizing pain ripped through his arms and legs. He couldn't hold a single thought.

Aldo found himself coming to a stop in a grassy ditch, hitting a fence post. He smelled manure. He heard the thundering of hooves as horses ran off.

He struggled to maintain consciousness. The pain was agonizing. He hurt everywhere. He felt warmth all over his face. He knew it was his own blood. He opened his eyes with effort. Above him loomed a line of dark silhouettes, brandishing long clubs.

Fascists.

Aldo felt his heart thunder with terror. The Fascists must have discovered their plans. He struggled to his feet, but his legs buckled under him. Pain exploded in his right knee. It must be broken. He pitched forward and crumpled to the ground. His blood drenched him. He smelled the metallic odor.

The men laughed, coming for him. "Bolshevik pig!" "You're under arrest, Communist!" "I see a gun on him, don't you?" "Yes, I see it, too!" "We have to defend ourselves!"

Aldo realized they were going to kill him, not arrest him. He tried to crawl away. His legs seared with agony. He panted and grunted like an animal. He clawed his way forward with his fingers.

"Come on, boy, run for it! Make it fun!"

A club whacked him from behind. He heard his scapula crack and splinter. Excruciating pain shot through his body. He refused to cry out. If he was going to die, it would be with bravery.

"Come on, get up and run, you good-for-nothing!"

The men began pounding Aldo with clubs, breaking his ribs. His elbow. His legs. He writhed in agony. Someone kicked him in the head. He began to lose consciousness.

Suddenly Aldo felt no pain. His life began to ebb away. He recited the Hail Mary. It was the hour of his death. His soul left his body, and he felt himself looking down on the young man lying beside a country road, being beaten by the men who had stolen his country.

He thought of his family. He loved them so much. He regretted that he had never let them know him, truly. He had kept himself to himself.

He regretted that he had never been loved by a woman. He would have been the most devoted of husbands. He hadn't wanted to leave his life, so soon.

Yet he knew he was going to a better life, an eternal one, in the embrace of a just and loving God.

And in his last moment, he felt the deepest anguish, for now he could no longer protect his beloved Marco.

CHAPTER THIRTY-SEVEN

# Marco
October 1938

It was a slow morning at Bar GiroSport, with Marco at the counter with Letizia, since Aldo hadn't come home last night. His parents had been surprised to wake up to Aldo's absence, and they had worried, so Marco had told them that Aldo had been seeing a married girlfriend and had undoubtedly overslept there. Now both sons were in trouble, with their parents angry at them for lying, and at Aldo for having an affair with a married woman. Marco simmered at the utter hypocrisy of his father's reaction, and resentment boiled within him.

He looked up from the counter, surprised to see his boss, Commendatore Buonacorso, entering the bar with his father. Marco wondered if he was getting a promotion, since things had been going so well at work. His father motioned him forward, so Marco asked Letizia to take over, left the counter, and saluted his boss.

"Commendatore Buonacorso, it's good to see you."

Buonacorso nodded, his expression unusually grim. "I'm here to speak with you and your parents."

Marco followed his father and Buonacorso into the kitchen, which had a small hallway before the cooking area and oven in the back. His mother looked up from the stove and wiped her hands on her apron as she came forward.

"Commendatore," she said, smiling, "I'm pleased to see you. May I get you something for breakfast?"

"No, thank you, signora." Buonacorso took off his hat. "Marco, is there a seat, perhaps?"

"Yes, Commendatore." Marco grabbed an old stool and pushed it toward his boss. "Sir, please, sit down."

"No, the seat is intended for your mother." Buonacorso motioned. "Signora, please. Sit down."

"Thank you, how thoughtful." His mother eased onto the seat, obviously impressed by the commendatore's manners.

Buonacorso cleared his throat. "Beppe, Maria, Marco, I'm sorry, but I have terrible news. There is no way to mince words. I regret to inform you that your Aldo is dead. He was an anti-Fascist. He was killed while transporting pistols to Rome, presumably for his comrades."

Marco gasped, horrified. It wasn't possible. He couldn't believe what he was hearing.

"No," his father said hoarsely. "This can't be. You must be mistaken."

His mother's hand flew to her mouth, her eyes widening with horror, but she made no sound.

"The incident took place last night, outside Orvieto," Buonacorso explained. "Aldo was stopped as he rode south to Rome. Five pistols were found in a package on his bicycle. He also had a pistol on his person. He resisted arrest and shot at the officers, almost killing one. Aldo was killed in self-defense."

"This can't be." His father shook his head.

His mother covered her face with her hands.

Marco's mind reeled. His lower lip trembled, but he found his voice. "Sir, there must be some mistake. Aldo was with his girlfriend last night. I'm sure he's still there. I promise you, he'll be home any minute."

"Marco, there is no mistake. These facts are true."

"But I know he's with his girlfriend, he went there last night. He goes there at night when he's supposed to be training, he's in love—"

"That is not where he has been going, Marco." Buonacorso frowned. "I cannot divulge further details, but OVRA has been surveilling the members of an anti-Fascist cell. The traitors have been meeting in the catacombs at night. Aldo has been identified as being there, routinely, among them."

Marco opened his mouth, but uttered no words. Aldo was gone. Tears flooded his eyes. He could barely hear the commendatore, who kept speaking.

"Aldo's body is in transit. He had his identity card on his person, and, Beppe, you will be asked to provide final identification of his body and sign the proper forms. My condolences."

His father remained in emotional control, his expression rigid. "Commendatore Buonacorso, I assure you that my son Aldo is no *traditore*. Aldo loved Mussolini and our country. You know I am a Fascist of the First Hour. I raised my family in Fascism. Marco is loyal to our party, and Aldo is the same way."

"Beppe, I understand this comes as a shock, so I won't speak further on the matter. I take my leave of you now, so that you may mourn together." Buonacorso put his hat back on. "As a matter of security, we will not report the details of this matter to the press. We will report instead that Aldo perished in a bicycle accident, and his body was found by police."

Smoky incense thickened the air, and Marco sat in his stiff black suit, facing the altar. Aldo's funeral Mass was almost over, though Marco hadn't heard a word. The colorful icon that depicted Madonna and Child against lapis lazuli flickered in the soft light of white tapers, and the only sound was the droning Latin of Father Donato and the occasional coughing of the congregation.

Marco, Emedio, and their mother had cried so much the past few days, but their father hadn't shed a tear, even after identifying Aldo's body, which had shown bullet wounds and signs of a beating, presumably the police venting their anger on his corpse. His father was deeply ashamed that Aldo had died as an anti-Fascist. It only stoked Marco's resentment against his father, for he himself mourned Aldo regardless of politics, and his love for his brother would never go away.

Marco remembered playing ball with Aldo in the Piazza San Bartolomeo all'Isola, then cuddling with him at night, since they slept in the same bed when they were little. Aldo had taught him how to fix a tire and operate the coffee machine. It was impossible to imagine life without Aldo's quiet, constant presence, for his brother had been as foundational as the cobblestones beneath Marco's feet.

The funeral Mass ended, and Father Donato swung a silver thurible on a chain, leaving pungent trails of gray smoke. Marco left the pew, then lined up beside Aldo's coffin with his father and the other pallbearers. They lifted the casket onto their shoulders with a whispered *uno, due, tre* and egressed slowly, moving into a shaft of sunlight in the middle of the aisle.

Marco bore his brother's casket outside, then loaded it into the undertaker's hearse. Mourners left the church, and he noticed Elisabetta among them, standing with Sandro and his parents. Her beautiful, dark eyes, flooded with tears, spoke to his heart. He stepped away to go to her, but heard his father's voice booming through the air.

"Marco, no, get in the car!"

Marco turned around, shocked to see his father charging toward him through the mourners, red-faced.

"Get in the car!" His father clamped Marco on the shoulder and yanked him away from Elisabetta. "This is your brother's funeral!"

"Papa, no—"

His father slapped him, and Marco's hand flew to his cheek. Elisabetta gasped. Marco's mother and Emedio recoiled, and the Simones edged away. His father grabbed Marco by the shoulder, but Marco broke his father's grip, confronting him.

"You want to tell me what to do, but I know what you did! I know who you are! I *know*!"

Clearly stunned, his father punched Marco, connecting with his left cheek, and Marco staggered backward, dizzy with pain. His mother wailed, Emedio shouted, and the mourners broke into horrified comment.

Marco ignored them, and all of the anger and resentment that had been intensifying within him exploded. He swung hard at his father, punching him in the temple. His father stumbled backward, arms flailing.

Emedio, Massimo, and Sandro rushed to break them up, but Marco cocked his right arm.

He didn't throw the punch.

His father looked him in the eye, realizing that Marco had pulled his punch, then lunged at him with the force of a freight train. The impact almost knocked Marco down, but Emedio, Sandro, Massimo, and other mourners surged forward and managed to tear father and son apart, yet both of them struggled against the restraint, torquing this way and that.

Even in the chaos, Marco knew that he was no longer under his father's control. He was his own man now, and nothing between them would ever be the same.

## CHAPTER THIRTY-EIGHT

# Massimo

### November 1938

Massimo hurried up the stairway in the synagogue. Another set of Race Laws had been issued this morning, and the Board was in an uproar. He reached the Sala del Consiglio, or the conference room, which was lined with bookshelves and dominated by a long polished conference table and chairs. Men sat in groups, holding copies of the new law. Rabbi Zolli was on the phone in his office, trying to compose the Community's response.

Massimo spotted his friends Luciano and Armando at the conference table. They were businessmen; Luciano in commercial real estate and Armando in banking. Luciano was tall and thin, but Armando short and round. Their faces were equally grave.

"*Ciao*, Massimo, sit down." Luciano pulled out a wooden chair. "Thanks for coming so quickly. This is a catastrophe."

"I know, it's very disconcerting." Massimo sat down, opening his briefcase.

"Disconcerting? It's *terrifying*." Luciano shook his head, pained. "When I left the house, my wife was in tears."

Armando frowned. "When I left the office, my *partners* were in tears. Anyway, what do you think?"

"I have a plan." Massimo took out his copy of the new laws, "Measures for the Defense of the Italian Race." "First, let's go through it quickly, for the end is what matters. The objective of the law is in Item 1, Measures Regarding Marriages, and Articles 1 through 7, relating to intermarriage between Jews and Gentiles. From now on, 'The marriage of an Italian citizen of the Aryan race with a person belonging to another race is prohibited.'"

"In other words, no intermarriage."

"Exactly." It was not lost on Massimo that under the new Race Law,

Sandro would no longer be permitted to marry Elisabetta. "Item 2, Article 8 defines what is a Jew, and Article 9 states that membership in the Jewish race must be reported and entered into official registers. This was codified before, if you recall."

Luciano scowled. "It's discriminatory treatment. Gentiles don't have to do any such thing."

Armando nodded.

"I agree." Massimo returned to the law. "These are laws that codify injustice. Nevertheless we move on. Article 10 provides that Jews may not serve in the military, act as guardians, or be owners or managers of companies related to national defense or companies of any kind that employ a hundred or more people." He looked up. "This is a terrible provision. Most of my clients own businesses that qualify. This will ruin my practice."

Luciano groaned. "Me, too."

Armando's face fell. "I'll go bankrupt."

Massimo remained on course. His friends needed his guidance, not his emotions. "Section D provides that Jews cannot own land valued over five thousand *lire*, which I believe we all do. Section E provides Jews can't own any urban buildings with a taxable value of over twenty thousand *lire*, which includes me."

Luciano pursed his lips. "We live in the suburbs, but my wife's family owns the house."

Armando plopped his chin into his hand. "I own my house, too. Or I used to, until today."

Massimo nodded. "One could form a corporate entity and transfer the property to it, transfer the property to non-Jewish members of the family or to trusted friends, or even transfer it to a charitable institution."

Luciano nodded. "But wouldn't that be considered a fraudulent transfer?"

"In theory, but not as a practical matter. From my research, there's only a handful of people set up to administer this law. They're going to be deluged with applications for exemptions. I doubt they'll get to questioning transfers of property, valid on their face."

Armando added, "True, no one has ever extolled the efficiency of the Roman bureaucracy."

Massimo moved on. "Article 12 provides Jews may not employ Gentile servants. We lose our housekeeper, Cornelia, who needs the job."

Luciano nodded. "We hired a nurse for my youngest, since my wife got so sick."

Massimo pushed his glasses up. "Article 13 excludes Jews from employment in any public capacity, including the Fascist Party. Many people in our Community are going to lose their jobs." He straightened. "But now we come to the most important part. The *discriminazioni*—the exemptions, or those to whom the laws do not apply. There are categories of exemptions. First, for various types of veterans, and under Number 4, those who were Fascists in the years 1919, 1920, 1921, and 1922, and the second half of 1924."

Luciano leaned over. "That's you, isn't it, Massimo? You're a Fascist of the First Hour, so you're exempted, aren't you?"

"Close, but not technically. I joined in 1923."

"We're not Fascists. There are no exemptions for us."

"Yes, there are." Massimo pointed to the last provision. "This brings me to my strategy. There is an express exemption for any Jew with 'exceptional merits,' to be evaluated according to Article 16."

Armando scoffed. "That's a catchall term. It doesn't mean anything."

"I beg to differ," Massimo corrected him. "Article 16 is going to be our salvation. The tax code works in the same way. It contains terms that *invite* ambiguity, and when I see them, I turn that disadvantage to an advantage." He ran his finger down the page. "For example, I think the exemption for exceptional merits applies to both of you. You both served in the Great War, and I believe one of you even received a medal for valor, didn't you?"

"I did," Luciano answered proudly.

"What else is a medal, if not an example of exceptional merit? I served as an army officer in the Twenty-Ninth Piedmont Infantry, and I will be sure to include my military service on my own application. Likewise, you're both leaders in the business community, which is exceptional, per se." Massimo grew encouraged. "Do you see? The provision has to mean *something*. All we have to do is come up with rationales to construe it in a way that exempts the most members of our Community."

Armando frowned. "But this law *intends* to discriminate against Jews. They're not going to give us an exemption for helping Jews, are they?"

"Good point, but this law also *classifies* Jews, as illustrated by the provisions regarding what constitutes a Jew. So, we are going to file applications for exemptions for as many Jews as we can and show how exceptional they are." Massimo gestured around the room. "These men are leaders of business, scholars, and professionals. We can make arguments for all of them."

Luciano's dark eyes lit up. "You know, we could give out titles to suggest that the duty they perform benefits the Community or Rome."

"Good idea!" Armando sat taller, rallying.

"*Great* idea!" Massimo smiled. "We'll centralize our efforts here, at the synagogue. Everyone can come, and we'll interview them, elicit useful facts about them, and draft exemptions for them."

Armando blinked. "But, Massimo, we're not lawyers. You'd have to supervise us."

"I will," Massimo agreed, though he'd never supervised anyone but his secretary. "Gentlemen, I know how unjust this law is and how dire our position, but we are the leaders of this Community. Everyone counts on us. We have to move to a solution. It will take work, but we can do it, as we did with the schools."

"Massimo, stand up, right now. Everyone, listen!" Luciano rose, then clapped to get attention. Heads began to turn, and every man faced him.

Massimo stayed in his seat, unaccustomed to the limelight, but Luciano hoisted Massimo up by his arm, and began speaking:

"Friends, as you may know, Massimo Simone is one of the best lawyers in the city. He has just told me a strategy for us to cope with these terrible Race Laws."

"What is it?" a man called out, then others joined in. "Tell us!" "What can we do?"

"Massimo will tell you!" Luciano called back, stepping aside.

"I will?" Massimo asked, nervous.

"Massimo, you explain it better than I do. Tell them."

Massimo picked up his notepad with a shaking hand. "I'll begin by explaining the law . . ."

## CHAPTER THIRTY-NINE

# Marco

November 1938

---

Marco walked through Piazza Navona much more slowly than the businessmen, shopkeepers, and tradesmen around him. It was his first day at work after Aldo's funeral, and he felt heartsick and grief-stricken, having been barely able to sleep. He wasn't speaking to his father, and they avoided each other. His mother had taken to bed, bereft.

Marco approached the grand archway to Palazzo Braschi and saluted. "Good morning, Nino."

"Sorry about your brother." Nino snapped his eyes forward, unusually official.

"Thank you." Marco passed through the vaulted entranceway and turned right to the glass doors, where Giuseppe and Tino stood guard, their demeanor similarly cool. Marco saluted them, too. "Good morning."

"Good morning, Marco. Condolences."

"Thank you." Marco realized that they must have heard that Aldo had died an anti-Fascist, but he wasn't about to let their hard eyes bother him. He headed for the grand marble staircase and reached the top floor, which was flooded with sunlight from its floor-to-ceiling windows. He crossed to Commendatore Buonacorso's office, as he always checked in before the day started.

"Good morning," Marco said to Pasquale, who stood guard by the arch, and they saluted each other.

"Condolences," Pasquale said, and Marco went to his boss's office and knocked on the mahogany door.

Buonacorso called him to come in, and Marco opened the door and saluted, but was taken aback at the sight. His boss sat behind his desk, but standing next to him was an OVRA officer built like a bear, with a bald head and a fierce glare. OVRA was Mussolini's secret police, a law unto themselves.

Marco felt a tingle of fear as he walked to the desk. "Commendatore Buonacorso, good morning. May I get you anything?"

"No." Buonacorso motioned. "Sit down."

"Yes, sir." Marco sat, and the OVRA officer glared at him without introducing himself, a bad sign.

Buonacorso frowned. "Marco, you're fired. You can't continue at *fascio* headquarters, now that we know you had a subversive for a brother."

Marco recoiled. "But Aldo truly wasn't like that, I promise you."

"How can you defend him?" Buonacorso's dark eyes flashed. "He tried to kill an officer of the law. He was a violent anti-Fascist and a Communist co-conspirator. He was transporting guns to use against *us*."

"He may have, but he paid the ultimate price, and—"

"Which is as it should be," Buonacorso interrupted sternly.

"I am not my brother, sir. I had no idea of his leftist politics. We never discussed it. He kept it to himself."

"Is that true?" Buonacorso arched an eyebrow. "You had no idea?"

"I swear to you, sir, I didn't know. You can't fire me for what my brother did."

"It's a matter of trust, Marco. I can no longer trust you."

"Sir, you can. I prove it every day, working for you. I've learned confidential information here. It never leaves this building."

*Bam!* The OVRA officer slammed his meaty hand on the desk and advanced on Marco, leaning into his face. "Your brother was a criminal subversive! We must assume you are, too!"

"But I'm not."

"Yes, you are!" The OVRA officer's glare bored into Marco. "He was in an anti-Fascist cell, and you are, too!"

Marco's mouth went dry. "I swear to you, I didn't know anything about it. I'm a patriot, a good Fascist, and I love Il Duce and our party. I would never do anything against—"

"I don't believe you! You're in it with your brother!"

"No, no, I swear to you—"

"You work here in order to spy on us!"

"No, that's not true. I didn't know."

"You showed off at the bar for Commendatore Buonacorso! You tricked him into believing you were a patriot!"

"My patriotism is no trick." Marco could barely respond to the rapid-fire accusations.

"You expect us to believe that he *never* told you? You *lived* with your brother! You *rode* with him!"

"He said he was seeing a married woman."

"You came home at the same time! You were seen!"

Marco tried to think through his fear, which was intensifying. "We planned it that way, for my father. We lied to him."

"So you *admit* you're a liar! You're lying to us! You were in cahoots with your brother and the other filthy pigs! Who are they?"

"I don't know, I'm telling you, I had no idea he was meeting with them."

"That's why your father fought you at the funeral! He found out you were an anti-Fascist!"

"The fight had nothing to do with Aldo. It was about my girlfriend." Marco flashed on Elisabetta, then thought of Aldo's girlfriend, or whoever she had been. "Wait a minute, listen, one of the anti-Fascists came to the bar that day. She was a pretty blonde, the one Aldo said he was having an affair with, the married—"

"You saw her?" The OVRA officer blinked. "A woman anti-Fascist?"

"Yes." Marco had forgotten about her, in his grief. "She's the one you need to talk to."

"What's her name?"

"I don't know, he never told me."

"Where does she live?"

"I don't know."

"You were in cahoots with her!" The OVRA officer shoved a clenched fist in Marco's face. "Is *this* what you want? I could take you to the *Questura* right now! I'll beat you until you talk! I want to, but your boss says no. He's a gentleman, I'm not!"

"Wait, listen." Marco got an idea. "I can find out who she is. It will prove I'm not an anti-Fascist."

The OVRA officer thought this over. "Do it! You have twenty-four hours! We'll be watching! Understand?"

"I understand."

"Twenty-four hours!"

## CHAPTER FORTY

# Elisabetta
### November 1938

Elisabetta stood in the kitchen at home, wiping her brow and surveying her handiwork. She had finally finished packing to move, and piles of boxes surrounded her. She had sold anything she could part with, like her mother's dresses, shoes, and handbags, which had fetched a tidy sum from the peddlers in the Ghetto. Her father's clothes had brought in far less money, and for sentimental reasons, she kept his wonderful watercolors, from his heyday as an artist.

Most of the furniture was gone, as she had sold everything she wouldn't need. She would have a single room from now on, which would simplify her life. She was trying to look forward, not backward. Such thoughts were more productive than thinking of her father's death. She had come to accept that she was better off without her mother.

She sank into the wooden chair, realizing for the first time that the room was very small. She had always thought of the kitchen as very big, and it seemed paradoxical to her that the kitchen would look smaller without anything in it, but it was true. She saw her home with new eyes, realizing that she was leaving this part of her life behind, now that she was an adult on her own. With Rico.

The cat looked over from his seat atop a tall stack of boxes, from which he had been eyeing her, neither disapproving nor approving, merely watch-ful. Rico was intelligent enough to understand that they were leaving, and that he was going, too, for he had seen her pack his favorite dishes, which would have allayed any anxiety he might have had.

"Don't worry, Rico," Elisabetta told him anyway, but his only response was to blink, then stretch the way he always did, first extending his front legs and arching his back, then his back legs, with his tail straight up in the air like an exclamation mark.

He crouched, looking down from the box, and Elisabetta realized he was getting ready to jump to the table, but his perch was too high and the table was too far across the room, a dangerous trajectory.

"Rico, no," Elisabetta said, warning him off.

Rico sat back down, generally disappointed in her for preempting his acts of bravery and athletic daring. He would be good company going for-ward, and she still had Marco and Sandro. She didn't want to risk losing one or hurting the other, which would happen if she made her choice.

Her thoughts were interrupted by Rico, who had nevertheless decided to leap from the tower of boxes to the table. Despite the danger, he landed perfectly, then sat down and tucked his tail around himself in a perfect circle, forming a period at the end of his own sentence.

Elisabetta chuckled, admiring Rico for taking the risk, as he trusted himself that much. She found herself wondering if she could learn some-thing from him. If she trusted herself more, perhaps she could choose be-tween Sandro and Marco. She remembered what Nonna had told her, that her heart had already made its choice and would tell her its secret, when she was ready to listen.

She found herself sitting among the boxes, in the hollow husk of her house, with only a male cat for female advice. She closed her eyes, quieted her thoughts, and opened her heart wide enough for it to release its secret, which fluttered out like a dove from a cage, flying heavenward.

In that moment, Elisabetta made a choice, and as soon as she did, her heart affirmed that she had chosen correctly, for the decision resonated within her. Joy suffused her, and her happy gaze met Rico's.

*Prego,* Rico said, with his eyes.

## CHAPTER FORTY-ONE

# Marco

### November 1938

Marco ran home over the Ponte Fabricio and found his father working in the outside seating area. They weren't speaking, but this was an emergency. Out of breath, he took his father aside.

"Papa, do you remember a blond customer who came to the bar the day Aldo was killed? She was pretty and sat outside. She met with him that day."

His father frowned. "No, I don't remember. Why?"

"What about the photographer, who takes pictures of the tourists, for money? The one you always shoo away?"

"You mean Corrado?"

"Yes, was he here that day?"

"I don't know. He's a pest though."

"Do you know where he lives?"

"No, but he works at a camera shop in Trastevere. On Via della Lunga-retta."

Marco took off, running full speed over the Ponte Cestio into Trastevere. He darted past mothers with children and deliverymen pushing barrows, then made a left, hurrying under ivy bowers. He ran until he spotted the camera shop up ahead, with a hand-painted sign and storefront.

He burst through the door, startling the elderly shopkeeper, who was small with flyaway white hair. He had been reading the newspaper with a magnifying glass, and he looked up from behind a display case that held an array of used Leica, Bencini, and Kine Exakta cameras.

Marco had no time for small talk. "Sir, does a man named Corrado work here? I need to speak with him."

"In the darkroom, in back." The shopkeeper set down the magnifying glass. "But he's busy."

"I can't wait." Marco came around the counter, and the shopkeeper edged backward, raising his arthritic hands.

"Don't hurt me!" he cried out, which caught Marco up short. He forgot that some people were intimidated by his uniform.

"I wouldn't hurt you, sir. I need to see him without delay. It's an urgent matter, about my family."

"Okay, I'll show you. The darkroom must remain light-tight." The shopkeeper led Marco behind the counter to a heavy curtain, which he moved aside, then knocked at a door, calling out, "Corrado, there's a man who needs to see you. He says it's urgent."

"Fine," Corrado called from within.

"Use the double door." The shopkeeper held aside the curtain, and Marco opened the door, found himself in a dark vestibule with another door, and closed the first door behind him. He opened the next door, entering a room that was completely dark, except for a small orange lamplight that illuminated a shelf of bottles and jugs, and a table with trays of liquid. An acrid chemical odor filled the air. A clothesline held drying prints and long strips of negatives, which curled from the bottom.

When Marco's eyes adjusted, he crossed to Corrado, who stood at an enlarger, shedding a cone of white light on a sheet of photographic paper. "Corrado, I'm Marco Terrizzi."

"So?" Corrado flicked off the white light, plunging them both into darkness except for the orange lamp.

"My family owns Bar GiroSport, and you take pictures of the customers in the outside seating area. Were you there Thursday afternoon?"

"I'm usually there, until your father makes me go."

"I need to see the pictures you took that afternoon."

"I only developed the negatives. I don't make prints unless somebody orders them, and nobody did."

"Then let me see the negatives."

"It'll cost you." Corrado slid the photographic paper from the machine, crossed the darkroom to the trays of chemicals, and slid the paper into the liquid. "If you want any prints, that'll cost you, too."

"I'll pay. But you have to do it right now."

"You'll pay for that, too. Rush jobs are extra."

"Fine."

Corrado turned away and started riffling through negatives hanging from the ropes. The stiff strips made a crinkling sound as they swung into each other. He stopped at one. "This roll is from that day, I believe."

"Can I see it?" Marco stepped over, squinting in the darkness, and Corrado unclipped the strip of negatives and handed it to him, holding it by the edges.

"Don't smudge it, in case I get a call. I give out cards with my number, and sometimes they change their minds."

"Okay." Marco took the negative strip, and Corrado handed him a photographer's loupe.

"Go in the vestibule outside. There's a lightbox there. You can look for yourself."

"Thank you." Marco went to the vestibule, where there was a skinny table with a lightbox on top. He located a switch on the box, and it came to glowing life. He placed the negative strip on the box, which illuminated the images in obverse, with white spaces where there was darkness, and vice versa.

Marco placed the loupe on top of the strip, and the images zoomed into magnified focus. The first few were photos of random women on the street, then couples at sidewalk cafés. He kept going until Tiber Island appeared, then the Piazza San Bartolomeo all'Isola. Toward the end of the strip were images from the seating area in front of Bar GiroSport.

Marco's heart began to pound. The first image was of an older couple, and the second of a family, smiling at the camera. The third was a shot of a pretty girl passing by, and in the background was an empty table in the seating area. He wondered if it was where the blond anti-Fascist had been sitting before she was in the stockroom with Aldo.

Marco moved the loupe to the next frame. It was a picture of another pretty girl passing the bar, but in the background was a clear photo of the blonde, taken as she was emerging from the bar.

Marco felt a surge of relief. He could prove his loyalty and his innocence. The blonde's face was fully visible, and the photo of her, once enlarged, could even be used to identify her.

He eyed her through the loupe, and her face stared back at him, spooky in the obverse, as if her head were a skull. He knew that once he identified her, she would be arrested and beaten for information.

Marco paused, reflecting. Aldo would want him to protect the blonde, not turn her in.

But Marco felt a flame of anger, too. The blonde had manipulated Aldo. She had sent him to Orvieto for guns. Aldo would be alive but for her and her ilk.

Marco had to think of himself, too. He needed to clear his name. To get his job back. He had bet his future on the party.

He made a decision.

"Corrado!" he called out, flicking off the lightbox.

## CHAPTER FORTY-TWO

# Elisabetta
### November 1938

Elisabetta hurried into the Ghetto, hoping to see Sandro. She felt sure he had been avoiding her. He had been teaching at the Jewish school, and she would stop by to see him after class, but he would always say he was too busy. She couldn't let another day pass without seeing him.

Elisabetta hurried along the street, reaching the school. Children of all ages gathered at the entrance, a gaggle of boys and girls with bookbags and scarfs. She spotted Sandro at the top of the steps, with the other teachers, and her heart gladdened. He looked handsome in a brown tweed jacket, white shirt, and brown tie, like a professor.

"Sandro!" Elisabetta called out, and Sandro turned in her direction. He saw her, and their eyes connected. A pained expression flickered across his face, and he went back inside the school, disappearing.

She hurried to the steps, climbed them two by two, and hustled inside, spotting him at the end of the hall. He went into a classroom, and she followed. She ran to the end of the hall and entered the classroom, which was a cramped room barely big enough for tables that had been repurposed for desks, with old chairs. Mismatched bookcases lined the left wall, and on the right were two windows that shed a cold light.

"Sandro, I want to talk—"

"No." Sandro stood at an old teacher's desk, taking a thick packet of papers from his rucksack. "I can't, I'm busy."

"You say that every time."

"Because it's true."

"I don't know why you're avoiding me." Elisabetta crossed to him, touching his arm. Up close, she could see that he had lost weight and his expression was drawn.

"I'm not avoiding you." Sandro pursed his lips.

"You are. What is it? Is it something I've done? Is it because of Marco?"

"No, no." Sandro looked away.

"I've been thinking of you, so much. I miss you—"

"There's no time for that anymore. I have too much to do, and I can't hear about how you miss me."

"I'm not here for me, I'm here for you. I know how much you're hurting, I can see it in your eyes."

Sandro averted his gaze again, his feet shifting. "Elisabetta, what of it? You can't do anything about it."

"I can listen and be with you."

"That doesn't change anything."

"But it helps." Elisabetta's heart went out to him. "Remember after the Deledda lecture, when we talked? I told you everything about my father, and you listened. It didn't change my father, but it helped me. And after my father's funeral, too? We always talk, and it makes things easier, and better."

"That's past, and everything's changed. My world has changed. My father is losing his clients. My mother is exhausted. Rosa left for London. Cornelia is gone. Everything is different."

"Not us, we're still us."

"People change. People betray you." Sandro's expression turned pinched, and a new bitterness edged his tone. "There's a divide between Jews and everyone else now. The walls of the Ghetto may as well be back up again. You're on the other side. You don't understand."

"So explain it to me. Tell me how you're feeling, tell me what it's like." Elisabetta felt her eyes fill with tears, but she held them off because they were his to cry, not hers. "First, getting thrown out of school, then this new law—"

"The one that says there's no intermarriage?"

"Yes, everything about the law is wrong, all of it."

"I don't have the same rights as everybody else anymore. I can't marry anyone I want. I can't marry a Gentile, you're officially my better."

Elisabetta felt stricken. "No, don't say that, it's not true. I'm not, and the law doesn't matter to me."

"Of course it does, it's the law."

"The law doesn't matter between us." Elisabetta held his gaze. "The law wasn't here a month ago, and who knows whether it will be here a month from now."

"I do, and it will."

"You don't know that." Elisabetta didn't know how to reach him, or even if she could. "You don't know what the future holds. It could be better."

"It could be *worse*."

"I'm saying the law is only politics. It will come and go. But these feelings we have for each other, they're not going away, they're here. *I'm* here, for you."

"What does that mean?"

"I love you," Elisabetta answered, meaning it with all of her heart. "I love you, and I will love you when this law passes, and when we get older, and whatever else happens or whatever time brings."

"You mean you're choosing me?" Sandro blinked. "Not Marco?"

"Yes. It's you, Sandro. It was always you."

"Your timing is impeccable, Elisabetta. Just when you can't have me, you want me." Sandro frowned, shaking his head. "The irony is too much. The law forbids it. My parents forbid it and—"

"None of that matters to me." Elisabetta stepped closer, resting her hand on his arm.

"It does to me. This ends."

"It never ends. It goes on and on, it's love."

"Not anymore, not for me. I don't feel the same as I used to about you, not anymore." Sandro straightened, setting his jaw. "I'm sorry."

Elisabetta's chest tightened. "You're just saying that."

"No, I mean it." Sandro regarded her, a chill in his blue eyes. "You made a choice, but I have one, too."

"Sandro, do you really mean this?" Elisabetta asked, her heart breaking.

"Yes, I do." Sandro glanced at the door, and the clamor of students echoed in the hallway. "My class is coming back. Please, don't make a scene."

"I'm begging you, give us a chance."

"No, Elisabetta. You need to go."

Elisabetta ran from the classroom, wiping tears from her eyes, and hurried down the hallway past the students. Her heart was in tumult, her gut wrenched. She loved him, but she had decided too late. It was all her fault. Sandro was lost to her now.

Elisabetta ran from the school and hurried through the Ghetto, holding back her tears. She ran to Trastevere, reached the house, and flew inside, avoiding Nonna's bedroom downstairs. She raced upstairs and ran to her bedroom, where she collapsed on the floor.

Finally letting the tears flow.

## CHAPTER FORTY-THREE

# Sandro
### November 1938

Sandro sat at the table, too nervous to grade papers. His mother gazed out the window, undoubtedly feeling the same way. The first course of dinner, *concia di fiori di zucca*, fried squash flowers, cooled aromatically on the table. His father was late, and Sandro knew it would drive his mother more crazy than usual, for good reason.

A white envelope sat on the table, still sealed, having been delivered in the day's mail. The return address was the Demorazza, which was the government agency that administered the Race Laws, so the envelope must contain the agency's decision on their family's exemption. His father had filed an application for one on their behalf, and they all hoped the exemption would be granted. They had been awaiting the decision and prayed that the agency went their way. Sandro would have opened the envelope, rather than sit in suspended animation and guess about its contents. But his mother believed the envelope was his father's to open.

So they waited.

His mother smoothed out her dark sheath, fiddled with her pearl necklace, and linked her elegant hands in front of her. He put away his papers in silence, giving up on getting anything done. The fate of his family lay within the envelope. If they weren't granted an exemption from the Race Laws, they would lose their house, for Jews could no longer own property under those laws. His father would lose his law practice, too, as Jews could no longer own businesses, either. If his father couldn't work, it would cut their family income. Worse, it would break his parents' hearts to lose a house that had been in the family for generations.

Sandro sighed. Unfortunately, even if they were awarded the exemption, it would not readmit him to school because the exemptions applied only to the property provisions of the law. Nor would it permit him to marry Elisabetta, whom he thought about all the time. He still couldn't believe that she had chosen him over Marco, and it was his dream come true. But it had come too late. He had sent her away for her own good. He had lied to her when he'd told her that he didn't love her anymore. Of course he still loved her, he always would. But he was no longer a suitable husband for her; he had no job, no prospects, and he couldn't even marry her anymore. Ironically, he loved her too much to tell her so, which left him miserable and aching, experiencing an odd sort of grief that mourned even the living.

His mother reached for the letter and held it up to the chandelier, trying to read through the envelope. "I can't see what it says."

"Mamma, just open it."

"No, your father wants to be the one, and I told him we would honor his wishes." His mother set the envelope down. "It will be his triumph."

"I hope so."

"I think we'll get the exemption," his mother said, as if reassuring them both. "He was practically a Fascist of the First Hour, an officer in the Great War, and he serves the Community."

"I'm sure we'll get it," Sandro said, though he wasn't sure.

"I'm sorry it won't permit your return to school."

"It's okay," Sandro said, though the opposite was true.

"How are you enjoying the Jewish school?"

Sandro knew the correct answer. "I like teaching, and it's good to contribute to the Community."

"But I'm sure you miss your friends, and working for the professor."

"Life is trade-offs."

His mother paused. "That's what I always say."

"I know, that's why I said it." Sandro smiled.

His mother smiled back, her sharp eyes regarding him, behind her glasses. "I wonder if that means you're listening—or you've stopped listening."

"It means I'm listening."

"How's Marco?"

"He's fine, working a lot."

His mother paused again. "And Elisabetta? How is she?"

"Fine, I assume. I don't see her. I'm not interested in her anymore."

"Oh." His mother blinked, her expression softening. "I hope you understood our objection."

"I do, but I don't agree with it."

"Even after this? These awful Race Laws codify a ban against intermarriage." His mother gestured at the white envelope, but Sandro couldn't suppress the resentment flaring in his chest.

"Mamma, if anything, that should make you question your view."

"What are you talking about? The Race Laws prove the necessity for standing together as Jews. Our Community is under dire threat."

"I choose not to discriminate against those who discriminate. It's a principled—"

"Oh, Sandro, fine," his mother snapped. "You're too smart by half, and I don't want to fuss. Do we need more upset? Should I have more worries than whatever is in that envelope?"

"So let's open it then." Sandro picked up the envelope, annoyed. "If you won't, I will."

"No, Sandro, don't. I forbid it." His mother reached for the envelope just as Sandro jerked his hand away. The envelope tore in two, leaving her holding one half and him the other. In that moment, the front door opened and his father entered, smiling until he realized that Sandro and his mother were fighting. His father set down his briefcase and hurried into the dining room.

"What's going on, you two?" he asked, mystified. "What's that paper?"

"It's from the Demorazza." His mother slid the other half of the envelope from Sandro's grasp and handed them both over. "I'm sorry."

"Papa, I'm sorry, too," Sandro said quickly. "It's my fault. I wanted to open it, and Mamma said we shouldn't."

"What have you done? This is an important legal document!" Appalled, his father slid the white paper from the left and right halves of the envelope, then placed both sides on the table, matching them up. His mother stood over his father's left shoulder, and Sandro came around his right. He looked down to see that the halves of the document were unevenly matched, but the ruling was legible—and horrifying.

*NEGATO*, read the handwritten scrawl, in capital letters.

"No," his father said, hushed.

His mother gasped.

Sandro felt stricken.

His father moved both halves of the paper up and down, trying to realign them, as if it would change the outcome. "No, no, no, no," he said, over and over.

"Oh no." His mother put a hand on his father's knobby shoulder, but his father didn't seem to notice.

"They would *not* deny us! They would *not* do this to us! They would *not* do this to me!" His father kept rearranging the two halves of the decision. "I'm *almost* a Fascist of the First Hour! I've done everything I can for the party! It would *not* do this to my family! It would *not* do this to *me*!"

"Massimo, please." His mother patted his father's back. "We will find a way—"

"Il Duce would not do this to me. My country . . ." His father looked up, shaking his head, his eyes wild and his lips trembling.

Sandro felt alarmed, having never seen his father so frantic. Tears came to his mother's eyes, and she edged away, as unsettled as he was.

Sandro realized he had to do something. He took his father by the shoulders and turned him so they faced each other. "Papa, we have to reason together, the way we always do. We can figure out what to do."

"We can't, we can't, we're ruined! I don't know what to do."

Sandro felt taken aback, but masked his dismay. "Can we appeal? Is there a provision for appeal of these rulings, like a regular court case?"

"No, no, no, nothing like that's in the law! The decisions are final!" His father looked at Sandro without really seeing him, or so it seemed to Sandro.

"Papa, let's think. There has to be some way to deal with this, and we will."

"I've gotten exemptions for so many others, how could they deny mine? Why would they deny mine? Why?"

"Are you sure it's final, even though it's just handwritten? It barely looks official. I'm wondering if it's some sort of notation or—"

"No, no! It's a final determination, many of them are handwritten denials. They're mere functionaries who decide these things! They're not lawyers, they're bureaucrats! They scribble!" His father started shaking his head again. "Perhaps I was a borderline case, in that I didn't join the party until 1923, and that's before 1924, when they opened the rolls again. But why would they rely on such a technicality? How could they turn against one of their own? It's a Fascist body, deciding against one of the most loyal Fascists in the Community, in all of Rome! They have granted so many other exemptions, ones that *I* wrote, that were *far* less deserving! How could they deny us? This is a disaster!"

"So there's no way out, under the law?"

"No!"

Sandro's mind raced. "What about outside of the law?"

"What do you mean?"

"I think there's a way," Sandro said, taking over.

## CHAPTER FORTY-FOUR

# Beppe
November 1938

B eppe was relieved to show the last of the customers out of the bar. He
was ready for bed, always exhausted lately, for he mourned Aldo so
deeply. His grief weighed him down, but he bore it privately, a father's burden. Sometimes he felt as if he would collapse of its weight; other times it
reminded him of his time in the Great War. He had served in the Third
Division of the Bersaglieri, an infantry unit of elite cyclists who carried not
only a rucksack, but also a bicycle, on their backs. He had been on the
Isonzo front in the snowy Dolomites and at Caporetto, a brutal defeat that
still caused him nightmares. The battle of Caporetto was infamous for its
desertions, but Beppe had fought on, day after day, battling the enemy and
his own despair. He felt the same way, grieving Aldo.

As he finished cleaning up, he wracked his brain for what he had done
wrong with Aldo. How he had missed so many signs. Why his middle son
had betrayed his country. Beppe felt as if he hadn't even known the boy, his
own beloved child. He would never have believed that Aldo would resort
to violence for any reason, much less against his own government. He had
failed Aldo as a father.

Beppe gathered a dirty napkin and took it to the counter. Marco looked
up from cleaning the coffee machine, but said nothing. Since the fistfight at
Aldo's funeral, he and Marco spoke only when they had to. Beppe experienced the rift between them as another loss, depressing him further. His
wife, Maria, had taken to bed, and neither Emedio nor prayer could console her. The Terrizzis had never been so miserable, and Beppe bore that
as his failure, too. The happiness of a man's family was his responsibility,
no less than putting food on the table.

He was heading to the door to lock up when he saw Massimo and Sandro
hurrying over the Ponte Fabricio toward the bar. It was an unusual hour for

a visit, but Beppe waved to them, and Massimo waved back. When the Simones reached the foot of the bridge, Beppe opened the door to welcome them.

"*Buona sera*, Massimo, Sandro."

Massimo and Sandro greeted him, hustling inside the bar.

Massimo frowned, his anxiety plain. "We're sorry to intrude this late."

"Not at all. Come in, both of you." Beppe closed the door behind them, turning the sign on the door to CHIUSO. "Thank you for coming to Aldo's funeral."

"Of course, and you have our deepest condolences. Aldo was a wonderful young man." Massimo patted Beppe on the arm, and Beppe was thankful that Massimo was tactful enough not to mention the fight with Marco.

"Please, sit down." Beppe pulled chairs out from the nearest table, Massimo and Sandro sat down, and Marco came over, carrying four glasses of red wine on a tray.

"*Buona sera*." Marco set the wine in front of them, then sat down.

Massimo and Sandro greeted Marco, and Beppe could see that there was something weighing on Massimo's mind. His old friend took a big gulp of wine.

"Massimo, what's the matter?"

"I need your help."

"Then you shall have it, brother."

"Absolutely," Marco added.

Massimo and Sandro seemed to ease, letting down their shoulders. Massimo met Beppe's eye. "You know about these new Race Laws, forbidding Jews from owning property or businesses."

"Yes, and you know my view. They're a disgrace. I loathe our party's discriminatory laws. I don't countenance the persecution of Italian Jews, and it's the wrong direction for the party and for Italy."

"Thank you for saying that. Sadly, the worst has happened. I was denied an exemption."

"Oh no!" Beppe recoiled, taken aback. He and Massimo had been reasonably certain that the Simones would get an exemption, and he certainly deserved one.

"If we can't get this reversed, we'll be ruined. We'll lose the house and my practice."

"Is there a way to appeal it?"

"None, legally." Massimo's forehead buckled. "I based my argument on my loyalty to the party. Remember the first day we met, when Sandro was born?"

"Yes, of course. I could never forget." Beppe gestured outside the bar. "We met right there, on that spot. You had just left the hospital, having been there all night waiting for Gemma to deliver Sandro. We stood out front, together. It was the March on Rome, in 1922."

Massimo nodded, his eyes briefly shining. "Then we went to Piazza Venezia and saw Il Duce speak. The crowd was packed as far as the eye could see. You were already a member of the party."

"Yes, I joined in 1919." Beppe suppressed a pang. So much had changed since then, not for the better. Fascism had betrayed the Jews, and Mussolini had set the party on a course to war, in alliance with Hitler. And now Aldo was gone, tainting Marco with suspicion of complicity.

"There's an exemption to the Race Laws for Fascists of the First Hour, like you. Those who joined from 1919 to 1922 and the second half of 1924. I joined in 1923, though I was going to meetings from the earliest days. So you see, it's only a technicality that I was denied the exemption."

"That's very true. I'll help you in any way I can. What can I do?"

"Beppe, you know so many people in the party. I was wondering if you could speak to someone and attest to my loyalty, from those early days. I'm sure your word could make a difference." Massimo turned to Marco. "And, Marco, you work at the *fascio*. I know you're well thought of there. Is there someone you could speak to for us, as well? Commendatore Buonacorso knows me, for as you remember, I introduced him to you. Perhaps you could remind him of my loyalty?"

"Of course, we'll talk to someone," Beppe rushed to say, though the timing couldn't have been worse. He and Marco had no influence since Aldo's betrayal, but he couldn't tell Massimo and Sandro the truth about Aldo's death. It was confidential, and shameful.

Marco pursed his lips. "I'll ask, too."

Massimo breathed with relief. "Thank you, both of you."

Sandro smiled. "Thank you, so much."

Beppe patted Massimo on the arm. "Now, let's have a drink, to old friends."

"To old friends." Massimo raised his glass.

"To old friends," Marco said to Sandro, hoisting his wine.

"Yes, to us," Sandro said, after a moment.

CHAPTER FORTY-FIVE

# Marco
November 1938

The next morning, Marco sat next to his father on a brocade bench outside Commendatore Buonacorso's office. They had given the photograph of Aldo's blond anti-Fascist to Buonacorso and had been told to wait here. That had been two hours ago, during which various Fascist officers, whom Marco didn't recognize, hurried to and from the office.

He perched on the edge of his seat, tense. His father was somber in the suit he had worn to Aldo's funeral. They had said barely a word to each other. Marco told himself to relax, but it was impossible. Everything was on the line today.

"Gentlemen," an officer said, appearing from the office. "Commendatore Buonacorso will speak with you."

"Thank you," Marco and his father answered, in unison. They rose, entered the office, and gave the Fascist salute, which Buonacorso returned, then motioned to two cushioned chairs in front of his desk.

"Please, gentlemen. Sit down." As they did, Buonacorso took a seat behind his desk. "I'm surprised to see you here, Beppe."

"I came to support Marco. Neither of us had any inkling of Aldo's shameful and traitorous activities. As Aldo's father, I should have known. If anyone is to blame, it is me. If anyone should be punished, punish me."

Marco looked over, touched at his father's words. "Papa, I'm responsible for myself."

His father ignored him, his attention on Buonacorso. "We understand each other, as veterans. I tell you, Marco's loyalty is as solid as mine. I trust that his production of the photograph will serve as proof."

Buonacorso nodded curtly. "Beppe, I appreciate your words. We all know of your loyalty. Your integrity. We understand now that neither of you had any idea of Aldo's treachery. Our friends in OVRA have the photograph and will investigate the woman. We feel satisfied that Marco was not collaborating with Aldo and the other anti-Fascists."

"Thank you. Then I assume that means he gets his job back, at the *fascio*." Marco startled, surprised at his father's boldness on his behalf.

Buonacorso stroked his mustache, then turned to Marco. "Marco, yes, you have your job back. We shall let this unfortunate episode pass and not speak of it again."

"Thank you, sir." Marco smiled with relief. "You won't be sorry, sir."

His father interjected, "That, I guarantee."

"Thank you." Buonacorso glanced over as the door opened behind them, and Marco assumed someone had come in, as he smelled cigarette smoke.

"One last thing, Commendatore," his father said, raising a finger. "You know our mutual friend Massimo Simone. He has been denied an exemption from the new Race Laws, to which I believe he is absolutely entitled. I'm sure you agree."

"Denied, you say? Massimo?"

"Yes, and this injustice must be rectified. His exemption should be granted, given his years of service and loyalty to the party. I vouch for him in every particular. I was hoping you would help him."

Buonacorso shrugged. "Beppe, I have no say in such matters, as much as I would like to help. It's outside the scope of my authority."

"I expected that was the case, so I wrote a letter on Massimo's behalf. I'm hoping that you will place it in the proper hands." His father reached inside his jacket pocket, extracted an envelope, and set it on the desk.

"I will, thank you." Buonacorso picked up the envelope, and just then, harsh laughter erupted from the back of the office.

Marco and his father turned around as two uniformed OVRA officers walked to the desk, their black boots clicking on the parquet floor. Marco shuddered to recognize one of them as the bearlike OVRA officer who had interrogated him about Aldo. The other OVRA officer was short and skinny, holding a cigarette between slim fingers. Marco didn't know him, but he was casting hard eyes at his father.

"Do you remember me, Beppe?" asked the skinny OVRA officer.

"Carmine Vecchio," his father answered matter-of-factly.

"Tell me, are you surprised to see me as a superior officer?"

"No officer is the superior of any trencherman."

Marco swallowed hard, as OVRA wasn't to be provoked.

"*Bah!*" Officer Vecchio dragged on his cigarette. "You haven't changed, you old warhorse."

"Thank you," his father shot back, unsmiling.

"How dare you!" Officer Vecchio snorted, and jets of smoke escaped his nostrils. "You should show me some respect, and also my fellow officer Stefano Pretianni." He gestured to the bearlike officer, who didn't react. "And by the way, you're in no position to ask favors for your Jew friends."

Marco's father didn't blink. "It's not a favor when it's deserved. Massimo Simone is a loyal Fascist. He served our country in—"

"What do *you* know about loyalty, Beppe? Your son Aldo was running guns for subversives right under your nose. God knows what Marco is really up to."

Marco jumped to his feet, on impulse. "I am loyal to this party, and so is Massimo Simone. He deserves that exemption."

His father rose beside him, more calmly, his gaze on Vecchio. "Carmine, you're still picking unnecessary fights, and I'm still ignoring you."

"What fight is unnecessary, Beppe? Was Caporetto? Is that why you ran like a coward?"

"I did no such thing."

"Prove it."

"I don't have to prove anything to you."

"You Terrizzis don't fool me. I'll be watching you every minute. I'm keeping my eye on both of you."

"Enjoy the view." His father turned his back and walked out with Marco behind him. They left the office, crossed the anteroom, and strode past the guards. They descended the grand marble staircase, side by side, roughly the same height and build, unmistakably father and son. But after what had just happened, Marco wondered if he knew less about his father than he had thought.

They reached the ground floor, strode through the archway, and left Palazzo Braschi. They stopped in order to part ways in Piazza Navona, crowded with people rushing this way and that.

"I'm going back to work." His father's eyes went flinty in the sunshine.

"I'll stay here," Marco said, newly awkward. In other circumstances, he would have hugged his father, grateful for the help in getting his job back. But the rift between them made that impossible. "By the way, how do you know Carmine Vecchio?"

"It doesn't matter."

"Do you think the Simones will get the exemption?"

"They should. I paid plenty."

"What do you mean?" Marco asked, surprised.

"What did you think was in that envelope, son?"

CHAPTER FORTY-SIX

# Massimo

21 November 1938

Massimo sat in his study, his head in his hands. On the desk in front of him was yet another set of Race Laws. By today's royal decree, he was no longer a member of the Fascist Party. He had been thrown out. He reread the law's main provision, hoping that the sentences would change. Nevertheless they remained the same, in black-and-white print:

Italian citizens who, according to the laws, are considered as belonging to the Jewish race are excluded from the PNF, the Partito Nazionale Fascista.

Massimo couldn't comprehend what was before his eyes. He was a lawyer, baffled by a law. The Fascists had betrayed him, even though he and other Jews had helped put Il Duce in power. Massimo had believed in Il Duce, even loved him. But Il Duce had betrayed him, too. The newspapers were calling it a "purge" of Jews.

The door to his study was closed, and Massimo could hear Gemma and Sandro talking in the kitchen. The law had upset them, but hadn't devasted them the way it did him. He didn't know who he was if he wasn't a Fascist. The party was more than politics to him. It was a rubric like the law itself, a system of orderly government that allowed men to achieve their fullest potential.

He thought back to the March on Rome, the beginning of the party's rise. It was only sixteen years ago. He had ties as old as that. Shoes, even. It was the year Sandro was born, and Massimo had felt so much hope back then, a new father to a new son, witnessing a new father to his beloved country. He had believed that his life and times had converged in a wonderfully auspicious way, especially as a Roman. He had expected the future to shine bright and glorious.

His gaze wandered around his study, with his framed diplomas and bookshelf filled with tax regulations and textbooks. They were artifacts of his past life as a tax lawyer, like a fragment of a marble column at the Roman Forum. He had become a ruin.

He caught sight of his reflection in the window. He looked haunted, and he felt so. He thought again of the exemption he had failed to obtain. If he had succeeded, he would still be a party member, but he had let himself and his family down.

He prayed that Beppe and Marco could make the difference.

# PART THREE

*Nessun maggior dolore*
*che ricordarsi del tempo felice*
*nella miseria.*

There is no sorrow greater than in times of misery,
to hold at heart the memory of happiness.

—Dante Alighieri, *Inferno*,
Canto 5, 121–23

## CHAPTER FORTY-SEVEN

# Elisabetta

July 1939

Elisabetta and Nonna had a nightly routine, sharing a nightcap of anisette, a sweet anise liqueur. Challenging times were upon them, as rumors of impending war were on everyone's lips. Business had taken a bad turn at Casa Servano, since the tourist trade was down and Trastevere Jews had been harmed by the Race Laws, which the *Trasteverini* regarded as an abomination.

Elisabetta thought of Sandro all the time, heartbroken that he didn't love her anymore. She loved him still and wept at night, missing him and worrying about him. She avoided Marco, not to lead him on now that she knew Sandro was the one. Luckily Marco had gotten busier at Palazzo Braschi.

"Eh, what a dreadful day." Nonna eased into her chair at the head of the walnut table, where an overhead lamp of milky Murano glass emitted a halo of light. The window was open, but the breeze was warm and barely moved the lace curtains. Via Fiorata was typically quiet at night, and the only sound was Rico purring on the cushioned chair, atop the doily that protected it from his cat hair. His eyes were closed and his paws tucked under him, his tummy full of branzino scraps.

"Things will get better, Nonna."

"Not before they get worse, girl."

Elisabetta sipped anisette from a tiny carved glass, which was one of hundreds that Nonna owned. It turned out that the old woman collected all manner of glassware and myriad sets of antique china, as well as breakfronts, credenzas, and display cabinets to store the collection. The cabinetry lined every room in the small, cheery house, set cheek by jowl, displaying stacked sets of Royal Doulton, Limoges, majolica, Capodimonte, Minton, and other china manufacturers. It was somewhat eccentric, but it made the house feel surprisingly homey.

There was a knock, and Elisabetta rose, crossed the living room, and opened the door to find Marco in uniform, with a grin on his face and a large, gaily wrapped box under his arm.

"*Buona sera*, Elisabetta!" Marco swept her up with his free arm and kissed her on the cheek.

"What a surprise!" Elisabetta said, flustered. "It's good to see you."

"Elisabetta, where are your manners?" Nonna called out. "Who's there? Why don't you invite him in?"

"Marco, please come in." Elisabetta opened the door wider, and Marco entered the living room, eyeing the array of cabinetry without comment. She showed him into the dining room. "Nonna, this is Marco Terrizzi, and Marco, this is—"

"Signora Servano." Nonna's hooded eyes narrowed. "Doesn't your father, Beppe, run Bar GiroSport?"

"Yes." Marco smiled pleasantly.

"Aren't you the one who serenaded Elisabetta at my restaurant?"

"Yes." Marco nodded.

"So you're courting Elisabetta?"

"Yes." Marco beamed.

"What are your intentions? Are they honorable or trifling?"

Elisabetta cringed. "Nonna!"

Marco straightened. "My intentions are honorable, and I love her."

Elisabetta felt moved, her heart responding, to her own surprise.

Nonna scowled. "But you're not a very diligent suitor, are you, Marco?"

He blinked. "Pardon me?"

"You haven't been here yet, have you? She's been here a while, did you know?"

"Yes, but I've had to work."

"So why do you come knocking at this hour?"

"I had to work late and—"

"You don't expect she's going out with you tonight, do you?"

"*Beh*, I was hoping we could get a *gelato*."

"Don't you know she has to work in the morning? Do you believe you can just show up and have it your way?"

"No, no, I don't—"

"Don't get any ideas, *capito*? You know she's a good girl, don't you? She's not like the others, do you understand?"

"I know she's not like the others."

"So why treat her as you do? If your intentions are honorable, why come by so late, for the very first time?"

Elisabetta wished she could flee, but Nonna was unstoppable, already waving at Marco's wrapped gift.

"Anyway what have you got there?"

"Oh, this is for her." Marco slid the gift from under his arm.

"You don't think you can buy her off, do you? Elisabetta, why don't you open your gift?"

"I will." Elisabetta was too mortified to meet Marco's eye as he handed her the present. "Thank you, Marco. What's the occasion?"

"If I tell you, then you'll know what—"

"*Basta!*" Nonna interrupted, with a snort. "Talk, talk, talk! I'm sleepy! Hurry up!"

Elisabetta burst into laughter, and so did Marco. She tore off the silvery paper, and he balled it up as she lifted the lid of the box and opened a layer of white tissue paper.

Nonna craned her neck. "How can I see? Why don't you hold it up?"

Elisabetta gasped when she opened the tissue paper to reveal a beautiful pink dress, sleeveless with a scoop neckline, its fabric a filmy chiffon with a pink satin ribbon at the waist. She lifted it up, and it felt lighter than air, made for a night she would never have, for a life she would never live, a dress so elegant, feminine, and fancy that it was fit for a princess, not a waitress.

Nonna scoffed. "Now where's she going to wear *that*?"

"Nonna, please." Elisabetta clasped the dress to her chest, overwhelmed. "Thank you, so much, Marco. This is a beautiful dress!"

"You're welcome." Marco smiled warmly, his dark eyes shining. "I've been invited to a fancy party, and I was wondering if you would go with me. You can wear the dress."

"What about shoes?" Nonna interjected again. "You think she has shoes for such a dress? Or do you expect her to go barefoot?"

"Nonna, I'll get my own shoes." Elisabetta's heart was still hurting from Sandro, but a fancy party sounded fun, and she hadn't had fun in such a long time, working every day and going to bed early every night.

Marco touched her arm. "Will you go with me, Elisabetta?"

"Yes," Elisabetta answered impulsively.

"That's enough!" Nonna glowered, pointing to the door. "Good night, Marco! Bye-bye! Sleep tight!"

Marco chuckled. "Good night, Signora Servano."

Elisabetta placed the dress back in the box, folding it with care and smoothing out the skirt. "Marco, I'll walk you to the door."

"No, you won't." Nonna waved her hand. "Marco, see yourself to the door, will you? That's not difficult, is it? Are you sighted? In full possession of locomotive power?"

"Signora Servano, yes, thank you. Good night, Elisabetta." Marco reached for Elisabetta's hand and kissed it softly, then strode to the door, and left.

Elisabetta felt her heart wake up, though she hadn't known it was sleeping. Marco did love her, and she felt herself wanting what he was offering, whether it was fun, romance, or true love, she wasn't sure. She knew only that she felt happy. She looked at Nonna, but the old woman was frowning.

"Nonna, what's the matter? Don't you like him?"

"Not for you," Nonna shot back, lifting an eyebrow. "I told you before. You can't be with him."

"But why not?" Elisabetta asked, mystified. "Why don't you like him for me?"

Nonna's expression softened to sadness. "Sit down, dear."

## CHAPTER FORTY-EIGHT

# Sandro

July 1939

Sandro hurried home as soon as he heard that yet *another* Race Law had been issued, restricting Jewish employment in scores of professions, including doctors. Sandro feared that his mother had lost her job, since Jews without exemptions had to be listed in special rosters, *elenchi speciali*, and their professional practice was limited exclusively to Jewish clients. His mother worked at Ospedale Fatebenefratelli, a Catholic hospital, and Sandro doubted that they had sufficient Jewish patients to justify keeping her on.

Sandro hustled through the Ghetto, past shopkeepers huddling over newspapers and distraught housewives clustered in teary groups. So many Jews had lost their jobs that the streets were lined with beggars, rag traders, and the newly poor, selling their possessions. Via del Portico d'Ottavia had gone from a thoroughfare bustling with happy families to a marketplace of despair.

Stores had closed and the butcher shop struggled, since kosher butchering had been prohibited under a set of Race Laws designed to prevent Jews from practicing their religion. Jewish periodicals had been ordered to cease publication, and intermarried Jews sought exemptions to define themselves as Gentile. Congregations diminished as Jews emigrated, and rabbis emigrated, too. The Fascist barrage of discriminatory laws, intended to exclude Jews from daily life and drive them from Italy, was doing its dirty work.

Suddenly Sandro realized he was going in the wrong direction, as his feet kept carrying him to their old house on Piazza Mattei. They had never gotten their exemption reversed, so his father's law practice had been shuttered and they had lost their house. They had moved into a smaller apartment in a lesser house that had a dingy gray façade, cracked like many others on the street, squalid compared with the refined Piazza Mattei.

Sandro reached the house, ran up the broken steps to the third floor, and opened the door to their new apartment. The air was stifling, and he dropped his rucksack on the floor of the cramped kitchen that doubled as a living and dining room. They used the living room for his parents' bedroom, and Sandro got a bedroom barely big enough for a bed. It might have been close quarters, but at least it was sunny, since its back window faced south.

"Mamma, I heard the news. Did the hospital fire you?" Sandro went to his parents at the kitchen table, their expressions somber.

"Yes," his mother answered quietly. Her eyes were reddish and puffy, and her face had fallen into resigned lines. She had on her gray linen dress and pearls, managing to look like her dignified self, though her heart must be breaking.

"I'm so sorry." Sandro gave her a hug, then sat down at the small wooden table. They had sold most of the other furniture—except for a bookshelf stuffed with Sandro's math books, Rosa's first-edition novels, and his parents' old textbooks—and all of their valuables, except for a breakfront containing their family menorah and silver candlesticks.

His mother paused, pursing her lips. "When the news came out, I had just delivered a beautiful baby girl, a big one, too." His mother swallowed. "It's hard to accept that it's over, just like that. I've worked there such a long time. I loved what I did. I loved the labor and delivery nurses, they're a very special group."

"I know." Sandro nodded, having heard her say so many times.

"And I feel terrible that my patients won't have a female doctor anymore. The first-time mothers, mainly. They feel more comfortable with me. I regret that I won't be there to help them."

Sandro knew that as a woman she had struggled against discrimination by the other doctors. "Were all the Jewish doctors fired?"

"Yes."

"In the other departments, too?"

"Yes, the lot of us."

"Even before the effective date," his father interjected, shaking his head. He had on his customary suit and tie, but his lapels looked worn.

"I don't blame the administrators," his mother added, with a sigh. "They had no choice. They have to follow the law. Giancarlo told me they hated to do it, and Moro cried when I picked up my discharge papers. Alberto took me and the others for coffee afterward. Sister Anna Domenica and the other nurses broke down and cried."

Sandro knew them all. He had met most of his mother's colleagues, when he would stop by the hospital after school.

"I blame myself." His father raked a hand through his hair. "If I had gotten us the exemption, you could have kept your job, Gemma. I should've gotten it for us. I deserved it. We deserve it."

"You tried your best, and so did Beppe. We did all we could."

"Not true." His father shook his head. "You know what I hear? There are rumors that some are bribing their way to exemptions. That there's a racket being run by the Under-Secretary of the Interior, Buffarini. He's a virulent anti-Semite, but he's fine with taking our money." He shook his head again. "I let you down, dear."

"You didn't, Massimo. There's no guarantee, even with a bribe."

"It's all my fault, all of it. I relied on reason. Law. Justice. I still can't believe they denied me."

Listening, Sandro began to worry about his father, who had changed after being ousted from the party, becoming melancholy. All the time his father brought up his failure to get an exemption, second-guessing himself over and over again. Lately, his father had even begun carrying a folder of notes, to an almost compulsive degree. As Sandro knew he would, his father opened it and began to read aloud, even now.

"Here's the latest exemptions granted so far, which prove my point. According to the last census, 3,502 Jewish families were entitled to an exemption. That's broken down as 406 families of those killed in action, 721 from families that were volunteers, 1,597 from families of those decorated with military valor, and 3 families of Fascist martyrs." His father ran a fingernail across a line of his handwritten notes. "But, here we go, as of today, 724 families of veteran Fascists were granted exemptions, of which we should have been one. We should have been! It *could* have been us, so easily. If the interpretation hadn't been so strict!"

His mother sighed. "We did our best, and even without my job, we're not destitute. We still have our savings and the bonds they gave us when they took the house."

"Right." Sandro nodded, relieved. Under the laws, the deed to their old house had been transferred to a special government office, EGELI, and in return, his parents had been given thirty-year bonds. The transaction was a poor bargain, since the bonds weren't for fair market value and didn't gain maturity for thirty years.

"Massimo, don't worry." His mother put an arm around his father's shoulders. "We have enough to keep us fed for a year, and perhaps by then, this nightmare will have passed. You handle the money, so you know better than I do."

"Gemma, uh, there's something I have to tell you." His father's lined face blanched. "We don't have as much as you think we do. We have less than half."

"What do you mean?" His mother frowned in bewilderment.

Sandro felt his stomach drop, but didn't interrupt.

"*Beh*, it's hard to explain." His father began riffling through his papers. "I keep an accounting of the money I've withdrawn, over time. It's in here somewhere."

"What?" His mother recoiled, horrified. "You've been withdrawing money from our account? What for?"

"I've been giving out loans at the synagogue."

"To whom?" His mother's eyes flew open behind her glasses.

"I loaned it to my clients, until they get the exemption, or in case they don't." His father kept riffling through his papers, and his words began to speed up, rushing over one another. "Gemma, there are so many people worse off than we are, and when I'm sitting face-to-face with them, knowing we have more than they, I extend a helping hand. It's as the Torah says, it's *tzedakah*, righteous giving, charity, and justice that we should share what we have, and I assumed you would agree."

"But they'll never be able to repay it. Nobody has a job anymore."

"I didn't anticipate that you would lose your job, and even so, we should have gotten the exemption, that's the thing, it was an injustice. I can show you on our original application—"

"Massimo, you shouldn't have given away money, or lent it, when there's talk of war. If that happens, we will need every penny."

"Listen, both of you." Sandro stood up, and a new sense of calm came over him. "We can't look to the past. Papa, you can't keep bringing up our exemption. Mamma, maybe he shouldn't have lent money, but it's gone now. We have to start over, going forward."

His mother moaned, stricken. "But we don't have enough to live on."

"Mamma, I make some money. We have half of the savings you thought. I will sit down, balance the books, and account for it all. I'm fairly good with numbers, if you recall."

"Wait, allow me to double-check one last thing." His father returned his attention to his file of notes, but Sandro plucked it from his grasp.

"Papa, I'm going to hold on to this folder from now on."

"My notes? No, no, no." His father's eyes flared with dismay. "Son, I need my notes—"

"I'll keep them for you."

As his father stared at him, Sandro realized that he was becoming the head of the household.

"Thank you, Sandro," his mother said, forcing a smile.

## CHAPTER FORTY-NINE

# Elisabetta

### August 1939

Elisabetta should have been happy, but her chest felt tight. She and Marco headed for the fancy party at Palazzo Braschi, joining the throng of dressed-up couples filing inside. She still felt stunned by what Nonna had told her, that her mother and Marco's father had been in a love affair, when Elisabetta was only a baby. She had always suspected that her mother had been unfaithful, but she never would have guessed it had been with Marco's father.

Heads turned to admire her and Marco, and she supposed they made an attractive couple, she in her beautiful pink dress and new pumps, and Marco in his dark uniform, his hair shiny, his face tan from the sun. She didn't know if she should tell him about their parents, or even if she should be seeing him, at all. Nonna had been firmly against it, but Elisabetta had been hoping to play the evening by ear. She loved Marco's company, and the notion of the party had captivated her, too. She had been living the life of a much older person, working all the time, and she had felt so sad after Sandro's rejection. She had to stop longing for him. He was gone.

Marco held her hand as they approached the palazzo, entertaining her with animated stories, and when they neared the entrance, he gestured at the elegant façade of Palazzo Braschi, which had been festooned with tricolor sashes and a massive flag with the Fascist *littorio* emblem. "The decorations are beautiful, aren't they? I helped put them up."

"Beautiful."

"I'm so glad you came tonight. I've missed you." Marco flashed his dazzling smile, and Elisabetta found herself wondering if her mother had been as charmed by his father. It made her uncomfortable, and she didn't want to think she was anything like her mother, and she felt suddenly wrong being with him. She had thought she could go through with it, but now she wasn't so sure. Cigarette smoke and heavy perfume filled her nostrils as the partygoers pressed together, bottlenecking at the palazzo entrance. She felt vaguely nauseated.

"This will be so much fun, don't you think? My boss is getting a big promotion." Marco squeezed her hand, looking over, then tilted his head. "Elisabetta, are you okay?"

"I'm sorry." Elisabetta let go of Marco's hand, turned around, and made her way back through the packed crowd.

"Elisabetta!" Marco hurried after her, but she didn't stop. He reached her in front of the fountain and took her by the arm. "What's the matter? Where are you going?"

"I have to leave. I can't be with you. I shouldn't have come."

"Why? What's going on, *cara*?"

Elisabetta felt the secret bursting within her. "There's something you don't know. Nonna told me something awful, about my mother—"

"I know already." Marco took her hands gently, and his expression softened. "I know about my father and the affair."

"What? How?" Elisabetta felt her face turn hot. She felt exposed and awkward. "It's so embarrassing."

"Sit down, please." Marco pressed her onto the ledge of the fountain, holding one of her hands.

"I'm so ashamed that she did such a thing!"

"As am I. I never would have thought it of my father. I'm barely speaking to the man. Nevertheless, what happened between them has nothing to do with us."

"What are you talking about? They're our parents."

"Exactly. Our parents are not us."

"Nonna doesn't think we can be together."

"You're your own woman, Elisabetta." Marco met her eye, his dark gaze unusually steady. "You and I have known each other since we were little. I've loved you that long, I swear it to you now. We are Marco and Elisabetta. That's who we are, and nothing between us has changed."

"I don't know." Elisabetta wished she could go along, but her feelings were bollixed up. "How can we be together now? What will your parents say? Your mother? Nonna says it's not practical—"

"Don't worry so much. Here we are, you and me. We're in the present, not the past. You look stunning in that dress, and we're going to a beautiful party." A slow grin spread across Marco's face, and his eyes glinted with mischief. "And we're going to dance—"

"We can't—"

"—just like this!" Marco encircled her waist with his arm and swept her into the air, spinning her around so that her dress billowed gaily, and Elisabetta felt herself dizzy and laughing, even as he spun her closer to Palazzo Braschi. She saw the fancy people around them as a blur and she clung to him, wrapping her arms around his neck, and when they reached the entrance, Marco set her down under the archway, where he kissed her softly, chasing her objections away.

Marco took Elisabetta onto the glistening parquet floor, guiding her through dance after dance, and she followed his lead, whirling past walls lined with painted friezes, oil portraits, and polished bronze sconces that shed a romantic light. The ballroom was grand, and couples danced to a wonderful orchestra playing in front of a stage under a large tricolor sash, strung between two marble columns. Painted murals covered the vaulted ceiling, and the only time they stopped dancing was to accept flutes of bubbly *spumante* from passing waiters.

Elisabetta found herself having fun, and by the third glass of *spumante*, she began to feel less worried, though she noticed that many of Marco's former friends seemed cool to him. She didn't understand why, nor did she know if Marco had noticed. He focused only on her, making sure she was having a good time.

Suddenly excitement rippled through the crowd, and everyone burst into animated chatter, turning to the ballroom entrance. The orchestra launched into a rousing rendition of *"Giovinezza"* as an entourage of Blackshirts marched into the ballroom, and the partygoers moved quickly aside to admit them.

"What's happening?" Elisabetta asked, standing on tiptoe.

Marco gasped. "Il Duce is here!"

The crowd gave the Fascist salute, chanting, "Duce, Duce, Duce!" Marco joined in, and Elisabetta felt stunned at the notion that she was in the same room as such a powerful man. She craned her neck to see him, astonished to find that Mussolini looked just like his image in the photos, posters, stamps, and coins. He had round, dark eyes, a prominent brow, and a strong jawline—a pugnacious visage at odds with his formal attire, a black coat with tails and a shiny top hat. His magnetism was undeniable even to Elisabetta, who was no Fascist.

The crowd and Marco cheered wildly as Mussolini climbed the steps of the stage to a lectern, surveyed the chanting partygoers, then motioned for silence as he began to speak. "Ladies and Gentlemen! Greetings! Tonight we celebrate the promotion of Commendatore Buonacorso, who has served our glorious party!"

All of a sudden, the tricolor sash above the stage came undone and began to flutter down, heading for Mussolini. The partygoers gasped, the Blackshirts shouted a warning, and Mussolini stepped aside just before the sash fell on the lectern.

The partygoers burst into astonished chatter, and Blackshirts leapt to the stage. Mussolini stood aside, and Blackshirts started calling for a ladder to reattach the sash. There was chaos at the lectern, with everyone running this way and that. The mishap threatened to reduce the momentous occasion to a cartoonishly silly scene.

"What an embarrassment for the *fascio*." Marco muttered to Elisabetta. "We don't have a ladder tall enough to fix the sash. The contractor took the big ladder with him."

"What will they do?"

"Excuse me, Elisabetta. Be right back." Marco left her side, made his way to the front of the room, spoke with one of the Blackshirts, and hurried to the stage. She watched in bewilderment as the partygoers began to notice him, their heads turning.

On the stage, Marco hurried to pick up the fallen end of the sash, hustled with it to the base of the tall column, and, remarkably, began to climb the column as if it were a flagpole, straddling it with his strong arms and legs.

Elisabetta's mouth dropped open. The partygoers responded instantaneously, cheering and applauding him. The band struck up a rousing march, and everyone clapped in rhythm as Marco shimmied up the column, climbing until he reached its very top, where he tried to reattach the sash.

Everyone looked up, waiting to see if Marco would succeed. Elisabetta marveled at his bravado. The crowd cheered him on. In the next moment, the sash was affixed. Marco signaled that he had done the job, then slid down the column in a controlled manner, landing safely at the bottom.

The crowd roared, and so did Elisabetta. Mussolini himself strode to Marco, shook his hand, and spoke to him for a time, then clapped him on the arm. Marco beamed from ear to ear, and the moment galvanized Elisabetta, as she knew it was once in a lifetime for him. The crowd hollered and clapped, and Marco was grinning as he left the stage. Blackshirts and his friends surged toward him, congratulating him, and Elisabetta realized that he had just fixed whatever had bothered them, in a way that only he could.

The crowd settled down, and Mussolini retook the lectern, beginning with thanking Marco, by name. Marco acknowledged the honor with a nod, then threaded his way through the crowd as Mussolini resumed his speech, from where he had left off.

Elisabetta didn't hear a word. She felt so full of pride in Marco, who kept his eyes on her even as he made his way through the crowd. Partygoers stopped him, shaking his hand and clapping him on the back, but Marco kept glancing up at her, as if he couldn't wait to return to her side.

He reached her grinning, and she practically leapt into his arms, kissing him. He kissed her back softly, then deeply, and Elisabetta felt him bringing her broken heart back to life. She felt won over, and the love she had for him rekindled.

Still there.

## CHAPTER FIFTY

# Marco

### September 1939

M arco hurried to meet Sandro, catching snippets of conversation from businessmen. They talked in worried groups, and everyone buzzed about the outbreak of war. Hitler had invaded Poland earlier this month, and Europe erupted in conflict and fear. Great Britain and France declared war on Germany, and Romans lived on tenterhooks. Italy had yet to enter the conflict, but Palazzo Braschi was on high alert. Marco had been working around the clock, and there was volatility in the very air.

He approached Piazza Bocca della Verità, which was out of the way and contained a small park, unusually quiet and peaceful. The piazza was in one of the oldest parts of the city, just outside the Ghetto, and the scale of the ancient buildings allowed for plenty of sunny sky. Only a few people walked by, and traffic was light on Via Luigi Petroselli and Via di Santa Maria in Cosmedin.

He spotted Sandro waiting for him on a stone bench, but the sight gave him cause for concern. His friend hunched over a newspaper, reading, but his posture was uncharacteristically stooped and he looked older in a worn brown jacket and tie. Marco had been worried about him, which was why he'd invited him to meet today.

"Sandro!" Marco called to him. "Remember we used to play here?"

Sandro looked up, then broke into a grin, setting aside the newspaper. "Just like the old days, eh?"

"Yes." Marco greeted him, sitting down. "We used to get so dizzy, running around the temple." He meant the Temple of Hercules Victor, a small, round building of Greek marble in the piazza, which was sur-rounded by tall columns holding up a roof of red tile. "It's a miracle we didn't get sick."

"You did, don't you remember? You threw up."

"I forgot." Marco chuckled. "We spent more time here than at school. And had more fun."

"Remember, you're talking to a teacher now."

"Oh, right." Marco looked over, eyeing Sandro with concern. "How is it going, brother?"

"Terrible."

*"Dimmi tutto."* Tell me everything.

"My mother lost her job and she volunteers as a midwife. My father spends all day at the synagogue." Sandro shook his head. "He's helping people, but something's wrong with him. He's not doing well, mentally. I think losing the house was too much for him."

"Oh no." Marco's heart felt heavy. "I'm so sorry we didn't get you the exemption. My father is still trying."

"Thanks." Sandro smiled, but shook his head. "I don't think it will work, though. My father says they're clamping down. It's so terrible to feel you don't belong where you always have. Now, because I'm Jewish, I'm not Italian. It changes everything."

"You'll always be Italian to me. We're the same, you and me."

Sandro's lower lip puckered. "No, we aren't, I know that now. I have a new clarity about this, and much else."

"What do you mean? We're the same. We always have been."

"No, I'm Jewish, and I always have been." Sandro met his eye evenly. "You think it's the same because you're not in my position. Your life hasn't changed, but mine has. We're not equal, according to the Fascists."

"But not all Fascists support the Race Laws."

"Nevertheless, they're responsible for them."

"I'm not," Marco said, pained. He felt suddenly aware of his black shirt. "I'm not my uniform, and you used to be a Fascist, too."

"I'm not anymore, and neither is my father. He still wants to be, but he was thrown out of his own party."

Marco felt a wrench in his chest, not knowing how to respond, and Sandro's expression softened.

"Look, I don't mind being different. I'm proud of my Jewishness. What I want is to be equal, the way I used to be. It's a terrible feeling not to be, and it's with me all the time. Now I feel inferior, less than others. Apart. Officially."

"I understand," Marco said, but he wasn't sure that he really did. Or that he could.

"You know what's worse? I don't feel safe outside the Ghetto anymore. Even here, where we used to play. I'm nervous in my own hometown."

"I'm so sorry, truly. You'll always be safe with me."

"I know that." Sandro smiled, but it vanished quickly. "But the world has changed, with the war. Do you think we'll enter? Do you hear anything at work, one way or the other?"

Marco sighed, for the question plagued him, too. "All I hear is that Il Duce doesn't think we have the gold reserves for war. He wants Italy to stay neutral."

"Unless he changes his mind, which he does all the time."

"How?" Marco felt a defensive twinge, having met Il Duce himself. He would never forget that night at the ball, when he had fixed the sash. Mussolini had shaken his hand, thanked him personally, and told him that he was an excellent example of a young Italian Fascist. But Marco could never tell that to Sandro. His best friend didn't need another blow, and the fact that Elisabetta had been with him at the ball would hurt Sandro, too.

"He changed his mind with the Race Laws, didn't he? Mussolini never had a problem with Jews before. That's why my father believed in him, and so did I. He turned on us. It's a rank betrayal."

Marco swallowed hard. It was true, and he had to acknowledge as much. "You're right, but I don't think he'll change his mind about the war."

"I dread to think of Italy, ever, as Hitler's ally." Sandro shuddered. "The Nazis are ruthlessly anti-Semitic, violently so. They turned on the German Jews, and rumors are they're attacking Polish Jews."

"But that won't happen here."

"I'm worried."

"Don't be." Marco touched his arm. "Sandro, what can I do? Can't I help you in any way?"

"No, thanks."

"But I'm making money these days. If you need any, I can—"

"No, no, we're fine." Sandro straightened up, and Marco changed the subject, not to offend him.

"How's Rosa?"

"Still in London. Her husband enlisted in the RAF. We get letters from time to time." Sandro bit his lip, his expression newly grave. "I hope she's not in harm's way. Italy would be fighting her husband, if we enter."

"But we won't."

"Again, I hope not," Sandro said, his anxiety plain, and Marco felt a wave of sadness. He would never have foreseen that his and Sandro's teenage years would be concerned with matters of life and death. He fell silent a moment, and so did Sandro, but they understood each other without words, in the way that only old friends can.

"Let's eat something," Marco said, breaking the spell. "I'm starving. I worked through lunch."

"You want to go somewhere?"

"No, I grabbed something for us, on the street." Marco reached for his rucksack, pulled out a paper bag, and took out a brown bag of *supplì*, releasing a delicious aroma.

*"Supplì?"* Sandro frowned, his lips parting.

"Yes, you like them, don't you?"

"Yes," Sandro answered, after a moment. "But I'm not hungry."

"You sure?" Marco asked, surprised. "I got four."

"No, thanks."

"Suit yourself." Marco popped a *supplì* into his mouth and bit down, releasing the deliciously salty taste of breading, rice, tomato, and cheese.

"I have something to tell you about Elisabetta." Sandro paused. "My feelings for her have waned. The stronger feelings I used to have for her have gone."

*"Davvero?"* Marco exploded with joy, hugging him. He had been falling more deeply in love with Elisabetta, and it would be wonderful not to have to vie with Sandro for her anymore. "What happened?"

"I don't know, I fell out of love." Sandro shrugged, but Marco realized what must have happened.

"You've met someone else, haven't you? Come on, tell me the truth."

Sandro hesitated, then smiled. "Yes, I have."

"What great news! What's her name?" Marco felt a wave of happiness for him, because Sandro needed a woman more than he knew. Every man did.

"Anna."

"Where did you meet her?"

"At school. She just moved here with her family. She's beautiful."

"And she likes you back?"

"Yes."

*"Bravo,* Sandro!" Marco's heart lifted, for them both. "So you're out of our competition? You promise?"

"Yes." Sandro nodded. "Elisabetta's yours."

"Thank you, friend! Now we both can be happy!" Marco flooded with relief. "I lost sleep, worrying she'd choose you."

"No, Marco. It was always you." Sandro smiled again, a little sadly.

"I wish you the best with Anna."

"And I wish you the best with Elisabetta."

"We're friends forever, Sandro. No matter what."

"No matter what," Sandro repeated, sealing the bond.

## CHAPTER FIFTY-ONE

# Elisabetta

October 1939

The late-day sun streamed through the lacy curtains in Nonna's bedroom, and Elisabetta entered to check on her. Nonna had fallen ill with bronchitis and lay in bed in her pink-flowered nightgown, covered by a white quilted coverlet. Her bedroom felt cozy, if crowded, containing four mismatched breakfronts of china, as well as the conventional bed, ladder-back chair, a pine night table, and a dresser. A ceramic crucifix hung over her headboard next to a faded photo of the last Pope, though Nonna refused to hang any of the present one. She was a Roman Catholic, but considered herself a higher power.

"Nonna, how are you feeling?" Elisabetta set a glass of water on her night table.

"Don't you remember from the last time you asked?"

Elisabetta smoothed down the coverlet, hiding her worry. "Your color is better today. You're improving."

"What would you expect? And when can I resume work?"

"As soon as the doctor says it's permissible."

"What does *he* know?"

"More than we do." Elisabetta patted Nonna's arm. If Nonna was cranky, she was feeling more like herself. "Can I get you anything before I go?"

"Would you please stop asking me questions?"

"Okay, I'll be home as early as possible."

"To plague me?"

"Yes, exactly." Elisabetta smiled. "Paolo will look in on you while I'm out."

"Where are you going? Why are you so dressed up?"

"I'm meeting Marco." Elisabetta had on her pale blue cotton dress with mother-of-pearl buttons, having come home to change after work.

"Why?" Nonna's hooded eyes narrowed behind her glasses. "What about his father and your mother?"

"That doesn't matter," Elisabetta answered matter-of-factly, not for the first time.

"Don't you know you're making a big mistake?"

"I told you, we're not going to live in the past."

"You can't live in the present without acknowledging the past." Nonna scoffed. "All Romans live in the present and the past, at the same time. Walk by the old Basilica di Santa Maria in Trastevere. You can't pretend it doesn't exist."

"What does that have to do with anything? The church is a building."

"So? That only allows you to see it better." Nonna wagged a knobby finger at her. "If Marco's past were a building, you couldn't deny its presence. Don't you understand my point? How will his father receive you? How will his mother?"

Elisabetta didn't want to fuss. "It's not Marco's past, it's his father's."

"If you marry him, you marry his family."

"Nonna, nobody's talking about marriage yet."

"But this is how it begins. Don't you know by now, I'm always right?"

"Nonna, this will be the one time you're wrong. Anyway, I have to go."

"Why don't you listen to me?"

"I do, Nonna. I just don't always obey you. *Ciao*." Elisabetta kissed her on the cheek, then petted the cat, sitting at the foot of the bed. "Rico, be a good boy."

"When is he *not* a good boy?" Nonna moved her toe under the covers, playing with him. "He's better than you. He obeys."

"No, he doesn't." Elisabetta left the room with a smile. "Goodbye."

"He obeys *me*!" Nonna called after her.


Elisabetta and Marco left the restaurant, a local seafood place on the Lungotevere Aventino outside the Ghetto. The city was still lively at this hour, and couples emerged from restaurants laughing and talking loudly, their conversations lubricated by wine. Elisabetta had sensed, even at Casa Servano, that everyone was trying too hard to have a good time. Romans worried all the time that Europe was at war, anxious that Italy would be drawn into the conflict. The night air was cool, smelling of car exhaust.

Elisabetta walked with Marco, feeling happy with him, hand in hand. He looked handsome in a light gray sweater and slacks, like his old self, and the shine on his hair and whiteness of his smile caught the lamplight as they passed.

"So, did you enjoy dinner?" Marco asked, with a smile.

"Very much, thank you," Elisabetta answered. They had shared a delicious meal of *orata al forno con finocchio*, sea bream with fennel, while they told each other stories about their jobs. Marco had done funny impressions of his boss that had made her laugh, charming her.

"You notice everything about restaurants now, like a professional." Marco smiled again.

"Do I?" Elisabetta asked, though she realized he might be right. She felt like a restaurant critic in other restaurants. She found all of them wanting compared to Casa Servano.

"You remarked that the water glass was spotted, and the waiter's shirt untucked."

"It was!" Elisabetta laughed, and Marco joined her.

"Let's take a walk, okay?"

"Yes, but only a short one. I can't be away from home too long, with Nonna unwell."

"How about the Giardino degli Aranci? It's nearby."

"That would be great." Elisabetta liked the Giardino degli Aranci, the Orange Garden, as it was a park with a natural grove of orange trees, a lesser-known gem of Rome.

"I used to go there at night, after Aldo passed, and look at the view."

Elisabetta heard Marco's voice soften, which she recognized as grief. She squeezed his hand gently. "I'm sorry. It must be so hard for you."

"You, too. They say losses are a part of life, but it doesn't make you feel better, does it?"

"No." Elisabetta reflected that he was right. "I'm worried about Nonna, being so sick."

"She'll be fine. She's strong. Women like her live forever, and you take wonderful care of her." Marco paused. "She doesn't like me, does she?"

"It's not about you, it's about what happened between our parents." Elisabetta thought a moment, as they strolled. "How are your parents?"

"My mother is still grieving Aldo, and there are days she doesn't get out of bed. Only Emedio can talk to her."

"I'm sorry."

"We'll get through it. Watch out, *cara*." Marco put an arm around Elisabetta protectively, as a cyclist whipped around the corner. "You know, I was in this neighborhood recently with Sandro. We met across from Bocca della Verità, like in the old days."

"Oh, how is he?" Elisabetta masked her interest. She wondered if Sandro had told him what had happened between them, then realized he probably hadn't, so as not to hurt Marco's feelings.

"He's busy teaching." Marco's face fell. "The Race Laws are crushing him and his family. I don't think he'll have much time for either of us, for a while."

"I'm sure. Poor Sandro." Elisabetta felt a deep pang. "Doesn't it bother you that the Fascists are passing such anti-Semitic laws? It was never like this before, and they're ruining Sandro's family and so many others."

"Of course it bothers me. I hate it, but there's nothing I can do." Marco pursed his lips. "None of my friends at Palazzo Braschi thinks these laws are just, but we lack any say. More and more, we've become afraid to speak out."

"Are you afraid?"

"Honestly, yes." Marco looked over, his dark eyes searching hers. "But my father and I tried to get Sandro's family an exemption, and we'll keep trying."

"I'm glad to hear that," Elisabetta said, feeling a surge of gratitude. She knew that Marco loved Sandro.

"Let's head this way." Marco gestured past the church, off Via di Santa Maria in Cosmedin. They walked uphill along the Clivo di Rocca Savella, a wide cobblestone walkway beside a tall wall, its surface rough with dark stones, bricks, and marble fragments of different sizes. The route steepened because the Giardino degli Aranci was on the Aventine Hill, one of the seven fabled hills of Rome.

Elisabetta held on to Marco's hand, negotiating the cobblestones in her fancy shoes. She felt relaxed and happy at his side, marveling at how easy it was to be with him. The breeze was stronger at elevation, carrying the fragrance of the bitter orange trees, naturally perfuming the air. There were fewer people on the street, and cars weren't permitted, so the traffic noises receded into the background.

They walked in contented silence, and in time entered the Giardino degli Aranci, a large park full of orange trees and umbrella pines, making a leafy bower against the dark sky. Gaslights shed a gentle light in soft halos, illuminating a light gravel path that divided the garden, which led to a large brick belvedere, a scenic overlook with only a handful of other couples.

Elisabetta enjoyed the warmth of his fingers over hers, their footsteps crunching on the gravel path. They reached the terrace and took in the beautiful panorama of Rome at night, bigger and more glittery than Elisabetta had seen it before, even from the balcony at Palazzo Braschi. To her right were the Roman Forum and the ruins, their marble glowing creamy white in the lights from underneath, but her gaze shifted from them to her beloved Trastevere, a humbler patchwork of red tile roofs and church domes across the Tiber, watched over by the serene, glowing dome of Saint Peter's Basilica.

"Isn't this magnificent?" Marco asked her.

"Beautiful." Elisabetta breathed in a deep lungful of air.

"I brought you up for here for a reason." Marco put his arm around her, and she tilted her face up, expecting him to kiss her, but instead he was holding out a diamond ring, twinkling in the ambient light.

Elisabetta blinked, shocked. Her heart leapt to her throat. She hadn't seen this coming.

"Elisabetta, I love you, and I've loved you all my life. My feelings have only grown stronger, every day. I know I can make you happy." Marco smiled down at her, his dark eyes shining and his expression intense with emotion. "I love you, I appreciate you, and I treasure all that is wonderful about you and always have, even from when we were little. I promise to spend the rest of my life making you happy. Nothing would make me happier. I would be the luckiest man in the world if you would accept this ring, and say yes to my proposal."

Elisabetta listened, astounded. Other couples were starting to look over, realizing they were witnessing a marriage proposal. They began to gasp, smile, and talk to each other excitedly, as if awaiting her answer with Marco, but she didn't know what to say. She didn't want to hurt Marco or embarrass him, though he didn't notice them, his gaze focused only on her, reflecting the devotion he had always shown her.

"Elisabetta, I know you struggle, always on your own, and you don't need to do that anymore. I have a real job and I can provide for you. We can make a family, you and I, and we can withstand all the troubles that the war, or hard times, or anything else may bring us."

"But what about your family?" Elisabetta blurted out, stalling. "Did you discuss this with them?"

"No, and I don't have to. My parents will get used to the idea, and if they don't, we'll leave them behind. You and I will live together in our own place, and if they don't like it, that will be their problem, not ours." Marco dropped to one knee, looking up at her with a heartbreaking smile. "Will you marry me?"

"Marco, I, uh, didn't expect this." Elisabetta watched his expression darken, and she hated to hurt him. She did love him, but she didn't know if she wanted to marry him, not yet. She was just getting used to seeing him again. She was trying to take care of Nonna and work. She remembered when she had dreamed about becoming a columnist or a novelist. She still had those dreams, somewhere inside her, and she wouldn't be able to fulfill them if she decided to get married.

"Elisabetta." Marco kept looking up at her, though a frown popped onto his forehead. "You love me, don't you?"

"Yes, but I don't know if I feel ready for—"

"I understand." Marco looked pained, but his expression remained loving. He rose from his knees, still holding her hands, and pressed the engagement ring into her palm. "I understand, this caught you unawares. We haven't been seeing each other enough. I've been working too hard and haven't given us the time that we deserve."

"Yes, that's it," Elisabetta rushed to say, though her heart hurt.

"Keep the ring until you're ready. It's only a matter of time."

"Are you sure?" Elisabetta asked, but when she heard herself, she realized that it wasn't the correct question at all. *She* was the one who was unsure. *She* didn't know if it was only a matter of time. And *she* didn't know if she should take the ring. But it was already in her hand.

"When you're ready, just say the word." Marco kissed her softly.

CHAPTER FIFTY-TWO

# Rosa

December 1939

It was a sunny, if chilly, day and Rosa felt relieved to be back on Italian soil. Her heart lifted to see the palm trees lining the Tiber, a sight she had missed in rainy London, and the Thames didn't compare to this river, pea-green and sun-kissed. She walked down Lungotevere de' Cenci, passing people on the sidewalk, loving the musical sound of her native tongue and noting the emotionality of her countrymen, who gesticulated as they spoke. She hadn't realized how different Italians were until she lived in London, and though she loved David and their circle of British friends, she was happy to be home, even in the circumstances.

Rosa had left London on an embassy flight, lucky to get a ticket to Rome, as travel was restricted. David was serving in the RAF, and she had been following the news of the Race Laws at home, which were systematically stripping Italian Jews of their citizenship, profession, and property. She sensed her parents needed her, even though their letters never said so.

Rosa reached the entrance to the Ghetto and passed the small white church of San Gregorio della Divina Pietà, an ancient church that had significance for Jews, especially poignant now. In the 1500s, the Ghetto Jews had been forced to attend Mass there every Sunday, as part of the campaign to convert them. The church's ivory façade showed a painting of a crucified Christ, above a biblical inscription intended as a tongue-lashing to Ghetto Jews: "I have stretched out my hands all day to a rebellious people, who walk in a way that is not good, following their own devices, a people who provoke me to my face continually."

Rosa looked away, shuddering. She took in Tempio Maggiore, the synagogue directly across the way, its bright lemony limestone a golden hue in the sunshine. The stained glass on its square dome shone multicolored, though she admired the solidity of the edifice itself. And from that structure, she drew strength.

Rosa continued down Via del Portico d'Ottavia, shocked by how much the Ghetto had deteriorated. Men and women sold used shoes, clothing, and pots and pans from barrows, pushcarts, and stalls. Via del Portico d'Ottavia used to be lined with busy shops, but most of them were closed. People picked through the items, milled about, talked, or even begged. Everyone looked bedraggled in clothes that were old or in need of repair. Gone were the happy, healthy, and boisterous families carrying home full bags of groceries, as well as the delicious aromas of *pollo arrosto*, roast chicken, and *pesce fritto*, fried fish, wafting from apartments.

Rosa felt oddly as if she had never been here before, and heads began to turn in her direction as she walked by. She realized that she stood out in her fine coat of red wool, with its fashionable peplum waist, matching hat, and brown pumps. She was dressed for London, not the Ghetto.

She picked up her pace, self-conscious. She passed stall after stall, then her eye was caught by a set of secondhand books, which tempted her. A woman was bent over, unpacking more books, and Rosa glimpsed the woman's gray hair, gathered into a twist that Rosa recognized immediately. She realized with mute shock that the woman was her mother. The books being sold were her own.

Rosa froze, horrified. Her mother had aged so much, with new lines etched into her lovely face and brackets deepening around her mouth. She wore her old tan raincoat, but it was stained, and her black leather shoes had flattened with wear. Her mother finished setting up the books for display, opening them so they stood on end, then looked up and spotted Rosa.

"Rosa, is that *you*? You're back?" Her mother threw open her arms, her eyes filming with happiness behind her wire-rimmed glasses.

"Yes, Mamma!" Rosa masked her dismay, set down her suitcase, and embraced her mother. "I'm so happy to see you!"

"It's so good to see you, too, dear! I've missed you!" Her mother hugged her tightly, and Rosa could feel that she had lost a significant amount of weight, but she concealed her reaction as she released her mother from the embrace.

"I thought I would surprise you. I wasn't sure I could get the flight."

"Say hello to everyone! You remember Vanda Della Seta di Veroli, and here's Celeste Sermonetta! Everyone, look, my Rosa's home!"

Rosa forced a smile as her mother began reintroducing her to everyone, making small talk, as if everything were normal. All of the faces looked older, the clothes ragged, and the men who used to work during the day were here. She assumed her neighbors and the parents of her friends had been expelled from their jobs. They had been handymen, teachers, electricians, accountants, shipping agents, scrap dealers, shop owners, tailors, knife sharpeners, shoemakers, and bakers.

Rosa remembered she'd left her suitcase on the street. She turned to fetch it, but it was already gone.

R osa sat in her old seat at the wooden table, but other than that, nothing was the same. The apartment was tiny and cramped, the kitchen barely big enough to contain the table. Of course there was no chandelier, only a glass fixture that cast harsh light. There was a window, but it didn't overlook the charming Piazza Mattei, just a dirty brick wall. Sandro pointed out that the apartment was sunny, making the best of things though he looked as drained and thin as her parents.

"Here, darling." Her mother set down a serving bowl that was only half-full of spaghetti, the tomato sauce thinned with water. There was no other course; no fish, meat, potatoes, or vegetable, nor was there bread or wine. Gone were the delicious meals from better times, the mouthwatering *braciola* or *aliciotti con l'indivia*, anchovy and endive casserole, served piping hot on platters.

"It looks wonderful, Mamma." Rosa exchanged a look with Sandro, who was undoubtedly reading her mind. Her mother doled out small portions, and after her father said a prayer over the meal, they began to eat. Rosa tried not to notice that they gobbled their pasta, truly famished. She ate, noting that her father returned his attention to a thick folder of papers, making notations. He had greeted her happily when he had come home, but since then, he barely lifted his head from the folder.

"So, Papa," Rosa began gently. "How have you been?"

"Fine," he answered without looking up, which wasn't like him. He'd always been chatty at the dinner table, but he was completely preoccupied. He was still dressed in his suit and tie, but it had become too large for him, its frayed collar leaving space around his neck. He was balder and grayer, too.

"What's in the folder, Papa? What are you doing?"

Her mother interjected, "Your father prepares exemptions from the Race Laws for members of the Community."

"Oh, that's good." Rosa turned to her mother. "And how are you, Mamma?"

"I'm fine, too."

"You must miss the hospital."

"Yes, but I feel needed here. I midwife and patch skinned knees." Her mother smiled briefly. "The Community has come together, and we help each other. We barter when we can, goods for services. Someone leaves us food and money in a bag on the door. We think it's one of your father's clients, in return for his legal services."

"That's nice." Rosa knew her savings would do them good.

"Your brother's been teaching mathematics at the Jewish school. He's a born teacher." Her mother pushed her empty plate away, and Rosa turned to Sandro, feeling a rush of love for him.

"Good for you."

"Thanks. I teach three classes of about forty students each. The ages are all over the lot." Sandro smiled gamely, but to Rosa's eye he looked thin, too. His cheeks were hollowed out of his handsome face, emphasizing his remarkable blue eyes. But they didn't have their usual brightness, as if hardship had diluted their hue.

"Do you hear from the professor?"

"No."

Rosa felt a pang for him. "What's going on with your independent study? Do you work on your own?"

"No, I don't have time. I have to prepare lesson plans and grade exams."

Rosa wanted to change the subject, but each one seemed worse than the last. "How's Marco doing, after Aldo's death?"

"He's coming around."

Rosa felt the loss of Aldo, whom she had always liked. "Poor Maria and Beppe. Emedio, too."

"Marco works for the *fascio*, at Palazzo Braschi. He and his father tried to help us get an exemption, but they couldn't. Good of them to try. What about Elisabetta?"

Rosa remembered that Sandro had been crazy about Elisabetta. "Whatever happened with you and her?"

"Marco liked her, too, and she chose him." A frown buckled Sandro's forehead, and somehow this struck Rosa as the saddest news of all.

"I'm so sorry."

"If I have to lose her to somebody, I'm happy it's him."

Rosa could see Sandro was hurt, but putting on a brave face. "So, you had your first heartbreak. My advice is to move on. You're a good catch. Are you seeing anyone?"

"No. I'm too busy."

"There's a lot of fish in the sea, Sandro."

Her mother interjected, "That's what *I* tell him."

"Jewish fish," Rosa added, to make Sandro laugh, which it did.

"I'm glad you're home, Rosa."

Rosa smiled, happy that she had come home, too. They needed her, tested in a way they never had been before.

Sandro asked, "You must be worried about David, eh?"

"Yes, of course," Rosa answered, as David was always in her thoughts.

"Then we'll worry together." Sandro reached for her hand. "As a family."

## CHAPTER FIFTY-THREE

# Marco
### February 1940

It was the dead of night in the Ghetto, and a cold drizzle began to fall, so Marco sped up on his bicycle. No one was on the streets, and everyone was asleep, which was why he always ran his secret mission this late. He had been dropping off groceries and money at Sandro's doorstep for months. He would ride to their new apartment, run up to the third floor, hang the bag on their doorknob, then steal away. He and his father didn't want the Simones to know it had come from them, as they would have felt embarrassed.

Marco pedaled down Via Catalana, the wide street that ran alongside the front of the synagogue, and his tires bobbled on the cobblestones. The light limestone of the Tempio Maggiore stood out in the darkness, and its square dome rose in a stormy sky. He turned right onto Via del Tempio and rode past the apartment houses, their shutters closed against the chill. A family slept in a doorjamb, huddling under a single blanket.

Marco looked away. It broke his heart to see the deprivation on the Ghetto streets, and he worried the situation was about to get worse. His boss and everyone at Palazzo Braschi believed that Mussolini had changed his mind, and that Italy was going to enter the war on Germany's side.

Marco headed home on Lungotevere de' Cenci, and the lights lining its banks were indistinct in the fog. He tilted his head down against the rain. There was little traffic, and he left the Ghetto. He never went there in his uniform anymore, even at night. Heads would turn and expressions vary from fright to disgust. He felt awful that the Jews feared the Fascists, but he couldn't blame them.

He pedaled harder, approaching the Ponte Fabricio. He slept badly these days. He believed in Fascism except for its new anti-Semitism, which tore him up inside. He didn't know what else he could do, except to make sure that the Simones didn't starve.

His father felt the same way. It was the only thing they had in common these days, still barely speaking.

Marco had almost reached the Ponte Fabricio when he detected a car close to him. He sped up, annoyed. The car sped up, too. He glanced over his shoulder to see a dark sedan. He didn't know why it was harassing him. He accelerated again, risky on slick asphalt.

The car gunned its engine and passed him, and Marco cursed. Suddenly the car veered in front of him and braked sideways, cutting him off.

Marco yelled, shocked. He couldn't brake in time. There wasn't enough space between him and the car. Instinctively he jerked his handlebars up. His bicycle jumped onto the sidewalk, narrowly missing the car's front grille. He dismounted rather than fall. The bike slid into the stone wall lining the Tiber.

"What the hell?" Marco whirled around in fury. The car was a black sedan. He realized it was the type used by OVRA, the secret police.

The driver and passenger sprang from the car, their dark silhouettes mere shadows in the gloom. They ran toward him. He recognized the driver's bearlike outline. Stefano. The skinny little one was Carmine.

"You're a piece of shit!" Stefano grabbed Marco by his collar and pinned him to the stone wall. Carmine watched, his hands on his hips. Meanwhile a bus began to honk its horn, its path blocked by their car. Cars on the Lungotevere piled up, unable to pass.

"Get off!" Marco wrenched away, ripping his shirt. They could kill him right now and get away with it. OVRA operated with impunity.

"Why were you in the Ghetto? You're a Jew-lover!"

"What I do is not your business!" Marco reached for his bike, but Stefano grabbed him again.

"You think we don't know what you're up to? Your lunches with your Jew friend? Your visits at night? There's penalties for fraternizing with Jews! You think the rules don't apply to you! You should die the way your brother did!"

Marco exploded in grief and fury. He punched Stefano, and Stefano slugged him back. The two of them started fighting, falling to the pavement. Marco rained a flurry of blows on the bigger man, raging out of control. Stefano hit him harder, grunting. Traffic tangled on the Lungotevere, honking.

Marco kept punching, ignoring agonizing pain. Carmine shouted to Stefano. Stefano sprang off Marco, leaving him on the pavement.

Marco staggered to his feet, doubled over. Blood from his face dripped onto the sidewalk. Rain poured onto his back. Stefano and Carmine jumped into their car, closed the doors, and sped off.

Once home, Marco washed his face in the bathroom. His right cheekbone was swelling, and the skin had split. His mother was asleep in bed, and his father stood in the doorway, his arms folded against his naked chest, a formidable figure even in his undershorts. The expression on his face was grave.

"Marco, there were two of them?"

"Carmine and his pet, Stefano." Marco rinsed blood from the sink.

"Stefano used to be an informer. He got kicked up to OVRA. They say he's sadistic."

"Sounds right." Marco had sensed that Stefano had enjoyed beating him.

"So they've been watching you."

"Evidently." Marco turned off the water and patted his face dry, gingerly. "They can go to hell. We can't leave the Simones without help."

"Of course not. I'll feed the entire Ghetto, to spite them."

Marco looked over, surprised to find his father smiling. "Are you enjoying this?"

"Absolutely." His father chuckled. "There's nothing like a good fight."

Marco smiled, feeling closer to his father. They had a common enemy, rather than each other. He rinsed blood out of the towel and hung it up on the rack. "So what do we do now?"

"The same thing as before, but smarter."

"How so?"

"I have ideas."

Marco unbuttoned his shirt and eyed his reflection in the mirror. Pinkish bruises swelled on his chest and abdomen.

"But how's the bike?"

CHAPTER FIFTY-FOUR

# Elisabetta

### March 1940

Elisabetta hovered outside Nonna's bedroom while Dr. Pastore finished his examination, as Nonna's bronchitis had worsened. Elisabetta felt on edge, worrying about Nonna, and she remembered Dr. Pastore from the day that her father had died. Dr. Pastore hadn't mentioned it, and she tried to dismiss thoughts of that awful morning now. Dr. Pastore had grown balder, wider, and more standoffish since then, though he came whenever Nonna needed him, even in the evening, as she was so well regarded in the neighborhood.

"Giuseppina, good night." Dr. Pastore stood in the threshold of Nonna's bedroom, holding his worn black bag. "Get some sleep."

"Then why keep me awake?" Nonna called back, and Dr. Pastore left the bedroom, closing the door behind him.

"How is she?" Elisabetta asked, holding her breath.

"Her usual difficult self." Dr. Pastore crossed to the front door, and Elisabetta dogged his steps, feeling defensive for Nonna.

"She doesn't like being sick. She knows the restaurant needs her. She feels her responsibilities acutely. She's been sick for a while—"

"She'll be fine, in time. She needs to rest and continue her medication."

"Why isn't she getting better? What's the matter with her? This has been going on for months."

"She has pneumonia now."

"Oh no. Is pneumonia better or worse than bronchitis?"

"It means she has mucus in her lungs." Dr. Pastore opened the front door, but Elisabetta stopped him, grabbing the sleeve of his suit jacket.

"I'm worried. When I came home from work, she was lethargic. That's not like her."

"She wasn't lethargic just now," Dr. Pastore said matter-of-factly.

"Because she perks up for you, and her son." Sometimes Elisabetta thought she was the only person who truly understood Nonna. "I see her day to day. I'm worried she's hiding how bad she's feeling. She's not a young woman."

Nonna called out, "Elisabetta, will you please quiet down? I'm sick, not deaf!"

Dr. Pastore rolled his eyes. "See? Not lethargic. The medication takes time. I really must leave. Goodbye."

"I'll call you if she worsens?"

"Yes." Dr. Pastore turned away, trundling off down the street.

"Good night." Elisabetta was just about to close the door when she spotted Marco, coming toward her in a nice jacket and slacks. They were supposed to go out for a drink tonight, but she had forgotten after she'd come home and found Nonna sicker.

"*Buona sera,* Elisabetta!" Marco kissed her quickly on the lips, smelling of a spicy aftershave she had come to favor, but not tonight.

"Oh, Marco, I'm sorry, I can't go out."

"Why not?" Marco's face fell. "It's a beautiful night."

"Nonna has pneumonia, and the doctor just left. She needs to rest. I should stay home."

"Okay, then, why don't I come in and visit? We don't have to go out."

"No, that won't work. We'll disturb her, and she needs to rest."

"Why don't we take a quick walk?" Marco touched her arm gently.

"No, I don't want to leave her alone."

"We won't be long, just around the block."

Nonna yelled from the bedroom, "Leave or stay, but kindly let me sleep, will you?"

Macro smiled, taking Elisabetta's hand. "Come on, *cara*."

"Okay." Elisabetta let herself be led out of the house, closing the front door behind her. Via Fiorata was one of the most charming little streets in Trastevere, with two-story houses with façades of peach, pink, and mint green. Flowerboxes were stuffed with daisies and ivy that cascaded down. The air smelled fresh, and the night sky was starry, but Elisabetta was preoccupied with pneumonia.

"So how have you been?" Marco gave her hand a kiss.

"Busy with Nonna."

"You know, she's not your responsibility."

Elisabetta looked over, surprised. "I love her, Marco."

"I understand, but she's still not your responsibility. She has Paolo."

"But I live with her."

"I know, but you can't live *for* her."

"I don't," Elisabetta shot back, defensive.

"Don't you?" Marco squeezed her hand. "We could go out a lot more, but you always want to stay home and take care of her."

Elisabetta knew he was right, but it bothered her. "I have obligations you don't have."

"You also have my ring. I wish you would wear it." Marco lifted her hand, eyeing her bare fingers. "It would look so pretty on your hand."

Elisabetta had no immediate reply. She kept the ring in her jewelry box and tried it on from time to time. But she never kept it on long.

"So what do you think, about getting married? Do you feel ready yet?"

"Not really, I'm sorry," Elisabetta forced herself to say.

"Why not?"

"For the same reason that I can't go out as much. I have so many responsibilities. It's just a hard time for me."

Marco stopped, looking at her with those dark eyes and a soft expression.

"That's what I'm for, to make those hard times easier. I want to do that for you, for the rest of your life. You work so hard, and I want to lighten your load."

Elisabetta felt touched, but she couldn't ignore her feelings. "I appreciate that, but I need to take care of my business on my own."

"We don't have forever. War seems a certainty now." Marco frowned. "With so much disruption, wouldn't it be good to have something we can count on? You and me, as man and wife? Living in our own place?"

"But I can't move out on Nonna. She has no one but me."

"Again, Paolo should do more. You're not family."

Elisabetta felt stung, unaccountably. "I feel like I'm her family."

"You're not. Blood is blood."

"Paolo has a wife and family, so he's busier than I am. Nonna's on her own, Marco. I live with her, and I can't turn my back on her. I won't."

"Okay." Marco took her arm. "But I still don't see why you won't wear my ring."

Elisabetta swallowed hard. "I don't feel ready to say yes, yet."

Marco sighed, pained. "Is it Sandro?"

"No," Elisabetta answered, but she wasn't exactly sure. "It's things I have to take care of and do, before I get married."

"Like what?"

"Like become a journalist or a novelist."

"But you're not writing anything, are you?"

"Not now, only because I've been so busy. My responsibilities come before the things I want for myself, and marriage, too. Can't you understand that?"

"No, I can't," Marco answered, gentle but persistent. "I can support you, so you won't have to work so hard."

"But these are my obligations. My life." Elisabetta meant what she said, but she also hurt to see the disappointment flickering across his handsome face. "Do you want your ring back?"

"No, of course not. Keep the ring, *cara*." Marco opened his arms, enveloped her in an embrace, and kissed her forehead. "I'll be more patient."

"Thank you." Elisabetta nestled against his chest. "Please try to understand."

"I will," Marco said, with a resigned sigh.

CHAPTER FIFTY-FIVE

# Marco
### April 1940

Marco hurried down the crowded sidewalk to the Piazza Venezia, his heart thundering with anticipation. He had been summoned to see Commendatore Buonacorso, who had been promoted to working for the Partito Nazionale Fascista, the National Fascist Party. The commendatore's office was now in Palazzo Venezia, which was the very seat of Fascist power, located in the heart of Rome. Il Duce himself had his office there and delivered his speeches from its iconic balcony.

Scores of Fascist officers in black uniforms hurried in and out of Palazzo Venezia, climbing into waiting cars or hustling off in groups. There was a stronger military presence in the capital and an undercurrent of urgency, now that war loomed larger. Palazzo Venezia had become the most important building in all of Italy, and Marco couldn't wait to see inside. It had been built in the 1400s and was medieval in aspect, with a crenellated roofline like a castle and its turret soaring into the blue sky.

Armed guards flanked the entrance, their demeanor exemplifying military professionalism, unlike the jovial guards back at Palazzo Braschi. Marco saluted them crisply, they saluted him back, then he was shown into a security office, where he identified himself. Fascist officers hurried to and fro, their expressions grave and conversations conducted in low tones.

There was no talking, laughing, or joking around, also unlike Palazzo Braschi.

Marco was ushered into the Hall of Feats of Hercules, a magnificent vaulted hallway of marble, covered with painted friezes of Hercules fighting lions, oxen, dragons, deer, and a centaur. He gazed at the grand murals in awe, realizing that he stood within shouting distance of Mussolini's office, the Sala del Mappamondo. Il Duce worked famously hard, so the lights remained on until late at night, though some gossiped it was for show. Il Duce also had a private bedroom attached to his office, where it was rumored that he would bed his mistress and other women.

Marco strained to hear Il Duce's voice, perhaps in conversation or on the telephone, but the hallway was quiet. He didn't know if he believed the gossip, as some were jealous of Il Duce and everyone had stories about him. Marco felt a personal connection to Il Duce since he had shaken his hand. Of course Marco loathed the anti-Semitic Race Laws, but perhaps if he worked here, he could maneuver himself into a position to change them.

Commendatore Buonacorso's new office was grander and more elegantly appointed than his old one, with a polished parquet floor, oil paintings, marble statues, and a crystal chandelier. His desk was larger and fancier, ornately carved, and Buonacorso looked more powerful merely because he stood behind it. Otherwise his appearance hadn't changed and he still sported his trimmed and oiled mustache, his neatly pressed dark uniform, and his shiny tall boots.

Buonacorso remained standing, unsmiling, his expression formal. He gestured to the chair opposite his desk. "Marco, sit down."

Marco obeyed.

"You know I think highly of you. I look out for you."

"Thank you, sir." Marco had been expecting a promotion, but he was getting the impression he had been wrong.

"Your fortunes have been up and down with the party, have they not?"

"Yes, sir."

"I was very proud of you the night of Il Duce's speech, when you leapt so quickly to corrective action. You turned an embarrassment into a victory for the *fascio*." Buonacorso met his eye, newly stern. "However, it has come to my attention that you had a recent encounter with OVRA. You have been fraternizing with Jews, rendering them aid and assistance."

Marco stiffened. Carmine and Stefano must have reported his midnight runs to Buonacorso.

"Marco, those who fraternize with Jews can be expelled from the party. You must know this. Hundreds have already been expelled. *Pietisti* are no longer tolerated. That applies to you."

Marco's heart sank. *Pietisti* were those who were compassionate toward Jews.

"I stood up for you with respect to your brother Aldo. I cannot do so again, if you continue to fraternize with Jews."

"But these are the Simones. They are close friends of my family. You know Massimo. His son, Sandro, is my best—"

"*Basta!*" Buonacorso raised a hand. "I don't want to know such things. Do you understand?"

"Yes, sir."

Buonacorso frowned. "I called you here to help you. I think you show great promise. I have groomed you to take your place in our party. It hasn't been easy, given your brother's treachery. I placed my own reputation on the line for you. It's time for you to grow up, son."

Marco swallowed hard.

"When we get older, we leave our childhood behind. Classmates must be cut loose. These are only historic relationships, and they must go. You cannot live in the past and still have a future. Do you follow?"

"Yes," Marco answered, but he wasn't sure he agreed.

"Marco, I know you well." Buonacorso narrowed his eyes. "I can tell you disagree with me. You follow your heart and not your head. Wise up! Don't be a *testardo*. If there is another such report from OVRA, you will be expelled from our party. Your father, too. Where would your family be then? If the Terrizzis are no longer in good standing, we'll find another bar. You can lose Bar GiroSport."

Marco blinked, shaken. It was true, if disturbing.

"Now you're listening." Buonacorso smiled tightly. "Do as I say. Trust my judgment. I have plans for you here. I am planning to offer you a position, in the eventuality that Italy enters the war."

*War.* The word echoed with gravity, especially in these halls.

"The stakes are higher for you now. In time of war, the decisions that one makes are crucial. That's true on the front lines, and on the homefront. From now on, if you help the Simone family, you risk your own."

Marco's gut wrenched.

"It comes down to you or them, Marco. Choose wisely."

## CHAPTER FIFTY-SIX

# Sandro

### May 1940

Sandro had no idea why Marco wanted to meet at the Spanish Steps, which was mobbed with students and bohemians on this temperate night. He searched for his best friend among the throng talking, drinking, smoking, singing, kissing, playing guitars, and posing for pictures in front of the Chiesa della Trinità dei Monti, the church at the top of the stairs, its alabaster façade and twin spires lit up.

No Marco.

Sandro made his way down to the landing, which was packed with people people sitting hip to hip. No Marco. Sandro began to descend the hundred or so steps, picking his way through.

Still no Marco.

Finally Sandro spotted his best friend against the side wall, sitting among a group of Dutch tourists wearing bright orange hats. Marco had on an orange hat, too, blending in with the Dutch. Sandro assumed Marco was playing a joke, as he made his way over and squeezed in beside him.

"Marco, why the hat?"

"It's new." Marco produced another orange hat and plopped it on Sandro's head. "Here's one for you, too."

"Are you kidding? I don't need a hat."

"Keep it on. It looks good on you. Watch out, ladies!"

Sandro laughed. "What's going on? Why are we meeting here, of all places? It's so noisy I can barely hear you. Were you in the neighborhood?"

"No." Marco glanced over his shoulder.

"Then why?"

"To see how you are, since the last time we got together."

"I'm fine, I guess," Sandro answered, mystified. "Rosa came home and she's helping out."

"That's good. How are your parents? My father sends his regards."

"Things grow worse, but we cope."

"And Anna?"

"Who?"

"Anna, the girl you like."

Sandro had forgotten about his fictional girlfriend. "Oh, Anna's fine."

"Are you in love?"

"Almost."

"A man can't *almost* be in love." Marco laughed. "Either he loves, or he does not."

Sandro needed to change the subject. "How have you been?"

"Fine. I might get a job at Palazzo Venezia. My boss got a promotion and he's trying to bring me over."

"*Davvero?*" Sandro managed to say, refraining from speaking further on the subject. "Good for you."

"Thanks, but I know how you feel." Marco's expression turned serious under his silly orange cap. "I'm hoping one day I can be in a position to fight these horrible Race Laws."

"I hope so, too," Sandro said, though he couldn't imagine Marco ever having such power.

"Things are tense at work, and I've come around to your view on the war. I was wrong before. I think we're going to enter."

"I agree." Sandro feared that if war came to Italy, things would get worse for the Jews, though he didn't know how that was even possible. Everyone in the Ghetto was out of work, food was growing scarce, and every day seemed to bring another new Race Law.

"Don't worry. I'll keep you posted. I'll let you know as soon as I know anything." Marco brightened. "Guess what, I proposed to Elisabetta."

"Congratulations!" Sandro patted Marco on the back, masking his anguish. He hadn't guessed Marco would propose so quickly, but he should have. He would love Elisabetta forever, but he had done the right thing in sending her away. He couldn't offer her anything, and Marco could offer her everything. She would be safe and happy if she married Marco.

Marco pursed his lips. "The only thing is, she didn't say yes, but she didn't say no. She said she needs time to think it over."

"So give her time." Sandro wondered if Elisabetta's decision had anything to do with him. On the one hand, he hoped it didn't. On the other, he hoped it did.

"I'm going to, but I don't see what difference time makes." Marco rolled his eyes. "We should get married without delay. I love her, and she loves me. She does everything on her own, like always. I feel bad for her, and now she has to take care of Nonna, who's sick."

"What's the rush?"

"I would rather be happy sooner, wouldn't you? I love and adore her. And I have needs." Marco snorted in frustration. "Rome is full of beautiful girls, yet I wait for Elisabetta. My brother took a vow of chastity, but I didn't."

"Just be patient." Sandro couldn't bear the thought of Elisabetta in bed with Marco. He shooed it from his mind.

"And she's talking about wanting to be a writer or something."

"She wants to be a novelist." Sandro flashed on the time after the Deledda lecture, when he and Elisabetta had sat outside, talking. Now it seemed like a magical night from another time.

"Am I supposed to wait for her to finish her novel? One that she hasn't even started?"

"It sounds as if she's too busy to write, with Nonna sick."

"Hmph! If she wanted to write, she would write."

Sandro felt a pang, for Marco and for Elisabetta. He loved them both, and he wanted Elisabetta to be happy and safe. It struck him that Marco could make her safe, but he himself could make her happy. Suddenly he got an idea. "You want my advice?"

Marco smiled crookedly. "You, give *me* advice about women?"

Sandro bit his tongue. He would never tell Marco that Elisabetta had chosen him. "Brother, for what it's worth, encourage her writing."

"How?"

"Her birthday is next month. Buy her a fancy notebook."

"How's *that* going to make her marry me?"

"It's not."

"Then why do it?"

"It will make her start writing, and she'll be happier. Isn't that what you want?"

"But *I* can make her happy. All she has to do is say yes."

"Writing will make her happy, and maybe if she's happy, she'll come around sooner."

"I should go." Abruptly Marco glanced over his shoulder. "When I get up, I want you to take my rucksack."

"Why?"

"It's for your family."

"What's inside?"

Marco pushed his rucksack over with his foot. "Groceries and things."

Sandro felt torn. His family needed the groceries, but he didn't want to accept charity. "No, thanks. My family is my responsibility."

"Please take it, Sandro. My father will kill me if I come home with that rucksack."

"Tell him I insisted, then. We have money, and we barter. Everybody does. One of my father's clients leaves us groceries in return for legal help."

Marco pursed his lips, and Sandro read his expression, since Marco could never hide his emotions.

"Marco, are *you* the one who leaves the food at our door? And the money?"

"Yes, but don't make it a big deal."

Sandro felt grateful, but ashamed to need the help. "Why didn't you tell me?"

"You wouldn't have taken it." Marco looked over his shoulder again, and Sandro realized what was going on.

"They know you're helping us, don't they? They've been watching you, haven't they? We're meeting at the Spanish Steps, where we never go, wearing these hats . . . I can't let you do this." Sandro took off the hat and pushed the rucksack back to Marco.

"Take the bag, please."

"No, thanks."

"On our friendship." Marco rose. "Please. I have to leave. I can't argue about it any longer."

Sandro relented, with a sigh. "Okay. Thank you."

"Good. My bike's around the corner, and I don't think I was followed. Nevertheless, wait five minutes, then go."

"Goodbye, Marco. Stay safe." Sandro watched Marco thread his way through the students, slip his orange hat into his back pocket, and vanish into the crowd.

Sandro heaved a deep sigh. He despaired that things had come to this, with his family struggling and Marco risking so much to help. It wasn't the life he had foreseen for himself, Marco, or Elisabetta. He prayed that they would survive whatever the future held in store. It terrified him to think that the three of them were sliding toward war, into the gaping maw of a monster that could swallow them whole, like Jonah into the whale.

Sandro picked up the rucksack and left, heartsick.

## CHAPTER FIFTY-SEVEN

# Elisabetta

### 9 June 1940

Elisabetta awoke to the sound of Nonna's coughing downstairs, and she lay in bed, waiting for it to stop. The older woman's health had been up and down, but Dr. Pastore had said that the warm weather would do her good. Elisabetta took off her sheet, about to get out of bed until she remembered that today was her birthday. She put her sheet back on and gave herself a moment to rest.

Sunlight brightened her bedroom, and her gaze fell on her father's watercolors of Trastevere, which hung on the wall opposite her bed. She couldn't feel completely happy on her birthday without him. He had always made a fuss on the day, though he hadn't had money for gifts. He made her feel special, and she mourned him still.

Sandro popped into her mind, as always, but she pressed that thought away. There was no point in thinking about him, if he didn't want her. Marco was taking her out to dinner tonight, and though she looked forward to it, she knew he would ask about the ring again. She loved him, but dreaded the pressure, for she couldn't give him the answer he wanted yet.

Rico picked his way to her, purring, and she stroked his back, feeling the vertebrae underneath. He was thin, but he wore it well, as he had the excellent self-esteem of every feline.

"Elisabetta!" Nonna called from downstairs, and she threw off her sheet in alarm.

"Be right down!" Elisabetta jumped out of bed, slipped into her bathrobe, and hustled downstairs, with Rico at her heels. She hurried to Nonna's bedroom and opened the door to find Nonna propped up on her pillows, holding a tiny white kitten in her lap.

"Happy birthday!"

"Oh my!" Elisabetta gasped, instantly charmed. "A kitten! Thank you!"

"Isn't she pretty?" Nonna stroked the kitten, which had a perfect triangle of a face, with round eyes as blue as the sea, a spongy pink nose, and wispy white ears.

"She is!" Elisabetta sat on the bed and petted the kitten, who purred immediately, a gratifying sound. "Where did you get her?"

"Teresa's cat had kittens, and they needed homes. Teresa brought her by earlier this morning."

"But you're not supposed to get out of bed. What if you fell?"

"You think I can't walk?" Nonna picked up the droopy kitten and placed her on Elisabetta's lap, and Rico looked up from the doorway, his tail curling into a question mark.

"Oh no, I wonder what Rico will think."

"I already told him. He has to get used to her, the way I got used to him. Old cats like us can change our ways." Nonna chuckled, but it turned into a cough.

"Are you okay?"

"Yes, and I feel good today. What do you want to name your kitten?"

"I don't know. She's as white as flour and chubby as a dumpling."

"So how about Gnocchi?"

"Perfect." Elisabetta laughed.

"I know you'll take wonderful care of her, because you take wonderful care of me."

"Thank you, Nonna." Elisabetta kissed her on the cheek. "I love you."

"I love you, too. Happy birthday. And don't tell me you're going out with Marco to celebrate." Nonna wagged an arthritic index finger at her. "If you keep this up, he's going to ask you to marry him."

Elisabetta felt a guilty twinge. She hadn't told Nonna about Marco's proposal, since she hadn't decided what to do. "Then I'll tell him I need time to think about it."

"Oh, good idea. Italian men *love* waiting." Nonna snorted. "By the way, he left you a gift this morning. I saw it when I got the kitten from Teresa."

"Marco, a gift?"

"Yes. He's trying very hard, isn't he?" Nonna turned to her night table, picked up a gift wrapped in silver paper, and handed it over.

Elisabetta read the card on top, recognizing Marco's oversized and sloppy handwriting, with some letters facing the wrong way.

*Elizabetta, Happy birthday! Begin a great novel today! I love you! Marco*

Elisabetta felt a wave of love for him, appreciating that he was trying to encourage her writing. She tore off the wrapping paper, and the gift was a notebook with lined pages and a painted sunflower on the cover. "Isn't that so sweet?"

"Why is his handwriting so bad? Is he dumb?"

"No," Elisabetta answered, defensive. "He's very smart."

"Then why can't he write? His letters look like a child's."

"Boys never have good handwriting." Elisabetta held the notebook to her chest, and Rico leapt to the bed. She watched to see how Rico would receive the newcomer, and so did Nonna. Gnocchi took the initiative, walking to Rico, and Rico purred loudly. "Look, he likes her!"

"I told you, he obeys me."

Elisabetta arrived home after work, having floated through her birthday on a cloud. Paolo, his wife, Sofia, and the busboys had bought her a cake, and her regulars had tipped generously for the occasion. It had been a wonderful day and was going to be a wonderful night. Marco had been on her mind, and she couldn't wait to see him.

She went to check on Nonna, but the older woman was asleep. Rico and Gnocchi were curled up together at the foot of her bed, so Elisabetta ran upstairs to get ready. She unbuttoned her work dress on the fly and slipped into her beautiful pink party dress, since they were going to a fancy restaurant. She jumped into her nice shoes, hurried to her bureau, and put on some new perfume, a freesia scent. She glanced in the mirror, loving the way the dress looked and grateful that Marco had bought it for her.

She paused, opened her jewelry box, and fished out the engagement ring. She slipped the diamond on her finger and turned her hand this way and that, watching the facets catch the light. It was lovely, and even more than the ring, she felt moved by Marco leaving her the notebook, this morning. That simple act showed her that he truly understood her.

Elisabetta made a decision. She picked up her purse and slipped the ring inside, just as she heard knocking downstairs on the front door. She flew from the bedroom and downstairs, hurried through the living room, and opened the door to find Marco in his uniform, smiling and holding a single red rose.

"Happy birthday, *cara!*" Marco presented her with the rose.

"Thank you, it's lovely!"

"As are you!" Marco kissed her on both cheeks, then embraced her, and Elisabetta loved the warm sensation of being in his arms again, breathing in the smell of his familiar aftershave.

"Thank you for the notebook, too. That was very sweet of you."

"Oh, you're welcome. There will be another gift with dessert, too. Shall we go?"

"Yes," Elisabetta answered, setting her rose down, and they left together, walking hand in hand. She felt so happy, and Via Fiorata had never looked prettier, with jasmine, pink-and-white oleander, and red geraniums blooming in windowboxes. The air was refreshing, and the late-day sun bronzed the small houses of mint green and melon stucco.

On impulse, Elisabetta stopped under a fragrant bower of wisteria at the end of the street. "Marco, I have something to say."

"What?" Marco turned to her with a smile.

"I love you, and I'm ready to get married." Elisabetta heard the words coming out of her mouth, and they sounded exactly right. She dipped her hand into her purse, withdrew the ring, and handed it to him. "Will you put this on my finger?"

"Of course!" Marco's dark eyes filmed, and he broke into a huge grin. He accepted the ring and slid it onto her finger. "Elisabetta, will you marry me?"

"Yes, I will!" Elisabetta laughed, giddy, and Marco embraced her and kissed her gently.

"Now we can celebrate your birthday *and* our engagement. I'm so happy!"

"Me, too!" Elisabetta slid her hand around Marco's back, and he slid his around hers, as they resumed walking.

"Hold up the ring. Let me see it."

Elisabetta extended her hand, wiggling her finger, and the little diamond twinkled in the sunshine. "It looks like a star, doesn't it?"

"It does."

Suddenly their attention was drawn by an older, ginger-haired man weaving toward them. She recognized him as one of her father's old drinking buddies, who had been at his funeral. He was obviously inebriated and his unfocused gaze kept shifting from her to Marco and back again. He was poorly dressed, with coarse features and a nose marked by broken capillaries.

"You!" The ginger pointed at Elisabetta, his brow furrowing. "You're Ludovico D'Orfeo's daughter, aren't you? You look like him!"

"Why, yes," Elisabetta answered, surprised. She had no idea why the ginger seemed angry at her. "Sir, I'm sorry. I don't recall your name."

"But I know yours! Your father called you Betta. Look at you now!" The ginger scowled. "If your father were alive, he would be *ashamed* of you!"

"What? Excuse me, sir. Who are you?"

Marco frowned. "Don't talk to her that way, friend."

The ginger snorted. "I'm not your friend. I don't want you to know me, and I don't want to know you. I know all I need to know by your uniform."

"Then you should call me brother, if you're loyal to Italy and Il Duce."

"Those are two very different matters! Dare I say more? Will you beat me? Ludovico *hated* your ilk for what you've done to our country!" The ginger turned to Elisabetta, his eyes blazing with drunken intensity. "The Fascists beat your father without mercy! They stomped on his hands! They broke all his fingers! Yet today you're with a filthy Blackshirt!"

Elisabetta recoiled, appalled. "No, no, that's not right. That's not how he broke his hands. He was in a bicycle accident—"

"Yes, it is! I knew him then. The Fascists did it, but he didn't want you to know. He didn't want you in danger from those thugs! Now you're in bed with one!"

Elisabetta gasped.

Marco stepped to the ginger. "Sir, move along and I'll forget you insulted my fiancée."

"Fiancée?" The ginger turned to Elisabetta and sneered. "You're marrying a thug! You dishonor Ludovico! You *disgrace* him!"

"No, no." Elisabetta felt shaken at the very thought. "I honor my father's memory. You're just wrong. Why would Fascists break his hands? He had nothing to do with Fascists. He was a peaceful man, a painter—"

"And you're a *whore*!"

"Sir!" Marco interjected, cocking his fist. "Don't make me!"

The ginger cursed, then staggered off.

Elisabetta felt shaken, jarred by a sudden snippet of memory. She remembered one of the times her father had tried to quit drinking. He had experienced delirium tremens, shaking uncontrollably, terrified that Fascists were coming to beat him. She had feared he was losing his sanity and dismissed it as delusion. But maybe it hadn't been.

Marco smoothed her hair into place. "I'm sorry about that idiot. He's just drunk, telling stories."

"But I just remembered something strange," Elisabetta said, then told Marco the story. She had told Sandro the same thing, after she had left the Deledda lecture in tears. Maybe there was a reason that the memory stuck with her. Maybe it was the truth, refusing to hide.

"It was undoubtedly a hallucination. It doesn't mean anything." Marco took her hand, and they resumed walking. "Let's not let this ruin our celebration."

"It's strange, though. My father's fingers . . . they went in different directions. He always said they healed poorly, or the joints locked, or something. I asked when I was little." Elisabetta could picture her father's hands in detail. Even as misshapen as they had been, his fingers had been long, an artist's hands. "He said it was because of the way he fell off the bicycle, but it could have been caused by someone stomping on his hand. Come to think of it, it makes more sense."

"Why would a Fascist stomp on his hands? For no reason?"

"I don't know, but what if it's true?" Elisabetta felt lost and bewildered. She had thought that the only secret her parents had kept from her was her mother's affair. This felt like another shock. She couldn't dismiss it so easily.

"It doesn't ring true to me." Marco blinked as they walked along. "Your father wasn't political."

"But he didn't like Mussolini."

"I admit, the party used to have a thuggish element. But that doesn't mean they beat people willy-nilly."

"But those injuries ruined him. It was when he started drinking. He couldn't paint again. He lost himself. He couldn't support us anymore. It was why my mother worked, even why their marriage fell apart."

"Marriages fall apart for many reasons. Ours won't." Marco smiled, as they reached the restaurant. "Here we are. Let's celebrate."

Elisabetta remained preoccupied, and Marco found them a table by the window. Her mind couldn't stop racing, even as he ordered them *spumante*, then talked through dinner, regaling her with his typically funny stories about work. She watched his lips moving, but heard nothing. All of her father's rants about Mussolini began to make more sense, and she was viewing them in a different light.

Marco kept talking, but her gaze shifted from his handsome face to the utter blackness of his uniform. All she could think of was death. She knew that the Fascists had risen to power via violence. She couldn't help but wonder if her father had been one of their victims, his elegant hands broken beneath the boots of a Blackshirt. Like Marco.

"Elisabetta, are you okay? You haven't eaten much."

"I'm not hungry." Elisabetta forced a smile.

"Your ring looks so pretty."

"Thank you." Elisabetta glanced at the diamond, which seemed to have lost its brilliance.

"You're not saying much."

"I'm tired, I guess. I had a busy day at work."

Marco nodded. "So did I, and I didn't get any sleep last night."

"Why not?" Elisabetta asked, trying to rally.

"The boss had an early meeting out of town. I had to pick him up at four thirty in the morning to get him there in time."

Elisabetta didn't understand. "You picked him up at four thirty? Then when did you leave me the notebook?"

Marco blinked. "What do you mean?"

"The notebook you left on my doorstep, for my birthday. When did you drop it off, if you had to pick up your boss so early?"

Marco's smile faded.

Elisabetta didn't understand what was going on.

Marco pursed his lips, his regret plain. "Okay, I admit it, I didn't give you the notebook."

"What?" Elisabetta asked, blindsided. "I thought the notebook was from you. You said it was."

"Does it matter?"

"Of course. I feel disappointed. I trust you, I always have. You mean you lied to me?"

"I'm sorry." Marco frowned, newly impatient. "I didn't know what to say, and I was on the spot. You were so happy, and I didn't want to admit it wasn't from me."

"But that's wrong." Elisabetta didn't know what to say. She had given Marco credit for the notebook. She had thought it showed that he understood her. It had been the thing that had made her decide to wear his diamond ring. But the truth was, he hadn't given her the notebook at all. He had lied.

"It's just a notebook."

"No, it's more than that. It's you, and me." Elisabetta struggled to think through her emotions. "I'm sick of lies, Marco. My mother lied to me. My father lied to me, if that ginger man is right. And now you, too? You?"

"I did it to make you happy."

"How? Why? Lies don't make me happy." Elisabetta spoke from the heart. "Not anymore."

"Then I'm sorry I lied."

"That doesn't erase it." Elisabetta realized then who must have left the notebook. There was only one other person who could forge Marco's handwriting, and who knew it was her birthday. She began to pull off her diamond ring.

"What are you doing?"

"I'm sorry." Elisabetta set the ring on the table. "I can't marry you. I don't feel sure anymore—"

"Over a stupid notebook?" Marco's eyes flashed with anger. "I love you, and you love me!"

"I told you, it's more than the notebook."

"Is it because I'm a Fascist? You knew I was a Fascist before!"

"But I didn't know you would lie to me."

"Fine! You don't want to marry me?" Marco snatched the ring off the table and put it in his pocket. "After I waited for you, all this time! After I was faithful!"

"Marco—"

"Do you know how much I adore you? And this is how you treat me?" Marco grabbed his water glass and hurled it at the wall, where it shattered. Water splashed, shards flew.

Elisabetta jumped up. The other diners gasped, shocked. The waiter and the manager started running over.

Marco stormed to the door, flung it open, and slammed it behind him.

## CHAPTER FIFTY-EIGHT

# Sandro

### 9 June 1940

There was a knock at the door, and Sandro looked up from the papers he was grading at the table. They had finished dinner, and Rosa and his mother were washing dishes and his father was making notes in his thick folder.

"I'll get it." Sandro rose and answered the door, shocked to find Elisabetta in the threshold. Her eyes were red as if she had been crying, but she was more beautiful than ever in a pink dress. He could barely stand this close to her without taking her in his arms.

"Sandro, may I speak with you, in private?"

"I'll be right back," Sandro called over his shoulder, then he shut the door behind them, trying to get his bearings. "Sorry, it's hard to find any privacy around here."

"Maybe away from the door?"

"They'll hear everything."

"Outside?"

"Worse. Let's go down to the landing."

Elisabetta descended the stairs, trailing a beautiful fragrance, and Sandro followed her, his heart aching. It killed him to see her again, and the emotions he had been suppressing for so long rushed back to him. They reached the landing, and she turned around, linking her hands in front of her formally, as if she had something to say.

"Sandro, did you leave a notebook on my step this morning, for my birthday? Did you forge a card to make me think Marco had written it?"

Sandro felt stricken. Elisabetta was right, and he didn't know what to say. He never thought she would figure it out. He had gotten her the notebook, knowing that Marco probably wouldn't. He had only wanted to make Marco look good to her.

"Sandro, please answer."

"He loves you, Elisabetta. Marry him."

"I'm not. I broke up with him tonight."

Sandro groaned, anguished. "I told you, I don't love you anymore."

"I don't believe you," Elisabetta shot back, then pressed herself against him and kissed him on the lips. Sandro kissed her back, feeling all the love in his broken heart.

"What the *hell*?" Marco appeared at the lower landing, his face red with outrage. "You're seeing each other behind my back?"

Sandro sprang away from Elisabetta. "Marco—"

Elisabetta shook her head. "Marco, listen—"

"No!" Marco's agonized gaze filmed with tears. "Sandro, you did it on purpose! You left the notebook without telling me! You did it to sabotage me!" He pointed at Elisabetta, wounded. "You betrayed me with my best friend! Good luck together!"

Marco turned away and flew down the stairs. Sandro went after him, but Marco bolted into the street.

"Marco, wait!" Sandro hurried after him, noticing the neighbors coming to their windows.

"Leave me alone!" Marco whirled around, on the run. "You can have her! I'm done with you both!"

Sandro stopped running. He knew that Marco was beyond reason when he was this emotional, for he had always been ruled by his heart.

"All of you Jews are liars!" Marco yelled. "Filthy liars!"

Sandro shuddered at the ugly words, echoing off the houses. His neighbors popped back into their houses, closing the shutters. He stood watching as Marco vanished into the darkness, his black uniform becoming night.

Sandro turned around and went home.

To send Elisabetta away, again.

<br>

## CHAPTER FIFTY-NINE

# Marco
### 9 June 1940

M arco hurried through the Ghetto, tears filling his eyes. His heart pounded, and his chest heaved. He was shaking with anger, stumbling over the cobblestones. He had never been so hurt. Elisabetta and Sandro were together. He had seen it for himself.

A man walking by gave him wide berth, and Marco kept his head down. He had loved Elisabetta and Sandro both, so much. He had trusted them both, without question. Their betrayal stabbed like a blade.

He raked his hair back, dazed and enraged. Wine clouded his head. He never should have shouted such insults. It was the only thing he regretted. He had wanted to hurt Sandro, as Sandro had hurt him.

He hurried past the synagogue, wiping his eyes, then heard a commotion behind him. He turned around to see Carmine and Stefano, the OVRA officers, stepping out of the shadows, on his very heels.

"Back in the Ghetto, eh?" Stefano clamped a hand on Marco's right shoulder, and Carmine clamped a hand on his left.

"Boy, keep walking."

Marco felt a bolt of terror. The OVRA officers flanked him, marching him forward. They must have been following him. He didn't know what to do. They were armed, and he wasn't. He had been crazy to go to Sandro's. He had been drunk and angry and blinded by love. And now it would cost him.

"So, Marco," Carmine said, under his breath. "Sounds like you finally wised up about the Jews."

"It's about time." Stefano hurried him forward.

"Where are we going?" Marco masked his fear.

"Palazzo Venezia. Buonacorso wants you."

"Why?" Marco asked, surprised.

"Tomorrow, Italy enters the war."

# PART FOUR

*È facile saper vivere.*
*Grande saper morire.*

It is easy to know how to live.
Heroic to know how to die.

—Arrigo Paladini

❧

## CHAPTER SIXTY

# Marco

### 10 June 1940

---

Marco stood in the hallway behind a packed crowd of Fascist officers, the cabinet, the Grand Council, and the staff filling the second floor of the Palazzo Venezia. Mussolini was about to give a speech from the balcony, declaring war on Great Britain and France. Marco's head spun with his turnabout in fortunes, which had flip-flopped in a single night. He was on the top of the heap, only the morning after he'd suffered the lowest of lows, catching his fiancée in the arms of his best friend. The betrayal made him sick to his stomach, but he hardened his heart. He vowed never to see either of them again.

Marco had worked all night without a moment's sleep. He had been pressed into service fetching coffee, bottled water, food, telegrams, and whatever Buonacorso and anybody else needed for today. Marco could scarcely believe that he was here on this momentous occasion. The gargantuan crowd on the Piazza Venezia was chanting so thunderously that it reverberated inside the building.

"Duce, Duce, Duce!" they roared.

The officers in front of Marco surged forward, and Marco watched from behind, trying to get a glimpse of Mussolini. War had been rumored for so long, and Marco had gotten a behind-the-scenes view of the hurried discussions, shouted phone calls, and officers with their heads bent together over maps and memoranda. Excitement coursed like an electrical charge throughout his body. He was embarking on a great adventure, and so was his country.

"Duce! Duce! Duce!"

The officers around Marco fell silent, and from the balcony came the sound of Il Duce being introduced. The crowd shouted so loudly in response that the officers covered their ears and turned to one another grinning, their eyes wide. The crowd kept roaring until at last the speech began.

"Fighters on the land, on the sea, and in the air!" Mussolini shouted. "Blackshirts of the revolution and the legions! Men and women of Italy, of the empire, and of the Kingdom of Albania! Listen!"

Marco stood spellbound as Mussolini continued to speak, his voice amplified by loudspeakers broadcasting the speech throughout Rome and every major Italian city.

"An hour that has been marked out by destiny is sounding in the sky above our Fatherland! The hour of irrevocable decisions! The declaration of war has already been handed to the Ambassadors of Great Britain and France—"

"Marco," someone said behind him, and Marco turned to see Officer DiFillipo, a minor official. "Go to the Communications Room. There's an unsecured telegram for me. Bring it up."

"Yes, sir." Marco threaded his way out of the room, into the hallway, and down the vast staircase to the sound of Mussolini's voice, ricocheting off the marble walls. He reached the basement, went down the hall to the Communications Room, and entered the windowless square, lined with telegraph machines. There was no staff member in the room, although last night there had been an aged functionary, who had given Marco all of the telegrams he requested, since he himself couldn't read them.

Marco went to the first machine, but there were no telegrams. He went to the next machine, but there were no telegrams there, either. Same with the third machine. Marco assumed they were being collected by somebody, since last night there had been so many. He noticed a door in the far wall, crossed the room, and opened it, startling a pretty secretary at her desk, typing as she ate *panna cotta*.

"Sir, oh my, may I help you?" The secretary jumped to her pumps, then shifted in front of the *panna cotta*, as if to hide the dessert.

"Yes, I was looking for a telegram to Officer DiFillipo."

"Oh, I just pulled that one." The secretary picked up a telegram and handed it to Marco, hastily wiping cream from her lower lip.

"Thank you. You don't have to hide your dessert from me." Marco smiled, noticing that she had lovely green eyes, dark red hair waving to her shoulders, and a body that filled every curve of her uniform.

"Please don't tell my boss. We set up the food for the reception, but it's supposed to be for the brass."

"Who can resist *panna cotta*?" Marco found himself flirting, for the first time in a long time. It felt strange, especially with Elisabetta's engagement ring in his pocket.

"Not me. It's my favorite."

"Mine, too. What's your name?"

"Fiorella, and I already know who you are, Marco." Fiorella smiled. "I saw you climb the pillar at Commendatore Buonacorso's party. You were amazing."

"Really?" Marco asked, perking up. He began to feel good, like in the old days. Fiorella was a beautiful girl, and there were so many desserts he had been passing up, to no end. From now on, he was going to eat everything.

"I know Tino at Palazzo Braschi, and he said you have a girlfriend."

"Not anymore." Marco pushed Elisabetta from his mind, by sheer act of will. "Do you have a boyfriend?"

"No, I don't."

"Then this is my lucky day." Marco brushed a strand of hair from her lovely eyes. "May I taste your *panna cotta*?"

"Yes, of course." Fiorella reached for her plate, but Marco stopped her with a gentle touch—then leaned in for a kiss.

Evening fell, and Marco walked home through a city throbbing with excitement. People filled the streets, restaurants, and bars, celebrating, arguing, and discussing the amazing news of the day. He had never felt better in his uniform, and though he wished he was old enough to enlist and fight, he would settle for working at Palazzo Venezia. He was riding high on adrenaline and pride, in himself and his country. Italy was going to war and she was going to win.

Marco reached Ponte Fabricio and climbed the bridge, breathing in the familiar dampness of the Tiber. His thoughts turned to Elisabetta because he was heading toward Trastevere, and he slipped a hand into his pocket, feeling for the diamond ring. It was still there, but she belonged in his past. Plenty of other girls were in his future. He was off to a fast start with Fiorella.

Marco descended the other side and saw his father hustling from one customer to the next, in a packed outside seating area. If they had been on better terms, Marco would have been excited to tell him about being hired at Palazzo Venezia. Marco wondered if those days were truly over.

He reached the bar and crossed to his father. "Papa, were you at Piazza Venezia for the speech?"

"No, I was busy here." His father frowned. "Where have you been?"

"Buonacorso brought me over. I work at Palazzo Venezia now. I was in the same room as Il Duce. It was a wonderful day for Italy."

"War may be necessary, but never wonderful." His father pursed his lips. "And I heard you were in front of Massimo's house last night, saying the most hateful things. Shame on you."

Marco's mouth went dry. "I didn't mean it, I was angry—"

"Go put on an apron, big shot."

CHAPTER SIXTY-ONE

# Elisabetta

September 1940

Elisabetta served coffee while the women took their seats around a long table at Casa Servano, ready for the meeting. The war had gone on over the summer, with awful bombing in London and other cities. Rome had been spared so far, and day-to-day life in the capital city continued mostly unchanged. Local businesses thrived due to the influx of dignitaries and military. There were shortages of men and food, but one bothered Elisabetta more than the other. She was through with love.

Nonna sat at the head of the table, having recovered from her pneumonia. "Ladies, settle down. We have to get started."

Elisabetta sat down behind her gleaming black Olivetti typewriter, with its black letters on lovely white keys. Women quieted their children and took babies onto their laps. There were seven of them, all mothers who ran restaurants in Trastevere since their husbands had gone to war. Nonna had formed an informal restaurant association to help guide them, for they had besieged her with questions. She was solely in charge of Casa Servano now, because her son, Paolo, had enlisted.

"We'll begin where we left off. Elisabetta, please read the minutes from the last meeting."

Elisabetta began. " 'We in the restaurant business are experiencing difficulties getting flour, olive oil, and butter from our regular suppliers. Rationing has been affecting flour, butter, olive oil, rice, and pasta. Our main problem is getting flour from our regular vendors at reasonable prices. Italy has always produced abundant supplies of wheat for flour. As you may know, the government devised the *ammassi* plan, whereby farmers who produced wheat would give it to a central collective, which would ensure the food was evenly distributed—' "

"You mean, ensure the *graft* was evenly distributed," Nonna interjected, and everybody laughed, then Elisabetta continued.

" 'Farmers are being sent to war, and farms are being shut down, so food production is suffering. In the provinces, families are becoming malnourished.' " Elisabetta felt a pang that this would happen in her country, which loved its food so well. " 'Wheat and flour supplies are diminishing, and the decrease is hurting us. A black market has sprung up, but it is not an alternative for us, as we require large quantities. Some of us reported ridiculous prices, like these: Flour, 260 *lire* per kilo. Sugar, 450 *lire* per kilo. Butter, 700 *lire* per kilo. Oil, 800 *lire* per kilo. Parmesan cheese, 600 *lire* per kilo. Salt, 350 *lire* per kilo. Rice, 250 *lire* per kilo. Eggs, 15 *lire* each.' "

Nonna clucked, and the women around the table shook their heads. The babies in their laps patted the tablecloth or played with napkins.

" 'At our last meeting, we distributed a list of suppliers that Casa Servano has found the most reliable and low priced. Feel free to use them.' That is the end of old business. We can proceed to new—" Elisabetta stopped talking when she heard the door opening and looked up, shocked to see that it was Beppe Terrizzi.

His large, muscular frame filled the doorway, backlit by the sunlight, and his build was an older version of Marco's. All of the women gawked at him, reacting to his dark good looks and powerfully masculine presence. Elisabetta understood instantly what her mother had seen in him, for she herself had seen the same things in Marco. The thought disturbed her, and she lowered her gaze to her typewriter.

Nonna acknowledged him with a nod. "*Ciao*, Beppe. It's been a long time."

"Yes, it has, Giuseppina. I heard about the meeting and thought I might attend, to help."

"Good. Feel free to take a seat."

"Thank you." Beppe brought over a chair and sat down at the other head of the table, opposite Nonna.

Nonna gestured. "Ladies, this is Beppe Terrizzi, the owner of the very successful Bar GiroSport, on Tiber Island. Quickly introduce yourself and say the name of your restaurant."

"I'm Isabella, from Franco's Ristorante," began the first woman, and Elisabetta tuned out, composing herself. She hadn't seen Marco or Sandro since her birthday, and she had exiled them both to the back of her mind. She had asked around to see if anyone knew whether Fascists had broken her father's hands. No one had any answers, not even Nonna.

After the introductions were finished, Nonna glanced at Beppe. "Last week I distributed a list of vendors that I have had good experiences with. I will make sure you get one."

Beppe lifted an eyebrow. "You share your vendors with the competition?"

Nonna blinked behind her glasses. "We don't regard each other as competition. We rise or fall together. I expect you to bring a list of your vendors to the next meeting."

Beppe nodded, his expression impassive.

"Now, is there any new business?" Nonna looked around the table.

"I have something," said Gaia, a young, dark-haired mother with a toddler on her lap. "I have some signs. I think they could increase business to our restaurants."

"Excellent." Nonna smiled, and heads nodded.

"I had them printed for everyone. My uncle is a printer and did it for free. I'll show you." Gaia dug in her tote bag, produced a stack of printed signs, and held one up. NEGOZIO ARIANO, or ARYAN BUSINESS, it read, meaning that the store was owned by Gentiles, not Jews.

Elisabetta stopped typing.

Nonna cleared her throat. "I would never put that sign in my window. It's offensive. Many of our neighbors in Trastevere are Jewish."

Gaia frowned. "With respect, I'm putting one up. Anybody else want a sign, for free?"

Leandra raised her hand. "I do, please. I put my family before anybody else's."

Isabella raised her hand, too. "I have three children to feed. I can't afford the niceties."

Gianna nodded. "I'll take two signs, one for me and one for my neighbor. She runs a dress shop."

Nonna leaned forward, placing her arthritic hands on the table. "Ladies, please reconsider. Trastevere is home to painters, musicians, and writers, a veritable artists colony. The effect of the Race Laws on Jewish artists has been devastating. They aren't permitted to work in public radio, theater, or music, or private entertainment. Textbooks by Jewish authors are no longer in use, nor are maps signed by Jews. They are our neighbors, our friends."

"I agree." Elisabetta nodded.

"Of course you do, you work for her." Gaia smirked, cuddling her baby.

Leandra frowned. "We didn't write the Race Laws. We're in business."

Nonna pursed her lips, her vexation plain. "When I formed this organization, it was to save Trastevere, not merely our businesses."

"Trastevere will survive if we do," Gaia shot back.

Nonna frowned. "No. We must lift our gaze from our own plates. A community is comprised of people, *all* of its people."

Gaia smoothed her baby's hair. "Giuseppina, we know you own many houses in the neighborhood. There will always be a roof over your head. I can't say the same thing."

The women nodded around the table, siding with Gaia.

"*Se posso—*" Beppe began to say, then all of the women looked to him, since he was known as a prominent Fascist. "No sign for me."

In the end, one restaurant owner after another took a sign. The only two who didn't were Nonna and Beppe, who agreed about nothing else.

It wasn't until the end of the day that Elisabetta had the chance to finalize her notes from the meeting. She sat behind the Olivetti, but she couldn't stop thinking about Beppe Terrizzi. His presence lingered, a ghost at the head of the table, and he loomed larger than life to her, since his past intertwined with her own. She wondered how long his affair with her mother had lasted, and how much of her childhood it had spanned. Why it had started, or how it had ended. She doubted she would ever know.

Nonna entered the dining room, holding her purse and a paper bag reeking of leftover fish. "Aren't you finished? It's time to go home."

"Not yet."

"How long can it take?" Nonna peered at the typed page. "You haven't started. What have you been doing?"

"I've been distracted. I was thinking about the meeting."

"That disgusting sign?" Nonna eased into her chair, setting down her things. "Weak people abound, strong people abide."

Elisabetta had heard her say that before, many times.

"There have always been anti-Semites, as there have always been fleas. Both are insignificant and brainless, having no purpose other than to torment their betters. I pray that someday we will be rid of them, but until then, we can only bathe, to keep them at bay."

"It was strange at the meeting, with Beppe there."

Nonna smiled slyly. "Oh yes, it killed him to agree with me."

"He agreed because of his friendship with Massimo Simone, Sandro's father."

"No, he agreed because I'm right." Nonna snorted. "Handsome Beppe Terrizzi. Did you see those women? The ones who weren't salivating were lactating."

Elisabetta chuckled.

"So is that what's been distracting you? Marco again? Or Sandro? When are you going to put them behind you? You don't think I hear you at night, crying like a little baby? Boo-hoo." Nonna imitated her.

Elisabetta felt taken aback. "That's not nice."

"Have we met?" Nonna arched a gray eyebrow. "Don't you think it's time to move on?"

"I'm not ready to start dating again."

"Was I talking about men? Why must it always be about men? Don't you remember when I told you, 'preserve your independence'?"

"Nonna, I can't be more independent than I am. I live like a nun."

"Virginity and independence are not the same thing. Sex, love, romance, men—that's all that fills your head. What about this, under your nose?" Nonna gestured at the Olivetti. "Remember when you wanted to become a writer? When I introduced you to Gualeschi? When Marco, Sandro, or whoever bought you a notebook? How much encouragement do you need, Elisabetta? How many others will dream your dreams for you? What will it take for you to become the woman whom God intended you to be?"

Elisabetta felt hurt, for Nonna sounded right.

"What are you waiting for? When do you want to begin your future? What time is better than now?" Nonna tapped the typewriter with her curved fingernail. "If you were Jewish, you wouldn't be permitted to write. You're throwing away a right denied to others, for no reason. By *fleas*."

Elisabetta felt ashamed. It was true. "But I don't know if I can write or what to write about."

"You live in fascinating times. Write about them on a typewriter made by the Olivetti family, which hates Fascism. If you can't write now, you're no daughter of mine."

*Daughter?* Nonna must have misspoken, but Elisabetta wasn't going to correct her.

Nonna eased from her chair. "Let's go home. The cats await, and that typewriter is portable for a reason."

## CHAPTER SIXTY-TWO

# Sandro

October 1940

---

Sandro and Rosa walked down Via del Portico d'Ottavia, under gray skies. They were on their way to buy bread from their black-market connection, a transaction that required the two of them. Sandro would make the purchase while Rosa served as lookout, the method a necessity because Jews caught buying on the black market would be fined, and if they couldn't pay, arrested. They had no choice but to buy on the black market because food and other essentials were scarce, especially in the Ghetto, where so many shops had closed.

They greeted neighbors as they passed, but the main thoroughfare was emptier than ever. Nobody was selling anything on the street anymore, after another set of Race Laws had revoked the licenses for peddling of any kind, which had the effect of denying income even to rag traders. Worst of all, last week, Mussolini had ordered all Jews to leave the country. Most Jews ignored the law, as they were too poor to travel to any country that would accept them.

"What do you think we should do about the new law?" Sandro asked, looking over at his sister. They often discussed important matters outside the house, so as not to upset their parents, especially their father.

"I think Fascists want us out. They made it official." Rosa shook her head, walking along. Her hair was up in a twist, and her face was lovely, if leaner. Like all of them, she had lost weight, so that her red coat fit loosely. Its bright color had dulled, and the lapel stitching had come free.

"We don't have the money to emigrate now, even if we wanted to."

"Correct." Sandro knew the numbers, and they kept him up at night. He stretched every *lira* they had left.

"And we have nowhere to immigrate to, now that the war is on. We can't go to Britain or France anymore, and Poland and the Netherlands are already under Nazi rule." Rosa looked over. "The only option left is Palestine, but I hear the waiting list is too long."

"I can't believe it's come to this. Still, I can't believe it."

"I can."

"I was wrong, and you were right, all along."

"Don't feel bad. You didn't want to believe it. You love your country. You couldn't imagine she would turn on you." Rosa shrugged. "What is a country if not her people?"

"Right." Sandro felt a rush of regard for her. "You know, you didn't have to come back. You put yourself in this, all over again."

"I'm with my family." Rosa smiled, but Sandro knew she was putting on a brave face.

"Papa's worse, don't you think?"

"Yes, he's anxious and preoccupied, all the time."

"I don't know how to help him, other than what I'm already doing."

"There's nothing, Sandro. You're doing enough."

They turned right, then left, heading out of the Ghetto, and it felt to Sandro that they were entering a different world. Outside, stores and businesses were thriving, and well-dressed Romans went about their quotidian business, living the life that the Simones used to live.

Rosa walked with her head down, a frown marking her pretty features. "I got a letter from one of my British friends, saying it's terrible in London right now. The city is being bombed, and everyone's hiding in the Tube at night. Now that Hitler's taken France, Britain stands alone. Churchill will never surrender, but I don't know if the Brits can stop the Nazis."

"How frightening." Sandro shuddered.

"It horrifies me that Italy is on Hitler's side—and I'm married to a Brit. My own country is trying to kill my husband. How can that be?"

"Everything is topsy-turvy. The Allies are on the right side, and we're on the wrong one."

"I had news of David. He got reassigned to a group called the SOE, a special operations division. They go behind the lines to disrupt the enemy in any way they can, blowing up rail lines and the like."

Sandro hid his dismay. "But he's a diplomat."

"I know. They picked him for his diplomatic knowledge and language skills. I heard that from our old embassy friends. The rest is top secret. I don't even know where he is." Rosa bit her lip, and seeing her anxiety, Sandro stopped her and gave her a warm hug.

"It's going to be okay."

"Is it?" Rosa released him, her eyes filming. They resumed walking, and she sighed. "Sandro, we talk about David and me all the time. But we never talk about you and Elisabetta. Every time I bring her up, you change the subject. What happened that night, on her birthday?"

"Nothing." Sandro's chest ached.

"Come on. You lied to me." Rosa lifted an eyebrow. "You told me that she chose Marco, but I heard what she said to you that night. She chose you, and you sent her away."

"It was for her own good."

"She didn't think so. She wants you. She told you so."

"Marco is better for her."

"That's her decision to make, not yours. You love her. You should have told her that."

"Why?"

"It's the truth. You don't need a reason for the truth."

Sandro wished it were that simple. "I couldn't see her now, even if I wanted to. Mixed couples are under surveillance these days. We can't have OVRA watching us. If they did, we couldn't meet our connection. How would we get food or anything else we need?"

Rosa was silent a moment, walking along. "We would figure it out. Elisabetta never gave up on you. She probably still hasn't."

Sandro didn't want to believe that was true. He didn't want to think he could have Elisabetta back, for it only kept his heart broken. All of the reasons he had let her go still existed, whether she saw Marco or not.

"Sandro, you should go to her. Just tell her you love her, and let the rest fall as it may."

"Oh, is that your romantic advice?" Sandro smiled, remembering a happier time when she had advised him about Elisabetta.

"Yes, and bring her flowers." Rosa smiled back.

"I brought her a book. And it worked."

"Ha!"

Sandro spotted their connection, a dirty little man with a cap pulled down, standing on the street corner. "There he is. He's waiting for us."

"Sandro, you really should tell Elisabetta."

"Enough. Keep an eye out for the police."

## CHAPTER SIXTY-THREE

# Beppe
### December 1940

Beppe carried two wineglasses to Massimo's table in the back of the empty bar. The two men had fallen into a routine, and Massimo would slip through the side entrance after closing time, have something to eat, and take home a bag of groceries.

"How was the *panino*?" Beppe sat down, noticing that every crumb of the sandwich was gone. His old friend had lost weight, and his worn brown suit hung on him. His omnipresent folder of papers lay open next to him, having grown even thicker.

"It was delicious. Did Maria make it?" Massimo pushed his plate away.

"No, Letitizia."

"How is Maria doing? Still upstairs?"

"Yes, but she's getting out more. She goes to Mass. Emedio takes her."

"It must be hard. I'm sorry."

"The war makes it worse. She reads the newspaper, the reports of the dead. She sees which ones are Aldo's age, or whether they're younger or older. She mourns them like her own."

"How sad."

"It's odd to be home in wartime, isn't it?"

"Yes."

Beppe and Massimo locked eyes, soldier to soldier. Beppe's old knee injury had prevented him from serving this time, and Jews were not permitted to serve.

Massimo sighed heavily. "Though I have to say, when I hear that the war is going badly for us, I don't know whether to rejoice or weep."

"I understand." Beppe sipped his wine. "We're off to a rocky start in the Mediterranean. The naval defeat at Taranto was an embarrassment. I'm hoping the Egyptian front goes better, but I feel ambivalent, too."

"Understood." Massimo opened his folder, slid a pen from his pocket, and made a note.

"On the other hand, it pains me to admit that the Germans have had success. Their blitzkrieg is something new, altogether. Hitler occupies much of Western Europe."

"Yes." Massimo made another note.

"I rue the day we joined forces with the Nazis. We're Hitler's vassals, that's all." Beppe watched Massimo take notes, which was becoming more frequent. "What are you writing, Massimo?"

"Important things I have to remember, they need to be written down." Massimo turned the folder around and showed Beppe a line of figures. "See, this is the census, in August 1938. There were fifteen thousand applications for exemptions to the Race Laws—"

"Massimo," Beppe interrupted him. "You told me this already, many times."

"Oh, I did?" Massimo blinked. "Did I show you the families who got exemptions based on exceptional merits?"

"Yes. Massimo, how are you feeling, brother?"

"As well as can be expected." Massimo turned the folder right-side up. "I'm proud of my work, I'm able to serve the Community. You know, I got the exemptions for many of those families. They were granted on applications I prepared or supervised. I wish I could have done it for my own family, I deserved it on the merits. I just missed that one year. I wish I'd joined the party earlier, like you."

"We've discussed this, many times. It's not your fault." Beppe paused. "I'm worried about you. You don't seem like yourself. You need a break."

"A *break*?" Massimo's eyes flared behind his glasses. "It's not like the old days at the office. The Community needs me, it's suffering. Nobody has work, there's no money, and we struggle daily to eat." His words sped up, running over one another. "I've trained people to file the applications. Sixteen people work for me at the synagogue, but every time we file one application, we find another family who needs one. It never ends."

"I understand that, but you can't solve everything yourself. I feel as if you're trying to redeem yourself for not getting the exemption."

"Perhaps I am, but what's the harm in that? I don't want another family to be in our position."

"I'll tell you the harm." Beppe kept his tone without judgment. "You're trying to redeem yourself for something that wasn't your fault. You're neglecting your family in the process. Be home more. That's your place."

"But I can't simply *stop*."

"I'm not saying stop. I'm saying cut down." Beppe closed Massimo's folder. "Your mind is on your work all the time."

"That's what Sandro says." Massimo frowned.

"He's right, your son. Talk to me about him, not this folder. How is Sandro these days?"

"I don't see much of him. I'm at the synagogue. He's off with Rosa or at school. He runs the house."

"What do you mean?"

"He's taken over the household finances, such as they are, so I can work."

"But it's not his place." Beppe frowned. "You're the head of the Simone family. Remember who you are. Resume your proper role. Everything else will fall into place. It will do you good."

"Maybe I will." Massimo straightened, blinking. "How's Marco?"

"He likes working at Palazzo Venezia, and at night he sees girls." Beppe paused. "Again, I'm sorry for those things he said at your house. I'm ashamed."

"Of course he didn't mean it. You apologized already. These are dark and hard times. There's suffering, and war."

"But wars end. That, we know. That, we have lived."

"Yes, they end." Massimo pursed his lips. "And then, they begin again."

I n time, Beppe slipped Massimo out the side entrance, then locked up. He left to go upstairs when he heard banging on the front door. He turned around to see Carmine Vecchio through the glass, a runty figure in his dark OVRA uniform.

Beppe went to the door and unlocked it, blocking the threshold. "We're closed," he said, matter-of-factly.

"You're feeding that little Jew. I saw you. I know you." Carmine's eyes glittered with malice.

"I feed every customer. The day that becomes illegal, throw me in jail."

"Simone is not a customer, he's a friend. You think you can get away with it because Marco works at Palazzo Venezia."

"My son has nothing to do with it. Your grudge with me goes back. You were a punk then, and you're a punk now."

Carmine wagged a finger. "Don't think I can't get to you."

"Go ahead. Try."

"Or your little Jew friend."

"Don't dare touch him."

Carmine snickered. "The Simones are your Achilles' heel. It's written all over your face."

"I warn you, don't touch him."

"I have OVRA behind me. What will you do to me?"

"Don't find out," Beppe answered, through clenched teeth. Out of no-where, the thought occurred to him to kill Carmine with his bare hands, right then and there. It was an instinct forged in combat, the reflex of a soldier to protect a brother of his company. He had done it in war. Many times.

"You don't scare me, Beppe."

"Because you're stupid." Beppe stepped back and closed the door, eye-ing Carmine through the glass. Beppe had always believed there were bat-tles that a man needed to walk away from, and battles that a man needed to fight.

Carmine had just become the latter.

## CHAPTER SIXTY-FOUR

# Elisabetta
### March 1941

Elisabetta and Nonna sat at the dining room table, nursing their night-caps of anisette. The house was quiet and tranquil, and the breeze through the open window billowed the lace curtains. Rico slept on his chair, with Gnocchi on hers, their seat cushions covered with white doilies to collect cat hair, which was a lost cause.

Nonna nodded. "We did well this week. We were even with last, so we're holding our own."

"You deserve the credit." Elisabetta smiled, pleased.

"Do I disagree? No!" Nonna laughed, and Elisabetta joined her. Casa Servano was still in business thanks to Nonna's strategy, which was serving only their house specialty, pasta. All other entrées had been eliminated, and Elisabetta bartered everything they had for flour and eggs. Others in the trade association had followed suit, focusing on their own various specialties. Beppe had never come to another meeting, though he had left them his list of vendors.

"Elisabetta, how are you doing with your book?"

"Fine, thanks." Elisabetta finished the last of her anisette, which tasted licorice-sweet. She had begun to write the night she first brought home the Olivetti, and what had started as a lark had turned into a discipline. She would start writing after their nightcap and not stop until she had finished five hundred words. Some nights it would take her until one o'clock in the morning, and other nights until almost dawn.

"When are you going to let me read it?"

"When I'm finished," Elisabetta answered firmly, since they had had the conversation many times.

"Why are you taking so long?"

"It takes time."

"You're not going on and on, are you?"

"No, I hope not." Elisabetta rose, smiling. "Now I have to get to work."

"Why can't I read it now? Don't you realize I'll have valuable suggestions?"

"I'm sure, and you can make them when I'm finished." Elisabetta picked up her glass, but Nonna stopped her.

"You think I don't know how to wash a glass? Now tell me, what's your book about?"

"You'll see, soon. Good night." Elisabetta kissed Nonna on the cheek, picked up the Olivetti, and went upstairs, her thoughts already turning to her book. The story had completely captured her imagination, and she realized that Nonna had been right. Writing had given her something to think about other than Sandro or Marco.

She entered her bedroom, switched on the light, and set the Olivetti on her desk. She changed into her nightgown, so she wouldn't wrinkle her dress, then sat down at her chair and took out her manuscript, setting it beside the typewriter. A Talkative Girl, read the title page, and under it was something she had wanted to write for years: By Elisabetta D'Orfeo.

She ran her palm over the smooth, cool page, then rested it on the manuscript, as if she could feel its heartbeat. The main character was a girl named Zarina, who was a lot like her, though Elisabetta hadn't intended that. She had made up the plot as she had gone along, and Zarina had acquired a vain and careless mother, a loving but feckless father, and a pet she loved very much, only it wasn't a cat, but a parakeet. And when Zarina had fallen in love with a young man who had fallen out of love with her, Elisabetta had realized that she was writing everything she held in her heart, all of the things she thought but hadn't said, which was when it had struck her that she was a talkative girl with no one to talk to.

And when she had gotten to the middle of the novel, she had found herself writing about an angel who appeared from nowhere, which was strange because Elisabetta hadn't intended to have any magical elements in her book. Then she had remembered that Grazia Deledda had magical elements in her novels, so she had kept writing, and when Zarina was in her most terrible trouble, the angel had fluttered to her side, taken her by the hand, and showed her the way to safety, and that was when Elisabetta realized who the angel was.

She picked up a piece of paper, loaded it into the typewriter, and rolled it up. Despite what she had told Nonna, she had finished writing the entire novel except for the dedication. She had been mulling it over all day, because she wanted to word it perfectly. She typed:

    For Nonna, my beloved angel

Her eyes blurred with tears, and her heart suffused with gratitude. Thanks to Nonna, she had let go of everything that had been locked inside her, forgiven her mother for leaving and her father for drinking. She had set herself free, so that she could finally breathe, and she did, inhaling and exhaling, just once.

*Fine.* The End.

She unrolled the dedication page, slipped it under the title page, and squared the stack of papers. She rose with the manuscript, left her bedroom, and padded downstairs in bare feet, to surprise Nonna with the news. She went to Nonna's door, where the light was still on, since Nonna always read until late.

Elisabetta entered the bedroom, but Nonna had fallen asleep with her glasses on and her book open on her chest. Elisabetta put the manuscript on the bed and went to her side. Nonna was sleeping with her head slightly to the right. Elisabetta hesitated to wake her, but she knew that Nonna would want her to.

"Nonna, wake up."

Nonna didn't stir, but she was a sound sleeper.

"Nonna?" Elisabetta touched her shoulder, and Nonna's head slipped down, but she didn't wake up.

Elisabetta's gaze fell to Nonna's body, which was very still. Her chest wasn't moving, nor was she snoring, as she often did.

Elisabetta reached for Nonna's hand, but Nonna didn't awake.

Elisabetta realized what had happened. She felt her chest wrench with the deepest sorrow. She held on to Nonna's hand, as if it were a way to tether Nonna to the earth even though she had become an angel, truly.

"I finished my book," Elisabetta said thickly, blinking tears from her eyes. "I'm so sorry I waited to show it to you."

Nonna didn't respond, of course, and Elisabetta realized what she had to do, for it was the last time they would be together. She released Nonna's hand, slid off her glasses, and folded them carefully, then set them on the nightstand. She removed Nonna's book from her chest and set that on the nightstand, too.

She picked up her manuscript. "Nonna, the title of my book is *A Talkative Girl*, so you know it's about me, even though it's fiction." She sniffled, composing herself. "So I'll read it to you, and I know you'll hear and that you're with me right now, together in our house, with our cats and our china. And I know you'll never leave me, ever. Because you always loved me, Nonna, more than enough."

Elisabetta wiped her eyes on the sleeve of her nightgown. It would take all night to read the book, and only when she was finished would she reveal the dedication, though she suspected Nonna knew that already, too.

"Chapter One," Elisabetta said, clearing her throat.

## CHAPTER SIXTY-FIVE

# Marco

### 13 April 1941

Bar GiroSport closed for Easter Sunday, and Marco climbed the stairs to the apartment, late for the holiday meal. He hadn't been home since yesterday and had missed Mass this morning, having been in bed with a woman who wasn't the churchgoing type. He entered the kitchen to find his father and Emedio at the table, having already eaten the first course. Both men looked at him with disapproval, but Marco pretended not to notice.

"*Buona Pasqua,* Emedio." Marco went to his brother and embraced him. "You never visit us anymore. Can't that Pope do anything for himself?"

Emedio released him, his manner judgmental in his black cassock. "Why didn't you come to Mass? It's the holiest of all days."

"I had to work," Marco lied. He couldn't tell the truth in front of his mother.

"On *Pasqua*? The office is open?"

"Not officially, but I had things to do for the bosses."

"That's no excuse."

"Are you my father now, Father?" Marco wisecracked, then went to his father, dressed for the holiday in his suit and tie. "*Buona Pasqua*, Papa."

"To you, too, Marco. You need a shave."

"Sorry." Marco remained distant from his father, but it mattered less to him than it used to. He spent all his time at Palazzo Venezia, where he received promotion after promotion. Everyone was delighted with his performance, and he was the youngest assistant in supply administration. His new boss was higher up than Buonacorso, and Marco was being groomed for leadership.

"*Buona Pasqua, figlio.*" His mother carried *abbacchio* to the table, a leg of lamb with rosemary, white wine, and anchovies, served with roasted potatoes.

"*Buona Pasqua*, Mamma. Sorry I missed the first course." Marco kissed her on the cheek and took the heavy platter from her, breathing in its delicious aroma. He set it on the table next to a ring of golden-brown Easter bread, braided with hard-boiled eggs dyed pink and green. It satisfied him to know that the abundance of the meal was due to him, bringing home extra food coupons from work.

"You missed Mass?" His mother began serving the lamb. Her mood seemed better, perhaps because of the holiday. She had on her best black dress, with her dark hair in its braid.

"I'm sorry."

"Our Lord sacrificed Himself for you."

"I know, I'm sorry."

"We lit candles for Aldo." His mother finished serving and sat down.

"Good." Marco sat down, glancing reflexively at Aldo's chair, which held only a newspaper.

Emedio caught his eye. "It's hard to celebrate today without him here."

"No, it's not," Marco shot back. He had hardened his heart toward Aldo, after what he learned about anti-Fascists at Palazzo Venezia. They killed soldiers and destroyed materiel and equipment. He had to work twice as hard to make the bosses forget what Aldo had done. Many knew, due to jealous gossip.

"Aldo was our brother," Emedio said, his tone corrective. "We mourn him still."

His mother frowned. "Marco? Why would you—"

His father raised his hand, which silenced her. "We all mourn our Aldo."

His mother blessed herself. "Of course we do, we always will. God rest his soul. Emedio, please say grace."

Emedio prayed while Marco fell silent.

His father nodded, picking up his fork. "Let's begin."

Marco took a bite of meat, and it tasted juicy and flavorful, owing to the anchovies. "So, Emedio, how are things for you, these days?"

"The war is keeping us very busy at the Curia."

His father interjected, "It's going badly for Italy. We were defeated in Egypt and pushed out of Greece and Albania."

Marco knew the details, even more than his father. "True, but the Germans have been a strong ally. They sent Rommel and his Afrika Korps to retake North Africa. My new boss says even the British admire Rommel—"

"Marco," his father interrupted him, frowning. "The Nazi successes are not ours. We are not Germans."

"I understand." Marco forgot that his father hated the Germans, since the Great War. "I meant only that they support us. They went into Greece and Yugoslavia, and they're always at Palazzo Venezia. I've become friends with one of the assistants. He's my age, and his name is Rolf Stratten."

His father looked down at his plate, clenching his jaw.

His mother chewed silently.

"You're friends with Nazis now?" Emedio reached for the newspaper that had been on Aldo's chair and pointed to the front page. "Did you see this?"

Marco tensed. He couldn't read the headline, but he recognized a photograph of the town of Ljubljana, in Slovenia.

"Look at this! A 'proud exchange of messages between Il Duce and the Führer.' What do you think of this?"

"What's your point?" Marco waved dismissively.

"Read it and you'll see."

"I don't have to. Who do you think gives the newspapers the information they print? I work at Palazzo Venezia, brother. I know more than you do about this war. And like it or not, the Germans are our allies."

"Enough of the Germans." His father scowled, and Marco dreaded what he had to tell him next.

"Papa, my new boss has been after me, about you. I suspect his information comes from Carmine."

Emedio interjected, "Who's Carmine?"

"Carmine is an OVRA officer who knows that Papa gives food and money to Massimo. OVRA doesn't like it. Neither does my new boss. He's mentioned it several times."

His father chewed another piece of lamb. "Ignore your boss, Marco. He's saying that because he has to, officially. That's how officers operate. They care only about the chain of command. It's bosses on top of bosses at Palazzo Venezia."

"Perhaps, but, Papa, you should stop."

His father didn't reply, hunched over his plate.

Emedio recoiled. "Marco, you want Papa to stop helping the Simones?"

"Yes." Marco's heart had hardened toward the Simones, too. He would never forgive Sandro for betraying him with Elisabetta. The pain had gotten worse over time, not better. Ironically, he missed them both. He hated them for that, too.

His father remained silent, still eating.

His mother looked down.

Marco couldn't let it go. "Papa, if you keep helping the Simones, you could get me in trouble. You jeopardize my career."

His father looked up, his dark gaze even. "Today is a joyful day. Your mother cooked this meal for us. In deference to her, and our Lord, I'm going to ignore what you just said."

Marco met his father's eye directly.

His mother bit her lip, but said nothing.

Emedio broke the silence. "Good for you, Papa. If you can help the Simones, keep it up. This persecution of the Jews is immoral."

Marco looked over. "Oh, what's the Church doing to help the Jews?"

"Our Holy Father is opposed to the Nazis precisely because of their anti-Semitism. If you remember not so long ago, when he was cardinal secretary of state, he helped to write the encyclical to the German churches, *Mit Brennender Sorge*. In retaliation, the Nazis opposed his selection as Pope. Germany was the only country not to send a representative to his inauguration."

"You're not answering my question. Now that Cardinal Pacelli has become Pius XII, what has he done for the Jews?"

Emedio frowned. "Didn't you hear his homily, broadcasted today? He said the war was a 'lamentable spectacle of human conflict.' And that it was 'a ruthless struggle' that has been 'atrocious.' He asked for charity on the homefront."

"But did his homily speak of Jews specifically? I doubt it."

Emedio pursed his lips. "That's because the Vatican must maintain neutrality, and it has a valid concern about the Communist threat. There are fears that retribution against the Jews will take place if our Holy Father speaks too specifically. Even so, there are those who urge a more active role, and I am one. I condemn Mussolini for the Race Laws. They cause untold suffering."

Marco felt anger flare in his chest. "Don't you think it's hypocritical to ask Papa to keep helping the Jews when the Vatican doesn't lift a finger? Why should my career be harmed for the Simones?"

Emedio's dark eyes widened. "Since when are you worried about your career instead of your best friend?"

"He's not my friend. He can go to hell for all I care."

"Marco!" His mother set down her glass, shaken. "What's come over you? You mustn't criticize our Holy Father, on *Pasqua* of all days. You've accepted too readily this godless view—"

"Maria, let me handle this." His father raised his hand again. "Marco, Emedio, this is not the day for this discussion. Let it drop."

Emedio stiffened. "Papa, I'm only trying to understand why Marco has changed so much—"

"I haven't changed. I've always been a Fascist."

"You used to love Sandro, but now you turn your back on him. You're befriending Nazis and following whatever Mussolini says."

"Mussolini is always right," Marco shot back, but even he realized it was from the Decalogue. "Who are you, to accuse *me* of following my leader without question? What about you?"

"Me? I'm a priest. You act like a big shot now, in your uniform."

"No more than you do, in yours."

Emedio recoiled, grimacing. "I serve God. Whom do you serve?"

"Il Duce and Italy."

"I know you better than that, little brother. It's not love of country that motivates you. It's love of self."

Marco felt stung, jumping to his feet. "I could say the same of you. Always the perfect son, the perfect priest, follows the rules—"

"What's come over you?" Emedio rose. "Your heart is turning as black as your shirt."

"No, it's not!" Marco found himself walking around the table to Emedio, but Emedio stood his ground, his eyes flashing.

"You've become like one of the mob who crucified Christ instead of Barabbas. The Fascist mob that blindly follows the leader—"

"Who are you to judge? You're a priest, not God himself!"

"—and you're too *stupid* to question—" Emedio started to say, but Marco grabbed him by his shoulders and pushed him back against the kitchen wall, knocking down the Learco calendar.

His father leapt to his feet.

His mother wailed.

"Don't you dare!" Marco raged at an astonished Emedio, then his father succeeded in yanking him off.

His mother covered her face.

Marco fled the apartment to the sound of her sobs.

## CHAPTER SIXTY-SIX

# Elisabetta

April 1941

Elisabetta swept the living room, so the house would be as presentable as possible. Sofia, Paolo's wife, had told her at work today that one of the family's female cousins, a refugee from the country, was moving into Nonna's old room. Elisabetta dreaded the thought of someone sleeping in Nonna's bed in her cozy little room, among her lovely china. Elisabetta had had no say in the matter, and she told herself to be charitable, for war was ravaging the provinces, sending people fleeing to the city. Housing was at a shortage, and Rome's population swelled from a million and a half to two million.

Elisabetta swept the dirt into the dustpan, feeling the heaviness in her heart. Nonna hadn't passed away that long ago, and grief had become a part of her body, folded into her very soul, like an egg kneaded into dough. Rico and Gnocchi mourned Nonna, too, restlessly looking for her in her bedroom or meowing at odd hours of the night. Otherwise they followed Elisabetta everywhere, and even now they watched her from the dining room, curled up on their respective chairs atop their doilies. She never scolded them, and being cats, they were free to express how they felt, unlike humans.

There was a vigorous pounding on the door, and loud voices on the front step. She leaned the dustpan and broom against the wall and went to the door, smoothing her hair into place. She opened the door, taken aback to find two middle-aged women, one short and one tall—and with them were eight scruffy children, boys and girls of varying ages. Their clothes were shabby and their faces dirty, and they carried bulging sacks and a rolled-up blanket of their belongings.

Elisabetta had been expecting only one person, but it would have been rude to say so. "*Piacere*, I'm Elisabetta and you must be—"

"*Madonna!*" The tall woman stepped inside the house, her mouth agape.

Her features were plain, her skin weathered, and she wore her long dark hair in a braid to her waist, country-style. She dropped her sack on the floor. "What a beautiful house!"

"*Che bella!* Look at these rugs, this furniture!" The short woman climbed inside after her, her face gaunt and her body bony, with scraggly brown hair and a worn brown dress. She looked around in astonishment, and the children piled in behind them, dropping their bags and sacks like a small invasion. They raced to the breakfronts and started opening and closing the doors, leaving smudgy fingerprints on the glass windows.

Flustered, Elisabetta kept an eye on the children. "I'm sorry, ladies. I didn't get your names."

"I'm Nedda Rotunno, and my sister-in-law is Martina Bellolio." The tall woman scanned the breakfronts, her dark eyes agog. "Giuseppina lived like a queen! We're in luck. We're going to love it here."

Elisabetta hid her dismay. "You mean you're *all* moving in? There's only the one bedroom downstairs, and I have the one upstairs. I was told only one woman—"

"We'll squeeze in with ease." Nedda turned to Martina, delighted. "How lucky are we? This china will bring a pretty penny. We're going to be rich!"

"Pardon me?" Elisabetta asked, aghast. "You can't sell Nonna's china. It's antique."

"Of course we can." Nedda gestured around the room. "This is a gold mine. It's all going to the estate sale, and so are these breakfronts. We'll make a fortune!"

"No, no." Elisabetta felt a wrench in her chest. "Nonna collected that china. She chose every plate and every pattern for a specific reason. Some of it is decades old. It took her years to amass—"

"*E allora?*" Nedda waved her off. "She's gone now, isn't she?"

"That's disrespectful." Elisabetta cringed. "You mustn't say such things, and you can't sell her collection. Sofia won't allow you."

"Yes, she already has. Sofia arranged the whole thing. The appraiser is coming this week and he's going to give us a price."

"That can't be right." Elisabetta recoiled. "Sofia didn't tell me, and she doesn't have a legal right to dispose of Nonna's property. Only Paolo does."

"*Beh*, Paolo's not here, is he?"

"No, he's at war, but he'll be back." Elisabetta fought back tears. "The china is what Nonna loved the most. It was hers, and she didn't ask for anything from anybody. She earned it all herself."

"Elisabetta, this is none of your business. You're only a freeloader." Nedda scowled, and just then one of the little girls dropped a plate, one of the blue-patterned Staffordshire that Nonna had loved, which shattered on the floor.

"Oh no!" Elisabetta reached for the broom, then hurried over to clean up. She knelt down, picked up the pieces, and put them in the dustpan. The characteristic *chink* of the shards could have been the sound of Nonna's own bones, as the china was made from bone and ash.

"You clumsy girl!" Nedda smacked the little girl in the face, provoking a wail. "Do you know how much that dish cost? We could have eaten for weeks! Don't touch the plates!"

"Don't touch the plates!" Martina joined in, and the children raced into the dining room like a horde.

"Look, a white cat!" a little boy howled, reaching for Gnocchi, who sprang from the chair in alarm, then froze under the table, arching her back.

"No, leave her alone!" Elisabetta dropped the broom and ran into the dining room.

"There are *two* cats!" shouted one of the little girls, when she discovered Rico on the chair. "Two! Two!"

"Catch them, catch them!" a boy squealed, and the children swarmed after the cats. Rico scooted smartly to the stairwell, realizing that these dirty little humans were to be avoided at all costs.

"Stop!" Elisabetta blocked the children's path as Rico and Gnocchi fled past them and up the stairs. "You must leave the cats alone!"

"Cats! Cats! Two cats!" The children exploded in excited chatter. "One is white and one is striped!"

"Nedda, Martina, please, I have a request." Elisabetta had to find a way to live with these people. "Please don't let the children tease the cats. They're accustomed to a quiet life."

"*Boh!*" Nedda scoffed. "The children are playing."

Martina nodded. "They love cats. We used to have a cat."

"We ate it!" a little boy called out.

Elisabetta recoiled, horrified. "You're kidding, aren't you?"

The boy burst into laughter. "We loved it! It was delicious!"

Nedda snorted. "Elisabetta, don't be so high and mighty. The bombs destroyed our farm. Our cow and goats were killed. Our husbands are in the army. I held my family together, and so did Martina. You don't have a family, so keep your snotty opinions to yourself."

"Fine," Elisabetta said, defensive. "You keep the children away from the cats. No harm can come to these cats. They're mine and Nonna's."

Nedda smirked. "She wasn't your *nonna*."

"She wasn't yours, either. Sofia told me to expect one woman, a cousin. Your last names are all different."

"Watch your step!" Martina raised her voice. "We could have you thrown into the street! We'll tell Sofia!"

"Good luck," Elisabetta shot back. "Sofia can't run the restaurant without me, so she'll never throw me out."

"We'll see about that!"

"Do it. But don't let your children harm these cats."

"Then get your ass upstairs! Stay out of our way, you bitch!"

"You stay out of mine." Elisabetta headed for the stairs, upset.

"And you can't use the kitchen anymore! You're not allowed!"

"I eat at the restaurant anyway!" Elisabetta ran upstairs and locked her bedroom door, resolving that the cats would never go downstairs again. From now on, she would feed them and move their litter box to her room. She sat down on the bed, petting them and trying to calm down. All three listened to the clamor coming from downstairs.

Suddenly she remembered that there was a storage closet on the second floor, where Nonna kept her soup tureens that were too large for the breakfronts. Elisabetta couldn't allow them to be sold off, too. She left the bedroom and hurried to the storage closet. She retrieved a tureen and carried it back to her bedroom, then returned to the storage closet again and again, until she had moved all of the tureens to safety.

When she was finished, she locked the bedroom door behind her and counted the beautiful tureens, which covered the floor. There were thirty-four, each with its matching lid and ladle. She scanned them with a loving eye, remembering how Nonna had shown her each one, educating her about its vintage and manufacturer. There was the ornate Capodimonte tureen, from an Italian manufacturer, with pink and yellow flowers and handles shaped like swans' necks. An older majolica tureen with bright orange and green flowers, with fluted ridges in the bowl. A Haviland Limoges tureen, with pink flowers and gold-rimmed accents on the rim, handles, and pedestal. Nonna's favorite was an authentic Minton of the Rococo Revival period, a rare pattern of blue and white flowers, its elegantly fluted lid filigreed with gold.

"Okay, let's go," Elisabetta said to the cats. She picked up one of the tureens and went to the small door on the far side of her bedroom, which led to a fire escape. It was on the back of the house and went to the rooftop, where she had a potted garden with herbs for the restaurant. The only access was through Elisabetta's room, so nobody could go there but her and the cats. Rico and Gnocchi loved their private sanctuary and they walked up, their tails as straight as exclamation marks.

Elisabetta reached the rooftop and set the tureen down among the pots, then went back downstairs, retrieved another tureen, and brought it up. She worked until all of the tureens were on the rooftop, and when she finally finished, she exhaled with relief. The garden would be even more beautiful, because now it would feature Nonna's tureens, planted in her memory.

Elisabetta felt her gaze travel upward into the dome of night sky, shaped like the underside of a tureen lid. She knew that Nonna was looking down on her, and Nonna understood that there was nothing more that Elisabetta could have done, except for rescuing thirty-four soup tureens and two cats.

## CHAPTER SIXTY-SEVEN

# Sandro

January 1942

---

Sandro stood outside the modest apartment house, on a residential backstreet in Ostiense in southwest Rome. Professor Tullio Levi-Civita had died in the house, just a few days ago. The professor had been sixty-eight years old, and a heart attack had taken his life. These days Sandro rarely left the Ghetto, but he had come after reading the death notice in the newspaper, published without any fanfare. Levi-Civita had received none of the memorials he deserved, the little man who was a giant in his field. Sandro wondered if anyone would ever even know of Levi-Civita, or if the Fascists would succeed in erasing him from history altogether.

An older woman dressed in fashionable clothes walked by, and when she glanced over, Sandro saw himself through her eyes, a thin young man with sunken cheeks, a worn muffler, and shabby clothes. He wondered if she could tell he was Jewish, for he felt his Jewishness now more than he ever had before, a paradoxical effect of the Race Laws.

It was a cold day, and Sandro wrapped his muffler closer, eyeing the house. He had followed Levi-Civita's career, or what had been left of it, after the professors had been expelled. Levi-Civita hadn't been permitted to teach anywhere, but Pope Pius XII had invited him to broadcast on the Vatican radio station, regarding new developments in science. Levi-Civita had become the first Jew ever to do so, but Sandro hadn't been able to listen because he had been teaching.

He was paying his respects now, as best as he could, a lone mourner. He felt the loss of the professor for himself and for the country they loved. No one would ever know what other groundbreaking advances Levi-Civita would have made, had he been allowed to continue working, teaching, and publishing papers. No one could ever say which students Levi-Civita would have mentored, who would have brought advances to follow, as science builds on itself like bricks in a wall. Sandro had hoped to be among those students, but that time had passed.

He thought of the other professors expelled from the University of Rome, as if he were walking through a cemetery, reading tombstones. There was Enrico Fermi, who had won the Nobel Prize in Physics in 1938. His wife, Laura, had been Jewish, so he had emigrated. There was Leo Pincherle, the grandson of the mathematician Salvatore Pincherle, who founded functional analysis in Italy. Federigo Enriques. Bruno Rossi. Emilio Segre. Sergio De Benedetti. Ugo Fano. Eugenio Fubini. Bruno Pontecorvo. Giulio Racah. Franco Rasetti. And so many others at the other departments at the universities of Rome, as well as Turin, Bologna, Pavia, Padua, Trieste, and Milan.

Sandro wondered if he ever would have accomplished something as brilliant as Tullio Levi-Civita. He doubted it, but he knew for sure that he would have tried. He had wanted to try, from when he was young, from as far back as when Professoressa Longhi had told him about the independent study. He would never forget the day he got the note from Levi-Civita himself.

Sandro looked at the house, one last time. There was a low wall of gray stucco in front, with pillars that flanked an iron gate to its entrance. He walked to the gate with his bicycle, said a silent prayer, and took a small rock from his pocket, then set it on the pillar.

A loving remembrance, from one Jewish mathematician to another.

CHAPTER SIXTY-EIGHT

# Elisabetta

May 1943

Elisabetta counted the money and ration cards from the dinner service, pleased that they had broken even again, a success in these difficult days. Food shortages were decimating the restaurant business, but she kept

Casa Servano going by making the pasta herself, hiring only a waitress, and getting occasional help from Sofia. Sugar and coffee were impossible to stock, but she made ersatz coffee from chicory and stretched the flour by adding chaff and ground potato peels. She brought in fresh herbs from her rooftop garden, which continued to be a haven for her and the cats, safe from Nedda, Martina, and the children.

Sofia entered the kitchen, taking off her apron. She was a pretty woman, but she had aged since Paolo had gone to war. Her brown eyes looked tired, tilting down at the corners, and gray strands threaded her dark hair. "I'm finished in the dining room. I have to get home."

"Good news. We made as much as last night." Elisabetta stuffed the *lire* into a canvas pouch and handed it to her.

"Thanks." Sofia reached for her purse and put the money pouch inside, exhaling. "How I loathe our Nazi customers. Every day there's more of them. They treat me like dirt."

"*Beh*, the joke's on them, since we take their money." Elisabetta hated the Nazis, too, so she had raised prices. Top Nazi brass had become regulars, even the German Ambassador to the Vatican, Baron Ernst von Weizsäcker.

"I know they're our allies, but it was a bad marriage from the outset." Sofia frowned. "Meanwhile Paolo's letters grow worse. He says it's a lost cause. I pray every night that the war ends soon. I don't even care if we lose."

"I feel the same way. I think we're getting close to the end, no matter the propaganda in the newspapers." Elisabetta sensed that the tide was turning against the Fascists, after defeats in Stalingrad and Tunisia. Everyone was whispering that Mussolini had led the country astray. She wondered if Marco's loyalty to Fascism had wavered, but she dismissed thoughts of him. She never did figure out how her father's hands had gotten broken.

"I worry about Paolo all the time."

"I'm sure." Elisabetta worried about Sandro all the time, too. The Race Laws had ground the Jews of Rome into oppression, and she could only imagine how Sandro and his family were faring. She used to walk through the Ghetto, hoping to catch sight of him, but she had stopped. Still, she never stopped loving him. The Fascists couldn't police her heart.

"The children miss their father. I leave the radio off or they ask too many questions."

"I'm sorry." Elisabetta gave her a brief hug. "If it makes you feel better, I spit in the pasta we serve the Nazis."

"You do?" Sofia burst into surprised laughter.

"Nonna taught me. I learned from the best."

"That, you did." Sofia's expression softened. "I miss her, too."

"We go on for her," Elisabetta said, patting her back. "Good night."

"Good night." Sofia left, and Elisabetta experienced a pang of mourning. She looked around the kitchen, letting her gaze linger on the pantry that had been Nonna's throne room. She found herself entering the pantry, running her fingertips along the wooden surface of the table, then using her fingernail to clean out the flour wedged into its grain. She felt as if she were touching Nonna herself, and so they remained together, in life and in death.

Elisabetta heard a noise behind her. "Sofia, did you forget something?" she asked, turning around, but it wasn't Sofia. Standing in the kitchen was a large, dark-haired man. She experienced a tingle of fear, realizing she had forgotten to lock the front door after closing. Crime was rampant in Rome these days, but the man didn't look malicious. He was as thin as a rolling pin, and his shabby jacket and pants hung on him.

"Sir, please go," Elisabetta said, just the same.

"Please, if you have any food to spare, I would thank you. My wife was killed when our farm was bombed, and I have nothing. I served in the army until I injured my foot."

"I'm sorry, but I have nothing to spare and a restaurant to run."

"I'm not asking for myself, but for my children. Two boys and a girl, my youngest. They won't eat much, I promise. If you could feed them, just this once, I would never bother you again." The man gestured to the dining room. "They're outside, skin and bones. If you don't believe me, see for yourself."

"Of course I believe you," Elisabetta said, giving in. "Please, sir, go sit down. I'll make you all some pasta."

She didn't need to see the children.

She already knew how they would look.

## CHAPTER SIXTY-NINE

# Marco

June 1943

Marco fell into step with his friend Rolf, and they walked along the Tiber on the Lungotevere dei Sangallo. Marco had been working around the clock at Palazzo Venezia, and he needed a break on such a nice day. The sun climbed high in a bright blue sky, and he always felt restored by the river, a natural oasis from noise, traffic, and worry. Tall palm trees lined the stone wall, which was set high above the riverbank. A damp, familiar breeze blew off the water, rustling their fronds.

He breathed in a fresh lungful, and Rolf sipped from his silver flask. The Nazi's dimpled cheeks had a boyishness that women loved, though his fondness for beer gave him a belly that strained the buttons of his uniform. Otherwise Rolf had an athletic frame, having been a stellar soccer player in his hometown of Osnabrück, in northern Germany.

"You're quiet, Marco," Rolf said in German. He looked over, his narrow brown eyes shifting under the black patent bill of his cap. His lips, which were thin, formed a flat line, uncharacteristically so.

"I'm tired," Marco answered, also in German. Rolf had taught him the language, and he had become fluent. But when he was tired, it felt effortful. "Do you mind if we speak Italian?"

"Not at all," Rolf answered, switching languages easily. He spoke Italian like a native, thanks to Marco.

"My boss is driving me crazy. I really needed to get out today."

"Here." Rolf offered his flask to Marco, who shook his head no.

"My boss would smell it on my breath. He stands so close when he talks, I smell his garlic."

"Mine would never know." Rolf capped the flask.

"Germans don't stand as close as Italians."

*"Genau,"* Rolf said, which meant exactly, a word that Germans used as

often as Italians used *allora*. He looked around, with a smile. "This is such a beautiful city."

"It was better before," Marco heard himself say, though he hadn't realized he felt that way.

"How so?"

Marco fell silent, having seen so many changes in Rome since Italy had entered the war. The city functioned and stores remained open, but the lines for food and other necessities were endless, and Romans looked harried, their faces showing the strain. Everyone's clothes were worn, and the military presence dominated the sidewalks and streets, with uniformed personnel and vehicles everywhere. He missed the carefree, pretty girls, walking this way and that, the lovers kissing at a café, and the noisy schoolchildren with *gelato* dripping over their fingers. Rome used to have *brio*, a life and spirit unique to this remarkable city, but it was gone.

"Marco?" Rolf asked, puzzled.

"It's just different, that's all."

"Well, I love it here. When the war is over, I think I may move here, like von Weizsäcker. He loves Rome."

Marco knew he meant Baron Ernst von Weizsäcker, the German Ambassador to the Vatican, who came to Palazzo Venezia from time to time. Weizsäcker genuinely liked Italians, in contrast to the Nazi brass, who carried themselves with an undisguised air of superiority. The entry of the United States into the war had gotten their attention, but the Nazis remained confident of victory.

"My boss is happy that things are going so well for us."

"Are they?" Marco thought of his father, who was turning out to be right about one thing. There was a difference in the way you viewed the war, depending on whether you were German or Italian. "The Allied bombing is destroying southern Italy and Sicily. The Allies won't let up."

"They're targeting the south because it supports the North African front."

"Whatever the reason, it's devastating to us." Marco realized Rolf didn't feel the same sympathy because Italy wasn't his country.

"Look on the bright side. They haven't bombed major cities like Rome, Venice, and Florence. I doubt they will."

"But they bombed Genoa, and it's a major city. Besides, my boss said it's not only the targets the Allies are choosing, but the way they're bombing. They're flying more missions, dropping a greater volume of smaller bombs." Marco had overheard a phone conversation the other day. "It's a brutal, relentless campaign. There's no food and no shelter. Italians are terrified. They didn't expect any of this. They feel betrayed. They're losing heart and belief in the war." Marco heard himself saying *they*, but he was Italian, so it should have been *we*.

"The Allies are trying to get Italy to drop out, in order to weaken the Axis. They think Italy is the weak link."

"We're not," Marco shot back, defensive.

"So then, it won't work. Italy won't quit."

"Of course not," Marco said, but he wasn't certain. He had sensed a new tension in the air at Palazzo Venezia and an undercurrent of blame that led to all manner of backstabbing and second-guessing. His boss griped privately that Italy had entered the war unprepared and that Il Duce spent afternoons in his private bedroom with women, words that never would have been uttered before. Marco was beginning to question the most fundamental of Fascist precepts. Maybe Mussolini wasn't always right.

"Let's stop a minute." Rolf took off his hat and rested it on the wall. He wiped sweat from his brow, making his short brown hair stick up.

Marco stood looking out at the Tiber, watching the moving current of the water. He loved its cloudy jade color and the little whitecaps of foam. He remembered those lazy, carefree days on the riverbank with Elisabetta, Sandro, and his classmates. It hurt his heart to think of it now.

"What are you looking at?"

"Nothing." Marco shrugged. "I used to do bike tricks on the riverbank, to impress a girl."

"Did you get her?"

Marco thought that one over. "No."

"Impossible to believe." Rolf took out his pack of cigarettes and plugged one between his lips. "What happened?"

"It doesn't matter now." Marco wanted to keep Elisabetta in his past.

"Her loss, eh?"

Marco didn't reply. Elisabetta was his loss, forever. His heartbroken gaze returned to the Tiber, then he spotted a group of men shoveling sand on the embankment, downriver. The men were naked to the waist, and some had bandannas on their heads as protection from the sun. One wore a hat made of folded newspaper.

Marco flashed on a memory. Elisabetta had worn a hat like that by the river, once. He found himself walking along the wall to get a closer look at the man.

"Where are you going?" Rolf lit his cigarette behind a cupped hand.

"I want to see what they're doing, below." Marco stopped when he got close enough. The man in the paper hat had gotten so much thinner, but Marco would have recognized him anywhere. It was Sandro.

Marco felt stricken. He had known that a Race Law compelled Ghetto Jews into forced labor, but he hadn't focused on it before. It horrified him to think that his old friend, who was a bona fide genius, was digging like a common laborer. His heart ached with the love he had had for Sandro, which must have lain dormant until now.

Suddenly Sandro lifted his face and looked up at Marco, holding his gaze. Marco's mouth went dry, and in that moment, he saw himself as Sandro saw him, a witness to his own actions, a Fascist standing with a Nazi. And Marco didn't recognize himself.

Sandro resumed digging, but Marco experienced an epiphany. He didn't know who he was anymore. He didn't know what he had become. He had performed so well at Palazzo Venezia this past year, a rising star. But his father had been right about that, too; there were bosses on top of bosses, like a ladder that never ended. Marco didn't know why he was climbing it anymore. He didn't even know where it led.

He felt embittered with shame, for all that he had said and done, for all he had become. He had once told Sandro that he wasn't his uniform, but he had been wrong. He had become his uniform, and now, he was disgusted with himself.

"Marco, do you know one of those guys?"

Marco blinked, shaken. "Yes. The one in the paper hat."

"Who is he?" Rolf blew out a cone of cigarette smoke.

"My best friend."

Rolf frowned. "Your best friend was a Jew?"

"Yes." Marco averted his eyes. "Let's go."

"Where? Back to work?"

"I don't know," Marco answered, lost.

## CHAPTER SEVENTY

# Elisabetta

### 19 July 1943

Elisabetta walked along, heading for San Lorenzo to meet a new black-market connection. San Lorenzo was a more congested neighborhood than Trastevere, and businessmen hurried on crowded sidewalks. Mothers tugged children by the hand, and old women rolled shopping carts behind them. Cars, buses, and trams honked on the wide streets.

She turned onto Via Cesare de Lollis, bordering La Sapienza, which reminded her of Sandro. It seemed like ages ago that she had gone with him to the Deledda lecture. Back then, all she had to worry about was choosing between two wonderful men.

Suddenly an air raid siren erupted through the loudspeakers on the street. She heard a horrifying hum vibrating through the air. She looked up in fear, and so did everyone else. A fleet of American bombers blanketed the sky, aiming directly for San Lorenzo. The Flying Fortresses. She knew from photos in the newspaper.

Chaos erupted. Women shrieked in terror. Men shouted. Everyone raced to get off the street. The air siren screamed. The planes zoomed toward them. Their engines rumbled louder and louder, a fearsome roar.

Elisabetta whirled around, not knowing if there was a shelter. Men and women jostled her, scattering in all directions. She raced with the panicked crowd to the nearest building, a shoe store. People pushed and shoved to get inside, frantic and desperate.

She pressed in with them, obeying instincts for survival. The roar of the planes deafened her. Everyone covered their ears, screaming, shouting, praying, crying. Mothers clutched their children, cowering. The planes darkened the sky and eclipsed the sun.

*Boom!* A blinding flash of light exploded in the middle of the street. The percussive blast sent her flying through the air. Brick and stones spewed as if from a volcano. She landed on the ground with everybody else, a stunned mass of humanity, wailing, crying, screaming, groaning, bleeding.

Elisabetta stayed conscious. Her head pounded. She couldn't hear a thing. It was as if she had gone deaf. She told herself she had to get moving. She had to find shelter. She tried to get up but a woman lay on top of her, motionless.

Elisabetta tried calling to her, but the woman didn't respond. Elisabetta realized the woman was dead. A little girl lay moving nearby, her head bloodied.

There was another explosion, then another. The ground shuddered. Black smoke billowed. The roof of the shop buckled and crashed.

Elisabetta screamed in sheer terror. She still couldn't hear herself. She struggled to her feet. Grit and debris blanketed her body. Cuts covered her arms and legs. Her purse was gone. She was missing a shoe.

*Boom boom boom!* Bombs exploded throughout the neighborhood. The explosions rocked the ground. Debris flew everywhere. Glass windows blew out of storefronts.

Elisabetta couldn't see through the smoke. Fires broke out on the buildings, flashes of horrifying orange amid wreckage. The air superheated. Black smoke rolled across the rubble, heavy with particulate. Her eyes stung, her nostrils clogged. She coughed, gasping. People staggered like shadows in an inferno.

The explosions kept coming. She ran this way, then that, colliding into terrified people doing the same. Everyone fled screaming. She whirled around, losing any sense of direction. She heard crying and realized it was coming from her. Her knees buckled. She fell to the ground atop the rubble and lost consciousness.

Elisabetta looked up, blinking, trying to gather her senses. Her head pounded. Her entire body ached. She lay backward on broken concrete, facing up. The sky was barely visible through the smoke.

Her brain struggled to function. The American bombers had gone. The attack was over. She had no idea how long she had been lying here. She could hear faint wailing. She tried to move. It hurt, but her legs and arms weren't broken.

She sat up slowly, feeling her face. Warm blood wet her hands. Her arms and legs were gashed. Gray soot covered her clothes and body. She couldn't breathe, her nostrils were full. She snorted black snot. Her mouth tasted gritty and dirty.

She staggered to her feet, looking around in horror. San Lorenzo had been leveled. She could see through to the next street. Fires flared and burned in the rubble and ruins. People and authorities were trying to put out the flames. Shops had been reduced to piles of brick, marble, stone, and twisted metal.

Carnage surrounded her. Severed limbs lay in the street like so much meat. Men, women, and children lay dead among the debris and rubble, bleeding from gruesome wounds. Hospital personnel and authorities ran back and forth with stretchers and black medical bags.

Blood was spattered everywhere. Everyone's clothes were soaked and stained, torn and shredded. Some people were still alive, moaning and crying, writhing in agony from mortal wounds. Among them was the detritus of human life. A spiral-bound notebook. A brown purse. Horn-rimmed eyeglasses. A briefcase.

The woman next to her lay motionless, her gaze fixed heavenward. A little boy lay next to the woman. Blood matted his hair. Tears dried in rivulets in the grime on his face. His lips moved, and Elisabetta realized he was alive.

She staggered to his side, kneeling down. "Are you okay?" she asked, and the little boy's eyes fluttered open, a bloodshot dark brown. His mouth formed words she couldn't hear. He raised his arms weakly, melting her heart, and she scooped him up.

"Mamma," the little boy whispered hoarsely.

"Okay, okay." Elisabetta scanned his little body for injuries. There were cuts all over him. She spotted a jagged shard of glass in his thigh. Blood leaked from the wound, flowing steadily down his leg.

"Help!" Elisabetta called out, hoarse. The medical personnel didn't come. Everyone alive was screaming for help. She started to remove the shard, but stopped herself. Instinctively she knew it should stay in place. It was plugging the vein. She had to stop the bleeding. He could bleed to death.

"Mamma, Mamma, Mamma," the little boy whispered, over and over.

"I'm here," Elisabetta said, frantic. She held the boy in one arm and clawed at her shirt with the other, ripping off her sleeve. She rested the boy on her lap, used both hands to twist the sleeve, and tied it quickly around his thigh, making a tourniquet above the shard of glass.

"Mamma," the little boy whispered, his eyes rolling back in his head. He must have been going into shock.

Elisabetta yelled for help again, but the medical personnel were busy. She remembered the hospital wasn't far. She could get him there. She gathered him in her arms, struggled to her feet, and started making her way. The boy went limp, and his lips kept forming the word Mamma, over and over.

"Help!" Elisabetta called out, stumbling through the rubble. Electrical wires sparked. Wood burned and smoldered around her. Gray smoke obscured the way.

She tripped and almost fell. She held the little boy to her chest. His legs dangled. His feet were bare. Blood dripped from his thigh wound, but less than before. Her tourniquet was working.

She kept going, calling for help. There was no path, no street. She passed mangled bodies amid the debris of buildings, collapsed walls, and crushed cars. Moaning and screaming emanated from piles of rubble, where people had been buried alive. She saw a crowd collecting at the end of the street. It looked as if there were authorities there, too. She headed in that direction and kept going. The crowd was shouting at something she couldn't see. She was almost there.

"Mamma . . ." the little boy whispered, and all of a sudden, his body went limp in her arms.

Elisabetta looked down in fear. His head drooped over her arms, his neck stretched. She kept going, holding him tighter. Tears spilled from her eyes.

"Help, please!" Elisabetta wailed, and heads turned in the back of the crowd. The faces were grimy and bloodied, their expressions dazed and deranged.

"The King is here!" shouted a man.

"What king?" Elisabetta asked, feeling as if she were walking in a nightmare. The little boy sagged in her arms, lifeless.

"The King of Italy! Vittorio Emanuele! The Pope was here an hour ago!"

Elisabetta craned her neck. She caught a glimpse of uniformed Republican guards and Fascists, forming a protective escort for the gray-bearded King Vittorio Emanuele III. It was bizarre, a King amid the hellish scene, resplendent in his uniform with its shiny brass buttons, fancy ribbons, and gold-braided epaulets. His elegant wife was in their gleaming black limousine, and a uniformed aide was giving money to the crowd.

"Keep your money, you bastard!" The crowd threw it back, jeering and spitting. "We want peace!"

"You're no good!" a woman yelled at the King. "Look what you've done to Italy!"

"It's your fault!" Another man hurled rubble at the limousine. "You got my wife and daughter killed! Their blood is on your hands!"

"You betrayed us!" an old woman screamed. "You ruined us!"

"Down with the King! Down with Mussolini!" The crowd began throwing rocks, turning violent.

Elisabetta edged away in fear and grief. She sank to her knees on the hard rubble, holding the boy to her chest. It was all too horrific. War and death. Kings and Popes. Bombs. Nonna. The boy. She couldn't take it anymore. She felt as if she were losing her mind.

Tears streamed down her cheeks. She kissed the boy's sweet face and told him that his mother loved him very much.

And she stayed with him until a nurse came and took them both away.

## CHAPTER SEVENTY-ONE

# Marco
### 25 July 1943

Marco was on the second floor of Palazzo Venezia, standing with a grim crowd of Fascist officers. In the early morning hours, the Grand Council had voted a motion of no confidence in Mussolini, and Il Duce was being escorted to the grand marble staircase. Many said it was the end for Mussolini, and that King Vittorio Emanuele III would be taking command of the armed forces. Italians hoped that the war would be over for Italy. Outside on Piazza Venezia, thousands were celebrating.

Marco watched, reeling, as Mussolini passed him. Il Duce looked haggard in a rumpled blue suit, and there was no trace of the powerful, magnetic man who had shaken his hand that night and run the country for over twenty years. Italy had taken major blows with the Allied invasion of Sicily and the bombing of San Lorenzo. More than two thousand people had been killed and thousands more injured in the bombardment, which had lasted over two hours. The Allies had sent some nine hundred bombers over the railway in San Lorenzo and Littorio, and two air bases at Ciampino. One of the B-17s had reportedly been piloted by American actor Clark Gable.

Marco heard the shouting surge outside, which told him that Mussolini's car had left Palazzo Venezia. The shouting went on and on, no longer the chanted "Duce, Duce, Duce," but hooting, hollering, and incomprehensible cursing. Everyone blamed Mussolini for leading the country into war.

Marco descended the marble stairs, ignoring the officers rushing this way and that. They would attempt an impossibly herculean task, that of righting a national government. It was rumored that the King was about to appoint Marshal Badoglio as the new Prime Minister, but Marco had grown up hearing his father curse Badoglio. Badoglio was a weak career officer responsible for the humiliating defeat at Caporetto, in the Great

War. Badoglio was supposed to negotiate the terms of Italy's surrender, without provoking Nazi retaliation or drawing the anger of the Allies. No one at Palazzo Venezia believed Badoglio could do the job.

Marco put it all behind him, walking slowly down the steps. He wasn't working today. He didn't know about tomorrow. He had been so wrong to believe in Mussolini. He was appalled that he had supported the war, which had caused death, starvation, and destruction. Vast regions of his homeland lay in rubble. Turin, Milan, Bologna, Palermo, Messina, Brescia, Catania, and Naples had been bombed. Half a million Italians were dead.

Marco left Palazzo Venezia, astounded at the jubilant, chaotic, and drunken crowd packing the piazza, ablaze with sun. Men, women, and children danced, waved flags and banners, sang, held up posters of the King, and played trumpets and horns.

He wedged his way between them, exhausted. Confetti fluttered through the air, and wine bottles were hoisted high. Men climbed ladders against the buildings and chiseled off Fascist emblems. Posters of Mussolini were ripped from kiosks. A plaster bust of Il Duce flew from a window and crashed onto the street, to gales of drunken laughter. A truck careened recklessly past, its bed full of cheering men, flying Italian flags and banners of the King.

Marco made his way through the mob. A woman kissed him, and another one gave him a bottle of wine, which he drank thirstily. He finally reached the end of the piazza, hoping to leave the crowd behind him, but more people flooded the streets from every direction. He couldn't share their joy, for they celebrated husbands and sons coming home, but he could only think of those who wouldn't. He didn't know what his fellow Italians had died for. Everyone had believed in the same tragic delusion.

Not Aldo.

Tears flooded his eyes. Marco realized that he would never see Aldo again, never ride with him, never tease him at dinner. He had kept his love for his brother locked inside, with his love for Elisabetta and Sandro, and there was so much love locked away in him, too much, his heart simply didn't have the chambers to hold it and it couldn't be contained anymore.

He hurled his wine bottle at a building, where it shattered into flying glass. A woman laughed raucously, and Marco kept going, making his way through the riotous crowd, staggering more than walking. He reached the Ponte Fabricio, traveled up and then down the footbridge, spotting his father in front of Bar GiroSport, wearing his long apron and organizing an unruly crowd outside the restaurant.

Marco had never been so happy to see his father, which gave him a deep pang of guilt. They had hardly spoken to each other in so long, but he let his legs carry him down the hill, like a car running out of fuel.

"Papa?" Marco called, and his father's head turned instantly, looking at him with an expression that mirrored his own love, anguish, and regret. His father ran to meet him and scooped him up in his strong arms, embracing him as if he were a little boy again, and Marco buried his face in his father's big, warm, sweaty neck, beginning to cry.

"I know, son," his father said quietly. "I know."

CHAPTER SEVENTY-TWO

# Sandro

26 July 1943

Sandro scanned the happy scene in front of the house, and the amazing news had drawn everyone into the street to celebrate. Mussolini was on his way out, and it appeared that Italy would exit the war. Ghetto Jews could see the end of their long, horrible ordeal. The Simone family sat among their neighbors, who were singing, laughing, and hugging each other at tables set up for an impromptu party.

Their street was too narrow to enjoy full sun, but a sliver of brightness was all they needed. There was no food to spare, but they shared. There was no wine or real coffee, but they made do with water and whatever else they had. They had suffered for five years, stripped of their citizenship, professions, jobs, homes, and savings. They had been brought to the brink of starvation, suffering sickness and deprivation. They had been denied justice and all of their rights, but they had persevered to see this glorious day.

"To Italy!" Sandro said, raising his glass of water.

"To Italy!" His father, mother, and Rosa raised their glasses.

Sandro sipped his water. He could only imagine the emotions his sister was feeling. She would be worried about David, as she hadn't had news of him since he had entered the special operations group. Italy might have dropped out of the war, but it raged on for Britain and the Allies against Germany and Japan.

Sandro touched her hand. "Rosa, I know David will be home soon."

"I agree." Rosa smiled back, gamely. "The end is in sight now."

"Yes, it is, darling," their mother said, putting her arm around her.

"It has to be." Their father's eyes danced behind his glasses. "I hope the Race Laws will be repealed, as the first order of business. The Community has already dispatched an emissary to the Badoglio government."

"I would love to go back to school." Sandro brightened, expecting that the Jewish faculty would return to La Sapienza—even if Levi-Civita hadn't lived to see this day.

"I can go back to the hospital," his mother said, delight etched into her weary features.

His father grinned. "I can reestablish my practice."

Sandro leaned forward. "So, Papa, how long will it take to negotiate the Armistice?"

"I don't know for sure. It's a tricky business. Badoglio is in charge, so it will be poorly executed. If he drags his feet, the Allies will teach him a lesson."

Their mother nodded. "Let's hope it comes quickly."

Sandro's thoughts strayed to Marco, back to the day he had been digging sand on the riverbank and had looked up to see Marco, with a Nazi. The sight had horrified him, but he knew his best friend was still in there, somewhere under the Fascist uniform. They would probably never again be close, since Marco suspected that he had been seeing Elisabetta behind his back.

Sandro's heart wrenched at the thought of her. He remembered when she had confessed her love to him, at school. By now, she had probably met another man, maybe even married. Elisabetta would never become his wife, but his heart would always belong to her.

"To a brighter future!" his father said, raising his glass.

### CHAPTER SEVENTY-THREE

# Marco

August 1943

It was almost midnight, but Marco was walking home, exhausted. He had returned to work at Palazzo Venezia, but he was already regretting his decision. The Badoglio government had yet to find its footing and still hadn't signed the Armistice. The feckless Badoglio delayed in choosing between the Germans and the Allies, trying to get Rome declared an "open city," or neutral zone. Both sides were losing patience with Italy. The Germans had withdrawn to the outskirts of Rome, under Field Marshal Kesselring, and the Allies had dropped leaflets on the city, warning that they would resume bombing if Badoglio didn't sign.

Marco walked down the Ponte Fabricio, unable to shake his melancholy. He still didn't know who he was anymore. He didn't know what to believe in. Fascism had been his identity for so long he didn't have another alternative. The Badoglio government wasn't offering any.

He passed a happy family on the bridge, and he wondered if he would ever have a wife and children. He slept with women, but his state of mind grew darker. He still thought of Elisabetta and would walk by her restaurant. He loved her, but he knew that she loved Sandro. Even if she wasn't with Sandro, she was lost to Marco.

He crossed the bridge and spotted his father closing the outside seating area. When he reached the bar, he said, "Papa, I'll get an apron and help you clean up."

"It's done. Get us some wine and meet me inside."

Marco went inside, poured them both a glass of red, and took it to a table near the side entrance. He sat down and sipped his wine, but it didn't improve his mood. His father entered, locked the door, and walked over, sitting down heavily.

"Marco, what's the matter?"

"Palazzo Venezia. The officers and the politicians. Badoglio's an idiot, like you said."

His father took a slug of wine. "So why don't you quit? Work for me."

Marco didn't want to fight. They were only recently getting along better. "Papa, I mean no disrespect, but I don't want to work at the bar for my life. It's your business, not mine."

"Then what do you want to do?"

"If I say I don't know, you'll be disappointed. I know I'm not living up to your expectations. I barely ride anymore, I work for Palazzo Venezia. They changed my title, but it's the same job." *And I can barely read,* Marco thought but didn't say.

"So? You are not your job, son. Life rarely meets our expectations. Do you think I've met mine? Did Mussolini meet ours?" His father shook his head, his face falling. "I made a terrible mistake."

"I made the same mistake."

"But I should've known better. You were taught to follow Mussolini, but I chose to. I ask myself why, over and over. I think I know, now."

"Why?"

"Years ago, the Unification tried to make us into one Italy. But we didn't know what that meant. We had no single national identity." His father met his eye, pained. "Italy had to figure out who she was, and Mussolini told her that she was the greatness that produced Rome. He might have been right, but he lost his way."

Marco felt the words resonate. He had been trying to figure out who he was, too. He had lost his way, like the land he loved.

"Mussolini is a bully, and I'll regret joining his party as long as I live. I had my doubts when he pushed the Race Laws, but I went along. So many people suffered. Poor Massimo."

"How is he?" Marco knew his father still sneaked the Simones food and money.

"He's praying for Badoglio to lift the Race Laws."

"And Sandro, how's he?"

"He's okay." His father paused. "So in my view, we've made mistakes, but we have an opportunity to set it right. You know what I always say, not every battle is worth fighting. But some are. We have one now, for Italy."

"I agree. That's what I tell people at work, but they don't listen."

"They're politicians. You know who's not politicians?"

"Who?"

"The Nazis." His father sipped his wine. "The Nazis aren't going to let Rome go. This city is the prize. The birthplace of Western Civilization. The home of the Vatican. The Eternal City. Kesselring is an Italophile. He wants to own Rome, possess her. He will try to take her, sooner rather than later."

Marco heard an edge in his father's words. "What are you saying?"

"I formed a group, mostly veterans of the Great War. That's where I go at night, when I say I have vendor meetings."

"What do you do?" Marco asked, astonished.

"Acts of sabotage."

Marco's mouth dropped open. "*You're* an anti-Fascist?"

"Yes, in our own cell, a network of partisans. Many other networks are forming. The Fronte Militare Clandestino della Resistenza under Montezemolo. The Comitato di Liberazione Nazionale. There's a power vacuum in Palazzo Venezia. Politicians and officers offer talk. We defend the city."

Marco felt his pulse quicken. "How long has this been going on?"

"Months."

"Does Mamma know?"

"No. Better for her if she doesn't."

"Why didn't you tell me?"

"You weren't ready. Now you are. I could tell by the way you walked down the bridge tonight. I've been watching you walk home since you were young. Remember when I saw you dodge that cat, riding home? That's when I knew you were ready to race. Now I know you're ready to fight. Join me."

Marco realized he had been watching his father, too, always expecting to see him at the foot of the bridge. "I fought for Fascism, now I'll fight for Italy."

"*Bravo.*" His father smiled. "But you have to follow my orders. I'm in command."

"Agreed." Marco raised his glass, and then had a heartbreaking thought. "To Aldo."

His father hoisted a glass. "To our Aldo."

CHAPTER SEVENTY-FOUR

## Marco
### 10 September 1943

Marco stood with his father and the partisans in a basement in Testaccio, a neighborhood south of central Rome. The Nazis were on the march toward the city. News of their imminent invasion had spread overnight. Shamefully, Marshal Badoglio and King Vittorio Emanuele III had fled the capital for Brindisi, out of harm's way. Badoglio hadn't even left behind a battle plan to defend the city. The Italian Army was on its own, with only partisans for support.

"Here, Marco." His father handed him an M91 Carcano carbine long gun. Its heft weighed in Marco's hand, and he felt the gravity of their mission. He had fired rifles in Balilla, but never faced a live enemy.

His father scanned the men with a steady gaze. "Any questions before we go?"

"Beppe, how many volunteers are there?" one of the partisans asked.

"Several thousand, deployed throughout the city."

"How many are with us?"

"Perhaps a thousand."

"Which of our army divisions will we be fighting with?"

"With us in the south are the Piacenza and Granatieri di Sardegna

Divisions. As for the Nazis, we fight regular Wehrmacht and Fallschirm-jäger, the paratroopers. Most of you know their reputation as elite line in-fantry. Our troops outnumber the Nazis significantly."

His father paused, scanned the men for more questions, then continued.

"Gentlemen, I'm not one for talk. Our mission is clear. Hold Porta San Paolo. Prevent the Nazis from passing through the gate into the city. Our infantry will be on the ground with heavy weaponry. We will fire from rooftops and houses. We have a battle plan. We will execute it. This fight could last all day. By its end, we will emerge victorious. We fight for free-dom and our magnificent city. We will hold Rome. *Viva l'Italia! Viva Roma!*"

They all shouted in accord. Marco shouldered his gun, swallowing hard.

The partisans left the house and jogged down the street. It was a lower-middle-class neighborhood, comprised of the meatpacking district and nondescript stucco homes. No sound came from the homes or shops. Their shutters and metal grates remained closed. The residents waited for the battle to begin, as they knew the Nazis would attempt to enter the city here. Invaders had done so since the ancient days of Rome, as far back as the Visigoths.

Marco jogged up the street, looking ahead. The Porta San Paolo, the Gate of Saint Paul, was a massive brick edifice called the Castelletto, as it looked like a medieval castle with a crenellated top over a gatehouse flanked by large turrets. In the center was the arch of the gate, which led to a fork that offered two ways to enter Rome, Via Mamorata to the west and Viale della Piramide Cestia to the east. To the south, the major artery from Porta San Paolo was Via Ostiense, and that was where the Nazis were expected to attack. Next to the Porta San Paolo was the ancient Pyramid of Cestius, which was embedded in the Aurelian wall, part of the earliest fortifications of the city. Its white marble glowed in the early morning light, and its apex impaled the rising sun.

Marco could see the Italian Army taking positions around the Porta San Paolo and the Pyramid. Soldiers grouped in loose formation, checking their equipment. A fleet of Italian tanks and motorized assault vehicles stood in front of the Porta San Paolo, and one tank was stationed under the arch of the gate. Soldiers loaded a row of self-propelled guns, the Obice 100mm Howitzers, held long guns in front of the gate, and set up tripods for machine guns along Via Ostiense.

"Marco, come," his father said, motioning.

Marco followed his father and his father's old buddy Arnaldo, another veteran. The three of them formed a group, and according to his father's plan, the other partisans broke into small units and fanned out among the houses. They began knocking on doors, asking the residents to let them use the windows and rooftops.

"Open the door!" his father said, banging on a weathered door at the southernmost end of the block.

"No!" called a shaky voice from within. "We don't want any trouble!"

"We defend you and your family! Open up! It's your duty as an Italian!"

The door opened, and they were admitted by an old woman, nervous and haggard. Marco's father persuaded her to let them use the house, told her to hide in the cellar, then led the way up to the rooftop, which was flat except for a small shed that contained the stair.

His father gestured. "Arnaldo, you take the south side with me. Marco, you take the north, but stand behind the shed. Use it for cover."

"But, Papa, I thought I would be fighting alongside you."

His father shot him a look. "Do as I say. Don't fire until I give the order."

Marco wanted to protest, but didn't. "When do they arrive?"

"We'll see. War is waiting. Go to your post."

Marco hustled to the shed and took a position at the same time as his father did, on the other side of the building. The Nazis would be coming up Via Ostiense from the south, so his father and Arnaldo were closer to the action. His father was protecting him by putting him in the back. But when the shooting started, Marco knew he'd move forward. He hadn't come this far to hide.

He looked down the sight of his rifle, taking aim down Via Ostiense. He visualized the Nazi troops and their Panzers invading his city. He could scarcely believe he was here. He had sat out the entire war, only to fight after the Armistice had been announced.

*Better late than never,* Marco thought.

The fighting began. The Italian Army and its civilian volunteers seized the upper hand from the beginning, firing on the Nazis as soon as they marched up Via Ostiense. The Italians waged a brave and bloody battle, and smoke and haze filled the air, the noise deafening. Shelling began, and soldiers fell on both sides, lying dead before the Castelletto and the Pyramid.

Marco kept shooting, without hesitation. He ran out of bullets and was resupplied by a runner, though he became frustrated at his position behind the shed. He couldn't tell from his vantage point if his bullets had found their targets. At a break in the action, he raced forward and started shooting from the front of the rooftop, at his father's side.

"Marco, get back!" his father shouted over the gunfire.

"I can take a better shot here!"

"Get back! Follow my orders!"

"You said I could fight! Why won't you let me?"

"Back to your post!"

Marco hurried back to his shed and resumed shooting, resenting his father for treating him like a little boy. He would be more effective if he had a better vantage point, as he was an excellent shot. The battle wore on, but the tide began to turn in favor of the Nazis. The Wehrmacht was relentless, their Panzers lightning fast. The Nazis shot and killed wounded Italians who were lying on the street.

Marco began to fear the battle was lost, but he fought on. His father fired like a machine with Arnaldo at his side.

Suddenly two Nazis burst through the shed door and onto the roof, forward of Marco. They raised their rifles to shoot Marco's father and Arnaldo, but Marco reacted instantly.

*Crack crack!* Marco shot both Nazis before they could fire. They spun horribly around, jerking with the impact of the bullets, then crumpled to the rooftop, bleeding from mortal wounds. Their ambush ended in a blink.

Marco lowered his gun, shaking with adrenaline.

"Marco, get up here!" his father shouted to him.

"Yes, sir!" Marco shouted back.

The fighting continued, and though the Italians fought bravely, they began to lose ground and run out of ammunition. Marco's father received notice that the Italian Army was negotiating a surrender. His father gave the order to retreat, and Marco, his father, and Arnaldo raced from the rooftop in Testaccio and hurried home.

The Italian surrender was signed in the late afternoon, and the army was on its own. The government was in a state of collapse, and Italians hid in their homes. The defeat broke Marco's heart, and his father's.

The Nazis invaded the Eternal City, turning their fury on its citizens and looting stores.

Rome was lost.

CHAPTER SEVENTY-FIVE

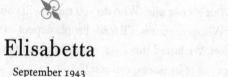

# Elisabetta

September 1943

It was a warm, cloudy morning, and Elisabetta hurried to work. The Germans had invaded and occupied Rome, and last night, drunken Nazis had looted shops and vandalized property, celebrating their triumph. Romans had stayed inside in fear, hiding behind their shutters. German tanks and trucks drove the Lungotevere Sanzio, and random gunfire echoed in the distance.

She hurried past the bakery, where a few women had already begun to form a line. Most stores remained closed today, their windows boarded up to prevent further vandalism. Shattered glass and smashed flowerpots littered the street, and tables in outdoor seating areas had been broken. Her paradise of Trastevere was no longer.

Two Nazis stood at the other end of the street, so Elisabetta turned right to avoid them, taking the long way. They were everywhere, even though Rome had been declared an open city. Nazis were supposed to be confined to the German embassy, the Rome radio station, and the German telephone exchange.

Elisabetta reached Casa Servano and opened the door to find Sofia waiting for her at the bar, wearing her brown dress, but no apron. "*Ciao*, Sofia."

Sofia crossed to her, plainly nervous. "I don't think we should open today. I was terrified coming here."

"We have to open. We can't lose another day. Our budget is too close to the bone."

"But Rinaldo's not coming in. We can't get another cook on such short notice."

"Then I'll cook. Is Michele coming?"

"I doubt it."

"Then we'll bus the tables ourselves. Sofia, you and I can run the place on our own."

"But it's not safe. Who do you think will come?"

"Whoever comes, I'll feed. People expect us to be open. We have a reputation. We lasted this long, when others didn't. I can't survive if this place goes out of business, can you?"

"Yes, I have Paolo's paycheck."

The answer caught Elisabetta up short. "Then we're in different positions. I'm opening today."

"Can't I talk you out of it?"

"Why would you want to?"

Sofia pursed her lips. "You sound like Nonna, answering a question with a question."

Elisabetta didn't reply, disliking Sofia's occasional sarcasm about Nonna. Secretly she would never forgive Sofia for selling Nonna's beloved china.

"*Ascolta*, Elisabetta, I have children. I left them with my neighbor again." Sofia tucked her purse under her arm. "I don't want to work anymore. I'm sorry, I quit."

"For good?" Elisabetta asked, dismayed. "But what about the restaurant? What would Paolo say? It's his family's."

"He'll understand. If you were a mother, you would understand."

Elisabetta felt like a mother to Rico and Gnocchi, but nobody thought that was the same thing except her. "Okay, well . . . thanks."

Sofia frowned, meeting her eye. "Aren't you sick of begging for olive oil from vendors? Of being cheated by the black market for eggs and flour? Of barely having enough gas for cooking, and counting our matches? No salt for weeks? Tea from blackberry leaves and dried orange peel? Why don't you just give up?"

"Is that an option?"

Elisabetta worked all morning to make pasta, *ravioli* only, to be served with fresh *pomodoro* sauce, and Castelli Romani the only wine. The dinner service was big, and the mood celebratory, as the Nazis were gloating over their victory. Wine enhanced their mood, and they sang song after song. She was in the kitchen when she heard Hitler himself broadcasting on the radio, threatening that Italy would pay dearly for betraying Germany and that Nazi retaliatory measures would be "very hard."

Elisabetta grabbed a platter of steaming *ravioli* and hurried out to the dining room. She managed to keep the customers fed, the glasses full, and the tables turned, and after the last customer had left, she locked the door and hustled to the kitchen to clean up. She made quick work of putting away the extra food, careful to save every leftover scrap. As she worked, Sandro was in the back of her mind, and she felt afraid for him. The Nazis were worse than the Fascists, especially when it came to the Jews.

She started to put the bread away, but stopped herself. She grated the bread, collected some tomato pulp, rice, and cheese, then dripped some olive oil in a pan and began frying. In no time, she had made twelve *supplì*, wrapped them in waxed paper, bagged them, then cleaned up and left. She hurried through Trastevere and over the Tiber, and though it was after curfew, restaurateurs were given an informal pass.

She reached the Ghetto, which was deserted. She hurried to Sandro's house, raced up the stairs, and set the *supplì* on his doorstep. She didn't leave a note because he would know it was from her. She hoped it would comfort him. He would know he was loved, even if he didn't love her anymore, and she wanted to give him that feeling, for it was all she had to give.

She hurried away from the Ghetto. Her heart felt happy and full, and that was how she learned that love warms the heart when it is given, regardless of whether it is received.

O nly minutes later, starving rats emerged from the shadows of San-dro's house, their noses twitching. They swarmed the *supplì* and devoured them all, including the bag.

### CHAPTER SEVENTY-SIX

# Marco

13 September 1943

M arco tensed as a Nazi soldier approached the counter at Bar GiroSport. The mere sight of the Wehrmacht uniform triggered a visceral hatred in him. The Armistice had been signed last week, and it made Marco sick to his stomach to see Nazis swarming all over Tiber Island. Only days ago, he had been shooting them from a rooftop, and now he had to take their coffee orders.

"*Kaffe, bitte,*" the Nazi said, reaching the counter.

"*Danke,*" Marco shot back reflexively.

"*Sie sprechen Deutsch?*"

"*Nur ein bisschen,*" Marco answered, meaning a little. He hit a button on the gleaming coffee machine, heating the pressurized water. Confusion had reigned today at Palazzo Venezia, with the bosses reeling from the Nazi occupation. Marco went in to learn information useful to the partisans.

"Here," Marco said, switching to Italian as he passed the coffee to the Nazi.

The Nazi took the coffee without paying.

"You owe me for that."

The Nazi laughed, then turned away.

Anger flamed in Marco's chest. He caught his father's eye as he was walking toward the counter, his expression grim. His father had been listening to a secret radio in the storeroom and he beelined for the counter, then came behind.

"I have news," he said under his breath. "Mussolini has been rescued by the Germans. He was being held in the Gran Sasso."

Marco masked his shock, in case any customers noticed.

"He's setting up a Fascist regime in the north. He's calling it the Salò Republic, after the town of Salò. It's a puppet government, and the Nazis are propping him up."

"He's trying to return to power?"

"Yes." His father picked up a rag, for show. "Badoglio will try to stay in power in the south, in absentia, supported by some army officers."

Marco felt stunned. "So there will be *two* Italian governments, competing with each other?"

"Yes, and the Fascist officers who had voted for Mussolini to remain in power have been released from prison, including Buonacorso. It makes your activities with the partisans more risky."

Marco's mind raced. "But I can learn more than ever before, too. Buonacorso trusts me."

"I know, but I fear for you. I can go on without you. I offer you that choice."

"I'm with you," Marco answered, unhesitating.

His father placed a hand on his shoulder, and Marco warmed to the touch. Neither of them had to say another word. The time for talk had passed. Now was the time for action. The Nazis infested Rome, presenting new targets of opportunity.

Marco was ready.

This time, to do justice.

## CHAPTER SEVENTY-SEVEN

# Sandro

### September 1943

---

Sandro felt intimidated, as he had never been to the offices of the Union of Italian Jewish Communities. At the head of the glistening conference table sat Dante Almansi, the President of the Union, who had formerly served as a Vice Chief of Police under Mussolini. Next to him sat Ugo Foà, who was President of the Jewish Community of Rome, also formerly a Fascist magistrate. Opposite them sat the Chief Rabbi of Rome, Israel Zolli, with his characteristic downturned eyes and round, horn-rimmed glasses. Chief Rabbi Zolli had asked Sandro's father to attend and serve as his legal counsel.

Sandro sat on a carved chair against the wall, which was lined with mahogany bookshelves full of leather-bound volumes in Hebrew and Italian. A glass display case contained an antique silver menorah, ornate candlesticks, and an array of other priceless Judaica. Elegant brocade curtains flanked tall windows, which were open to the balmy afternoon, as the meeting began.

"So." President Almansi smiled politely. "Chief Rabbi Zolli, it's always good to see you, but what is the purpose of this meeting? You called it in great haste, causing some disruption to President Foà and myself."

"My apologies, but these are terrible times for our Community. Exigent times, in fact, and quotidian business cannot hold sway." Chief Rabbi Zolli shifted forward. "Roman Jews are under grave threat since the Nazi occupation. I have studied the matter, and it is my considered opinion that we need to encourage them to evacuate and emigrate. We need to disperse and disband Italian Jewry."

Almansi recoiled, alarmed. "What an extreme suggestion! I don't share your concerns."

"Nor do I," Foà added, with a deep frown. "What are you saying? Run away? We live here! Even so, Chief Rabbi, where would everyone to go? Who has the means to travel or move?"

Sandro could see that neither Almansi nor Foà were going to agree with Chief Rabbi Zolli, who had always been an outsider. Unlike Almansi and Foà, born of storied Italian families, Chief Rabbi Zolli was a naturalized Italian from Eastern Europe, and his demeanor tended to be excitable, unlike the reserved Almansi and Foà. Even Sandro's father disagreed with him.

"I can speak to those concerns," Chief Rabbi Zolli answered, agitated. "I say we close the synagogue and our office, draw down our Community bank account, and use the money to fund the safe escape of our members. We can also prevail upon the Vatican to hide more of us in convents and monasteries. We must act immediately."

Almansi's lips parted in disbelief. "The synagogue, closed? What about services on the High Holy Days?"

"We must cancel them. It's too dangerous to hold them. The Nazis could swoop down on all of us. We're too vulnerable when we collect in one place."

Almansi threw up his hands. "There's no need for such dire and unprecedented actions. You'll spread fear and hysteria. Furthermore, it would be unduly provocative to the Nazis."

Foà chimed in, "Rabbi Zolli, you're panicking without cause."

Chief Rabbi Zolli frowned. "I'm not panicking, I'm reacting. You're doing nothing!"

Almansi lifted a graying eyebrow. "There's nothing that needs doing. We loathe the fact that we are occupied, but that necessitates no call to action. The Nazis have instituted martial law, so order is the rule of the day. We need to stay the course—"

"No, we don't!" Chief Rabbi Zolli shot back. "You're underestimating the threat. Italian Jews are in mortal peril, now that Nazis have taken Rome. I no longer feel safe walking the streets of the Ghetto. Many of my congregation feel the same way. You don't need me to tell you about the deportations elsewhere."

Almansi shook his head. "Rome has always stood on different footing. We will remain that way, due to the presence of the Vatican."

"I have to reiterate, I truly think you are underestimating the threat."

Almansi hesitated. "Chief Rabbi Zolli, if you must know, we have had assurances there will be no trouble, from those in whom we have unshakable confidence, highly placed in government."

Chief Rabbi Zolli scoffed. "Then I am hereby requesting that we destroy the Community's list of Jews resident in Rome. As you may know, there are two lists, one of those who contribute to the Community in the graduated income tax, which includes almost all of the city's Jews. The secondary list is the index cards containing the names, addresses, birthdays, and genealogy of every Jew living in Rome."

"Destroy them? Out of the question." Almansi's hooded eyes flared. "Those are the official records of the Community. They represent the history of our very members."

"Then I'm not asking your permission. No matter your disagreement, I intend to destroy those lists, close the synagogue, and tell my congregation to disperse—"

"No, you may not and you will not." Almansi scowled. "Chief Rabbi, you lack the power over any such things. Your jurisdiction concerns religious questions raised within the Jewish Community of Rome. The actions you propose have nothing to do with religious matters. As such, they lie outside the scope of your authority."

Chief Rabbi Zolli turned to Sandro's father. "Massimo, is that correct?"

"Allow me to check." His father motioned to Sandro, who crossed to him with the heavy briefcase, set it down, and unlatched the top. His father riffled through the files and extracted a sheaf of papers while Sandro returned to his seat.

His father read the papers, then looked up. "Chief Rabbi Zolli, President Almansi and President Foà are correct. They retain authority over governance and administrative matters such as these. You have authority only on religious questions."

"Hmph!" Chief Rabbi Zolli returned his attention to President Almansi and President Foà. "Nevertheless, would you stand on such a legal technicality against me? I am the leader of my congregation. Lawyerly distinctions should not overrule my opinion."

"Again, we disagree." Almansi's mouth set in a firm line. "In times like these, we need to keep a cool head. We need to communicate confidence and self-assurance. We will survive the occupation as we have always survived, as a community."

"But—"

"This meeting is over."


On Saturday morning, Sandro and his father filed into the synagogue amid a throng of male congregants, their heads covered with white *capellini*, or skullcaps, and their shoulders draped with white *tallit*, or prayer shawls. The service was about to begin, and his mother and Rosa climbed the steps to the women's balconies, while Sandro and his father went to their seats on the main floor.

His father greeted his friends, and Sandro looked around the synagogue with new eyes. His gaze took in the white marble columns at the *bimah*, the gold brocade curtain over the ark that held the sacred Torah scrolls, and the ornate brass chandelier, shedding a gentle light. Above them all was the square dome, with its vault painted a rainbow of gorgeous colors, culminating in a glass window to the sky. The beautiful synagogue embodied the peace that Sandro had newly found in Judaism, like a healing salve.

Before they sat down, his father took Sandro aside. "I have bad news. There's a substitute rabbi today."

"Where's Chief Rabbi Zolli?"

"Nobody knows."

"Is he sick?"

"No," his father answered gravely. "He's gone into hiding."

## CHAPTER SEVENTY-EIGHT

# Marco

September 1943

---

Marco, come." Marco's father motioned to him, entering the bar from the side door. The place had just closed, and his father had been meeting with the partisans.

"What's going on?" Marco left the counter and followed him into the storeroom, where they shut the door.

"Look." His father took off his backpack and extracted a cascade of tangled iron, which looked like a bunch of junk. He disentangled a large iron thing from the pile and held it up.

"What's that?"

"A *quattropunto*, a four-pointed nail. It's made of two long iron nails bent in half and soldered together, with a sharpened point on each end."

"What does it do?"

"It pops tires. If you throw it onto a road, one sharp point will always stick up. It always rests on three other points, like a tripod. It's primitive, but effective. It was used by the Roman Army. We used it in the Great War, but I had forgotten about it."

"It's so simple." Marco tested the sharpness of the spike with his finger. It pricked him instantly, drawing a bubble of blood.

"After the battle of Porta San Paolo, one of our fighters, Lindoro Boccanera, was hiding in the military museum there. He noticed an exhibition of artifacts from the Great War, including the *quattropunto*. He proposed we resume its production."

"Where did you get these?"

"From a farrier in Trastevere. He's making them for us."

*Trastevere.* Marco got distracted, thinking of Elisabetta. He would always associate her with the neighborhood, which he now avoided.

"Next, we strike—" His father fell silent when the door opened, then they both looked over.

His mother stood in the threshold, her hair in mild disarray from cleaning the kitchen. Her mood had steadily improved, though Marco sensed she would never be the same. His father had told him that she had realized they were partisans after Porta San Paolo, but she would turn a blind eye. Marco didn't think she looked blind right now.

His father said, "Maria, please close the door."

"Don't tell me what to do in my own house." His mother regarded them with a cold stare. "What's that junk on my floor?"

"*Quattropunti.*"

"Weapons?"

"Yes."

Her dark eyes narrowed. "You planning something new?"

"Yes."

She pursed her lips. "Beppe, if anything happens to Marco, don't come home."

"I understand," his father said matter-of-factly.

"*Ever* again."

"I know."

His mother closed the door without another word.

Marco had to smile. "She doesn't mean that, does she?"

"Yes."

"No, she doesn't."

"You don't know her like I do."

"What would she do if you came home without me? Would she leave you?"

"No, she would kill me." His father chuckled, but Marco couldn't let the joke pass, thinking about his father's infidelity.

"Papa, what happened with you and Elisabetta's mother?"

His father's face fell. "I'm not proud of that."

"How did it happen?"

"It began with Ludovico, Elisabetta's father. She was just a baby then, like you." His father eased onto a stack of boxes, setting the *quattropunte* on the floor. "I met Ludovico when he came to the Piazza San Bartolomeo all'Isola, to paint the Basilica. He was very talented, and I would bring him coffee. Then one day, on his way home, he painted over the party emblem on a wall in Trastevere. He covered it with a perfect painting of the Basilica."

"Oh no."

His father's expression darkened. "You know, in those days, thugs abounded. Carmine Vecchio was one of them."

Marco's ears perked up. "The OVRA officer?"

"Yes. He saw the painting, but didn't know who had done it. He asked me if anyone came to paint the Basilica, but I told him no. That night I warned Ludovico to get out of town. That's when I met Serafina and I . . . fell in love."

Marco felt uncomfortable, as it was hard to hear. "Real love?"

"I wouldn't have strayed for less. But she wasn't who I thought she was. She was selfish. Now, I know better. I know how lucky I am."

"And you and Mamma are happy?"

"Yes. Marriage is hard work, but it's worth it." His father smiled, his relief plain. "Anyway I told Ludovico and Serafina to get out of town, but he came back early and was ambushed. I suspected Carmine and Stefano Pretianni, but I could never prove it. They crushed his hands, so he couldn't paint again. It was cruel, and unjust."

Marco shuddered. So it had been true, what the ginger had told Elisabetta. "Were they punished?"

"No, they were promoted." His father shook his head. "Ludovico spiraled down after that. Couldn't paint, couldn't earn money. He started drinking. I gave him what I could. I couldn't stop thinking about Serafina. That's when it began." His father pursed his lips, but held Marco's gaze. "I'm ashamed to say that I betrayed him, and your mother."

"How did she find out?"

"She followed me one night, with a knife."

"Mamma, a *knife*?" Marco asked, in disbelief.

"Make no mistake about her. She's quite something, your mother. She was protecting her family." His father heaved a sigh that filled his big chest. "I made a terrible mistake. I broke her heart. I'll spend the rest of my life making it up to her."

"How did Elisabetta's father find out? He's the one who told me."

"Ludovico? Serafina probably told him. It wasn't her first affair. I heard she left him for someone else. He probably blamed me for everything, and I accept that. It's in the past."

Marco couldn't agree. "No, it's not."

"Yes, it is."

"If it were, it wouldn't have mattered to you if I saw Elisabetta. You didn't want me to see her because she was Serafina's daughter. That's why you hit me at Aldo's funeral, isn't it? Your past became my present, Papa."

His father cringed. "You're right. I was embarrassed that you knew."

"So you understood me."

"Of course. You could never hide your feelings, from when you were little. I could see hate in your eyes. Disrespect, for me."

Marco felt a rush of love for his father. "Not anymore."

He smiled. "As for Elisabetta, you're better off without her."

Marco couldn't stay silent. "No, Papa, I'm not."

CHAPTER SEVENTY-NINE

# Massimo

26 September 1943

I t was Sunday evening, and Massimo masked his nervousness as he got out of the car with Presidents Almansi and Foà. They had been summoned by Lieutenant Colonel Herbert Kappler, head of the SS in Rome, to a meeting at Villa Wolkonsky, a historic Italian estate in the southeast of the city, which was now serving as the German embassy. Almansi and Foà had asked Massimo to accompany them as counsel, but none of them knew the purpose of the meeting.

Guards escorted them onto the property, and Massimo passed a massive Nazi banner with a black swastika against a field of blood red. Dread filled him, but he reminded himself to remain calm.

The men were escorted along a stone path to the massive villa, which had been the residence of the British Ambassador before the war. The grounds were beautifully landscaped, and Massimo hated to see this Roman jewel in Nazi hands. Set on the Esquiline Hill, Villa Wolkonsky was said to encompass five verdant hectares. Waning sunlight filtered through the fronds of its many palm trees, and the fragrance of lemon and lime trees scented the air. Thirty-odd bays of a Roman aqueduct built by the Emperor Claudius stood in the distance, and Villa Wolkonsky itself lay ahead, a magnificent home with squared wings, classic balustrades, and a porticoed entrance.

They reached the entrance, a grand door flanked by Nazi soldiers, then were escorted into an elegant office dominated by an ornately carved antique desk, with upholstered chairs in front. Massimo felt his heart begin to hammer when Lieutenant Colonel Kappler rose from behind the desk and strode toward them. The Nazi was fearsome in his gray uniform, its black collar embroidered with the runic SS insignia. He looked to be in his forties, with a widow's peak in his light brown hair, framing a wide face with large eyes. He had a straight nose, thin lips set in a strong jaw, and a scar that creased in his left cheek.

"Good evening, gentlemen." Lieutenant Colonel Kappler extended a hand, and Foà shook it with a nod.

"I am President Foà. Good evening."

"Thank you for coming. It's good for us to meet, face-to-face. Please introduce me to your colleagues."

Foà made the introductions, then Kappler shook hands with Almansi and Massimo, who felt a tingle of disgust at the Nazi's touch.

Kappler gestured to the chairs opposite his desk. "Please sit down."

Foà, Almansi, and Massimo did so, and Kappler seated himself behind the desk. A Nazi flag stood behind the desk chair, next to walnut shelves lined with books.

"Gentlemen, I regret any inconvenience this may have caused your schedules."

Foà nodded. "We were pleased to oblige."

"If you would, first provide me some background. How many Jews are there in Rome?"

"About twelve thousand," Foà answered. "There are maybe fifty thousand Jews in Italy, as a whole."

"I thought there were more in Rome." Kappler cocked his head. "Do most of the Jews in the city live in the Ghetto?"

Foà shook his head. "No, many have moved away."

"But the converse is true, is it not? Everyone who lives in the Ghetto is Jewish, correct?"

"Yes."

"So." Kappler's expression darkened quickly, like a sudden storm. "I will come to my point. You may be Italians, but that is of no importance to me or Germany. We consider you Jews, regardless of your nationality. Therefore, you are our enemy. We will treat you as such."

Foà didn't reply, nor did Almansi. Massimo's mouth went dry.

Kappler sniffed. "I called you here to convey a demand. We need gold for new arms. Within thirty-six hours, you will pay us fifty kilograms of gold. If you pay, no harm will come to any of you. If you do not, two hundred Jews will be arrested and deported to Germany, then sent to the Russian frontier or elsewhere."

Foà and Almansi exchanged horrified glances. Massimo hid his terror, refusing to give Kappler the satisfaction. The Nazi had presented his extortionate demand as if it were a mere business transaction, as if gold could be traded for human beings. Fifty kilograms was such an astronomical amount of gold that Massimo doubted that the Ghetto Jews could come close in such a short time, if at all. They had been left impoverished by the Race Laws under Fascism, and conditions had grown even worse under the Nazi occupation. The two hundred people to be deported could include Gemma, Rosa, Sandro, or himself. His neighbors, friends, or clients. His Community. Anyone.

Kappler broke the silence. "Gentlemen, if you have no questions, you may go."

Foà cleared his throat. "I have a question or two. When does the time begin to run on the thirty-six hours?"

"Now."

Foà recoiled, aghast. "Colonel Kappler, it will be impossible to find that much gold in such a short time. Isn't there any way you can extend the deadline?"

"It depends." Kappler leaned back in his chair. "If I perceive that you are proceeding with dispatch, I may be flexible. I may also be able to provide you with cars and light trucks to transport the gold in a secure fashion."

"No, thank you." Foà paused. "Instead of gold, could we pay the equivalent amount in *lire*?"

"No. American dollars or British pounds are fine, but not *lire*. I can print as much of your money as I want."

"In the event that we cannot obtain the gold in time, would the two hundred Jews deported include those converted to Catholicism or the offspring of mixed marriages?"

"I don't make any distinction." Kappler pursed his lips. "All Jews are Germany's enemy. I have already carried out several operations of this type, and it has ended well, so far. Only once did it not. That time, a few hundred Jews paid with their lives."

Foà and Almansi looked stricken, and Massimo struggled to maintain emotional control.

Kappler rose, motioning to the guard. "Gentlemen, this meeting is concluded. I will see you here on Tuesday at noon, with the gold. Until then, goodbye."

Massimo felt shaken to the core as the guard escorted him, Foà, and Almansi back through the gardens. He held his head high, but his knees had gone wobbly. The three men were led to their sedan, and they drove off. Nobody said a word until Villa Wolkonsky had vanished from the rearview mirror.

Foà, who was driving, spoke first. "How will we come up with that much gold? By Tuesday at noon? It's not possible!"

Almansi shook his head. "If evil has a face, it is Kappler's."

"May I suggest a plan?" Massimo spoke up from the back seat, having gathered his wits. "First, we should work through the night, call our few wealthy members, and establish a donation center on the second floor of the synagogue. Second, we should call a meeting of the board for tomorrow morning. Third, we should make an announcement to the Community tomorrow, so everyone can contribute. We'll pull out all the stops."

"I agree," Almansi said, after a moment. "Good organizational thinking, Massimo."

"Yes." Foà glanced at Massimo in the rearview mirror.

Massimo's mind raced. "We should also call Palazzo Venezia and the Vatican, too. They should be pressed to help."

"Agree," Foà and Almansi said, in unison.

Massimo looked out the window. Darkness descended as the car sped toward the Ghetto. The three men fell silent again, each left to his own fears. The task that had befallen them could not be more impossible. They had been charged with protecting innocent men, women, and children. They would try with all of their collective might, will, and heart to succeed.

It was Sunday night.

They had until Tuesday at noon.

The clock was ticking.

# PART FIVE

I loved the Italians too much. Now I hate them.

—Field-Marshal Albert Kesselring

Then one of them took my arm and looked at my number and then both laughed still more strongly. Everyone knows that 174000s are the Italian Jews, the well-known Italian Jews who arrived two months ago, all lawyers, all with degrees, who were more than a hundred and are now only forty; the ones who do not know how to work, and let their bread be stolen, and are slapped from the morning to the evening.

—Primo Levi, *If This Is a Man* (1958)

## CHAPTER EIGHTY

# Sandro

26 September 1943
Sunday Night

Sandro knew something was wrong when he heard hurried footsteps on the stairs. He looked up from his papers, and Rosa placed a finger between the pages of her book. His mother dried her hands on a dishcloth just as his father burst through the door. His sparse hair was flyaway, and his manner panicky.

"Do we have any gold?" he asked, his eyes round with alarm.

"Gold?" his mother answered, bewildered. "Are you crazy?"

"Think, dear. We must have some. What about your jewelry? Your wedding band?"

"It's all gone, you know that. I gave my ring for the war in Ethiopia, and we sold the rest of my jewelry."

"We *must* have some gold somewhere." His father rushed to Rosa. "Don't you have any jewelry left? Something David gave you?"

"No, we sold my wedding band, too. I have nothing of value left. Why?"

"The Community has to come up with fifty kilograms of gold by noon on Tuesday. If we don't, the Nazis will deport two hundred of us."

His mother gasped, horrified. "What are you talking about? That can't be true."

Rosa stood up slowly. "The Nazis want to make a bargain? Fifty kilograms of gold? For *people*?"

"Yes, and there's no time to lose." His father swallowed hard, his Adam's apple going up and down his skinny neck like a lift. "We called Angelo the goldsmith. He says fifty kilograms of gold is about twelve thousand rings."

His mother's hand flew to her face. "Oh no."

Rosa's lips parted in outrage. "This is extortion, plain and simple! How will we *ever* come up with that much gold?"

Sandro said nothing, trying to keep his wits about him. He knew that the Community couldn't produce that much gold in such a short time. Nobody had any money, much less gold. Since the Nazi occupation, conditions had gone from bad to worse. Ghetto Jews foraged daily for food, and some were starving. Tuberculosis was rampant in such close quarters, and his mother delivered babies that were stillborn. Everyone prayed for salvation, counting the days until the U.S. reached Rome, fighting northward from Sicily.

"Massimo, why do they want so much gold? Why now?"

"They need money for their war effort. Gemma, we don't have time to discuss it. We need to look for gold." His father crossed to the cabinet near the beds, which used to hold the family menorah and antique candlesticks.

"But tell me, how did this come about?" his mother asked, following him.

"Kappler summoned Foà, Almansi, and me to Villa Wolkonsky. He told us the demand." His father began searching the cabinet, which held his papers and their clothes.

"Massimo, *you* met *Kappler*?"

Sandro felt a bolt of fear. Kappler was the notoriously brutal head of the Gestapo, which had its headquarters across town on Via Tasso, where people were beaten, tortured, or worse. Everyone said that the screams could be heard throughout the neighborhood.

Rosa stood motionless, her gaze terrified. "Papa, how will they choose the two hundred? And where will they be deported to?"

"I don't know more than I told you. Help me look! There might be an earring, a trinket, a charm, however small." His father rooted through the cabinet, tossing out papers and shirts. Rosa and his mother joined in.

Sandro watched them, knowing the search was futile. He didn't know what to do. He was supposed to be a genius, but he didn't have any answers. He didn't know who among them would be deported. He knew only that Elisabetta would be safe.

"Sandro, help us!" his mother snapped. "Hurry!"

## CHAPTER EIGHTY-ONE

# Sandro

27 September 1943
Monday Morning

───────────

By the next morning, the news of the Nazi demand for gold had spread, and the Ghetto was gripped by panic. President Foà, President Almansi, and Sandro's father had called families all night, asking for contributions. They had also solicited Rome's municipal government, but it had declined. A crowd of families filled the piazza outside the synagogue, waiting for the doors to open and ready to give what little gold they had.

Inside, the synagogue buzzed with activity. Foà and Almansi kept phoning for contributions in their offices, and Sandro and his father set up a collection station in the Sala del Consiglio. They moved the conference table, so the donors would stand on one side, and on the other would be the staff, which included goldsmith Angelo Anticoli and his two assistants, to weigh the gold and verify its quality, and Renzo Levi, a *ragioniere*, an accountant, to keep track of each donation. Sandro's job was to double-check the calculations, and he sat at the end of the table. He arranged his sharpened pencils and paper in front of him, as if for the most important test of his lifetime.

"Let's start the collection," Sandro's father said, with an authority that his son had never seen in him.

The synagogue doors were opened downstairs, and men and women came upstairs and began forming a line to make their contributions. They were Ghetto Jews, since they lived the closest. Fear strained their expressions, their clothes were shabby, and they held their meager treasures in clenched hands, purses, or bags. Some lifted Star of David and other necklaces from their necks, and others unfastened small gold earrings. One older man took a bridge of false teeth from his mouth to offer his gold fillings.

Sandro's heart lifted at each contribution. Everyone around the table watched as each ring, brooch, or necklace was weighed, its quality noted, a receipt written, and the figures double-checked. After a few contributions, someone would ask how much gold had been collected thus far, and Sandro began announcing a running tally.

His father greeted people in the line, and his mother and Rosa arrived to help. Sandro and the others thanked each donor, no matter how small their contribution, and the Community was so close, he knew the families. Ascoli. Sermonetta. Piperno. Piazza. Sonnino. Limentani. Fiorentino. Funaro. Caviglia. Di Tivoli. Del Monte. Sabatello.

Sandro had grown up with them all, and before the Race Laws stripped them of property and livelihood, they had been shopkeepers, tinsmiths, bakers, salesmen, tanners, and peddlers. They had gone to school together, shopped together, and worshipped together. They were his friends and neighbors, and it horrified him to think that two hundred of them might be deported.

The morning wore on, and the initial enthusiasm began to wane. The line thinned to a few donors, then to an old woman with a locket. Simple arithmetic told Sandro that if they collected gold at this rate, it would take them an entire month to accumulate the required weight. He stopped announcing the running tally, as the answers were intensifying their collective anxiety. The Ghetto families had given all they had, but they had far too little.

Sandro exchanged grave looks with his father, who stood with his mother and Rosa. None of them had to say a word, for the terrifying truth was plain to see. They grew deathly quiet. Their expressions fell into tense and drawn lines. The lethal deadline hung over them all.

His father crossed to Sandro and leaned next to his ear. "Chin up, for all of our sakes."

Sandro forced a smile.

"I have to go out, son. I'll return in a few hours."

"Where are you going?"

"I'll tell you later. Keep up the good work, and have faith."

## CHAPTER EIGHTY-TWO

# Massimo

27 September 1943
Monday Afternoon

Massimo reached Vatican City, breathless from the walk, then hurried up the majestic Via della Conciliazione. Crowds filled the massive Saint Peter's Square, and among them he spotted Emedio, who was waiting for him in front of Saint Peter's Basilica. Massimo had telephoned him, told him about Kappler's demand, and asked for help.

Massimo scurried to him, his tie flying, and Emedio hustled forward, his cassock billowing. They met in the middle and embraced, clinging to each other a moment longer, as men do in times of distress.

Massimo released him. "Thank you for seeing me."

"Of course. I'm sorry about your terrible trouble."

"It's horrifying, but we're doing everything we can. Thank you for responding to my call, Emedio." Massimo caught himself. "I'm sorry, should I call you Father Terrizzi here?"

"No, you needn't." Emedio smiled warmly. "Let's go. I know time is of the essence."

"It absolutely is." Massimo checked his watch, and it was already five minutes after two o'clock.

"This way." Emedio gestured to the left of the Basilica, and they fell in step toward the Bernini Colonnade. "I heard that Almansi and Foà have already petitioned our Holy Father for help. I believe they just left."

"What did the Holy Father say? Will the Vatican help?"

"I hope so, but I'm not privy to that information. I'm glad you called me, though. Sometimes a back channel can accomplish what a formal method cannot, especially in Vatican City. Diplomacy is the watchword here."

"That's what I thought." Massimo hurried to keep pace with Emedio, who had long legs. "I would be grateful for anything you can do. Fifty kilograms is an enormous amount of gold."

"Yes, I know. Come this way." Emedio led him under the Bernini Colonnade. "We're going to the Collegium Teutonicum, the German College."

"*Inside* the Vatican?" Massimo had never been within the walls of Vatican City.

"Not technically. The German College is on extraterritorial ground, like the German Cemetery and the Holy Office, where I work."

"Oh." Massimo still thought it was remarkable, and they hurried under an arch flanked by the Swiss guards in battle dress uniforms. "So what's your idea?"

"I'm going to introduce you to Monsignor Hugh O'Flaherty. He's helped a lot of foreign Jews get to convents and monasteries. He's even helped them move into Vatican City."

"Jews live in Vatican City?" Massimo asked, astonished. They hustled past a small cemetery set in a grassy hillock, surrounded by spiky cypresses and graceful palm trees.

"Yes." Emedio nodded. "We have many Jewish refugees living at the College of Cardinals. There are over a thousand rooms in Vatican City, but only two hundred or so are occupied. Monsignor O'Flaherty has also hidden foreign Jews in apartments throughout the city, where they live freely."

"How does he do that?" Massimo hurried to keep pace with Emedio. They were heading for a grand stucco building painted a soft golden hue, rising six or seven stories into the sky. Two levels of vaulted arches marked its entrance, which was at the other side of a beautifully landscaped courtyard.

"Monsignor O'Flaherty's rank at the Vatican is *scrittore*, a writer, but he does whatever he thinks is needed, on his own initiative. Between you and me, I doubt he could operate without the tacit approval of our Holy Father. The monsignor has cultivated a confidential network of *padroni di casa* to help him, some fifty priests and theological students."

"How does the monsignor rent the apartments?"

"Under assumed names, backed by false *documenti*."

Massimo thought it was ingenious. "Where does he get the money?"

"From rich donors who want to help. He knows a lot of people in high society because he's an expert golfer. He even taught Mussolini's son-in-law, Count Ciano, to play at the Rome golf club."

"What about the Nazis? How does he get away with this?"

"It's very dangerous." Emedio frowned with concern. "Kappler himself has targeted the monsignor, but he's dedicated. He even disguises himself for his missions, so we call him the Pimpernel of Vatican City."

Massimo's heart lifted with hope. "He sounds like an amazing man. Do you think he'll help?"

"I can't promise anything, but I believe you can convince him."

"So do I," Massimo said, though he wasn't sure. They reached the entrance to the Collegium Teutonicum, where priests and nuns stood talking in small groups. Standing alone in one archway was a monsignor with round, wire-rimmed glasses under his low-crowned black hat, in a long black robe with red facings. Remarkably, he was built like a world-class athlete, at about 188 centimeters tall.

"That's Monsignor O' Flaherty," Emedio said, pointing.

"He's so tall!"

"So are you, Massimo."

"On the inside, maybe."

"But that's where it counts, isn't it?"

<br>

CHAPTER EIGHTY-THREE

# Sandro

27 September 1943
Monday Afternoon

---

Sandro checked the calculations for a gold necklace contributed by the De Veroli family, then thanked them and handed them the receipt. But there was nobody else in line. There were simply no other contributions.

His mother and Rosa maintained their smiles, but Sandro could tell it was effortful. No one knew where to look, averting their eyes from each other. The staff at the table busied themselves straightening papers or brushing away dust. Angelo coughed, the only interruption of the silence. Gloom burdened the room, as if the very air had acquired a weight measurable on one of the scales.

There was a commotion as new contributors arrived, and Sandro looked up to see that they were Beppe, Maria, and Marco. His throat thickened, and he felt moved that the Terrizzis had come. His gaze connected across the room with Marco's, and he could see pain and sympathy etched into his best friend's expression.

His mother and Rosa embraced the Terrizzis. "Maria, Beppe, thank you," Rosa said, wiping her eyes under her glasses.

Maria hugged Rosa. "We'll do anything we can to help."

Beppe's rugged face softened. "We're deeply sorry, Gemma. It's outrageous that this should happen in Rome."

Sandro hadn't realized until this moment how much he had missed his best friend. Seeing Marco again brought back memories of a better, sweeter time, of a past they shared, riding bicycles, horsing around in the street, and walking through Rome together, from when they were little boys.

His mother showed the Terrizzis to the table. "Look who's here, Sandro," she said, composing herself.

"Marco—" Sandro started to say, but words fell short. He rose, came around the table, and embraced his old friend.

"I've missed you, brother. I'm sorry this is happening, too. I'm sorry for what I said that night."

"Thank you." Sandro released Marco, touched. "And about Elisabetta, I want you to know, I never—"

"None of that matters now," Marco interrupted him gently, his gaze glistening as he squeezed Sandro's arms. "We're best friends, you and me. We said it once, but I forgot our bond. I stand with you. We stand together."

Sandro blinked. He felt the same way, and he could discern a new maturity in his old friend. "Thank you."

"Here, take this." Marco reached around his neck and took off a gold chain with a small crucifix, which Sandro had seen on his neck since boy-hood.

Maria reached for her gold necklaces, one with a filigreed crucifix and the other with a *corno*. "Take mine, too."

Beppe handed over a thick envelope, then took off his necklace, with a crucifix and a gold saint's medal. "I'm hoping the money will come in handy if you need to buy additional gold."

Sandro accepted the envelope and the necklaces. "Thank you, all of you."

CHAPTER EIGHTY-FOUR

❧

# Marco

27 September 1943
Monday Afternoon

———————

Marco left the synagogue with his parents, threading through the families filling the piazza, clustering in distraught groups, talking and holding each other. His heart went out to them, and he felt a deep wave of shame for having ever worn a Fascist uniform. He would never forgive himself for the harm and damage he had done.

Suddenly a black limousine pulled up on the piazza, being driven by a chauffeur, an unprecedented sight in the Ghetto. Heads turned as the limousine parked, and Marco and his parents looked over to see none other than Massimo emerging from its back seat, his face a mask of urgency.

Massimo closed the limousine door, hastily greeted a few families, then caught sight of the Terrizzis. He rushed over, throwing open his arms. "Beppe, Maria, Marco! You're here?"

"Of course." Marco's father embraced Massimo. "We came as soon as we heard. We saw Sandro and made a contribution."

"Thank you, I love you all. Emedio helped us, too. Look what I have."

Massimo put his hand in his pocket and extracted a pile of gold necklaces, which dripped between his fingers. "These are from friends of Monsignor O'Flaherty. One even had her driver take me home."

"*Bravo*, Massimo!" his father and mother said, delighted.

Marco eyed the jewelry, fearing that it wouldn't make much difference toward the colossal amount that the Nazis had demanded.

"I have to go." Massimo returned the jewelry to his pocket, glancing at his watch.

"Good luck," Marco said, managing a smile.

CHAPTER EIGHTY-FIVE

# Elisabetta

27 September 1943
Monday Night

Casa Servano had a full house for dinner, and Elisabetta had been busy in the kitchen from the moment she'd gotten in this morning. Her one-pasta menu had become routine, and food shortages had grown worse since the Nazi occupation. Tonight they were serving *spaghetti alle vongole*, spaghetti with clam sauce, and she had made the pasta, cleaned the clams, and chopped fresh garlic, oregano, and parsley.

The kitchen filled with steam, and Elisabetta wiped her brow, standing behind the dented cauldrons of boiling water, one to cook pasta and the other to steam clams. On a third burner was a heavy saucepan for clam sauce, the heat low enough to warm the olive oil but not high enough to brown the garlic. Timing was everything, and Nonna always said *spaghetti alle vongole* was a dish that only the best cooks got right.

The new waitress, Antonia, hustled into the kitchen and emptied her tray. She was eighteen years old, with a sweet, wide face, dark eyes, and curly black hair that she wore in a braid. She was new to Rome, a refugee with hands calloused from harvesting wheat.

"Elisabetta, I need two servings." Antonia crossed to the stove. "I just seated table seven. It's that fancy German baron. You know, the regular."

"Baron von Weizsäcker." Elisabetta tossed two handfuls of pasta into the boiling water, scooped handfuls of clams into the steamer, and cranked up the heat on the olive oil, throwing in fresh garlic.

"Right. He's here with another Nazi. You'll never guess what I heard him say."

"What?" Elisabetta asked idly, stirring the pasta with a wooden spoon. She could tell from the smell of the hot water it had the right amount of salt, not too much.

"The Nazis are blackmailing the Jews. If the Ghetto doesn't give them fifty kilograms of gold by tomorrow, they'll deport two hundred of them."

Elisabetta looked up, horrified. Her first thought was of Sandro. "That can't be. Are you sure you understood them? How good is your German?"

"I heard about it before, too. I thought it was a rumor."

Elisabetta hadn't heard a thing, having been inside all day. "Give me your tray. I'll serve them myself."

"Why?"

"We'll see." Elisabetta accepted the tray, and when the pasta was ready, took it from the boiling water, strained it, and plated it. She scooped the clams onto the pasta, drizzled hot olive oil with garlic over the servings, then tossed each dish and topped them with fresh parsley. She set the plates on the tray and hustled from the kitchen.

Baron von Weizsäcker sat at a table with a Nazi officer, in uniform. Weizsäcker had on a suit instead of his uniform, as was his habit, though he always wore his Nazi lapel pin.

Elisabetta beelined for his table. "Good evening, Baron von Weizsäcker. How nice to see you. We're serving one of your favorite dishes tonight."

"I heard, Elisabetta! The *alle vongole.*" Weizsäcker smiled, with nice, even teeth. An Italophile, he had the bearing of a cultured aristocrat, with thinning blondish-gray hair, hooded eyes set close together, a patrician nose, and refined lips.

Elisabetta placed his meal in front of him. *"Buon appetito,* Baron."

*"Grazie.* The presentation is wonderful. The parsley looks so fresh."

"Thank you. I grow our herbs in my garden."

"Of course you do. Every detail is perfect." Weizsäcker gestured to his tablemate, a beefy Nazi with a lengthwise scar on his left cheek. "Elisabetta, this is Colonel Kappler."

"Pleased to meet you, Colonel Kappler." Elisabetta shuddered inwardly. Kappler was the feared head of the Gestapo, and if he was around, the rumor about the Ghetto could likely be true.

"Nice to meet you." Colonel Kappler nodded stiffly.

Weizsäcker interjected, "Elisabetta, I've been telling Colonel Kappler that Casa Servano serves the finest food in Rome. Nonna made the best pasta I've ever tasted, and you're a very worthy protégée."

"Thank you. *Buon appetito,* Colonel Kappler." Elisabetta reached over the table with the steaming plate, then pretended to trip. The plate flew into the air, flipped over, and landed upside down on Kappler's lap.

"Och!" Kappler jumped up, grimacing. Hot oil stained his crotch, as if he had urinated on himself, which Elisabetta couldn't have planned if she tried. He brushed *spaghetti* from his pants, and clamshells clattered to the floor.

"Oh no!" Weizsäcker recoiled. The other diners craned their necks, and a nervous murmur rippled through the restaurant.

Elisabetta faked a gasp. "Colonel Kappler, I'm so sorry! How clumsy of me!"

"Elisabetta, get a rag!" Weizsäcker snapped.

"Yes, sir!" Elisabetta escaped to the kitchen.



After closing the restaurant, Elisabetta hurried to the Ghetto, where she found the piazza in front of the synagogue packed with distraught families hugging each other and talking in groups. Men hustled to and from the synagogue, which was open. Light streamed through its tall windows of stained glass, glowing orange, yellow, green, and blue against the night sky.

Elisabetta scanned the crowd for Sandro, but didn't see him. She spotted a young couple in worn brown coats and crossed to them. "Excuse me," she said. "May I ask, do you know what's going on? I've heard a terrible rumor that the Jews have to raise gold to give to the Nazis."

"Yes, it's true," the wife answered, her forehead knit with fear.

"It's a nightmare." The husband shook his head, his mouth downturned in a thick beard. "Every family is contributing, but few have valuables or money anymore."

"I'd like to help." Elisabetta took from her purse an envelope containing the earnings of the day. "I don't have gold, but I have money."

"How kind of you. You can bring your contribution to the second floor of the synagogue. Ask for a lawyer named Massimo Simone."

Elisabetta hid her reaction. If Sandro's father was there, then Sandro would be, too. She would have loved to see him, but she doubted that he wanted to see her. He hadn't contacted her after she had left him the *supplì*.

She handed the man her envelope. "Will you take it in for me, instead?"

"If you wish." The husband accepted the envelope. "What's your name? I'll tell them you contributed."

"No, thank you." Elisabetta turned away, hurrying from the Ghetto.

**CHAPTER EIGHTY-SIX**

# Sandro

28 September 1943
Tuesday Morning

The deadline was only hours away, and Sandro, his family, Presidents Foà and Almansi, Angelo, Anticoli, and his assistants, the accountant Renzo Levi, and the secretary Rosina Sorani were in the Sala di Consiglio, exhausted. They had been collecting gold in dribs and drabs for hours on end. Their hopes had soared and plummeted, but they had made more phone calls, knocked on more doors, and tracked down every member of the Community for contributions. They had even bought fifteen kilograms of gold with cash they had collected.

Now they stood around the table, waiting to see if they had reached their goal. Angelo placed a single earring on the brass scale. The fulcrum squeaked just the slightest. They all held their breath.

Angelo straightened, grinning. "We did it!"

Everyone cheered. Sandro hugged his father. The women burst into tears, clinging together. Almansi and Foà shook hands, beaming with joy. Angelo, his assistants, and Renzo clapped each other on the backs.

Against all odds, they had succeeded, and faster than anyone had expected. The gold filled ten boxes on the table, five kilograms in each. They even had enough money left over to put 2,021,540 *lire* in the Community's safe, in the synagogue. Last night, the Vatican had offered to loan them any shortfall, but the Community had hoped to rely only on themselves.

"Son." Sandro's father released him, his eyes glistening behind his glasses. "Well done."

"You, too, Papa."

Foà cleared his throat. "I thank all of you for your herculean efforts. We did this together. It is a tribute to the love, strength, and power of our Community."

Almansi nodded. "I will call the Vatican and thank the Pope, but I am extremely proud that we did not fall short. That said, we still have time, so I would delay before we announce our wonderful news to the Community. As much as I want to relieve their suffering, I think we should keep up the collections, to be on the safe side. I also think we should call Colonel Kappler and ask for an extension. I don't want him to think we met his deadline too easily."

"Very wise." Foà turned to Sandro's father. "Massimo, do you agree?"

"Yes, on all points. If we tell the Nazis we met their demand, they'll just ask for more and put us back where we started." His father turned to Sandro. "Son, what do you think?"

"I agree," Sandro answered, pleased to be asked.

The Nazis ended up extending the deadline, and when it was time, Foà, Almansi, and Massimo traveled to Villa Wolkonsky with the gold. For some reason, Kappler wasn't there, and they were redirected to his office at Via Tasso, an unwelcome turn of events. At first the Nazis claimed the gold was of insufficient weight, but after protest, they reweighed the amount and had to relent.

The Jews of Rome were saved.

## CHAPTER EIGHTY-SEVEN

# Marco

### 29 September 1943

It was just before dawn, and the vast sky in the countryside was a warm golden orange at the horizon, cooling to sheer blue as it thinned to atmosphere. The moon was only the slimmest of crescents, barely a curved white line, like the obverse image of a shadow. Marco, his father, and the partisans had just assumed their firing positions, propped up on their elbows and lying belly-down along the deserted dirt road with a steep hill. They were waiting to ambush a Nazi convoy, due to pass in half an hour.

Marco looked down the sight of his long gun, which he aimed at the crest of the hill. His father had learned of the convoy late last night, so the partisans had mobilized quickly. They lay hidden by a hillock that bordered the road, and behind them was an abandoned lemon grove. Rotting lemons soured the air. Bees droned around Marco's head.

His father looked over, next to him. "Marco, when it starts, keep your head down."

"Who are you more afraid of, the Nazis or Mamma?"

"Do you have to ask?" His father smiled.

Marco felt closer to his father than ever. "Papa, you be safe, too."

"I survived Caporetto, I can survive anything."

Marco was surprised, as his father never said the word Caporetto out loud.

"Get ready." His father took aim. "They're coming."

"How do you know?"

"I feel the vibration within my chest."

Marco fell silent and felt the telltale vibration. Not long after, the mechanical rumble of heavy engines came from the far side of the hill, a steep grade. The convoy was said to consist of three covered trucks carrying supplies, escorted by two VW Kubelwagens, one in front and one behind. The gears ground as the trucks labored up the incline on the far side.

Marco tensed, readjusting his aim. The engine sound intensified, and he waited for the order to fire. It would come from his father. The battle plan was for the partisans to hold fire until the entire convoy was on the downward slope of the hill.

Marco looked down the barrel and reminded himself to be patient.

In the next moment, a Kubelwagen crested the hill.

Marco swallowed hard, keeping his head low. There were four Nazi soldiers in the Kubelwagen. It descended the hill, picking up speed.

Marco felt his heart hammer. A truck crested the hill with two Nazi soldiers in the cab. It followed the Kubelwagen closely. The second truck crested the hill, then the third.

Marco's mouth went dry. Another Kubelwagen containing Nazi soldiers crested the hill. The entire convoy was moving fast on the long downward slope.

All of a sudden the partisans near the bottom of the hill threw a slew of *quattropunti* onto the road. The Nazi vehicles had too much momentum to stop. The first Kubelwagen hit the *quattropunti*. Its tires popped and began to deflate.

"Fire!" shouted his father. Marco and the partisans started shooting. The Nazis in the Kubelwagen were caught unawares, shot as they reached for their weapons.

The first truck crashed into the Kubelwagen, too heavy to stop. The second truck joined the pile-up. The third truck tried to drive off the road.

Hillocks blocked them on both sides. The driver of the second Kubelwagen tried to veer out of the way. Momentum carried him downward into the pile-up.

The partisans rained bullets on the convoy. Smoke filled the air. Nazis returned fire but fell under the barrage.

Marco and the partisans kept firing. The Nazis jumped from the trucks only to be cut down. In time, no Nazis were firing back.

"Cease fire!" his father shouted, signaling. Marco and the partisans stopped shooting. One of the partisans had gotten hit in the hand, but they hadn't lost a single man.

The battle was over. Marco felt adrenaline ebb from his body, leaving him shaking. He eased to the ground and set down his gun. He scanned the carnage. The *quattropunti* had done their job. The partisans had won.

His father sat down beside him, putting an arm around him. Neither said a word. The partisans ran down to the road, climbing into the covered trucks to see what supplies they held.

Nazis lay dead and dying, their bodies in horrifying positions. Their sightless eyes stared at the sky. Their Wehrmacht uniforms had gone black with blood. Smoke wafted above the carnage, and the odor of cordite overpowered the citrus smell.

Marco couldn't tear his eyes from the gruesome scene. This battle was different from Porta San Paolo. Here, he was close to the soldiers he had killed. He could see their faces, and they were young men like him. Not long ago, they had been his allies. His friends. Rolf.

Marco felt despair, despite the victory. He had believed in Fascism, and they had believed in Nazism. Yet he was alive, and they were dead. There was no difference between him and them. They were all young men who believed in the wrong thing.

Marco prayed this was the last war, but he knew it wouldn't be. Men were fallible, and they would always believe in the wrong things. He sensed that he had just learned something that his father had already known, but neither of them spoke.

The sun began to rise, sending golden rays between the cypresses and lemon trees. Father and son turned instinctively to watch the sunrise.

Marco kept his eyes on the sun until they hurt.

## CHAPTER EIGHTY-EIGHT

# Elisabetta

### 29 September 1943

Elisabetta hurried to work. She hadn't slept for worrying about Sandro. The newspapers contained no news of the Nazi demand for gold, nor did the radio offer anything. She had already asked two men on the street if they knew whether the Ghetto had come up with the gold. Neither had any idea what she was talking about.

She spotted a little old man walking, wearing a dark suit and a *capellino*, a skullcap. She caught up with him, touching his elbow. "Excuse me, sir, may I ask you question?"

"Of course, young lady."

"Do you know if the Ghetto was able to come up with the gold?"

"Yes," he answered, a smile creasing his lined face. "We did."

"Thank God!" Elisabetta threw her arms around him.

He didn't seem to mind.

## CHAPTER EIGHTY-NINE

# Sandro

### 29 September 1943

Tonight was the eve of Rosh Hashanah, and Sandro and his father were in the synagogue early in the morning, putting the Sala di Consiglio back in order with the secretary, Rosina. Sandro felt happy and proud that the Ghetto Jews had survived their ordeal. He had never admired his father more, having seen him rise to the challenge.

Suddenly the grinding of heavy engines came from the piazza. Sandro exchanged glances with his father, and Rosina's eyes flared in alarm. The three of them hurried to the window and looked outside in horror.

Panzer tanks with long tank guns were driving to the very doors of the synagogue. Behind them were Kubelwagens full of Nazis and two large covered trucks.

Rosina emitted a frightened cry.

"Oh no!" Sandro felt a bolt of terror.

"What are they *doing*?" his father asked, clutching the windowsill.

They watched as Nazis in Wehrmacht uniforms jumped out of the vehicles, unloaded sawhorses from the truck, and cordoned off the piazza. A black sedan with Nazi flags pulled up, and a Gestapo captain emerged from its back seat, with a plainly nervous President Foà. Families in the piazza began to gather behind the cordon.

"Let's go." His father led the way, and they hurried downstairs, reached the ground floor, and met Foà and the Gestapo officer as they entered the synagogue.

Foà gestured to the Nazi, tense. "This is Captain Mayer of the SS. Captain Mayer, allow me to introduce—"

"I have no time for chitchat," Mayer interrupted him, unsmiling. "We need to search the synagogue for radio equipment. We believe that you Jews have been in secret contact with the Badoglio government."

Foà added, "Captain Mayer's men searched my house this morning, looking for such evidence. Of course, he found none. I assured him that none of us has any such contacts."

"Of course not." Sandro's father turned to Mayer. "There is no reason to search the synagogue. This is a place of worship. There is no radio equipment here or anything of the sort. This is outrageous."

Sandro bit his tongue, frightened for his father. Nazi soldiers armed with submachine guns were already pouring through the door, positioning themselves behind Mayer in a show of lethal force.

"Stand aside," Mayer said to them, then barked an order in German. The Nazi soldiers aimed their guns at Sandro, his father, and Rosina.

His father straightened. "Captain Mayer, you need not threaten us in this way. I merely sought to explain—"

"Move aside!"

They did so, and Mayer issued another order, causing the Nazi soldiers to lower their weapons. On the next command, the Nazis flooded the sanctuary, jogged down the aisles in their black boots, and rifled through the carved wooden seats. There were locked wooden boxes at each seat that contained prayer books, and they smashed the lids with the butts of their guns.

Sandro and the others watched, terrified and aghast. One cadre of Nazis hustled to the alms boxes, also locked, and broke them open the same way. Yet another cadre hurried to the front of the synagogue, climbed the steps to the *bimah*, and headed for the ark, which held the sacred Torah scrolls and other holy books, behind a brocade curtain.

Sandro clutched his father's arm, and they stood in stunned disbelief as the Nazis yanked the curtain aside, exposing the holy books. They picked up two scrolls and threw them on the floor, a profanity.

Sandro's father gasped. "Captain Mayer, that's vandalism! Those soldiers are in a sacred area, where only rabbis are permitted. There is no radio equipment!"

Foà's eyes rounded with alarm. "Captain Mayer, you can't do this! This is a violation of Jewish law, and I cannot sanction—"

"Silence!" Mayer shouted. "I have orders to search the synagogue from top to bottom. You lost the war and are now under martial law. Quiet or I'll have you taken to Via Tasso."

Sandro's heart hammered in his chest, and he looked over, horrified to see Nazis swarming the stairwell, running upstairs and down.

"Now, we go upstairs, everyone!" Mayer gestured to the stairwell, and Sandro and the others followed him and ascended to the second floor, only to be greeted by an appalling sight.

Nazis were ransacking the bookshelves in the conference room, tossing books and papers onto the floor. One side of the room held locked file cabinets, and Nazis broke them open and rifled through the contents.

Other Nazis arrived with cardboard boxes and started packing the papers and files.

Sandro's father frowned. "Captain Mayer, those are records of the Community. Why are they being confiscated? You said you wanted only to search."

"We can search more effectively off the premises." Mayer pointed at the bookshelf against the far wall. "Foà, what are those bound volumes?"

Foà hesitated. "The minutes of our meetings of the Jewish Council and financial ledgers."

Mayer gave orders in rapid German, and Nazis tore the volumes and financial ledgers from the shelves and loaded them into boxes. "Foà, what are those index cards?"

Foà's lined face fell. "The names, addresses, and genealogy information of our members."

Mayer gave more orders, and Nazis began boxing the index cards. "Foà, I know the Community has a safe. Where is it?"

Foà sighed in resignation. "In my office."

"Show me. Signora, remain here, please. The others, come with me."

Foà crossed to his office and opened the door, followed by Sandro and his father. The room contained a desk covered with papers, a wooden cabinet, and a bookshelf filled with books, photographs, and a menorah of engraved silver. Sandro had never been in the office before.

Foà opened the cabinet door, revealing a black safe. "Here."

"Open it."

"The key's in my desk." Foà pulled out his desk drawer, produced a small gold key, then unlocked the safe.

Mayer looked inside. "How much money is that?"

"About two million *lire*."

"Leave. I must use the telephone." Mayer motioned them out and closed the door, while they waited in coerced silence. Sandro exchanged looks with his father, who looked angrier than he had ever seen him. Around them, Nazis ransacked cabinets and confiscated files, papers, and index cards. Sandro strained to eavesdrop on Mayer's phone call, but couldn't make out the German words.

After a few minutes, Mayer opened the door and gestured to the safe. "Foà, I have new orders from Colonel Kappler to seize that money. Get a small box and pack it up for me."

"But it's ours." Foà's lips parted in dismay. "We collected it in response to his demand for gold."

Sandro's father interjected, "Captain Mayer, you have no legal basis for taking Community property. You called it a seizure, but it's common robbery, a criminal act."

Mayer glared at him. "Such defiance! I'll report you to Colonel Kappler, Simone."

Sandro cringed, terrified for his father. "Captain Mayer," he blurted out, "my father is a lawyer and he's only trying to protect the Community."

"Captain Mayer, please, I'll comply." Foà quickly picked up a box of correspondence from his desk, but Mayer grabbed it from him and dumped the letters on the rug.

"Get out, we'll do it!" Mayer motioned them out again, and they stood aside as he barked orders to his soldiers, who fetched more boxes and began emptying the contents of Foà's office.

As the morning wore on, Captain Mayer and the Nazi soldiers loaded the Community's papers, files, minutes books, financial ledgers, and other property onto the covered trucks in the piazza. Sandro, his father, Foà, Rosina, and families on the piazza, among them Sandro's mother and Rosa, watched in horrified silence.

It struck him that tonight was Rosh Hashanah, and the Jewish New Year 5704. He had hoped things would be better.

Now, he feared they would be worse.

Later, Sandro huddled with his parents and Rosa around the kitchen table, having finished a meager lunch of *spaghetti* with diluted *pomodoro* sauce. Sandro felt disturbed after seeing the Nazis vandalize his synagogue, a sacred house of worship. He hated that there was nothing anyone could do to stop the Nazis, in any way. If the Fascists had ruined the Ghetto Jews, the Nazis intended to destroy them.

Rosa shook her head. "I have to say, after seeing those tanks, I'm frightened for our lives, truly. We should go into hiding. We know people who can help us, like Emedio and Monsignor O'Flaherty."

"You think so?" Sandro asked, uncertain.

"Yes, absolutely. Others have, even Chief Rabbi Zolli. Why don't we? This could be our last chance."

"Well." Sandro's father sighed, his expression gravely troubled. "I admit, what I saw today opened my eyes. The Nazis . . . *enjoyed* vandalizing the synagogue. That excuse about the radio was a pretext to terrorize us and steal from us. Greed fueled them, but so did hatred. I always thought that we'd be safe in Rome, but I never anticipated that the Nazis would occupy us. I'm sorry, I should have." His father glanced at his mother, then back at Sandro and Rosa. "You two should know that your mother and I have been talking. We think it would be prudent for both of you to go into hiding."

"What?" Rosa recoiled. "What about you and Mamma?"

"We're staying here. We place our faith in God."

Sandro shook his head. "We won't go without you."

His mother touched Sandro's hand. "You can, and you must. I can't go, and your father feels the same way. But we don't want to take further risks with you two."

Rosa touched her hand. "Mamma, you'll both be trapped here."

"We're not trapped here, we're needed here. I'm the only obstetrician in the Ghetto, and you know that many of my deliveries are complicated these days, by malnutrition and illness. I have a patient who will go into labor any day now, Cecilia from around the corner. It's her first child, and she's been sick with pneumonia. I can't abandon her."

Rosa frowned. "But after her? Can't you go then?"

"No, there will be Regina, and Clara. They're both in their ninth month. There are simply too many women here who need me."

Sandro turned to his father. "Papa, you, too?"

"I'll stay with your mother." His father managed a smile, rallying. "I can't turn my back when everyone is most in need. So many Jews in the Ghetto lack our advantages. They couldn't go into hiding, even if they wanted to. They look up to me now. I'll stay to help Foà and the others—"

"Then we'll stay, too," Rosa interrupted him, sounding as determined to stay as she had been to go.

Sandro understood her change of heart. "Yes, we all stay."

His father's gaze met his own. "Son, are you sure?"

"Yes." Sandro hadn't known that he felt this way until this very moment. "We're Ghetto Jews. This is where we belong, with our Community."

His father held out his hand, palm up. "Then let us pray."

## CHAPTER NINETY

# Sandro

### 30 September 1943

Sandro, his father, and President Foà stood in the sanctuary while carpenters fixed the lockboxes, seamstresses repaired the curtain, and cleaners mopped the floor. The Nazis had done significant damage, and Sandro had spent the morning trying to find whatever ledgers still existed, then figuring out how the Community would pay for the restoration, given that the Nazis had also stolen their money.

Sandro startled at the sudden sound of cars, driving up to the synagogue on the piazza. He, his father, and Foà turned to the open doors, and the workers stopped abruptly. Everyone stiffened to see Nazis pulling up in a line of Kubelwagens.

Foà shook his head. "What do they want now?"

Sandro's father answered, "My guess is, anything of value. The libraries, the *argenterie*."

Sandro turned to his father. "Can't we stop them, Papa?"

"We can try." His father led the way, and they hurried down the aisle, meeting two Nazi captains entering the synagogue, ahead of armed soldiers. The captains were both bespectacled, reedy, and unarmed, and though they wore Wehrmacht uniforms, they didn't appear to be fighting men. Sandro detected in them a scholarly air, like the professors he had met at La Sapienza.

His father met them, but did not extend a hand. "Gentlemen, I am Massimo Simone, and this is President Foà and my son, Sandro. What is the reason for your visit today?"

The taller Nazi captain pursed thin lips. "We're from the ERR, the Einsatzstab Reichsleiter Rosenberg, a Wehrmacht division responsible for cultural artifacts and rare books. We are Orientalists, and I myself am a professor of Hebrew language studies at the Hohe Schule in Berlin. We understand you have two very important libraries here, the Biblioteca della Comunità and the Biblioteca del Collegio Rabbinico Italiano. We wish to browse the collections."

"For what reason?"

"For our academic interest."

His father shook his head. "That's not possible. The libraries are private and secure—"

"Show us the libraries." The Nazi captain gestured to the soldiers behind him. "Force is possible, should you refuse."

"If you insist," Sandro's father said pointedly.

Foà added, "You must follow proper procedures in handling these artifacts."

The Nazi captain sniffed as if insulted. "We are familiar with procedures for handling such items. We brought cloth gloves."

Foà, Massimo, and Sandro led the Nazi captains and soldiers upstairs two flights, and they reached the third floor, where Sandro had never been before, as it was off-limits. The stairwell emptied into a small conference room containing a round mahogany table and chairs. Beyond that was a large room with a wall that had glass on its upper half, so that Sandro could see inside. It was more akin to a rare book room than a library, lined with full bookshelves and document cabinets, with greenish shades over the windows to filter out sunlight.

Foà headed to the library. "As I say, you must be careful handling—"

"Let me confirm the salient facts," the taller Nazi interrupted, as they walked. "In terms of value, it is our understanding that the Biblioteca della Comunità is one of the most important collections in Europe. It is said to contain rare texts, illustrated scrolls and manuscripts from the days of the Caesars, and original drawings from the earliest Popes. Is that true?"

"Yes," Foà admitted reluctantly, as they reached the library.

"Is it also true that, taken together, the collections represent artifacts and history of early Judaism and early Christianity?"

"Yes." Foà sighed, taking a keyring from his pocket.

"Where are the catalogs of these treasures?"

Foà pointed through the glass. "On the bookshelf at the left, though we haven't catalogued everything yet."

"We'll be confiscating the catalogs."

"What?" Foà recoiled.

Sandro's father interjected, "But you said you wished only to browse. You may not confiscate any of the collection."

"The catalogs are not part of the collection per se. They are essentially indices made by you. We wish to enter the library now. You stay here." The two Nazis entered the library, then closed the door behind them.

Sandro, his father, and Foà stood on their side of the glass, watching. One Nazi crossed to the catalogs, and the other began scrutinizing the books. Sandro hated feeling so helpless, and he could see his father fuming, his thin skin mottled with emotion and his gaze trained on the Nazi captains.

"This is a disaster," Foà moaned. "We need to stop them from sacking the library. They'll ship everything to Germany. The plunder of such precious articles would be a loss for Italian Jewry and Italian culture forever. It's our patrimony."

Sandro's father nodded. "We'll fight back, using the full force of the law. I can prepare papers to file today, enjoining the ERR in court from any confiscatory action. I will courier an authorizing letter to Almansi for his signature, as only the Union has the authority to administer these libraries."

Foà nodded.

"We need allies, so I would courier a letter to the Vatican, too. They should want to keep the collections in Rome. The *Questura* and the Badoglio government should have the same interest."

Sandro interjected, "We can even call La Sapienza and other academic institutions. All of them should want to keep the collection in Rome. It has enormous educational value."

"Right." Foà looked encouraged. "When do we start?"

In unison, Sandro and his father answered, "Now."

## CHAPTER NINETY-ONE

# Marco

6 October 1943

Marco had an errand to run for his boss and hurried down the sidewalk. He turned the corner, but was stopped by a large crowd blocking the sidewalk. They seemed to be watching something going on across the street, their backs to him. Their mood was grim, and they massed on the sidewalk and spilled into the street. Traffic had been detoured, which was highly unusual in this busy district.

Marco knew something was wrong. On the other side of the street was the headquarters of the *carabinieri*, Rome's military police. He hustled around the crowd and got a clear view of a horrifying sight. Nazi soldiers surrounded the entrance to *carabinieri* headquarters, perhaps a hundred of them. A long line of covered trucks, maybe fifteen, idled in front of the building and down several blocks, escorted by Kubelwagens. Nazis guarded the vehicles and the sawhorses, cordoning off the headquarters.

Marco watched, shocked, as in the next moment, a cadre of Nazis emerged from the building with thirty *carabinieri* in handcuffs. He didn't know what was going on; he couldn't imagine that the *carabinieri* had done anything wrong. An angry murmur rumbled through the crowd, and many cursed the Nazis or made obscene hand gestures at them. The Nazis loaded the *carabinieri* into the back of a covered truck.

Marco kept watching, appalled to see another cadre of Nazis leaving the building with more *carabinieri* under arrest. The Nazis loaded the second group of *carabinieri* into another covered truck, and then followed with another group and another, in waves of arrests. As soon as one group of *carabinieri* was loaded, the truck drove off and another group would be brought out, loaded, and taken away in custody.

Marco realized with horror that the Nazis were arresting the *entire* police force. The very thought had been inconceivable, until now. This was a major operation, in the center of Rome, but the Nazis had pulled off a total surprise. He hadn't heard a whisper about it at Palazzo Venezia. The partisans didn't know about it, either.

Marco felt terrified for the city he loved and for his fellow Romans, who would be utterly defenseless against the Nazis from now on. The crowd watched in fear, their hands to their mouths. Some cursed or wept, and others turned away, despairing.

Marco stopped counting at five hundred *carabinieri* arrested. He doubted many were left inside, if any. He raced home to tell his father.

## CHAPTER NINETY-TWO

# Sandro
### 13 October 1943

Sandro stood with his mother, Rosa, and the other distraught families behind a barricade that had been erected by the Nazis, around the piazza. Armed Nazi soldiers guarded the entrance to the synagogue, in a terrifying display of lethal force. The Nazis were about to confiscate the contents of the Biblioteca della Comunità and the Biblioteca del Collegio Rabbinico Italiano, some ten thousand priceless books and artifacts. Legal opposition to prevent the plunder had been to no avail, for the Nazis were beyond the reach of any law. Nor had any institution intervened: neither the Vatican, the Badoglio government, the *Questura*, nor La Sapienza.

Sandro's father was inside the synagogue with Presidents Foà and Almansi, in a last-ditch effort to stop the Nazis. Sandro knew it would be futile. His only consolation was that his father and the others had taken matters into their own hands in the past few days, having anticipated that legal methods would fail. They had hidden some of the most precious artifacts from the collection in the homes and gardens of sympathetic families throughout Rome. They had even drained the *mikveh*, or ritual bath, in the synagogue and hired a tile setter to hide artifacts in its walls.

But this morning, without warning, the Ghetto had awakened to find two massive freight cars parked across from the synagogue on the Lungotevere de' Cenci, on the tracks of the Circolare Nera trolley line. Armed Nazis guarded another barricade around the freight train and detoured traffic away from the typically bustling boulevard. The insignia on the train was the emblem of the German national railroad, so everyone knew where the train had come from and where it was going. The Nazis had hired Otto & Rosini, an international shipping company, to transport the collection to Germany, and their O&R workmen were inside the synagogue, packing.

Sandro's father emerged from the synagogue and crossed the piazza. He held his head high as he passed the Nazi soldiers, and if he was afraid, he didn't let it show. Sandro felt a rush of admiration for him. He had seen his father grow in stature during these dark days, and the Community had come to regard him as a leader.

His father approached the barricade, his expression somber, and the families surged against the cordon, shouting questions at him.

"Massimo, how can they take our libraries? They belong to the Community!" "We paid the gold! How much more can they take from us?" "Were you able to stop this? It's a crime in broad daylight!"

Sandro's father motioned for calm. "Friends, I have disappointing news. We could not stop this confiscation, though we tried our very best." He paused as the families reacted with groans and murmurs, then he resumed. "However, we have warned them that we will take legal action if any of our artifacts are sold off, after they are out of the country. The Germans assure us that they have no intention of doing that. In addition, we have formally requested return of the artifacts after the war—"

The families burst into chatter, interrupting him, when an O&R man in a worksuit emerged from the synagogue carrying a box. He was followed by another O&R man with a box, then another. The workmen walked to the freight train, toting fragile books and centuries-old manuscripts in boxes, as if they were common pots and pans.

Suddenly, a book flew from an open window on the upper floor of the synagogue. The book opened in midair, and its ancient pages flapped like a flightless bird.

Sandro's father whirled around, crying out, "No, it will break!"

Sandro gasped as his father ran toward the synagogue, raising his arms. Amazingly, his father caught the book on the fly. The families cheered, clapping.

Inexplicably, the Nazis threw another priceless book out of a different window. Sandro's father turned around, then scrambled to catch that book, too. He did so in the nick of time, right before it hit the cobblestones. Just then, another book flew from yet a different window.

The families' cheers began to fade, as the Nazis kept throwing priceless books out of the windows, faster and faster. His father ran back and forth in his suit, his tie flying. He tried in vain to catch all of the books, but it was impossible. In no time, it was raining rare books. His father struggled to hold the books he'd already caught, almost tripping.

"Papa, stop!" Sandro looked on, dismayed. The Nazis were playing a humiliating game. The families reacted with angry shouting. The Nazi guards brandished their guns at the families. The situation turned dangerously volatile. He had to do something.

"Sir!" Sandro called to a Nazi. "Let me get my father, will you?"

"Go!" The Nazi scowled, motioning with his long gun.

Sandro ducked under the barricade, hurried to his father, and took some of the books from him. "Papa, stop!"

"These books are hundreds of years old!" his father said, anguished and out of breath, his glasses awry.

"Stop now." Sandro and his father gave the books to an O&R man who came over with a box. The Nazis kept tossing books out of the windows. Pages came loose, sailed through the air, and fluttered to the ground like trash.

Sandro took his father's arm, and they hustled back to the barricade. All around them, precious books plummeted to the piazza and broke on the cobblestones, their spines coming unglued. The crowd rushed the barricade, trying to pick up the pages.

The Nazis shouted in German, aiming their guns at the families.

The families quieted in fear, weeping and praying. Sandro hurried his father under the barricade, where his mother and Rosa clucked over him, righting his glasses. His father recovered his composure quickly, and the families surged to him, asking him questions again.

Sandro spotted a young woman at the far side of the crowd, with her head turned away. Her dark curls gleamed in the sunshine, and she had on a pretty blue-checked dress, like Elisabetta used to wear. His heart leapt to his throat, and he found himself threading his way to her.

"Elisabetta?" Sandro said, but when the woman turned to face him, she wasn't Elisabetta at all.

"Excuse me?"

"I'm sorry . . . I thought you were someone else." Sandro edged backward into the crowd. He should have known better. He had thrown Elisabetta away, and she probably never thought of him. Her love for him was a thing of the past.

He remembered that night at La Sapienza, how they had kissed under the stars. He found himself wondering if she had ever written the book she had wanted to.

Sandro made his way toward his family, trying to forget her.

**CHAPTER NINETY-THREE**

# Sandro

15 October 1943

Sandro stood beside Rosa's bed, worried about his sister. She had been sick for over a week, her stomach hurting. She could barely keep anything down. Her pretty face was drawn and pale, and her eyes had lost their shine.

His mother rested her palm on Rosa's forehead. "Darling, your fever is too high. I think we need to get you to the hospital while you can still walk."

"I'll be fine," Rosa said weakly.

"No, you need treatment."

Sandro agreed with his mother. "Mamma, what do you think is the matter?"

"I can't diagnose her properly without testing. It could be so many things."

"What should we do? Papa won't be home until late." Sandro had left his father at the synagogue, getting things in order after the sacking of the library.

"You and I can take her. I don't want to wait for Papa. We'll leave him a note." His mother straightened, her mouth set with purpose.

Sandro nodded. "Good, let's go."

"Mamma, no." Rosa shook her head. "I don't need to go, and it's after curfew. Sandro, tell her no. The curfew—"

"Don't worry. If they stop us, we'll explain that it's a medical emergency."

"Assuming they care," his mother muttered.

Sandro sat with his mother in the waiting area, while Rosa was being examined. Dr. Salvatore Cristabello, one of his mother's former colleagues, had been delighted to see her again, though he had done a discreet double-take at her shabby brown dress and the change in her appearance. Sandro realized that his mother had gone from slender to gaunt, and when he caught sight of his reflection in a glass window, he saw that he had, too.

Dr. Cristabello emerged from the door, professional in his crisp white coat, with sparse gray hair and thick bifocals. He had a warm, friendly face, but his expression looked grave as he walked toward them.

"How is she?" His mother rose to meet him, followed by Sandro.

"She'll be fine, and her vitals are good, but I'm going to admit her. I believe it's gastrointestinal, a parasite or the like. We're seeing a lot of that, considering the contamination of the food supply."

"I was thinking the same thing."

"We're giving her fluids and testing blood and urine. It will take a while to get the results back. You should go home and get some sleep."

"I'd like to stay over, if I may."

"Fine. I think I can sneak you in."

"Thank you, Salvatore." His mother turned to Sandro, touching his arm. "Go home, dear. Keep your father company."

"But I want to stay, too. We left him a note."

Dr. Cristabello interjected, "Sandro, I can pull a few strings to get her into your sister's room, but not you, too."

"Okay," Sandro agreed, reluctantly.

"Good boy," his mother said, kissing him on the cheek.

Sandro left the hospital, and the Ponte Cestio was only steps away, leading to Trastevere, and Elisabetta. A powerful wave of emotion swept over him, and he yearned for her. He couldn't fathom how he had lived this long without her.

Sandro couldn't deny himself for another minute. His heart led the way, and he turned right over the Ponte Cestio, crossing the bridge and entering a Trastevere he barely recognized. The streets were deserted, and restaurants and shops permanently closed. The windows in the houses were dark, blacked out in case of an air raid. Trash and rubble lay on the streets, and flowerpots lay in shards. Trellises went unplanted, and their broken slats clung to walls. A bower of ivy hung overhead, a sole survivor that needed no care and therefore got none. Like him.

Sandro walked as if in a fever dream, his steps leading him to the woman he loved. He would beg her to take him in and shelter him, and he would hold her close and they would be together finally, the way they were meant to be, the way God intended before man intervened, and Fascists, and Nazis, and hate, and laws, and injustice. He drew closer to her house and kept walking, praying that somehow his dream would come true and he would finally be with her.

Sandro turned onto her street, and not a soul was in sight. He reached her house, a two-story sliver of gold stucco that radiated like sunshine. The lights were off and the shutters closed. Elisabetta had to be asleep.

He thought of Marco serenading her, but Sandro couldn't sing. He had no song, he had nothing anymore. Despair swept over him, and he realized he had no future to offer her, no accomplishments, no alleged genius, not even a healthy body, and he felt flayed to his very bone, nothing but his rawest self, longing for her.

Sandro collapsed to his knees, landing on the cobblestones. He slumped over, his head down, and the tears he had held back burned his eyes. He doubled over, breaking down, incapable of anything but sorrow.

"Sandro?"

Sandro could have sworn he heard Elisabetta calling his name. It was a voice he had loved for so long, and it emanated from far above the street, perhaps from heaven itself. He must have been hallucinating, truly descending into madness.

Nevertheless, he looked up.

## CHAPTER NINETY-FOUR

# Elisabetta
### 15 October 1943

Just before bedtime, Elisabetta went to the rooftop with the cats, holding a candle in a jar for light. It had rained while she was at work, which presented a problem for the flowers in the tureens, as they had no drainage. She had to drain them, for she couldn't let water rot the roots. It was probably one of the reasons that priceless soup tureens weren't used for planting.

She set the lamp on the table and went about her chore, tilting each tureen and letting the water run out onto the roof. Gnocchi and Rico picked their way from pot to pot, mincing on delicate paws to avoid the puddles. Their noses took in the various smells, giving them information only they received, since animals had abilities that far exceeded humans, especially cats. And especially Gnocchi and Rico, who were geniuses even among their own.

Elisabetta reached the Capodimonte tureen, then noticed that Gnocchi was heading toward the narrow ledge surrounding the roof. Elisabetta worried whenever the cats walked on the ledge, as she feared they could fall.

"Gnocchi, please get down," Elisabetta said, but Gnocchi wasn't about to stop what she was doing, even something so dangerous. That was how strong was Gnocchi's will, and her self-confidence.

Elisabetta approached the ledge cautiously, not wanting to provoke the very disaster she was trying to prevent. She knelt at the ledge, extending her hand, but Gnocchi only turned away, showing her furry *didietro*, as she could be cheeky that way.

Elisabetta looked over the ledge, taken aback to see a man standing in front of the house. He was tall and thin, and his hair was light enough to catch the moonshine. Something inside her recognized him instantly, despite the darkness. She wondered if it was really him or if she was in some strange sort of waking dream. It made no sense that he would be in front of her house in the middle of the night.

In the next moment, the man fell to his knees.

Elisabetta gasped. "Sandro?"

The man looked up, and it was him.

"Elisabetta?" Sandro rose, looking up. "Is that really you?"

"Yes! Is it really *you*?"

"Where are you? Why are you up there?"

"Why are you down *there*?" Elizabeth shouted, excited. "Come up and see me! Go two houses down and around the back, there's an alley."

"I'll be right up!" Sandro ran off.

Elisabetta jumped to her feet, hurried across the roof, and reached the landing of the fire escape. A few minutes later, Sandro came running down the alley, a silhouette racing toward her, and she felt her heart surrendering to the love she had felt for him for so long.

"I love you!" Sandro called to her.

"I love you, too!" Elisabetta felt her heart flood with happiness, and Sandro reached the fire escape, grabbed the bottom, and climbed onto the lowest landing. He bounded up the steps, and Elisabetta reached for him just as he swept her up in his arms, lifting her off the stairs, swinging her onto the rooftop, and kissing her once, then again.

Elisabetta kissed him back, ardently, fully, embracing him. His arms enveloped her, and all of the heartache and fear and worry melted away, and she felt sheer joy in his embrace, and in the next moment, he set her back on her feet, looked down at her with a smile, and cupped her face in his hands as if she were something precious, as delicate as antique china.

"I've missed you so much, Elisabetta."

"I've worried so much about you."

"We're alive. And I think the worst is over."

"Thank God," Elisabetta said quickly, as if they couldn't catch up fast enough.

"Did you hear about the gold?"

"Yes, I was there, I gave money."

"You gave? Why didn't you tell me?"

"And the *supplì*, did you like the *supplì*?"

"What *supplì*? What are you talking about?" Sandro stroked her cheek. "I'm so glad you're here, I can't believe you're really here, on the roof of all places." He looked around, marveling. "What is this place? It smells so wonderful! What have you got up here? Flowers? Plants? I smell basil!"

"I grow herbs—"

"Peppers? Tomatoes? Food!" Sandro released her and turned to the tomato plants. He grabbed a tomato and bit into it, laughing. "Oh my God, this is delicious! This is so good I could cry! You grow all this food? And basil? I love fresh basil! I miss it so much!"

"Yes, here." Elisabetta pinched off a sprig of basil and stuck it in the buttonhole of his jacket. "As good as any flower."

"Better! And these flowers, too? It smells like heaven! My God, Elisabetta, this is paradise! An oasis! You're a dream!"

Elisabetta reached for him, kissing him, tasting tomato on his lips and tongue, and Sandro embraced her, kissing her back, letting go of the tomatoes, dropping them on the rooftop, and she could feel his hands and fingers as hungry as he was, moving down her body, wanting her.

"Elisabetta, listen," Sandro said gently, his expression soft. "Tonight, can we forget the past, set aside everything that came before, and everything that will come? I don't know what the future holds. All I can offer you is my love, my deepest love, from the very heart of me and all that I am inside. That's all I have, my darling. Can you accept that? Can you offer me yours? Can you give me tonight?"

"Yes, yes, yes."

Sandro kissed her, and Elisabetta kissed him back with full abandon, and in time she led him to her chaise longue with its flowered cushions and pillows, tucked under the wisteria that enclosed them like a fragrant room made of flowers, and still they didn't stop kissing even as they lay down, and Sandro showed her tenderness and passion and comfort when he made love to her, and Elisabetta accepted the gift she was being offered, and gave her gift in return.

And afterward, they fell asleep in each other's arms, under the stars and amid the flowers and the plants and the cats.

CHAPTER NINETY-FIVE

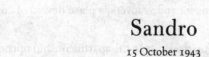

# Sandro

15 October 1943

Sandro woke up, holding Elisabetta. He felt a cold drizzle on his feet and realized it was beginning to rain. They were both nude on the chaise longue, and the bower of wisteria covered them. The sky was still dark, though he didn't know what time it was. The candle in the jar hadn't burned down very far. He hated to go, but his father would be home worried about Rosa.

"Elisabetta?" he said softly, but she didn't stir. He disentangled himself from her, dressed quickly, and gathered her clothes. He went to the chaise longue and lifted her up, cradling her close to his chest.

She murmured in her slumber, burying her face in his neck, and he carried her down the fire escape, with the cats following. There was a door ajar at the first landing, and he went inside a small bedroom, lowered her onto the bed, and covered her. He glanced around her room, which was as neat and pretty as he would've expected, with a desk and a bureau against the wall.

Elisabetta turned over, away from the pale light coming in through the open door, and he lingered another moment, allowing his gaze to absorb every centimeter of her, wishing he could remember every detail forever.

Sandro lay her dress over the back of her chair and found a pencil on her desk, to leave her a note. His gaze fell on the notebook he had left on her doorstep for her birthday. He opened it, expecting to find the pages covered with her handwriting, but instead it was blank. He wrote her a note, returned to the bed, and kissed her softly on the cheek. He could still smell the scent of wisteria that clung to her hair.

"I love you," he whispered, and Elisabetta mumbled something he couldn't understand.

He left, closing the door behind him. He descended the fire escape, then reached the bottom, held on to the lowest step, and dropped to the ground. The drizzle turned to rain, and he hurried down the alley, finding a new strength. He flew through the dark streets of Trastevere in a world of his own, a paradise that life opens for young lovers, a place devoid of curfews and Nazis.

He raced to his house, ran up the stairs to the apartment, and opened the door to find his father dozing in his chair, in his worn suit and tie. The lights were on, and a newspaper lay on his lap. Sandro went to his side. "Papa?"

His father opened his eyes, concerned. "Oh, I must have dozed off. How's Rosa? I would have gone to the hospital but for the curfew. Where's your mother?"

"Rosa's fine. She has something intestinal, and Mamma decided to stay at the hospital."

"Good." His father's frown eased. "I expected you sooner. Have you been at the hospital all this time?"

"No." Sandro didn't hesitate. "I went to see Elisabetta, and before you say anything, I love her and she loves me. As soon as the Race Laws are repealed, I'm going to ask her to marry me."

His father lifted a graying eyebrow. *"Mazel tov."*

Sandro blinked. "You don't disapprove?"

"After all we've been through? This war has left me tired of fighting. If you love her, then marry her. You're a wonderful son. You should be happy." His father opened his arms, and Sandro hugged him, moved.

"Thanks, Papa."

"Now, let's get to bed."

They did, and Sandro fell asleep to the sound of rain, his slumber deep and peaceful. But it was only a few hours before he and his father were awakened by a pounding on their door.

CHAPTER NINETY-SIX

# Sandro

16 October 1943

Sandro woke up. It took him a moment to realize that someone was banging on their door. His slumber had been so deep that his head ached. Only hours ago, he had been with Elisabetta in her rooftop garden.

He jumped out of bed, turned on the light, and hurried to the door. His father scurried behind, hooking his glasses behind his ears. It began to dawn on Sandro that something was terribly wrong. The Pontecorvo boys were crying downstairs. There was shouting in German outside. Boots thundered on the cobblestones. The heavy engines of trucks rumbled in the distance.

Sandro twisted the knob just as the door flew open. Two helmeted Nazis burst into the apartment, one short and one tall, armed with submachine guns.

*"Mani in alto!"* the short Nazi shouted, pointing his gun at Sandro and his father.

Sandro gulped with fear. He and his father raised their hands, the two of them terrified, standing in their undershorts. Sandro struggled through his fright to think clearly. He didn't know what the Nazis wanted. He wondered if it had to with their defiance of Captain Mayer. But the noise outside told him they weren't alone.

The short Nazi kept the gun trained on them. Rain dotted his helmet and wool greatcoat. The tall Nazi crossed to the telephone and cut the wires, then began searching the apartment.

Sandro's heart hammered. He didn't dare look at his father. At least his mother and Rosa were safe.

The short Nazi dug in the pocket of his greatcoat, pulled out a wrinkled sheet of paper, and thrust it at them wordlessly.

Their hands still in the air, Sandro and his father looked at the paper. It was a list of everyone who lived in their apartment house, with their ages and dates of birth. It must have come from the Community records, taken from the synagogue. His name and his father's were next to his mother and Rosa's.

"*Wo?*" The short Nazi pointed to his mother's and Rosa's names. "*Wo? Wo?*"

Sandro knew the word meant "where" in German. The Nazi was asking where his mother and Rosa were. "*Todt,*" he answered quickly, which meant "dead."

"*Was ist?*" The tall Nazi pointed at Rosa's bed, which they had squeezed in next to Sandro's.

Sandro thought fast. "*Todt,* the two of them, last week."

"*Hier!*" The short Nazi handed Sandro another paper.

Sandro and his father read it together, horrified:

(1) **You and your family and all other Jews belonging to your household are to be transferred.**

(2) **You are to bring with you:**

    (a) Food for at least eight days;

    (b) Ration books;

    (c) Identity card;

    (d) Drinking glasses.

(3) **You may also bring:**

    (a) A small suitcase with personal effects, clothing, blankets etc.;

    (b) Money and jewelry.

(4) **Close and lock the apartment/house. Take the key with you.**

   (5) **Invalids, even the severest cases, may not for any reason remain behind. There are infirmaries at the camp.**

   (6) **Twenty minutes after presentation of this card, the family must be ready to depart.**

Sandro's hand trembled as he held the paper. They were being taken to a labor camp.

"*Zwanzig minuten!*" the short Nazi shouted, then the Nazis left, slamming the door behind them.

Sandro reached for his father, and they clung together. His father had never felt so thin and frail. Sandro wanted to weep, but he couldn't surrender to emotion. "Thank God Mamma and Rosa are at the hospital. They're safe."

"Yes, but we had a deal with Kappler." His father broke their embrace, agitated. "We held up our end of the bargain."

"You think they're taking two hundred of us? Is that what's happening?"

"It has to be. They're not honoring the deal. This is bad faith. A material breach, as a matter of law."

"But what can we do now? We have to go. We can't make a legal argument."

"There must be law. There must be honor. We met with Kappler himself."

"Papa, we have to get ready. We don't have time for a legal discussion. The law won't help us now. The Nazis are the law." Sandro hurried back to his bed.

"We made an oral contract, son." His father stood still, shaking his head. "We performed our side of the bargain. This is a *clear* breach."

"Papa, we need to get dressed." Sandro put his identity card and clothes in a backpack, and his father went to the cabinet and took out his shirt.

"I assume Almansi and Foà will call Kappler. He'll have a lot to account for, that's for sure."

"Don't forget your identity card." Sandro packed drinking glasses and ration cards. "I'll get the rest."

"I wonder how Kappler will justify this. It's simply indefensible."

"I have the keys." Sandro took them from the drawer and pocketed them. "We'll leave the door unlocked for Mamma and Rosa."

"The Vatican will intervene, of course." His father put on his shirt, shaking his head. "Justice will prevail, in time. We will be sent home from the labor camps. Colonel Kappler's word was binding."

Sandro got his notebook, tore off a blank page, and grabbed a pencil, realizing it would be the second note he had left tonight. He started to write his mother's and Rosa's names, then remembered that he had told the Nazis that they were dead. He wrote instead:

*Don't worry about us. We'll see you when we can. We love you.*

Sandro set down the pencil. "Are you ready?"

"Almost." His father knotted his tie. "Put the note in the can of tea, so your mother finds it. You know how she loves her tea."

"Good idea," Sandro said, wondering anew about his father's state of mind. He doubted his mother would be making tea when she got home and found them gone.

He left the note on the table.

## CHAPTER NINETY-SEVEN

# Marco

### 16 October 1943

Marco woke up to find his father bent over his bed, already dressed. For some reason, the light was on in his bedroom. "What, Papa?"

"Get up, we have to go." His father's expression was grim. "The Nazis are mobilizing around the Ghetto."

Marco thought instantly of Sandro. He flung aside the sheet and leapt out of bed. He could hear his mother praying in their bedroom.

"I *thought* it was too quiet last night." His father pursed his lips, shaking his head. "I should have known they were up to something."

"Are the others coming?" Marco crossed to the chair, grabbed his pants, and slid them on.

"In time. We're closest, so we're on our own. The Nazis are cordoning off the Ghetto. They're setting up roadblocks at the synagogue, Via del Portico d'Ottavia, Via di Sant'Angelo in Pescheria, Piazza Costaguti, and Piazza Mattei."

Fear constricted Marco's chest. Sandro and his family lived near Piazza Costaguti. He threw on his shirt and buttoned it up.

"A German convoy is heading down the Lungotevere de' Cenci." Marco jumped into his shoes.

"How big is the convoy?"

"Thirty trucks with escorts, and more coming." His father left the bedroom, and Marco bolted after him.

"Oh no. That's a huge operation."

"Yes, and the trucks are empty. The Nazis are going to fill them with people." His father hustled down the stairwell with Marco.

"How can that be? The Ghetto gave them the gold. That was the deal."

"I think the deal was a ruse to buy time. They never intended to keep it."

"What, why?"

"It takes time to stage an operation this big. They must have been planning it for a while. It's why they arrested the *carabinieri*." His father reached the bottom of the stairwell and hustled to the stockroom, with Marco at his heels.

"So you think they're taking two hundred Jews?"

His father opened the storeroom door and turned on the light, without reply.

"Papa? Are they taking the two hundred anyway?"

His father met his eye, wearing an expression that Marco had never seen on his face, a mixture of sorrow, anger, and determination. "Son, I think it's too many trucks for only two hundred."

"What do you mean?" Marco asked, his heart pounding. "What are you saying?"

"I think the Nazis are taking all the Jews. I think they're emptying the entire Ghetto, like they do in Germany. It's a *rastrellamento*."

Marco cursed. "No! That can't be! Everyone?"

"Everyone." His father reached behind the cans on the shelves, where they hid their pistols.

Marco felt shocked, struck dumb with horror. But then he experienced a darker emotion. Pure rage.

His father retrieved two guns, pocketed one, and handed Marco the other. "It's loaded."

"Let's go," Marco said, palming the gun.

CHAPTER NINETY-EIGHT

# Marco
### 16 October 1943

Marco and his father raced up the Ponte Fabricio. Rain fell in sheets, drenching their heads and shoulders. They reached the crest of the bridge and got their first look at the Ghetto. The sight horrified and enraged them.

Hundreds of Nazis swarmed the other side of the river. A barricade cordoned off the Ghetto from the rest of Rome. A long line of covered trucks blocked the Lungotevere de' Cenci. Kubelwagens were parked everywhere. Nazis guarded a barricade at the foot of the bridge, and a crowd had gathered there.

Marco realized his father had been right. It had to be a *rastrellamento*, a roundup, of the Ghetto Jews. There were too many Nazis, too many trucks, and too much activity for it to be otherwise. He never would have believed that anyone, even the Nazis, could get away with this in Rome, under the nose of the Vatican.

Marco and his father ran down the bridge, slowing as they approached the back of the crowd, which was distraught. Men and women comforted each other, clinging together, praying, and crying. Marco struggled to maintain control of his emotions. The heavy trucks rumbled in idle, spewing exhaust. He simply could not allow Sandro and his family to be loaded onto them and taken to a labor camp.

Marco whispered to his father, "We have to do something."

"No. We wait."

"For what? We just can't stand here." Marco's fingers encircled the handle of the gun in his pocket.

"Don't. You'll get everybody killed. Be patient."

Suddenly a burst of gunfire came from the north side of Ghetto, where Sandro lived.

"No!" Marco cried out, startled.

His father shot him a look. A wave of fear ran through the crowd. Women gasped, men cursed the Nazis. An old man shook his head, tears filling his cloudy eyes. A woman covered her face, sobbing.

"Papa, I have an idea."

"What?"

"Follow me."

CHAPTER NINETY-NINE

# Sandro

16 October 1943

Sandro left the house with his father, holding a small bag of belongings and some bread. Nazis filled Piazza Costaguti, shouting orders, shoving terrified families into lines, and holding barking German shepherds. Shouting and crying echoed from other streets. Earlier there had been gunshots.

Sandro and his father joined the line of families forming diagonally, across the piazza. Nazis held them at gunpoint, their faces shadowed by helmets. The bedraggled families huddled together in the pouring rain, their expressions drawn with fear.

Sandro suppressed dread as his father shivered next to him. He spotted the other tenants from their house in their line. The Pontecorvos with their three boys, Giacomo, Carlo, and Datillo, who kept crying. The Lanzanas with their girls, Amelia and Aida, and the boys, Alvaro and Giuseppe.

Nazis were rousting neighbors from their houses. The DiConsiglio family; Ester with Ada, six years old. Marco, only four. Baby Mirella, not even a year old. The Sabatello family; Giovanni with Graziella, Letizia, Italia, and Franco. Liana, only eight years old.

Sandro saw some of his students, their young faces showing abject terror. Families clung to each other. Husbands comforted wives. Mothers sheltered children from the rain, like hens expanding their wings. Everybody held suitcases and small bags. They were being made to wait while other families were prodded into line at gunpoint.

Sandro realized that the Nazis weren't counting people. That meant they weren't taking only two hundred Jews. There were already more than that lined up on Piazza Costaguti.

He scanned the scene and came to a terrifying conclusion. The Nazis must have been taking *all* of the Ghetto Jews. It was an inconceivable horror, but the evidence was all around him. Men, women, children, without exception. Old and young, able-bodied and infirm, carried in chairs by their family members. He could see the evidence, all around him. It was a *rastrellamento*, a roundup.

Sandro fought back his fear. He couldn't succumb now. He had to save his father and himself. He struggled through his panic to figure out a way to escape.

He evaluated the surroundings. Their line faced south, toward Via del Progresso. The Nazis would probably lead them down that street, then to Via del Portico d'Ottavia, the main entrance to the Ghetto. There must be trucks parked on the Lungotevere de' Cenci, waiting to transport them. That would explain the mechanical thrumming vibrating through the air, even in the rain.

Sandro's mind raced. There had to be a way out. A group of Nazis guarded a roadblock directly behind them, which cut off Via Arenula, due north. He counted how many. Ten Nazis. Too many to get past.

Ahead lay a smaller, narrow street, Via in Publicolis, that led to Via del Piatto. A lone Nazi stood at the far end of Via in Publicolis, but no blockade had been set up. The Nazis on Piazza Costaguti weren't looking that way. No one was. All attention was focused on Via del Progresso.

Sandro kept his eye on the Nazi on Via in Publicolis. The line of families shifted forward, but he took his father's arm and discreetly held him back. They kept their position, letting other families go in front of them.

His father glanced up, questioningly. Rain dotted his spectacles and flattened his sparse hair to his head.

Sandro shook his head slightly, no. He was wondering if he and his father could take down a Nazi. The chance was slim.

But it was, nevertheless, a chance.

CHAPTER ONE HUNDRED

# Gemma

16 October 1943

Rain pelted the window of the hospital room, and Gemma awoke in the chair next to Rosa's bed. She had slept surprisingly well, since the hospital had fed both of them last night, the first good meal they'd had in ages. She felt relieved to see Rosa still sleeping peacefully, her color mildly improved.

Salvatore appeared in the threshold, his expression grave. His white coat was rumpled, as it was the end of his shift. He motioned her into the hallway, and Gemma rose and crossed to him.

"What's the matter, Salvatore? Did you get test results?"

"No, but I have terrible news." Salvatore placed a steady hand on her shoulder. "The Nazis are rounding up the Ghetto. They started early this morning."

"What?" Gemma asked, shocked. Tears sprang to her eyes. She shook her head. "No! A *rastrellamento*? This can't be happening, it can't be. Massimo and Sandro are home. I have to leave."

"No, Gemma, don't, you're safer here. We have a plan in place."

"What are you talking about?"

"The Nazis are on their way here. They're coming to take the Jewish patients. We're going to move Rosa, right away."

"No!" Gemma gasped, stricken.

"We have to act quickly. We're setting up an isolation ward for the Jewish patients—"

"Why?" Gemma recoiled. "You'll be doing the Nazis' work for them."

"You know us better than that." Salvatore's expression softened, his eyes sympathetic. "Giovanni has a plan to save Rosa and everyone else."

"How? What sort of plan?" Gemma knew he meant Dr. Giovanni Borromeo, the hospital administrator. Giovanni was a brilliant physician and professor of medicine, but she wanted details.

"Allow me to explain."

CHAPTER ONE HUNDRED ONE

# Marco

16 October 1943

"Here's my thinking." Marco ran with his father, back over the Ponte Fabricio. "The Ghetto is cordoned off at the Lungotevere de' Cenci. That's where the trucks are. That's where the Nazis are bringing everyone. Right?"

"È vero." His father ran, unbothered by the rain. They reached Tiber Island, ran past Bar GiroSport, and ran over the Ponte Cestio.

"So we should approach from the north end of the Ghetto, at Piazza Costaguti. The opposite end, away from the action. There will be roadblocks there, but they will be more lightly guarded."

"Understood. The Nazis will be busy at the south side of the Ghetto, not the north." Marco and his father took a right turn and ran up the Lungo-tevere degli Anguillara, on the west bank of the Tiber.

"Yes, and the north side is closer to the Simones' house. If the Nazis are lining them up, that's where Sandro and his family will be."

His father looked over, his dark curls dripping. "Let's pick up the pace."

Marco accelerated. Lights were going on in the houses along the river. Phones would be ringing. People would be waking up to horrific news.

His heart hammered like a piston. His legs churned. His breath became rhythmic. Raindrops slaked his face, blurring his vision. He shook them off and kept going.

He matched his father, stride for stride.

## CHAPTER ONE HUNDRED TWO

# Sandro

### 16 October 1943

Sandro kept his eye on the lone Nazi guard on Via in Publicolis. The line of families had shifted forward enough. He and his father stood directly across from the entrance to the street.

Sandro shifted his gaze to the Nazis guarding their line. They stood at a distance, near its head. They weren't looking in his direction.

He checked Via in Publicolis again. The Nazi there had turned away, too. It was time for Sandro to make his move.

He squeezed his father's arm, signaling him. His father looked up. San-dro shifted his gaze. They took a step toward Via in Publicolis.

Just then, two more Nazis approached the lone Nazi on Via in Publicolis. One lit a cigarette, cupping the flame against the rain.

Sandro's heart sank. It was too risky now. He quickly nudged his father back in line with the other families.

He wracked his brain for another means of escape. He needed a subterfuge of some kind. Maybe he could tell the Nazis that he had left the gas on. Gas came on for mealtimes, and it was around breakfast time. The Nazis wouldn't want to start a fire that could rage out of control.

He decided that it wouldn't work. The Nazis probably wouldn't let them both go back to the apartment, only Sandro. He didn't want to leave his father.

Their line grew longer, extending almost all the way across the piazza. His gaze fell on the other families. He knew all of them. The elderly Angelo Fornani with Alberto and little Alberto, six years old. The grandmotherly Teresa Campagnano with Vito and tiny Donato. Augusto Capon, an older gentleman whose daughter had married the Nobel Prize–winning physicist Enrico Fermi.

The Scudi family was prodded into the line, but Matteo Scudi was having a problem controlling his elderly mother, Aurelia, who had become senile and often said inappropriate things. Aurelia began shouting curses at the Nazis, and Matteo tried to silence her, placing his hand over her mouth. Sandro, his father, and the other families turned to watch in alarm.

Nazi guards rushed to Matteo and Aurelia and tore them forcibly apart. Aurelia cursed the Nazis louder. Matteo begged her to stop. Suddenly one of the Nazis struck Aurelia in the head with the butt of his gun. A gruesome fan of blood sprayed from her head. She dropped to the cobblestones, spasmed, then went motionless.

Matteo screamed, and his wife held him, turning him away from the agonizing sight. Aurelia was dead.

Sandro felt tears film his eyes. His father covered his mouth, stunned. The line recoiled, and children cried louder. Rain drenched her body, and her blood spilled in the crevices between the cobblestones with the rainwater. The Nazis stepped over her. They left her lying there, cruelly.

Sandro looked away, shocked and terrified. His thoughts were frantic. He had to think of something. He and his father had to escape.

And it had to be soon.

# Gemma

16 October 1943

---

Gemma hurried to push the gurney bearing Rosa down the hospital hallway. The Nazis were on their way. Rosa and the other Jewish patients had been given a sedative to avoid the risk of any emotional outburst, according to Giovanni's plan. Gemma had to hope it would work. She was betting Rosa's life on its success.

Gemma tried not to think of what was happening in the Ghetto. She could only pray that Massimo was taking care of Sandro and himself. She couldn't leave the hospital until Rosa was safe. She felt torn between her two children, both in mortal peril.

She remembered that Sandro had wanted to stay at the hospital, last night. If she had said yes, he would be here, safe. Instead she had barely kissed him goodbye. She tried to remember the last thing she had said to him. She thought it was *good boy*. She should've said *I love you*. How had she not said *I love you*?

She took a right turn down another corridor, near her old Obstetrics & Gynecology wing. Her years as a practicing physician came back to her. She knew the freshly painted white walls. The waxed tile floor. The bulletin board with posters for lectures that she was too busy to attend. She'd had such a sense of purpose in those days, but nothing mattered like today.

The entire hospital had swung into action, executing Giovanni's plan. Nuns and lay nurses were setting up the isolation ward. Jewish patients were being identified and moved there. The staff worked as one, for no one was better in an emergency than physicians and nurses.

She took a left turn and lined up behind other doctors, nuns, lay nurses, and orderlies. She spotted doctors she knew from Endocrinology and

Rheumatology, and nuns and lay nurses from Labor & Delivery. They were all moving Jewish patients into the isolation ward. She had never felt more honored to be among them.

In time, Gemma wheeled Rosa into the isolation ward, to a bed by the window. Rosa slept soundly, and Gemma kissed her on the forehead, struggling to remain in emotional control. With God's help, this would not be the last time that she kissed her daughter.

Gemma helped move all of the other Jewish patients into the isolation ward, and after it had been filled, the doctors returned to their rounds and the nurses to their stations. It was all according to Giovanni's plan, which required them to pretend that this was a normal day at the hospital.

She stood outside the closed door of the isolation ward with Sister Anna Domenica. They both looked over to see Salvatore striding toward them, his expression grim.

"Ladies, it's time." Salvatore reached them. "The Nazis are downstairs, twenty of them. They're talking to Giovanni. He's going to tell them the cover story and stall them as long as he can. Leonida is typing a patient list now. All of the names will be false. She'll stall them, too."

Gemma suppressed her fright. The thought of Nazis in the hospital terrified her.

"Gemma, we need to hide you."

"Of course." Gemma had been so focused on Rosa and the others, she hadn't thought of herself. "What about a supply closet?"

"No, they'll search everywhere."

"What should I do? Should I pose as a patient in the isolation ward?"

"No, we need you."

"But between my clothes and the weight I've lost, they'll know I'm Jewish if they find me."

Sister Anna Domenica interjected, "Gemma, they won't find you if you do what I say."

# Marco

16 October 1943

Marco and his father raced up the span of the Ponte Garibaldi. They gained momentum on the downward slope. Rain gusted in sheets off the Tiber. Clouds blackened the sky.

Rome was awakening. People appeared on the street under umbrellas. Traffic was picking up.

Marco feared that they were running out of time. He accelerated, and so did his father. They reached the end of the bridge and ran up Via Arenula, a major artery north of the Ghetto.

His father glanced over, his broad chest heaving. "Marco, we won't make it in time. We need to change plans. Take Via del Pianto."

"Okay."

"Yes. Even so, there may not be time."

"We have to try."

"Of course."

# Gemma

16 October 1943

Gemma and Salvatore stood in front of the closed door of the isolation ward. According to Giovanni's plan, Salvatore was pretending to be the head doctor of the ward and she was a nurse, dressed in Sister Anna

Domenica's habit. It turned out to be the perfect disguise, since its volumi-nous black folds disguised the unhealthy thinness of Gemma's body, and its stiff wimple and veil covered her hair.

Giovanni and a Nazi captain were striding toward them, followed by a cadre of Nazi soldiers. Gemma stiffened with fear, and even the sight of her old friend Giovanni didn't reassure her. He was in his forties, with thin-ning gray hair, large, almond-shaped dark eyes, a gray mustache, and a calming smile. The Nazi towered over him, a heavyset man with a square jaw, in a greatcoat dotted with rainwater.

Giovanni motioned to the Nazi. "Captain Weber, please meet Dr. Crista-bello and Sister Anna Domenica."

"Captain Weber, pleased to meet you," Salvatore said, extending a hand.

"You, too." Captain Weber shook his hand.

Giovanni cleared his throat. "Dr. Cristabello, Captain Weber and his men are here to arrest our Jewish patients. I've informed him that we keep no re-cords of our patients' religions. He and his men have searched the hospital. They have found no Jewish patients. Your isolation ward, for patients with Syndrome K virus, is the only place left to check. However, I have informed him of the extremely contagious nature of the Syndrome K virus."

"Thank you, Dr. Borromeo." Salvatore turned to the Nazi, his manner professional. "Captain Weber, I am in charge of the isolation ward and—"

"Tell me about the Syndrome K virus."

"In layman's terms, Syndrome K is a lethal and highly transmissible virus. If you or any of your men enter this isolation ward, you will contract the virus. In addition, if an infected soldier takes the virus back to his unit, he will infect everyone in proximity."

Gemma kept her lips sealed. There was no such thing as the Syndrome K virus. It was a brilliant ruse fabricated by Giovanni, exploiting the germ-aphobia of the Nazis. The name of the ersatz virus was an inside joke, as the K in Syndrome K referred to Field Marshal Kesselring, the Nazi com-mander.

Weber nodded, his lips tight. "How does the virus spread?"

"It's airborne, which is the deadliest means of transmission. We believe it attacks the brain. Early symptoms occur in two or three days. They are headaches of excruciating severity, then paralysis, and death." Salvatore cleared his throat. "We suspect that Syndrome K traveled here from Africa, via human host. As you know, Italian soldiers fought in North Africa. Libya, El Alamein, Benghazi. We can only imagine the bacteria they returned with, and the Syndrome K strain is foreign to European soil. Its lethality is such that no doctor goes inside that ward. Even the families of these patients aren't permitted to visit them."

"How do you treat them?" Weber asked, as the Nazi soldiers standing behind him exchanged nervous glances.

"There is an elderly nun who has volunteered for the task. She enters only in an appropriate mask and gown, but that is insufficient protection. She is already experiencing headaches. Soon she will be a patient herself."

"You're quite a coward, Doctor."

Salvatore didn't blink. "I must consider the greater good. We can't afford to lose a physician. We're understaffed as a result of the war. Frankly, nothing helps these poor souls. They're dead in two weeks, in agony."

Weber frowned. "I wish to see for myself."

Salvatore didn't move. "I implore you, do not enter the ward. You can look through the glass window."

Weber peered into the ward through the glass. The Nazi's cold blue eyes scanned the beds, including Rosa's. Gemma felt her heart beat harder. Seconds passed like hours.

Weber sniffed. "The patients merely look asleep."

"I assure you, they are dying. They are heavily sedated on morphine."

"Are any of them Jewish?"

"I don't know. We are a Catholic hospital. We treat the sick. We can provide you a list of their names. I believe a secretary is preparing the list as we speak."

"So I've been told, but it's taking too long. My orders are to arrest the Jewish patients, no matter how sick." Weber frowned, and the Nazis behind him exchanged nervous glances.

Salvatore folded his arms. "I understand that you have orders. However, I warn you, your men will die as a result of following them. Is it worth killing them for perhaps a single Jew, who will die anyway? Won't your superiors blame you if they contract Syndrome K? What will happen to you in that event?"

Weber fell silent, in thought.

Gemma held her breath.

The Nazi soldiers shuffled their feet, restless.

Weber nodded. "We'll take our leave now, Doctor."

"A prudent choice, Captain."

## CHAPTER ONE HUNDRED SIX

# Sandro
### 16 October 1943

Sandro's mind raced, but he couldn't come up with an escape plan. Nazis swarmed everywhere with guns and dogs. There was no realistic way out. They would be shot. More families were forced to the line at gunpoint. No age was too young or too old.

Sandro fought an increasing panic over whether they were truly going to a labor camp. He didn't see how children or babies could work. Every home was being emptied. He shifted forward as the Spizzichino clan joined the line. Settimia, Adelaide, Allegra, and Alberto, with the children Enrica, Franca, and little Mario, who had just started walking.

Sandro's gaze landed on his father, who stood beside him, his head tilted down against the rain. His father's hair dripped in rivulets down his neck, exposing the pinkness of his scalp. His nape had thinned so much that it was hard to see how he held his head up.

Sandro put an arm around his father, and his father looked up through his rain-spotted glasses. "Papa, I love you," he said simply.

"I love you, too, son." His father smiled shakily. "They can't take that from us, can they?"

"No, they cannot," Sandro answered.

But he thought, *Even if they take everything else.*

# Gemma

16 October 1943

Gemma raced to the hospital exit, desperate to get to Massimo and Sandro. Her black robes flew behind her, as she had stayed in the nun's habit as a disguise. She hadn't gotten to say goodbye to Rosa, who was still under sedation, but she felt assured that her daughter would be safe, now that the Syndrome K ruse had worked.

Gemma reached the door, flung it open, and launched herself into the downpour. She could hear the thrumming of heavy engines from Trastevere. Bar GiroSport was closed. She ran up the Ponte Fabricio, heading to the Ghetto. No one else was on the upward slope of the bridge. Cold rain drenched her veil and shoulders. Random gunshots echoed from the Ghetto. Her heart pounded with terror.

She ran up the span as fast as she could. Her habit grew heavy as it got wet. Her body had gotten so weak. She reached the crest of the Ponte Fabricio. The sight left her breathless with horror.

Nazis had cordoned off the entire Ghetto. Beyond the barricade, men, women, and children were being lined up at gunpoint, huddling together like gray shadows in the rain. Nazis were herding them all into trucks blocking the length of Lungotevere de' Cenci.

Gemma realized that Massimo and Sandro could be among them. She was too far away to make out their faces in the downpour.

Tears of sheer fright sprang to her eyes. She felt something mentally snap inside her. She was trained for an emergency, but never one like this. This was the worst thing she could ever imagine. Massimo and Sandro were being taken away? All of the Ghetto Jews? Everyone she knew?

She raced down the slope of the bridge. She reached a crowd of onlookers and shoved her way forward. Men and women moved quickly aside for her, making the Sign of the Cross on their chests.

Gemma kept going, beginning to sob. She felt as if she were losing her mind. She couldn't believe this was happening. She had to get to Massimo and Sandro.

She reached the barricade, which was guarded by armed Nazis.

"Massimo, Sandro!" Gemma found herself grabbing the sawhorse, and in the next moment, she was trying to yank it down.

The Nazis whirled around to face her.

Raising their guns.

CHAPTER ONE HUNDRED EIGHT

# Marco
16 October 1943

Marco and his father reached Via del Piatto, a narrow cobblestone street lined with homes on the north side of the Ghetto. They stopped running, panting hard from exertion. There was no roadblock, and only a lone Nazi guarded the path, turned away to face Piazza Costaguti.

Marco felt for the gun in his pocket. He considered picking the Nazi off.

His father stayed his hand, again. "Don't. We're too late. Look."

Marco shifted his gaze. Beyond the guard, a line of families was moving out of the piazza, toward the loading zone at the south side of the Ghetto.

"Change of plans."

"What?"

"After the Nazis arrested the *carabinieri*, they held them at the Collegio Militare before they shipped them north. They'll do the same thing now. They're creatures of habit. No place other than the Collegio Militare can hold that many securely."

"Agree." Marco understood. He had gone to the Collegio Militare many times when he had worked at Palazzo Venezia. The Collegio Militare was used by the Defense Ministry to train officers, and special ceremonies were held in its elegant courtyard. He couldn't imagine what it looked like full of hundreds of distraught civilians.

"We could be at the Collegio Militare in fifteen minutes, over the Ponte Mazzini. If we left now, we would be in place before the trucks arrived."

Marco disagreed. "Maybe, but I want to go back to the Ghetto entrance. I want to see the Simones with my own eyes. There's still a chance they won't be taken."

"There's no chance of that, son."

"But I know Sandro. He'll think of a way to get away."

"Not this time." His father looked pained. "They're all being taken."

"I want to see Sandro." Marco spoke from the heart. "I need to."

"Okay. We go back." His father turned around, and the two of them took off running, back down Via Arenula, over the Ponte Garibaldi, and onto the Lungotevere degli Anguillara. Nazi trucks plowed through Trastevere's streets, arresting Jews there, too.

Marco and his father ran faster, fueled by desperation. They were superb athletes and endurance cyclists. They had logged kilometer after kilometer on country roads, city roads, and back roads. Never before had they asked so much of their bodies. Never before had so much been required.

They bore down and flew. Their chests heaved with exertion but they ignored it. Their thighs burned but they didn't feel it. They had wind to carry them. They had energy to burn.

They accelerated into the rain and the storm.

# Gemma

16 October 1943

---

The Nazis aimed their weapons at Gemma, as she tried to pull down the roadblock. One Nazi menaced her by raising the butt of his gun. She ducked instinctively, and the crowd reacted with outraged shouts.

"Stop, she's a nun!" "You can't shoot her!" "God will punish you, Nazi pig!"

The Nazi swung the butt of his gun at her, but a man in the crowd yanked Gemma backward. The gun butt cleared her head but landed on her forearm.

Gemma cried out in agony. The pain stunned her.

The onlookers reacted with horror, hollering anew at the Nazis. The Nazis menaced the crowd with their weapons.

Men spirited Gemma away from harm, through the crowd. Tears poured from her eyes, and sobs wracked her body. All she could think of was Massimo and Sandro. She struggled to get back to the barricade even as the men brought her to the side of the bridge and eased her down.

"Sister, how is your arm?" they asked her. "Is it broken? Did those bastards break it?"

"Let me go! I want to go back!" Gemma shook her head, sobbing. "Massimo! Sandro!"

"Sister, you can't. They'll shoot you. You must stay here."

Suddenly Gemma saw two figures running over the bridge, their outlines unmistakable. It was Beppe and Marco. They stopped at the sound of her shouting, then turned to her.

"Gemma?" Beppe called to her, uncomprehending.

# Marco

16 October 1943

Marco, his father, and Gemma stood together on the Ponte Fabricio, watching the Nazis do their worst. They marched a line of families toward the trucks, menacing them with guns and barking dogs. Fathers in the line protected children, who wailed in terror. Wives clung to husbands and wept. Grandmothers covered their faces. Invalids and the aged were carried in arms or on wooden chairs.

Nazis loaded families like cattle. Once full, a truck would take off, driving north on the Lungotevere de' Cenci, heading for the Collegio Militare.

Marco, his father, and Gemma held each other, praying that Massimo and Sandro wouldn't be among them. They stood in mute fear as family after family was loaded into the trucks, and truck after truck took off, driving north. The line seemed to be diminishing in time, with no sign of Massimo or Sandro.

Marco felt his hopes lift, against all odds. Maybe Massimo and Sandro had escaped, as Gemma and Rosa had, and were hiding somewhere in safety.

But then Massimo and Sandro came into view, walking side by side in the rain. Gemma wailed in anguish, and Marco's father held her tight.

"Sandro!" Marco yelled. He waved his arms.

Sandro snapped his head around, spotted Marco, and nodded. Next to him, Massimo gave a little wave, a heartbreaking flash of an open palm, then father and son were loaded into the back of the covered truck.

Gemma collapsed, and Marco's father gathered her up and took her home.

Marco stayed behind, standing as a witness. Sandro and his father were being taken away, and there was nothing he could do to help them. He had never felt so enraged, or so helpless, in his life. Tears welled in his eyes.

The Nazis loaded Sandro's truck until it was full, then latched its back, and drew down its canvas flap, as if crime could be covered by mere cloth.

Marco watched as the truck bearing Sandro and his father lurched off and disappeared up the Lungotevere de' Cenci, with the others heading to the Collegio Militare.

Marco's tears poured down, like the rain.

CHAPTER ONE HUNDRED ELEVEN

# Elisabetta

16 October 1943

Elisabetta slept like a baby, dreaming that she and Sandro were getting married. She saw herself in a beautiful white dress, Sandro in a dark suit, and everyone gathered around them, smiling and happy, even Nonna.

Elisabetta's parents were there, too, watching and smiling, happy and whole, together as a couple. Her mother looked beautiful, and her father good-looking in his bohemian way, with his beard trimmed and his eyes sparkling with animation, not dulled by drink.

Marco was in the dream, too, darkly handsome in his dark suit, for he was Sandro's best man, and in a way, he was hers, too. She would always love Marco, and Marco would always love her, and she, Sandro, and Marco would love each other the way they always had, from as long as they had known life.

Gnocchi and Rico were there, too, watching from their own cloud that was nowhere near the edge of any roof, and there were tall tomato plants and peppers and basil and oregano growing all around them, and white roses climbing trellises and pink bougainvillea covering the walls, and purple and white wisteria dripping from a perfumed bower, among cypress trees and tall, curving palms.

In her dream, love was a garden she had grown for Sandro.

---

Elisabetta woke up alone, in her bed. She realized that Sandro must have carried her down, then left. She felt a pang of regret at not having said goodbye, but a warm rush of love filled her. She could remember the taste of his kiss on her lips and his touch on her body.

Soft gray light filled her bedroom, and she reached over to scratch Gnocchi's chin. Gnocchi moved her head around, making sure no spot was missed, having observed that humans often became distracted during prolonged stretching sessions.

Elisabetta heard a woman's scream outside. Gnocchi swiveled to the sound, and Rico woke up. She rose, threw on her bathrobe, and hurried up the stairs to the roof. She crossed to the front of the rooftop, horrified at the scene on the street below.

Nazis were arresting her neighbors, the Diorio family. Michele Diorio, his wife, Augusta, and their two little girls. Michele tried to protect Augusta, and the little girls cried as they were forced into a covered truck. Other families were already inside, clinging to each other.

Elisabetta gasped. She couldn't imagine what was going on, except that she knew that the Diorios were Jewish. The loud rumbling of heavy trucks emanated from the Lungotevere Sanzio, reverberating in the rain.

She felt a bolt of fear, thinking of Sandro. She hurried downstairs, dressed quickly, and flew out the door.

# Marco

16 October 1943

Marco ran up the Lungotevere Sanzio with his father, having left Gemma at the house with his mother. Covered trucks were driving away from the Ghetto, heading up the Lungotevere de' Cenci and turning left on the Ponte Mazzini.

Marco and his father caught sight of the Collegio Militare, a massive rectangular edifice with a gray stone façade at its entrance and lower floors, changing to lighter stucco at its second-floor balcony and upper floors. Criss-crossed bars covered its oblong windows, making a grim presence on Piazza della Rovere, only a kilometer away from Saint Peter's Basilica in Vatican City.

Marco wondered what was going on behind the Vatican walls. He hoped Emedio and others were trying to help. He prayed the Pope would intervene on behalf of the Jews. Nobody had before, even after the Race Laws. The Jews were forever on their own.

Marco kept running, fighting a sense of dread.

# Elisabetta

16 October 1943

Elisabetta ran through Trastevere, past Nazis on motorcycles. Jews were being rounded up throughout the neighborhood. Shutters and shops stayed closed. No one was on the street. She had to get to the Ghetto.

She kept running, splashing through puddles, finally reaching Tiber Island. She took a left turn over the Ponte Cestio and raced past Bar Giro-Sport. It was dark and closed. Marco and his family must already know.

Elisabetta kept going, distraught. She prayed this wasn't a *rastrellamento*. She hoped she wasn't too late. She tore up the span of the Ponte Fabricio. Rain pelted her face and soaked her dress.

She reached the crest to a horrifying scene. There was a roadblock in front of the Ghetto. Nazis were ordering men, women, and children into covered trucks, which were pulling away. She ran down the bridge, frantic. A crowd stood in front of the roadblock. She jumped up and down, hoping for a glimpse of Sandro. She didn't see him.

She tapped an older woman, next to her. "My God, what's going on? Is it . . . a *rastrellamento*?"

"Yes," the woman answered, crestfallen. "I just saw my oldest friend loaded into a truck like an animal."

Elisabetta felt her heart break. "No, no, it can't be true. They're not taking everyone, are they? They can't!"

"I tell you, they are. I've been standing here all morning. They are taking every Jew they can get their hands on. They're *emptying* the Ghetto."

Elisabetta couldn't surrender to panic. "My boyfriend, he lives on Piazza Costaguti. Have they taken from the north side already?"

"I don't know. My advice to you, go to the Collegio Militare. That's where the Nazis are taking them. Your boyfriend might be there already."

Elisabetta turned around and took off.

# Sandro

16 October 1943

Sandro scanned the courtyard at the Collegio Militare, trying to figure out a way to escape. He had never been here, but he was getting the lay of the land. The building was an elegant, two-story edifice of classrooms with floor-to-ceiling windows, each one topped by intricate scrollwork. A vaulted colonnade ringed a vast, stone courtyard, and at the front of the colonnade were five graceful arches, under the Latin motto ROMANA VIRTUS ROMAE DISCITUR. Roman Valor Is Learned in Rome.

The refinement of the building belied the horror of its use today. Terrified families filled all of the classrooms inside, and the rest were outside in the courtyard, like Sandro and his father. They stood under the colonnade, trying to stay out of the rain. They sat in groups, covering their heads with jackets, clothes, and newspapers. Women held children and nursed infants. Men stood and prayed in circles, as today was the Sabbath.

Nazis conferred at a security desk at the front of the courtyard, or walked among the families, brandishing their weapons and intimidating them. New truckloads of families would arrive at regular intervals, and more terrified men, women, and children would be packed into the courtyard, which was already full to bursting. Relatives, friends, and neighbors recognized each other and reunited tearfully.

"Sandro, please rest a bit." His father sat under the colonnade, his back against the wall of the building.

"I'm fine."

"What are you looking at?"

"Just looking."

"It's good to know that your mother and Rosa are at the hospital. We can only pray they're safe there. Please, sit."

"I'm fine, Papa." Sandro eyed the courtyard, wondering if Elisabetta had found his note. His heart wrenched at the thought of leaving her, Rosa, and his mother.

"Sir, I'm not Jewish!" yelled a woman, threading her way through the crowd to the security desk at the front.

Sandro watched the woman speak to the Nazis, then she joined a group of people being lined up on the left. He realized that the Nazis were releasing Gentiles who had been rounded up accidentally.

Sandro blinked. Maybe there was a way.


CHAPTER ONE HUNDRED FIFTEEN

# Elisabetta

16 October 1943

Elisabetta ran back over the Ponte Fabricio, heading for the Collegio Militare. Her heart lodged in her throat. All she could think of was Sandro. She reached Tiber Island and kept going, turning right up the Lungotevere Sanzio.

Her mind raced with questions. When had he gone? Why hadn't she awakened? A wave of guilt overwhelmed her. If she had been awake, she could have convinced him to stay. She could have delayed him. If she had, Sandro would be safe with her now.

She stumbled and almost fell. She straightened up and started running again. She had to get to him. She had to see if she could help him. She had to tell him she loved him and would always.

She powered forward, running hard in the rain.

# Marco
16 October 1943

Marco and his father reached the Collegio Militare, where armed Nazis had cordoned off the building's entrance. A distraught crowd thronged outside the barricade. Men and women waved notes in the air, hoping to communicate with their loved ones inside.

"Marco, listen." His father drew him close, his chest heaving. "You stay here, I'll go around the other side. I'm hoping one of our friends will be here."

Marco knew that his father meant their fellow partisans. "I'll look, too."

His father took off, and Marco scanned the faces around him, but saw no partisans. He threaded his way to the front of the crowd, then overheard two Nazi guards talking on the other side of the barricade, having a mundane conversation in German. The Nazi on the left was saying that he loved *cervelatwurst*, but the Nazi on the right preferred *bratwurst*, saying his wife never overcooked it.

Marco got an idea. He approached the Nazi on the right, who had narrow brown eyes and a face pockmarked from adolescent acne. "I agree with you, friend," he said in German. "I loathe overcooked *bratwurst*."

The Nazi cocked his head, impressed. "You speak excellent German."

"I am German. I was raised there, but moved here when I was little. I'm from the north, in Osnabrück." Marco knew of the city from his old friend Rolf. "It's a lovely town. We used to take trips to Bremen on the weekend."

"I'm from Köln," the Nazi offered, but Marco didn't know anything about Köln, so he got to the point.

"My mother sent me here. I'm hoping you can give me some information. One of her friends knows a Jew who got sent here. Where are they being sent from here? Just give me some information to shut her up. You know how they nag."

The Nazi nodded. "They're going to a labor camp in the north, out of the country."

"When?"

"Monday morning, around nine."

Marco hid his alarm. It was sooner than he'd expected to hear. "Do me one more favor. Isn't there a way I can talk to the guy? His name is Sandro Simone."

The Nazi snorted. "No, it's not allowed. There's about a thousand Jews in there, so I can't find him anyway."

"If you let me in, I can find him."

"Ha! You've got balls, friend." The Nazi turned away and walked over to his friend, and just then, Marco heard a woman calling at the back of the crowd.

"Sandro, Sandro!"

Marco turned around and spotted her in the rain, waving a note in the air. He should have known she would come. She managed to look beautiful, even with wet hair clinging to her face. "Elisabetta!"

"Marco?"

Marco made his way to her, and Elisabetta came forward to meet him. He embraced her, moved by her tears.

"Is Sandro here?" she asked, sniffling, as he released her.

"Yes, with his father. His mother is at my house."

"What can we do?" Elisabetta wiped her eyes.

"Let's go home, we can talk about it."

"No, I want to give him my note. Will you help me?"

"I can try, but even if I could get the guard to take it, they won't know which one is him."

"Yes, they will. He has basil in the buttonhole of his jacket. I put it there, last night."

Marco's mouth went dry. He didn't know when Elisabetta and Sandro had started sleeping together, but even a fool could tell that she was deeply in love. "Let me have the note then."

"Thank you." Elisabetta handed him a crumpled piece of paper. "It tells him I love him."

"I assumed that, *cara*," Marco said, masking his pain.

# Marco

16 October 1943

Marco, his parents, Elisabetta, and Gemma gathered around the Terrizzis' kitchen table. His mother served rolls with jam, and they were on their second pot of ersatz coffee. He and his father had changed from their wet clothes, and Marco's mother had lent a dark dress to Elisabetta and a flowered one to Gemma, who slumped at the table, her eyes puffy behind her rimless glasses. Her arm was bruised, and she rested it under an icebag. Bar GiroSport was closed, the only time since Aldo's funeral.

"Let's collect our thoughts," his father said, exhaling heavily.

"Yes." Marco's mother put an arm around Gemma's sloping shoulders. "We have to keep our hopes up. I've been praying all morning."

"Thank you, Maria." Gemma sniffled, so forlorn in the cheery dress that she looked like a pile of broken flowers. She had told them how the hospital had saved Rosa and the other Jewish patients with the Syndrome K ruse. In any other circumstances, it would have struck them as funny.

His mother added, "I called Emedio and begged him to see what he can do for Massimo and Sandro. He said he will talk to the powers that be."

Gemma wiped a tear from underneath her glasses. "I can't bear to think of Massimo and Sandro in a labor camp. I hear horrible stories about the conditions there."

Marco's father patted Gemma's hand. "We can't let that happen. We have to free them."

"Are you going to try?" Gemma asked, hopeful. "Really?"

"Of course. We have to think of a way." His father glanced at Marco. "Right, son?"

"Yes," Marco answered without hesitation. He felt a stab of anguish when he flashed on Sandro being loaded onto the truck and Massimo's little wave.

"Here's the problem." His father finished his coffee. "The Collegio Militare is too secure, too well protected to break Massimo and Sandro out. It would be disastrous."

Gemma deflated, her mouth turning down.

"Come Monday morning, they're on trains to the north." His father frowned in thought. "However, the trains have to stop once or twice before they leave the country. We could find out where they stop from partisans in the north. We could ambush the trains at one of the stations."

Marco shook his head. "Papa, that won't work."

"I know. Too many innocent lives would be lost, and we wouldn't know which train car held Massimo and Sandro."

"It's too bad they're not going to a labor camp in Italy, like Fossoli. We'd have a chance there."

His father blinked, puzzled. "What camp at Fossoli, son?"

"It's a transit camp, used for temporary detention. The Nazis send POWs there. My boss at Palazzo Venezia was involved in supervising its construction. It was built last year, only six kilometers from the Carpi train station. They were building a new section, the last I heard."

Gemma rallied. "I know the town of Fossoli. It's in Carpi, a small town outside Modena. I grew up in Reggio, and my parents ran an *acetaia* and made *balsamico*."

"That's the place." Marco nodded.

His father pursed his lips. "It doesn't matter. They're not being sent to Fossoli. They're going out of the country."

Elisabetta rose abruptly. "I have to go."

Gemma looked over, puzzled. "Where?"

Maria frowned, worried. "Why?"

Marco stood up. "Elisabetta, you're not going out there alone. It's not safe."

His father stood up, next to him. "Neither of you are going anywhere without me."

"You both can come." Elisabetta set her jaw, grabbed her bag, and hurried to the stairwell. "But I'm in charge."

# Elisabetta

16 October 1943

———

Elisabetta was shown to a tastefully decorated office with brocade curtains, damask-covered chairs, shelves lined with leather-bound books, and oil landscapes of Tuscany in heavy gilt frames. She had asked Marco and his father to wait across the street because she had a personal relationship with Baron von Weizsäcker, from the restaurant. She knew that the Baron was fond of her and she hoped to use that goodwill to help Sandro and his father. She had thought of a plan, and Marco and his father had agreed that it might work. This was the first step.

Weizsäcker rose from behind an ornate desk, his blondish gray hair perfectly in place. His hooded eyes had a pleasant, if puzzled, glint at her presence, and he was typically well-tailored in a dark suit with a gray silk tie. He had an aristocratic air that previously would have made Elisabetta conscious of her humbler origins, but the war had changed her. Social class mattered less to her than it used to, and she had learned that there was only one class that mattered in war. Survivors.

"Elisabetta, come in and sit down." Weizsäcker smiled with his nice, even teeth, gesturing to the chair across from his desk.

"Thank you." Elisabetta took a seat, and Weizsäcker returned to the cushioned chair behind his desk.

"I'm accustomed to seeing you across a delicious entrée, not a desk."

"I know." Elisabetta managed a smile. "Thank you for agreeing to see me."

"Not at all. What is it you wanted to discuss?"

"First, I want to apologize for the last time you were at the restaurant, with Colonel Kappler. I'm sorry about my clumsiness."

"Oh?" Weizsäcker lifted a gray eyebrow. "I don't think it was accidental."

Elisabetta hesitated, disarmed. "Baron, you're right. You and I have known each other for a long time. Nonna always called you a gentleman. Colonel Kappler is not of your ilk."

"Discretion dictates that I keep my own counsel." Weizsäcker pursed his lips. "Now, why did you wish to see me?"

"Baron, I'm here asking for a favor. The Jews were rounded up from the Ghetto today and brought to the Collegio Militare. One of them is my boyfriend, Sandro Simone, and the other is his father, Massimo."

Weizsäcker's expression darkened, but he didn't interrupt her.

"Sandro is a brilliant mathematician, and his father is a respected tax attorney. Isn't there any way you can get the Simones out?"

"No." Weizsäcker frowned, leaning back in his chair. "You're mistaking my function. I am the German Ambassador to the Holy See, a member of my government's Foreign Office. As a career diplomat, my aim is to smooth out differences, not to create them."

"But there must be something you can do. You're so well-respected, so important. You must have *some* influence. Please, help the Simones. I'm begging you." Elisabetta leaned forward, unable to hide her urgency, but Weizsäcker's expression remained matter of fact.

"I couldn't, even if I wanted to. It's simply outside the scope of my authority."

"But it's horrible, what happened today. It's wrong, it's criminal. You must know that, Baron. You can't agree with this. You can't do this to the Jews of Rome. I'm sure the Pope doesn't—"

"Again, I have no power to order their release."

Elisabetta swallowed hard, trying to maintain her composure. If she didn't succeed here, all was lost. "Then I have a much more modest request. If you can't have the Simones released, can't you at least have them sent to a labor camp in Italy, instead of out of the country? There's a labor camp at Fossoli. It's in the town of Carpi, near Modena."

"Again, you're mistaken." Weizsäcker spread his palms. "The camp at Fossoli is not a labor camp. It's a transit camp, a way station before deportation."

"But Italian Jews are being sent there, aren't they?"

"Yes, but only temporarily."

"And I understand the camp is building a new section, too. I assume it uses prisoners to do manual labor, doesn't it?"

"I have no idea." Weizsäcker cocked his head. "How do you know all this?"

"I asked around. I have to help Sandro and his father. Please, Baron, can't you get the Simones sent to Fossoli? They can help build the new section. They're both strong and able."

"What difference does it make to you, whether they go to Fossoli or out of the country?"

"If the Simones go to Fossoli, it gives me more time to petition for their release. I intend to ask everyone I can. There are so many important people among our clientele, like you. I'm going to ask every one of them to help. I have a chance if Sandro and his father are sent to Fossoli, but not if they're deported." Elisabetta paused. "And I have friends in Carpi, our balsamic producers. You love the *balsamico* we serve. Nonna used only the best *acetaia* there. Maybe I could visit Sandro, if he was sent to Fossoli."

"You're putting me in a terrible position."

"I know, but I can't help it." Elisabetta felt tears in her eyes. "I love Sandro, and he loves me."

Weizsäcker frowned, but had no reply.

"Baron, I'm appealing to you, as a gentleman. We have a relationship, don't we? One of mutual respect? If you deny me this request, how can you ever look me in the eye again?"

Weizsäcker lifted an eyebrow, mildly amused. "Are you holding Casa Servano as hostage?"

"Yes," Elisabetta shot back, unsmiling. She sensed a tiny shift in the balance of power between them. She found herself standing, instead of begging. "If you deny me, you can't eat at my restaurant, ever again."

# Beppe

16 October 1943

Beppe climbed the stairs to their apartment with Marco and Elisabetta behind him, but when he reached the kitchen, what he found left him breathless with rage. The bearlike Stefano Pretianni from OVRA held Gemma, pressing a knife against her throat. Her eyes had gone round with terror behind her glasses. Carmine Vecchio stood behind Maria, his hand clamped on her shoulder. His wife sat frozen in a chair, her face a mask of mute horror.

Carmine sneered. "Welcome home, Beppe."

Beppe suppressed the fury in his chest. He knew instinctively he had to proceed with caution. "Let the women go. Your fight is with me."

Marco added, "And me."

Carmine's dark eyes glittered with malice. "I finally got you where I want you, Beppe. I'm turning you and your family in. You're hiding a Jewess. She gets what she deserves."

"No!" Beppe shouted, but Stefano yanked his knife across Gemma's throat, slicing it open.

Gemma's eyes flared in agony. Blood spurted from the gruesome gash. She emitted a hideous gurgling sound.

Beppe roared, launching himself at Carmine and Stefano. Marco appeared at his side, running at the men. Stefano released Gemma, who collapsed to the floor, bleeding. Maria and Elisabetta rushed to her side, screaming in horror.

Beppe punched Stefano in the face. Stefano reeled backward, his nose exploding in blood. He dropped his knife.

Marco headbutted Carmine, who crumpled, stunned. Marco slugged him, but Beppe spotted Carmine slip his hand in his pocket. Beppe knew it was a gun, so he charged Carmine. The gun went off with a deafening report.

Beppe grabbed Carmine by the ears and banged his head against the wall, knocking him senseless. Carmine got off another shot as he slid down.

Beppe snatched Stefano's knife from the floor and plunged it deep into Carmine's chest. Carmine's eyes popped.

Meanwhile Marco punched Stefano, who punched him back harder. Marco staggered, reeling. Stefano turned to the stairwell to run away.

Beppe lunged after Stefano, grabbed the big man, yanked him off-balance, then threw him into the wall, headfirst. The impact stunned Stefano. Marco punched Stefano again, knocking the big man backward. Stefano's arms flailed. He fell, groaning. Blood poured from his broken nose.

Beppe picked up a chair, stalked to Stefano, and beat him with the chair until his skull showed. Stefano lay motionless, and Beppe dropped the chair with a clatter.

"Beppe!" Maria screamed, behind him. "You're bleeding! You've been shot!"

"I'm okay," Beppe told her, but warm blood bubbled in his throat. He remembered the coppery taste from the Great War.

"Papa, no!" Marco shouted, his eyes wide.

"Don't worry." Beppe looked down to see crimson bursts on his chest, blooming like grotesque flowers. He didn't feel anything. He knew that he was losing blood fast.

"Beppe!" Maria rushed to his side.

Beppe dropped to his knees. He was going into shock. He had seen enough to know. Men had died from such wounds at Caporetto.

"Beppe, don't leave!" Maria sobbed.

Beppe tried to reassure her, but he fell to the side.

Maria knelt beside him and turned him onto his back. Her tears dropped onto his face.

"I love you, my wife," Beppe told her, his words drowned in blood.

"Papa!" Marco appeared on his other side, anguished. "No!"

Beppe reached for Marco's arm. "Take care of your mother."

Beppe closed his eyes, feeling his soul edge away from them, seeking the hands of God. He took comfort in the faith that he would see Aldo soon, and he and Aldo would both perish on the side of justice.

He let go of his mortal life and all of the years he had spent walking the cobblestones of Rome and the rocky soil of Abruzzo, ending the sum total of the days granted him by God, each one spent in an Italy he had loved and bled for, a country of passion and emotion, as gloriously turbulent as the human heart.

His soul ascended to a higher and better life.

One that never ended.

## CHAPTER ONE HUNDRED TWENTY

# Marco
### 16 October 1943

Four people lay dead in the Terrizzi kitchen, and the gruesome scene spurred Marco into action, despite his grief. He called Emedio and told him the terrible news, and Emedio came and comforted their mother. Then he called Arnaldo, his father's old war buddy, who arrived with a car, wrapped the corpses of Carmine and Stefano in blankets, and took them from the apartment, to dump them in the Tiber on the outskirts of the city. It was Marco's plan, which ironically exploited the lack of *carabinieri* and the Nazis' ruthless preoccupation with rounding up the Jews.

After that, Marco called Nino Venuti, a local undertaker who agreed to a false story of his father's death. The public would be told that Beppe Terrizzi, the former professional cyclist and popular proprietor of Bar Giro-Sport, had died suddenly of a heart attack, at his home. His wake would be held on Monday, and his body would lie in an open casket, dressed in a suit that would hide his wounds. His funeral Mass and burial would be held the next morning, and nobody would suspect the truth.

Marco would have preferred a Jewish undertaker for Gemma, but the

Nazis had taken them all. He had to settle for Nino, who arrived at the house with two assistants, older men like him, balding and dressed in black suits.

"My God." Nino scanned the kitchen, appalled.

Marco kept his gaze averted, not to succumb to emotion. "What about for Dottoressa Simone? I told you she was Jewish. You said on the phone you would do right by her."

"We will bury her tomorrow morning, timely under Jewish law. I have a simple pine casket and have arranged for a plot near the Jewish section in Verano. It would be too dangerous to bury her in the Jewish section. I falsified her death certificate. It's the best we can do, in the circumstances."

His mother looked up from the table, tearful. "Thank you, Nino. Gemma was a very dear friend of our family."

"My deepest condolences, Maria." Nino gestured to Gemma. "Now, if I may, my assistants and I will take Dottoressa Simone first."

"We have said our final goodbyes to her." His mother nodded, but she and Elisabetta wept again as Nino and his assistant went to Gemma with a black velvet sack, trimmed with gold braid. They laid it flat on the floor, unzipped it, and carefully placed her body inside. They zipped up the velvet bag, fetched a canvas stretcher, placed Gemma's body on it, then carried it downstairs.

Marco cleared his throat. "I should say goodbye to Papa now, before they take him."

His mother looked over, sniffling. "You don't have to, now. They'll give us time before the viewing."

"Right." Emedio nodded, his arm around her, and Marco realized he hadn't had a chance to tell them about their plan.

"Mamma, I'm sorry, but I can't stay for the viewing, and I might not be back for the funeral."

"What?" his mother asked, shocked. "What do you mean? You have to be there. It's your father's funeral."

"I can't stay. We think that Elisabetta persuaded Baron von Weizsäcker to send Sandro and Massimo to Fossoli, instead of out of the country. That means I have to be in place before their train arrives. I have to leave today."

"Oh no." His mother nodded, crestfallen. Her lower lip trembled, and

Emedio hugged her closer. She nodded in resignation. "I suppose your father would understand."

"Yes, he would. He and I talked about it on the way home, before . . ." Marco couldn't finish the sentence.

"And Gemma would, too. You honor her memory, trying to help Massimo and Sandro." His mother frowned, wiping her eyes. "But you aren't going to Fossoli alone, are you? Can't Arnaldo go with you?"

"No, he has to deal with Carmine and Stefano."

"I'm going with him," Elisabetta interjected, and they all turned to her. Marco shook his head. "Elisabetta, you can't. It's dangerous."

"Then it will be dangerous for us both."

Marco looked at her a long moment, then turned to the sound of Nino and his assistants climbing up the stairs. The undertakers entered the kitchen with the stretcher and another black velvet bag. His mother began to cry softly, and they laid the velvet bag on the ground beside Marco's father. They were about to move him when Marco stepped forward.

"Let me take care of him," Marco heard himself say.

Nino looked over, sympathetic. "No, Marco. We can."

"I want to." Marco crossed to his father, knelt down beside him, and placed his hands underneath his father's big shoulder, then shifted it onto the velvet bag. Then he did the same thing with the other shoulder, moving him bit by bit.

His father was heavy, but Marco focused his effort. He kept shifting his father over, then sliding the velvet cover of the bag over him. He covered both sides of his father's body, then zipped the bag partway up, from the bottom.

He heard his mother and Elisabetta weeping, and Emedio praying, but his heart focused on this final task. His tears fell onto the velvet, though he hadn't known he was crying. He zippered the bag until it reached his father's chin.

Marco let his gaze take in his father's face one last time. Beppe Terrizzi was a strong man with strong features, his skin weathered by sun and marked by age, still with the scar on his lip, from where the wolf had bitten him, as a boy. Looking at that scar, Marco realized that his father had been born with a heart that fought and loved with equal ferocity, so it was perhaps inevitable that he and his father would fight each other at times, but also would always love each other, just as strongly.

Marco knew that of the three Terrizzi sons, he himself was the most like his father, and that was why his father had expected the most from him. For his father always expected the most from himself.

He kissed his father on the forehead, feeling the warmth ebbing from his father's skin. "I love you, Papa," he whispered, through his tears.

And he knew his father heard him.

## CHAPTER ONE HUNDRED TWENTY-ONE

# Rosa

16 October 1943

Rosa sniffled, her tears finally subsiding. Maria had come to the hospital to tell her that her mother was dead, along with Beppe, and that her father and Sandro had been rounded up. The news had overwhelmed Rosa, engulfing her in sorrow and grief. Maria had comforted her, and even cried with her, which helped her through the initial shock. The word of her mother's murder spread to Dr. Cristabello, Sister Anna Domenica, and her mother's former colleagues, who had come by to pay their respects. Even now, nuns looked over in sympathy as they swept through the ward, their black habits stark against the whiteness.

Rosa wiped her eyes, trying to fathom the loss. She hadn't even gotten to say goodbye to her mother, but everyone had told her the amazing story about the Syndrome K ruse and her mother disguised in Sister Anna Domenica's habit, of all things. Her mother had risked her own life to save Rosa's, and Rosa loved her so much. She wished David were here, but he was in harm's way, too. Fear for him made her want to cry all over again.

"I'm so sorry." Maria held her hand, her eyes swollen and bloodshot. She had on a black dress, but no jewelry, and Rosa remembered the gold crucifix she had contributed to satisfy the Nazi demand for gold, which had been a cruel lie.

"What an awful day." Rosa pressed Maria's handkerchief to her eyes. "And Papa, and Sandro, too . . ."

"I didn't mean to burden you when you're ill. But I felt you should know as soon as I could tell you."

"I appreciate that, thank you." Rosa blew her nose, her eyes stinging. Her chest felt hollow and empty, her mouth dry. She still had a fever, but her own illness was beside the point now.

Maria squeezed her hand. "It is so hard to imagine your mother gone, and Beppe. It's impossible."

"I'm so sorry about Beppe." Rosa had never felt closer to Maria. The two families had always been friends, but now they were joined forever, having a tragedy in common. A wave of despair washed over Rosa, knowing that there would be no justice for her mother's murder, or for Beppe's. War welcomed and concealed the most heinous of crimes.

"Beppe tried to save her. I know he died the way he wished to, as a fighter."

Rosa patted her hand. "He was a remarkable man, an oak, and you know my father loved him."

Maria nodded, managing a smile. "Marco was devastated. It's hard on him, after Aldo."

"I'm sure." Rosa remembered Aldo, with a pang. "I'm grateful to Marco for trying to save Sandro and my father." She paused, her head fogged with grief. "But who's helping Marco, if not Beppe?"

"Elisabetta."

"That's all?" Rosa couldn't hide her despair. There had to be a way she could help. She started to rise, but eased back, weak and dizzy. "Maybe I can talk to the doctor—"

"No, you need to get well." Maria patted her hand. "By the time you're ready to leave the hospital, Emedio will have false documentation for you, and a place to live in the Vatican."

"How can I go, with Papa and Sandro in such jeopardy?"

"You *must* go, for them." Maria leaned forward, her dark eyes flashing. "Your father and Sandro love you, and it will ease their burden to know that you're safe."

"How will they know where I am?"

"Marco will get to them, and he will find a way to tell them. Think of your mother, Rosa. I know, as a mother, that she would want you to live the life that God gave you. Your survival will be her triumph." Maria tilted her chin up, in teary defiance. "Live in honor of her memory."

Rosa listened, hushed. She could almost hear her mother saying those same words.

"Rosa, I know we're not the same religion, but we both believe in a just and loving God. I believe that He brought us all together, so we can be family for each other, now." Maria looked at her, her love plain in her anguished eyes. "And think of your father, too. I have shared glasses of wine with him, at the bar. What is his toast, most of the time?"

Rosa knew the answer. *"L'Chaim."*

Maria nodded. " 'To life.' "

Tears filled Rosa's eyes. They felt true, and she let them flow.

CHAPTER ONE HUNDRED TWENTY-TWO

# Elisabetta

16 October 1943

Elisabetta stood next to Marco at the train station, waiting for the train to Carpi. She felt agonized by the horrific events of the day, and he had to feel worse. Neither of them spoke, and she had never seen him so somber. He looked around, dry-eyed, but his dark gaze didn't settle anywhere, as if it couldn't rest, even for a moment. He usually stood tall, but his broad shoulders sloped as if he had caved in on himself.

Men and women around them on the platform talked, smoked, and read books and newspapers. Elisabetta scanned the headlines, but she saw no reports of the *rastrellamento*. The Vatican still hadn't made any statement, and she was beginning to fear that they wouldn't.

Elisabetta wondered if she and Marco had a realistic chance of saving Sandro and his father. Marco had a plan, but he hadn't shared it with her yet, and she hadn't pushed the matter, given his grief. Evidently he had been a partisan, so presumably he had experience with fighting, but she didn't. Balilla training for boys was shooting long guns, but for girls, it was exercising with hula hoops.

She checked the clock, concerned that the train hadn't yet boarded. She consulted the train schedule, which was printed in tri-fold and posted in front of them, in a case with a glass front. "Marco, look at this. Shouldn't the train be leaving already? It's ten minutes past time. Do you think something's the matter?"

Marco didn't even look at the schedule. "I don't know. Want me to ask someone?"

"No, it's okay." Elisabetta noticed he didn't read the train schedule. She flashed on his poor handwriting, filled with misspellings.

"Here, we're about to board." Marco pointed as travelers surged toward the train, and he and Elisabetta joined them. He helped her up the steps, then climbed in behind her. The train car was hot, dirty, and smoky inside. They found two seats and sat down.

The train lurched off, leaving the station, and she looked out the window, which was filthy. The sky darkened as the afternoon wore on, and they wouldn't arrive in Carpi until nighttime.

Marco shifted in his seat. "You should take a nap. We could be up all night."

"I'm not tired."

"Yes, you are."

"How do you know?"

"I know what you look like when you're tired. Your eyes narrow. You squint."

Elisabetta wondered if he was right. She looked over, but Marco was scanning the other passengers, who kept up their chatter, smoking and reading. The train gathered momentum in a noisy clacking rhythm, and they left Rome behind.

"Elisabetta, close your eyes. I'll wake you when we get there."

Elisabetta couldn't sleep, and she knew Marco wouldn't either. "I'm sorry about your father."

"Thank you."

"We can talk about it, if you want to. I know how much you admired him. He was a great man."

Macro looked down at her. "Your father was great, too. I know that now."

Elisabetta didn't understand. "What do you mean?"

"You remember that night, when we were going to dinner? We ran into the ginger-haired man, who yelled at you? Who said your father's hands were broken by Fascists?"

"Yes." Elisabetta remembered, intrigued. It was the night she had given Marco his ring back.

"He was telling the truth. My father told me the story."

"Really?" Elisabetta asked, in disbelief. She shifted up in the seat. "What happened?"

"Your father painted over a Fascist slogan, on a wall in Trastevere. That's why they broke his hands. My father warned him, and he went out of town, but came back too soon." Marco lowered his voice. "You know the OVRA officers that killed my father and Gemma? They were the ones who did it."

"Oh my." Elisabetta shuddered. "I had no idea. Of any of this."

"Your father didn't want you to know. That's what the man said. He lied to protect you."

"I never suspected he lied. I believed him." Elisabetta's chest wrenched with regret. "I was so wrong."

"No, you should have believed him. You loved him."

"But I didn't appreciate him. I didn't know him as well as I thought I did. I'm proud of him, but I'm finding this out too late."

"It's not too late. You can have a feeling of pride in him the rest of your life. It's good that you found out, even now."

Elisabetta felt a pang, looking at the countryside whizzing past the window.

Marco cleared his throat, hoarsely. "That's how I feel about my father. I will always be proud of him."

Tears came to Elisabetta's eyes, but she held them back. She felt profoundly sad for her father, for Marco, for his father, and for Gemma. For Sandro and Massimo. For Nonna. For the Ghetto Jews. For Rome.

"And I do have a plan. I'll give you the details when we get there. You want Sandro, so I'll get him for you." Marco kept his eyes front. "You love him, right?"

"Yes."

"I love him, too. I would have chosen him, too." Marco paused. "But it doesn't mean I don't love you."

Elisabetta looked up at him.

Marco managed a shaky smile. "Now go to sleep, *cara*."

## CHAPTER ONE HUNDRED TWENTY-THREE

# Sandro
### 16 October 1943

Sandro and his father had been in the courtyard all day. The rain had stopped, but the sky stayed cloudy, darkening. The families sat in groups, hungry, thirsty, and frightened. Sandro had been watching them all day, and he had finally thought of a plan. "Papa, stand up."

"Why?"

"I have an idea." Sandro extended him a hand and lifted him to his feet. "What is it?"

"Look, the Nazis are letting anyone go who's not Jewish." Sandro pointed to the front of the courtyard, where the Nazi officers had their security desk. Behind them was a short line of Gentiles and *Mischlinge*, the German term for half-Jewish and half-Gentile, being readied for release.

"We can't convince them we're Gentile. I was a board member. My name must be on every record they have."

"I know, but hear me." Sandro leaned close to his father. "I've been watching all day, seeing our friends and neighbors. I kept noticing the families who are here, but then I realized I was making a mistake. I should have been noticing the families who *aren't* here."

"What do you mean?" His father looked up, intrigued.

"You know who I *haven't* seen? Matteo and Giovanni Rotoli. They aren't here."

"From across the street?"

"Yes."

His father shrugged. "They must not have been home when the Nazis came."

"Exactly." Sandro felt his heart beat faster. "Matteo and Giovanni aren't here, so we can assume their identity. Remember, Matteo isn't Jewish, only his wife, Livia, is. That makes Giovanni, his son, half-Jewish. If the Nazis look up Matteo and Giovanni Rotoli on any list, they will appear as *Mischlinge*. We can pass as them. We know everything about them."

"You're right." His father smiled, straightening. "We should try."

"Follow my lead." Sandro made his way through the crowd, with his father behind him. They reached the front of the courtyard, where a Nazi officer stood at a lectern.

"What do you want?" The Nazi frowned under the bill of his cap.

Sandro willed himself to stay calm. "Sir, I'm Giovanni Rotoli and this is my father, Matteo. I'm *Mischlinge* and my father is Gentile, a Roman Catholic. We live on Piazza Costaguti and were taken by accident."

"Why didn't you say so before?"

"We were in a classroom. Please, we don't belong here."

"Show me your identification cards."

"We had to leave without them, in a hurry." Sandro held his breath as the Nazi officer began riffling through papers on his lectern. Behind him, other Nazis were lining up the Gentiles for release. The difference between deportation or salvation was centimeters.

"Ah so, Rotoli." The Nazi pointed at the Rotoli surname on the papers, then glanced up. "Fine. Get in the line, hurry. Go."

Sandro masked the relief that flooded his heart. He turned to take his father's arm, and together they walked around another Nazi, guarding the line for release.

"Get in line!" the Nazi guard said, then looked back at Sandro. "Hey you, what's in your buttonhole?"

Sandro looked down at his jacket. In his buttonhole was the basil from

Elisabetta's garden, drooping now. She had given it to him last night. "Uh, it's just some basil."

"Where did you get it?"

"My girlfriend," Sandro answered, puzzled.

"Ha! She gave me a note for you. You're Sandro Simone?"

Sandro froze at the sound of his real name. His father looked over in fear.

The Nazi at the lectern whipped his head around. "Simone? You filthy Jew, you said your name was Rotoli!" He yanked Sandro out of line, then cocked his arm to punch him.

Sandro raised his hand to protect himself.

But the first blow was already landing.

CHAPTER ONE HUNDRED TWENTY-FOUR

# Marco

16 October 1943

---

Marco and Elisabetta disembarked at Carpi and found themselves at a small deserted train station that was more like a shed, open on three sides. The only light came from a bare bulb in the ceiling, and the air carried the smell of horse manure and an oddly acidic odor, perhaps from *balsamico*. He took his flashlight and compass from his backpack.

Elisabetta looked around. "This is really the middle of nowhere."

"There's only vineyards, like Gemma said." Marco felt a pang of grief, but suppressed the emotion. He was on a mission, and Gemma would have wanted him to succeed.

"So, which way do we go?"

"Hold on." Marco consulted his compass, then started walking. "This way. The transit camp at Fossoli is due northeast, on the other side of Carpi."

Elisabetta fell into step beside him, and Marco shone the flashlight ahead of them. They walked down a dirt road, and there was nothing on either side, no homes or vineyards. About two kilometers ahead, he could see Carpi, a small cluster of lights and shadowy tile rooftops.

Elisabetta looked over. "So what now?"

"I'd like to get as close to the transit camp as possible, to see how it works and get the lay of the land."

"How long will it take to get there?"

"Probably an hour, maybe less."

They walked along, and in time crossed an intersection and a directional sign, with arrows aiming different ways.

"A sign." Elisabetta pointed.

"I see."

"It says Fossoli is straight ahead."

"That's the way we're going." Marco kept walking, breathing in the country air, which reminded him of Abruzzo, where his parents were from. His family had gone there to visit his grandparents from time to time. His father always talked about how he and his mother had fallen in love there and moved to Rome together, as if life were a grand adventure.

"Marco, why didn't you tell me you can't read?"

His mouth went dry. His face warmed.

"It's nothing to be ashamed of."

Marco didn't know what to say. Of course it was something to be ashamed of. He walked straight ahead, so she couldn't see his expression.

"Marco?"

"I can read."

"I don't think you can." Elisabetta's tone was sympathetic, not accusatory, which only made him feel worse.

"Well, I can."

"Then what did that sign say?"

"I don't need it. I rely on my compass. I have an excellent sense of direction."

"Just tell me what it said."

"It said we're going the right way."

"You know that's not the point. It had the names of towns nearby and the distances."

"Look, I admit, I don't read as well as you or Sandro. You read books, and he's a genius. I'm smart, just not as smart as you guys."

"Yes, you are."

"No, I'm not." Marco wanted to believe she was right, but she wasn't. That damn train schedule had given him away.

"Marco, come on, you're very smart. I know you, I see what you do. Look at what you did today."

"Today my father died."

Elisabetta touched his arm. "Even so, you figured out a story for Nino the undertaker and a plan for Arnaldo. You spoke good enough German to fool that Nazi. You even got him to agree to give Sandro my note."

"He did it because you're beautiful. Even Nazis like beautiful girls." Marco shook his head. "And I doubt he gave it to Sandro anyway."

"My point is that you're very intelligent."

"Then what's the matter?" Marco blurted out, since it was a question he had asked himself over and over. "Why is reading harder for me?"

"Tell me what happens when you read."

Marco sighed, pained. "I don't know."

"What do you see, on the page?"

"Everything looks mixed up."

"Do you think it's your eyes? Do you need glasses?"

"No, I see fine." Marco had already eliminated these possibilities.

"What happens when you write?"

"I don't know what to write. I don't know what to make anything look like."

"I bet I can help you."

"I bet you can't." Marco walked faster. "Let me tell you the plan. That's what matters now."


Marco and Elisabetta reached Fossoli, found a vineyard, and lay on their stomachs between rows of grapevines, behind a thick underbrush. The transit camp was across from them, far enough to avoid their being seen. Its lights illuminated the night sky, unnaturally bright in the countryside. They had an unobstructed view, since the grapes in the vineyards in between had been harvested, the earth tilled in rows.

Marco scanned the transit camp through the binoculars, reconnoitering. The camp was a long rectangle, set lengthwise on Via dei Grilli, running east to west and surrounded by three layers of post-and-barbed wire fencing. There were no guard turrets or watchtowers. The prisoners' barracks were long brick houses with small square windows, situated in rows on the east side of the camp and set perpendicular to the road. There were ten barracks in a row and eight rows of barracks, which flanked an aisle that ran down the middle of the camp, running parallel to Via dei Grilli.

He shifted his binoculars to focus on the west side of the transit camp, where there were smaller structures, evidently offices and barracks for Nazi guards. Behind the transit camp on the southwest side, situated along Via Remesina, was a construction site, apparently where the Nazis were building the extension. Ditches had been dug for foundations, framed with wood. Bricks, wood, and building materials sat piled next to the frames and shovels, picks, spades, and other tools.

Marco returned his attention to the transit camp proper. It was late and no prisoners were about, so they must have been inside the barracks. Nazis guarded the perimeter, stationed at every eighth post. Some looked around, others smoked. One left by the south gate, disappeared into the darkness, and reappeared after a few moments buckling his belt, so presumably he had gone to urinate.

"What do you see?" Elisabetta whispered.

"The layout and other details. It's what I expected."

"Can I look?"

"Yes." Marco handed her the binoculars, and Elisabetta held it up to her eyes.

"It's such a big camp."

"Not very."

"There's a lot of guards."

"Not too many."

"Are you sure we can do this?" Elisabetta lowered the binoculars, revealing a grimace.

"Yes," Marco answered, though he wasn't. "Let me go it alone. It's too dangerous, I told you."

"No, I want to do it. You need me for the plan, now."

"Still, I can think of another plan. Are you sure?"

"Yes." Elisabetta raised the binoculars.

Later, they walked along by moonlight, crossing vineyards and horse pastures. They came upon a large *acetaia* with a small stone farmhouse, a barn, a chicken coop, and two outbuildings. They sneaked through rows of vines to the outbuildings, and Marco turned on his flashlight and shone it inside.

The first outbuilding contained *balsamico* barrels, reeking of fermenting vinegar, and the other held stacked burlap bags. They chose the latter and went inside. The air smelled musty, and cobwebs draped from the low rafters.

Marco cast the flashlight on the burlap bags. "We can sleep here. We'll be gone by dawn."

"Good." Elisabetta eased into the earthen floor, leaning back against the bags. "I'm so tired, I could sleep sitting up."

"I'll wake you up when it's time. I always know." Marco sat beside her, turning off the flashlight and plunging them into darkness. His eyes adjusted to his surroundings. Moonlight streamed through the small window.

Elisabetta didn't respond.

Marco looked over to find her already asleep. He exhaled, then let himself feel his own fear and anguish. Their mission was dangerous, with slim odds of success. He would lay down his life for Sandro and Massimo, but he would never forgive himself if anything happened to Elisabetta. He considered sneaking out while she slept and executing the plan alone, but he did need her. And she would have been furious with him.

He leaned back on the burlap bags, closed his eyes, and rehearsed his plan in his mind. Tomorrow was the first step, and the more he thought about tomorrow, the less he thought about his father's death, and Gemma's.

# Elisabetta

17 October 1943

Elisabetta walked along Via Remesina, swinging a bottle of wine. Bees buzzed in the vineyards, and the air smelled of fermenting *balsamico* and freshly cultivated earth. It was a sunny Sunday afternoon, perfect for a young girl to visit her grandparents, which was her false story. This was the next step of their plan, and its success depended solely on her. She had freshened her dress and combed her hair into place, as she needed to look her best. Marco was watching her through his binoculars, from the ravine.

She tensed at the sight of armed Nazis with dogs, ahead at the transit camp. A group of them were guarding the prisoners laboring on the construction site, at the back of the camp. Dump trucks with muddy tires were parked on the site, and lumber and tools had been stacked here and there. She reached the site, and the dogs began barking at her.

Nazi guards and prisoners watched her pass by. The prisoners returned to their toil, but the Nazis smiled or winked at her. One Nazi blew her a kiss, which revolted her, but she waved back.

She kept walking, reminding herself that she had an important role to play. She felt newly stronger, having learned the truth about how her father's hands had been broken. Now she was proud of him, rather than ashamed. He had sacrificed to resist the Fascists. She felt as if she were truly his daughter, doing her part to defy the Nazis.

She reached the end of the construction site, walked along the side of the transit camp, and turned right on Via dei Grilli, heading for the main entrance. Inside, Nazis going in and out of the offices stopped to watch her walk by, smiling and waving. She smiled and waved back. The gates were open to construction traffic, and a group of Nazis surged forward to meet her, greeting her in German and broken Italian.

She smiled, waved, and made eye contact with as many Nazis as possible, for her goal was to be memorable. She was never good at flirting, but she didn't have to be, for they seemed hungry for female attention. Suddenly one of the dogs lunged at her, baring its teeth.

Elisabetta jumped back, startled. "Oh!"

"I'm very sorry, miss," the Nazi said, in poor Italian. He reprimanded the dog, which quieted. "He's really very friendly. Would you like to pet him?"

"No, thanks." Elisabetta made a funny face, and the Nazis laughed, evidently charmed.

"Do you live nearby, miss?"

"No, my grandparents do. I'm visiting." Elisabetta felt satisfied that she had made enough of an impression. "Well, I'd better go now. Goodbye."

"Will you come again sometime?"

"I'll try," Elisabetta answered, knowing she would be back sooner than they expected.

CHAPTER ONE HUNDRED TWENTY-SIX

# Marco

### 17 October 1943

It was almost midnight. Darkness concealed Marco and Elisabetta, who were lying in the ravine side by side, on their stomachs. Marco held the binoculars to his eyes, watching the transit camp. The prisoners were in their barracks. The construction site was quiet. The Nazis guarded their posts along the perimeter fence.

"What's going on?" Elisabetta asked, looking over.

"Nothing." Marco watched the Nazis, who examined their fingernails, brushed dirt from their coats, or smoked one cigarette after another. "They stand there, looking at the same vineyards night after night. That will help us, when the time comes. They're bored to death."

"That's why they were so interested in me today."

Marco lowered the binoculars. "That's not why. You're a beautiful girl, carrying wine. It's what men dream of."

"Men like wine that much?"

"No. Men like women who like wine that much." Marco returned the binoculars to his eyes. "Still, you did well. You were brave."

"Thank you."

"The next step will be harder, and there's always the possibility that Baron von Weizsäcker didn't get Sandro and his father sent here. If the Baron failed us, we're in trouble."

"I think he did it."

"Why?"

"I make the best pasta in Rome."

Marco smiled, falling in love with Elisabetta all over again. His heart ached for her, and he worried these feelings would never leave him.

He stole a glance at her in the moonlight, but her eyes were on the camp.

## CHAPTER ONE HUNDRED TWENTY-SEVEN

# Marco
### 18 October 1943

The next day, Marco and Elisabetta were lying in the ravine, having camouflaged themselves with underbrush. It was already late afternoon, and they were still waiting for Sandro and his father to appear. If the train had left Rome this morning, then Sandro and his father should have already arrived, assuming that they had been on the train.

Marco tried not to be discouraged. Elisabetta had fallen silent. He focused the binoculars on Via Remesina, the road from Carpi station. There was no sign of anyone. So far, the only traffic on that road or Via dei Grilli had been a mule cart, a farmer on horseback, and an old truck from an *acetaia*.

He shifted left, to the transit camp. It looked like business as usual, with

Nazis on post at the perimeter. A group of Nazis guarded the construction site, where the prisoners labored. No preparations were being made to receive new prisoners, which worried him.

Marco watched and waited, then finally noticed something coming down Via Remesina toward the transit camp. In the next moment he realized that it was a few Kubelwagens, a Nazi escort. They must have come from Modena or elsewhere. Perhaps that accounted for the delay.

His heart began to pound. The vehicles drew closer. He could see that behind them walked a bedraggled procession of men, women, and children.

"They're coming." Marco kept the binoculars to his eyes.

"Do you see Sandro?" Elisabetta asked, excited.

"Not yet." Marco watched the shifting view of families trudging down the road. They clung to each other, downcast. He searched every face, hoping it was Sandro's or his father's. The heads bobbed and moved, a shifting mass of men, women, and children.

He spotted Sandro, walking with his arm around Massimo, who was limping slightly. "I see him!"

"Thank God! Can I look?"

"Not yet. I don't want to lose sight of him." Marco watched as the Kubelwagens and the line of families turned the corner toward the entrance to the transit camp. The Nazis opened the gates and allowed the Kubelwagens to enter. Other Nazis hustled to the line and hurried the families inside with guns and barking dogs.

Marco watched as the families filed in. In time, Sandro and his father entered the transit camp and were hustled inside. The Nazis forced in the remaining families, then closed the gates. The families massed in front of the barracks, instinctively forming a group. Dogs barked and strained on leashes, terrifying the children. Mothers cradled babies, and fathers picked up toddlers.

Nazis brandishing weapons separated the men from the women and children, sending the men to the east and women to the west side of the barracks. Husbands and wives reached for each other, crying at being torn apart. Children screamed for fathers and grandfathers. They were forced to split up at gunpoint or menaced with the butts of rifles.

"What's happening?"

"The Nazis are separating men from women."

"And Sandro?"

"He and his father are getting in lines for the barracks." Marco waited to see which barracks Sandro and his father were assigned to. Soon they were shoved in front of the third barracks from the east and forced to line up outside. The barracks had a white sign that Marco couldn't read.

"Please, can I see?"

"Yes. He's in front of the third barracks from the end, on the left." Marco handed her the binoculars. "Each barracks has a white sign. What number is their barracks?"

Elisabetta raised the binoculars. "I see him! And he still has the basil! I wonder if he got my note."

"What number is their barracks?"

"Fifteen. I wish we could go in there right now."

"Not until nightfall. Stay with the plan."

"Oh no, something's the matter with his face!" Elisabetta moaned. "Do you think they beat him?"

Marco felt enraged at the thought.

It was time for action, and tonight couldn't come soon enough.

## CHAPTER ONE HUNDRED TWENTY-EIGHT

# Elisabetta
### 18 October 1943

A cloud cloaked the moon, and Elisabetta and Marco hurried ahead in utter darkness. Their clothes were dark so they blended in. They raced across an open pasture to the east side of the transit camp. There were no grapevines or ravines in which to hide, and they were vulnerable, covered only by night. They approached the transit camp, crouching down.

They stopped at a tall umbrella pine tree near the back entrance, close to Sandro's barracks.

The transit camp was quiet. The prisoners were inside the barracks, asleep at this hour. The Nazi guards stood at their regular posts. Elisabetta couldn't see their faces under their helmets, but it didn't matter if she remembered them. It mattered only if they remembered her, from when she had pretended to be a country girl, carrying wine.

Elisabetta and Marco split up at the umbrella pine, without exchanging a word. There was nothing to say, and they both knew the plan. She stayed behind the tree while Marco ran to the construction site, on the west side of the transit camp. There was no perimeter fence around the construction site, and it was unguarded at night. A few lamps there had been wired on posts, but they weren't lighted.

Elisabetta crouched behind the tree, hidden. Marco would reach the site any minute now. He would set a small fire, which would grow, giving him time to get back to her.

She was supposed to count off five minutes, then go into action. Her heart pounded in her chest, and she forced herself to count slowly. She told herself to stay calm. She would do whatever it took to save Sandro.

She didn't see Marco, but she had to trust that he would come in time. She counted to two minutes, then three, four, and five.

It was time.

"Hey, you!" Elisabetta called to the nearest Nazi guard, stepping out from behind the tree, with a smile.

The Nazi raised his gun, and a bolt of fear coursed through her body.

"It's only me," she called out, waving.

The Nazi lowered his gun, and Elisabetta breathed easier, remembering the German phrases Marco had taught her.

"I remember you, handsome. Do you remember me?"

"*Natürlich,*" the Nazi answered, keeping his voice low. He glanced behind him, checking to see if anyone was watching them.

"I like you the best. I need a man." Elisabetta struggled through her fear to remember the German words. "I'm so lonely."

The Nazi stood still, neither answering nor moving.

Elisabetta held her breath, not knowing what to do. She had to improvise. She pulled up her skirt in the front, leaving no mistake about her meaning. "Please, I like you the best. I need a man. I'm so lonely."

The Nazi turned in the direction of the other guard, then shouted to him in rapid German. Elisabetta prayed to God he wasn't informing on her. The other guard only nodded, so evidently he wasn't.

The Nazi started walking toward the back exit of the transit camp, then let himself out the gate, unbuckling his belt as if he had to go to the bathroom.

Elisabetta slipped back behind the tree, watching the Nazi come closer. Her heart thundered in her chest. She checked the construction site. She couldn't see if the fire had started. She could only hope Marco was on his way back to her.

The Nazi made a terrifying silhouette advancing on her, backlit. She wanted to scream, but instead she forced a naughty giggle.

The Nazi shadow loomed larger. She could hear him chuckling, in excitement. His belt jingled, and he unzipped his pants.

Elisabetta struggled to control her panic. The Nazi was almost there, saying something in German. She was supposed to reach out her arms, but she was too frightened. She didn't see Marco anywhere.

The Nazi embraced her roughly. He kissed her hard on the mouth, tasting of cigarettes. His hand slipped under her dress, sliding up her thigh to her underwear.

She forced herself not to struggle. The Nazi thrust his tongue into her mouth. Tears came to her eyes. The Nazi leaned her back, then pressed her to the ground.

Elisabetta scrambled backward, stalling. The Nazi thought she was teasing. He scrambled after her, chuckling. He gripped her arm, pulled her under him, and climbed on her with his full weight.

Suddenly the Nazi's head was jerked backward. His body was lifted off of her. Marco materialized above the Nazi, grabbing his head.

The Nazi's eyes widened with fear. Marco twisted the Nazi's head deftly, breaking his neck with a crunch of vertebrae.

Elisabetta rolled away, swallowing her horror.

The Nazi collapsed, dead.

# Marco

### 18 October 1943

Marco walked toward the back exit of the transit camp. He kept his face down under the dead Nazi's helmet. The Nazi's uniform fit him well, and he buckled his belt as he approached the transit camp, as if he had urinated. The Nazi guard opened the gate for him, and Marco grunted his thanks. He entered the transit camp, crossed to the dead Nazi's post, and stood on guard.

He glanced toward the construction site, praying that the fire grew soon. He had set it near some electrical wire behind a pile of bricks, then mixed in flammable solvent and oily rags. The fire wouldn't show until it was blazing, and the Nazis would assume it was negligence, rather than intentional. He didn't want it to look like sabotage, or they would lock down the transit camp.

Marco stood behind Sandro's barracks, which were quiet. The plan was working, so far. He had gotten to Elisabetta in time. She had looked terrified, but she had done the job. He checked the umbrella pine, knowing she would be hiding behind it, recovering.

He shifted his gaze to the construction site. He noticed a faint orange brightness behind the pile of bricks. The rags must have caught fire. They were beginning to burn.

Marco turned, patrolled Sandro's barracks, and peered in the windows, as he had seen the Nazis do. He glanced in the first window, then the second. The only thing he could discern in the gloom were sleeping forms, in rough wooden rows of beds. He had been hoping to spot Sandro inside, but it was too dark.

Marco passed the third window and heard snoring, a distinctly human sound that wrenched his heart. He wished he could save every one of them.

He returned to his post. He glanced at the construction site. The brightness was growing. None of the Nazis was looking in that direction.

*War is waiting,* he thought of his father saying.

Marco's first impulse was to suppress thoughts of his father, but instead he used the memory to strengthen him. Surely his father was with him now, watching over him. Everything that he had learned about right and wrong, and justice and injustice, came from his father.

Tonight, Marco prayed he would do justice.

## CHAPTER ONE HUNDRED THIRTY

# Marco
### 18 October 1943

ire!" yelled a Nazi. Panic rippled through the guards. All of the helmeted heads turned to the construction site. The Nazis ran to the fire, which had ignited the solvent and rags. Orange flames raged into the sky, licking the night air.

"Fire, fire!" Marco joined in, with flawless German. He pointed at the fire. The Nazis around him left their posts and ran where he pointed.

Marco ran to Sandro's barracks and tore open the door. The men inside recoiled in terror, but he couldn't reveal he wasn't a real Nazi. He couldn't risk how the men would react. Nothing could go wrong now.

"Get back!" Marco shouted in German. He looked wildly around for Sandro and his father. Men huddled together, cowering in fear. He spotted Sandro against the wall with Massimo, who was putting on his glasses.

"You, come with me!" Marco rushed to them, grabbing Sandro in one hand and Massimo in the other. He hustled them to the door and scanned the camp to see if it was safe to leave. All of the Nazi guards were at the construction site, trying to put out the fire. Some tried blankets, others water. There was no time to lose.

"Sandro, Massimo!" Marco whispered, leading them outside. "Come with me. Hurry."

"Marco?" Sandro's mouth dropped open. He took his father's arm. "Papa, he's getting us out of here."

"But I can't walk on my ankle." Massimo limped. "It's worse than before."

"We have to go." Marco glanced at the construction site. The fire raged higher, and the Nazis tried to put it out. The conflagration burned bright. No one was looking their way.

Massimo turned to Sandro, stricken. "Son, go without me. I'm too slow. I can't keep up."

Sandro shook his head. "Papa, I can't leave you."

"You must. Go. I love you."

"Massimo, please." Marco looked over, frantic.

"Marco, take Sandro." Massimo's eyes glistened. "Do it for me. I beg you."

"No," Sandro insisted, but Massimo wrenched his arm from his son's grasp and darted back inside the barracks.

"Papa!" Sandro started to go after him.

"Sandro. Come with me, now." Marco grabbed Sandro's arm, giving him no choice. The Nazis were at the fire. They were still preoccupied, but it wouldn't last long.

Marco yanked Sandro to the exit, tore open the gate, and swung it closed. He kept his grip on Sandro and ran him to the umbrella pine.

Elisabetta showed herself, taking Sandro's hand. "Sandro!"

"Elisabetta?" Sandro asked, shocked.

But there was no time for conversation.

Marco, Sandro, and Elisabetta raced into the darkness.

# Sandro

18 October 1943

Sandro's eyes filled with tears as they ran from the transit camp. Elisabetta held his one arm and Marco held the other, propelling him forward. He felt agonized at having abandoned his father. Guilt buckled his knees, weakening him. He knew he should go with Marco and Elisabetta, but he wanted to turn and run back.

"My father—" Sandro couldn't finish the sentence.

"We had no choice."

"We could have made him come."

"No."

"We could have tried."

"No, Sandro. He never could have made this run. We have to run for the next hour, over pastures and vineyards. It's too much for him."

"They won't retaliate against him, will they?"

"Did they check your names when they assigned you the barracks?"

"No, they only counted heads."

"So they don't know who you are. Your father is a brilliant man. He'll take care of himself."

Elisabetta squeezed his hand, and her grip gave Sandro the strength to keep running. Tears streamed down his cheeks. All around him was pitch black. His legs felt weak. His breath turned ragged. His heart pounded with exertion. He struggled to keep up.

"Sandro, listen," Marco said, as they ran. "The Nazis will realize a guard is missing. They'll find the dead guard with ease. They're going to search the transit camp and the houses in Fossoli and Carpi. We can't stay in the area."

"Right," Sandro said, his chest heaving.

"We can't go to Carpi train station. That's what they expect."

"So where are we going?"

"South, to the train station at Modena. The last train to Rome is in an hour and fifteen minutes. We timed your escape to make the train. If we miss it, we'll have to hide overnight."

"Okay." Sandro got the message. They had to make the train. It was life or death.

"I don't think the Nazis from Fossoli will be sent to Modena. They can't spare men."

"There could be Nazis in Modena."

"I know. I have false papers for you. Your new name is Giovanni Longhi."

"After Professoressa Longhi." Sandro remembered the math teacher, a lifetime ago.

"I have a change of clothes for you, too. When we get to the train station, we split up. Act like we don't know each other. You and Elisabetta will go together. You'll be a couple."

Elisabetta looked over at Sandro. "We are a couple."

Marco was barely panting. "I'll keep an eye on you two, but you're on your own."

"Will the Nazis at Modena know there was an escape?"

"Yes, I assume so. My hope is they'll expect us to hide around Fossoli rather than try to run to Modena. So we have surprise going for us, again. If we just keep traveling south across the fields, we'll be fine."

Elisabetta squeezed Sandro's hand. "This is all Marco's plan. How to get you out of the camp, everything."

"Not true." Marco looked over. "Elisabetta makes great pasta."

"What?" Sandro asked breathlessly. "Marco, thank you. I don't know how I can repay you."

"Take care of her, that's how."

# Elisabetta

18 October 1943

Elisabetta held Sandro's hand, and they walked through the cobblestone streets of Modena toward the train station. Marco was a block ahead of them, and men and women passed them. She had shaken the dirt from her shoes, and Sandro had changed into Marco's white shirt and dark pants, cinched by a belt. He looked fine except for the welt on his right cheek, from a Nazi blow.

Elisabetta felt terrible about leaving Massimo behind, and Sandro was somber. Ahead, Marco joined the people heading into the station, a long, square building with a series of arches at its entrance. She realized that he would have a hard time finding their platform, since he couldn't read train schedules. She hoped he would figure it out or ask someone.

Elisabetta and Sandro crossed the street and entered the train station. The ceiling was vaulted, and it was a large space, with doors on the far side that led to the platforms and tracks. There were only a handful of travelers, carrying valises and newspapers. Luckily, there were no Nazis in sight.

"Giovanni, let's check the track number," Elisabetta said, using Sandro's false name, in case anyone overheard. He pursed his lips, and she could tell he was nervous, so she squeezed his hand.

Sandro eyed the schedule. "Our train will be here any minute, on track seven. We're right on time."

"Good." Elisabetta glanced over to see Marco passing through the door to the platforms. "Let's wait outside, shall we? It's a nice night, and I'm sure we can pay on the train."

"Good idea." Sandro forced a smile, and they headed outside. They crossed to the platform for track seven. Their train approached, its round light rumbling toward them. The travelers perked up and formed a rough line.

Elisabetta's heart filled with happiness. All she and Sandro had to do was board and act like a couple in love, which they were. They were almost home.

Suddenly two Nazis emerged from the train station, smoking cigarettes. She spotted them out of the corner of her eye, but kept her smile in place. Sandro must have seen them, too. He stiffened, turning away.

Elisabetta worried about him. On impulse, she kissed him. He kissed her back, surprised at first, then she felt him catch fire. She pressed herself against him, feeling all the love she had for him.

"I love you," Sandro murmured, when he released her.

"I love you, too," she told him.

The train pulled into the station, its engine grinding and wheels slowing rhythmically. The other travelers to Rome lined up to board, flowing around them. She kept Marco in her sight, and he lingered to the side and behind them, pretending to read a newspaper. She knew he had seen the two Nazis and wouldn't board until after she and Sandro did, making sure they were safe.

The Nazis walked toward the platform, apparently to board the train. They chatted and smoked in a relaxed manner, but Sandro stared straight ahead, his back ramrod straight. Elisabetta felt alarm at Sandro's reaction and glanced at Marco. Their eyes connected, and she knew he was having the same concern. In the next moment, Marco set his newspaper on the bench.

The line of travelers shifted forward, boarding the train. Elisabetta and Sandro moved up, but Sandro kept his face front. The Nazis joined the line behind them, laughing together, as if they had shared a joke. Elisabetta didn't understand what they were saying, and Marco was too far away to hear.

Sandro kept staring straight ahead. Elisabetta caressed his arm, trying to reassure him. Marco shifted closer to the two of them, slipping off his backpack.

Elisabetta knew Marco had a gun inside.

The line moved forward.

Elisabetta stepped closer to the train, and so did Sandro. The Nazis followed, then one of them spoke to Sandro.

# Marco

18 October 1943

Marco slipped his hand inside his backpack. His fingers encircled the handle of his gun. He forced himself to wait. Two Nazis were standing behind Sandro and Elisabetta. One of the Nazis was saying something to Sandro, trying to get his attention.

Sandro stood oddly stiff.

Marco moved close enough to hear what they were saying.

The first Nazi chuckled. "Did your girlfriend hit you?" he asked Sandro, in broken Italian.

Sandro turned around, stiffly. He didn't laugh. His mouth went tight. "No . . . uh . . . I got hurt when, uh, when—"

"He fell down the steps," Elisabetta interjected, with a sly grin. "If I hit him, it would leave a bigger mark."

The Nazis burst into laughter. Sandro managed a smile, but it was shaky. Marco placed his finger on the trigger.

The first Nazi winked at Elisabetta. "I don't believe you. I think you did hit him."

"Like this!" The second Nazi cocked his arm and pretended to punch Sandro, but Sandro flinched in reflexive fear.

The first Nazi's smile faded. "What are you so worried about?"

The second Nazi eyed Sandro hard. "Show us your identity card."

"Of course." Sandro put his hand in his pocket, produced the false card, and held it out, but his hand trembled visibly.

Elisabetta stiffened.

Marco kept his finger on the trigger.

The Nazi made no move to take the card. Instead he watched Sandro's hand shake, prolonging the excruciating moment.

The conductor appeared in the stairwell of the train. "All aboard, all aboard!"

The Nazi gave the conductor a stern look. "Hold the train. We're not ready to leave yet."

The conductor nodded nervously, then disappeared.

The Nazi lifted his gaze from the trembling card to Sandro. "You seem very nervous. What are you hiding? What have you done?"

Sandro swallowed hard. "I haven't done anything."

"Something tells me you have." The Nazi snapped the card from Sandro's hand, skimmed it, and started to return it. But as soon as Sandro reached for the card, the Nazi pulled it back, toying with him.

Sandro's hand shook, suspended in the air.

Marco aimed his gun, still in the backpack.

The Nazi pulled his pistol on Sandro. "You're coming with us."

Marco withdrew his gun.

The Nazi whipped around, aimed at Marco, and fired.

"No!" Sandro threw himself in the path of the Nazi's bullet, and it struck him in the chest.

Sandro's shirt exploded in blood. He flew backward through the air, his arms flailing.

Elisabetta screamed in anguish.

Marco shot both Nazis, rapid-fire. They dropped to the platform, dead.

"No!" Elisabetta raced to Sandro, who lay bleeding on the platform. She threw herself on him, hugging him. She burst into tears, screaming and sobbing.

Marco raced to Sandro's side in horror. Sandro's blue eyes faced heavenward, fixed. His body was utterly motionless. Sandro was gone, his blood leaking from the mortal wound in his chest.

Marco felt his heart shatter. His best friend was dead, having given his life for him.

"No, no, no!" Elisabetta cried, her head against Sandro's chest. His blood stained her face and smeared her cheeks.

Marco forced himself to think through his agony. The train left, undoubtedly to avoid trouble. Men and women fled the platform into the station. He had killed two Nazis. More would come soon.

Marco had to get Elisabetta out of here. He didn't know where or how. He put his gun away, shouldered his backpack, and looked around, frantic.

The tracks began to rumble. A freight train appeared, southbound. Its locomotive was a dark shadow barreling towards the station. It was several tracks over, traveling too fast to be stopping in Modena. It was their only chance.

Marco grabbed Elisabetta by the shoulders. "Come with me!"

"No, no!" Elisabetta wouldn't let go of Sandro. She sobbed, holding his body, even as his chest bled.

"We have to go!"

"I can't leave him! I won't!"

"We have to! Now!" Marco yanked Elisabetta from Sandro and threw her over his shoulder, crying and screaming. He jumped off the platform with her and hurried across the tracks.

The freight train roared toward them. Its horn blared, warning him off the tracks.

Marco scanned the cars on the train. The first few were wood, with closed doors. Then he spotted a coal car with an open top and a ladder on the side.

The freight engine reached them and churned past at speed. Its locomotive thundered, but it slowed slightly as it approached the station. He tightened his grip on Elisabetta. Wind, dirt, and smoke blasted his face.

Marco readied himself. Elisabetta screamed. The train roared. The coal car zoomed closer.

He launched himself at the ladder, holding Elisabetta.

# Marco
18 October 1943

The train hurtled south, barreling through the night, and Marco and Elisabetta lay atop the hard coal. He held her as she wept, her body racked with sobs. The roar of the train deafened him, and it sped through town after town.

Wind flew over them, sending coal particulate everywhere, stinging their eyes and filling their nostrils. Coal smudged their clothes and covered their arms, turning them both black, as if they had become the hue of mourning.

Marco looked up at the sky, agonized over losing Sandro. The clouds concealed the moon and the stars. All he could see above was darkness, impenetrable. He wondered where the blackness ended, or if it ever did, like grief itself, having no bottom, top, or sides, but was limitless, borderless, surrounding him.

Elisabetta wept, and Marco felt her anguish, for he had gone to Fossoli to get Sandro for her. She loved Sandro, and Sandro loved her, and they belonged together. Marco had planned to sacrifice himself for Sandro, but his plan had failed. Instead, Sandro had sacrificed himself for Marco. The wrong man had died, and Marco knew it.

He gazed up at the black and empty sky.

He closed his eyes and saw the same void.

He cried with Elisabetta, all the way to Rome.

# Marco

19 October 1943

Marco slumped at the kitchen table, heartbroken. Coal dust covered his clothes and stung his eyes. His mother set another cup of coffee in front of him. She had cried with him, after he told her what had happened in Modena. She looked utterly drained and exhausted, still in the black dress she had worn to his father's wake.

Emedio sat at the table, in teary silence. Elisabetta was still in the bathroom, sobbing in the bathtub.

His mother sat down next to him, touching his arm. "Marco, drink your coffee."

"I don't want it, thanks."

"You gave your all. You can't blame yourself. Sandro wouldn't blame you. He loved you."

Emedio nodded, equally drained. "I'm sorry, brother."

Marco sipped his coffee, which did nothing to wash down the coal particulate, an irritant he couldn't ignore. Grief, guilt, and rage formed a bolus that lodged in his throat. He looked across the table at his brother. "Oh, Emedio, how nice. And will you pray? Will you pray for Sandro?"

Emedio blinked. "Of course, I have been."

"And what good did it do? What good did your prayers do Sandro? What good did they do Massimo or the other Jews? Or Papa, or Gemma?"

"Marco, you're upset—"

"Yes, I am. Why isn't anybody doing anything? If they had, Sandro would be alive. So would Papa and Gemma. Massimo would be here. It's madness! Why isn't anybody stopping this?" Marco found himself rising, his emotions coming to a boil. "Don't give me prayers, brother! Don't give me sympathy! Papa fought for what he believed in! So do I! I would kill every last Nazi with my bare hands! Sandro died because nobody did anything!"

"No," Emedio said, his tone hushed. "You have to look for the love and for God—"

"Don't be so naïve!" Marco exploded. "There was no love there, only hate! Where was God when the bullet ripped through Sandro's heart? Why didn't God take me instead? I wanted Him to!"

His mother gasped. "Marco, don't say such things!"

"Marco, listen to me." Emedio looked up, shaken. "Sandro made the choice to save you. God was there, in him. Sandro was love, not hate. Don't betray him now. Don't answer the love he showed with hate."

Marco felt stunned by his brother's words. Their impact stopped him. He felt ashamed to be shouting at his mother and brother, on the night of his father's wake. Their agonized expressions told him he was in the wrong.

He slumped down into the chair. He felt bewildered, devastated, crushed. His head dropped to his hands. His gaze found the pale stain darkening the floorboards. It was from his father's blood.

Behind him, the bathroom door opened, and Elisabetta came out in a fresh dress, her expression stricken.

"I want to go home," she said quietly.

## CHAPTER ONE HUNDRED THIRTY-SIX

# Elisabetta
### 19 October 1943

Elisabetta climbed the stairs to her bedroom, numb with grief. Marco had walked her home, but they hadn't said a single word. They existed in a hell that was shared, but also, somehow, private.

She reached her bedroom, unlocked the door, then closed it behind her. The bedroom was dark, except for a pale moonbeam filtering through the window, so faint as to appear ghostly.

Gnocchi and Rico began meowing, part greeting, part protest. Rico remained at the foot of the bed, his shadow as dark as the coal on the train. Gnocchi was visible, with her white fur glowing in the moonlight.

Elisabetta felt like crying, but no tears were left inside her. Only an emptiness, and a tearing in her chest that felt like she also had been shot through the heart. She had been shocked when Sandro had dived in front of the bullet, but she shouldn't have been. That was who Sandro was, as a man. Marco, too. Each would have given his life for the other, and for her, and Sandro had.

She began unbuttoning her dress, walking over to her chair. She noticed that her notebook lay open on her desk, which was odd. She turned on the light and saw a note, which read:

*Elisabetta,*
*We had one night, but I want a forever of nights.*
*I love you forever.*

*Your Sandro*

Her throat caught with emotion. Tears filled her eyes. She ran her fingers over the handwriting, feeling its indentures. She picked up the open notebook and held it against her chest. She knew that she would love Sandro forever. She wouldn't stop just because he was gone.

She found herself walking to the back door and up the fire escape. She crossed the garden to her chaise longue and lay down, holding the notebook against her chest. She closed her watery eyes, and in the next moment, she heard a loud flapping and fluttering above her, in the sky.

She looked up to see hundreds of starlings flying in front of the moon, their silhouettes twisting, turning, and forming all manner of elegant shapes. She knew that the flock was a murmuration, a natural phenomenon not uncommon this time of year, but it was remarkable just the same. Appearing on this heartbreaking night, it felt like a sign from Sandro, as surely as the note she held against her chest.

She watched the starlings shift and form elongated parabolas and ellipses, the mathematical shapes that he had loved so well. She realized that

Sandro was with her still, and would always be, even if he was above and she was below, him in the heavens and her on the ground, among her plants and flowers and animals.

Together they were the land and sky, the world entire.

And it was a world of love, and loss.

# Marco

19 October 1943

Marco, his mother, and Emedio stood in the aisle of the open-air building that held his father's vault, at his funeral. Almost two hundred mourners filled the place, flowing outside into the sun, on both sides. Their body heat and the humidity of the afternoon intensified the cloying fragrance of the bouquets lining the wall. It made Marco almost woozy. He hadn't slept at all last night, experiencing an emotional exhaustion that nevertheless rendered sleep impossible.

His father was to be buried in one of the gray marble vaults that lined the aisle on both sides, stacked five high. Each was a meter square and about three meters deep, containing a coffin. A bronze plaque was affixed to the front, engraved with the name of the deceased and dates of birth and death, which Marco couldn't read. His father's plaque wasn't ready, so Nino had put up a piece of paper with his father's name. Marco couldn't help but feel that his father deserved so much more. The vaults reminded him of the file cabinets at Palazzo Venezia.

His mother stood beside him, having cried throughout the funeral Mass, leaning against Emedio. Marco had barely listened to the Mass, though he had knelt and responded when required, then borne his father's pall and accepted condolences from the mourners. They had included the partisans, veterans of the Great War, his father's old friends from cycling, their neighbors, bar regulars, vendors, hospital employees, ex-Fascists, and *tifosi*.

The *tifosi* referred to his father by his proper name, Giuseppe Terrizzi, having read about him, collected his pictures, and memorized his race times.

*He could have been one of the greats,* one of them had said.

*He was,* Marco had blurted out, then had fallen silent for fear of saying the wrong thing. It was all he could do lately, the wrong things. His plan had failed. He had gotten his best friend killed. Elisabetta had come to the funeral today, which he appreciated, but he couldn't look her in the eye. He didn't know how to go on. He mourned Sandro, his father, Gemma, and Aldo. His grieving heart heaped one loss on top of the other, and their collective weight buried him.

After the cemetery, there was a family luncheon at Bar GiroSport, during which Marco could barely speak. His presence was in body only, and his actions were mechanical. He ate little, then cleared the tables, and when it was over, he knew what he had to do. He crossed to his mother's side, placing a hand on her arm.

"Mamma, may I be the one to go tell Rosa?"

Marco walked down the hospital corridor. He had spent so much time in a military uniform that the civilian suit felt strange on him. It occurred to him that a suit was a different sort of uniform, one of a successful man, and if so, he wore it as an actor does a costume. He wasn't successful at anything. He had failed, and now he would have to tell Rosa that her brother was dead and her father left behind.

He reached the end of the hallway and a closed door, with a glass window. He had already told Dr. Cristabello about Sandro and Massimo, which had saddened him. Dr. Cristabello had told him that the hospital was maintaining its Syndrome K story in case the Nazis came back.

Marco looked through the window and spotted Rosa, resting in a bed near the window. He put his hand on the knob, but stopped when he caught sight of his own reflection in the window. He looked haunted, like a ghost trapped in the glass. How could he tell her that he had gotten Sandro killed? He would have to find the strength, for her. He would tell her about her brother's bravery, and his sacrifice.

Marco opened the door.

## CHAPTER ONE HUNDRED THIRTY-EIGHT

# Massimo

### 22 October 1943

Massimo perked up, thinking that being of such short stature had paid off. Families from the transit camp were being transported in a wooden freight car, otherwise used for farm animals. There was a splintered slat partway up one side, which made a small opening, and Massimo kept his nostrils to the hole, breathing fresh air. It was a lucky break, for the stench was nauseating, since everyone had to defecate and urinate in the corners of the railcar.

The trip was nightmarish, spent in total darkness. Massimo hadn't eaten in days, and neither had anybody else. He was so thirsty he felt woozy. Once or twice his knees buckled, but there wasn't room to fall, and his sprained ankle throbbed. Children had stopped asking for food and water, but babies kept crying, a heart-wrenching sound. An infant near him had died in her mother's arms.

He dozed standing up, but he peeked through the opening from time to time. He could see where they were going, and it was mostly country, then mountainous, undoubtedly the Alps.

He didn't know their destination, but he assumed it was northward, as the air had grown progressively colder, then frigid. Everyone in the car was accustomed to a warmer climate and dressed too lightly. Again, Massimo counted himself lucky, since he still had on his suit jacket and was the only man wearing a tie, which he regarded as the last vestige of his dignity.

The rhythmic clacking of the wheels began to slow down. Massimo sensed they had reached southern Poland. He guessed that they would be at the labor camp, as he had heard rumors that the other Ghetto Jews were being sent there, too. He brightened, hoping there would be food and drink. Perhaps the Nazis would let them rest before they put them to work. The rumor was that the name of the labor camp was Auschwitz.

Massimo hoped that the camp would need a lawyer. He resolved to make his profession known to the powers that be. He felt certain that even Nazis would see his value and use him for billing, ledger keeping, or the like. He had always managed to turn every disadvantage to an advantage. This time would be no different.

People started noticing the train was slowing, and they burst into nervous chatter and frightened tears. Families clung together, but Massimo felt lucky, again, that his family had been spared the labor camp. Sandro had gotten away from Fossoli just in time. The Nazis had found the dead guard but hadn't known who had escaped. The very next morning, Massimo and the other Jews had been marched to the station at Carpi, herded onto the freight trains, and sent north.

Massimo's heart filled with relief to think of Sandro, Gemma, and Rosa in Rome, safe at the hospital or with the Terrizzis. As a father, he could be at peace only if he knew his family was safe and content. He knew he could count on Beppe to take care of Sandro, Gemma, and Rosa until he got back from Auschwitz.

Massimo hoped his stint in the camp would fly by quickly. If he had to perform manual labor, he would endure. He had survived Fascism, and he would survive Nazism. The war would end, and his family would be reunited in Rome, where Simones had lived for centuries.

The train was grinding to a stop. Massimo put his eye to the opening to see what was happening. It was dark.

But in the distance, there was light.

# Elisabetta

### November 1943

Elisabetta worked alone in the restaurant kitchen, since it was too early for the others to arrive. She was making angel hair pasta, folding egg into the dough, then kneading it. It softened and warmed in her palms, almost like a living thing, a human heart shaped with her fingers.

She grieved Sandro, but kept it to herself. She couldn't stop thinking of how violently he had died. She couldn't make peace with leaving him at the train station. Sometimes she remembered the happy times, sitting with him at La Sapienza or remembering their first kiss, on the riverbank. Whether she thought of the happy times or the sad, she cried nevertheless. It struck her as a paradox, that either happiness or sadness summoned tears.

She sprinkled more flour across the dough, then resumed kneading. She still had a business to run. She went to work every day, scrounging for supplies from vendors, bargaining with the black marketeers, and balancing the ledger book. She had come to understand that suffering was a part of war, part of life. Everyone was suffering. The men, women, and children of the Ghetto had yet to return. She missed Massimo, Gemma, the Diorios across the street, and her Jewish customers who had vanished that day. She didn't have the heart to go back to the Ghetto. She couldn't face the emptiness there.

She kept kneading, almost finished. She didn't want to overwork the dough or let her thoughts run away with her. Since Sandro's death, the Nazis had grown more oppressive and violent, and every day they issued new orders. Arrests and beatings in the street became commonplace. Everyone prayed for salvation, believing the Allies would be here by winter, but it was almost Christmas. More refugees arrived every day, displaced and starving.

She dusted flour from her hands, and her thoughts turned to Marco. He was the only person who understood how awful she felt, and he felt the same way. He worked at Bar GiroSport with the same numb sense of duty that she had. He would come by the restaurant once or twice a week, and she had begun to teach him to read. She had started with his name, and they had drilled and drilled. She didn't know why he couldn't read better, but she knew he was trying.

Elisabetta wiped her hands on a dishcloth. She headed for the tiny bathroom off the kitchen, shut the door, and used the toilet. When she pulled up her underpants, she noticed that they were still white, and unstained.

Her menstrual period was overdue.

She had never been late.

Until now.

CHAPTER ONE HUNDRED FORTY

# Elisabetta

December 1943

A month later, Elisabetta was leaving the kitchen, drying her hands on her apron. She entered the dining room, which was empty except for Marco, who sat alone at a table, ready for his lesson. The restaurant had closed for the night, and she and Marco had fallen into a comfortable routine. He would come at the end of his workday, and she would give him a practice sheet of reading and writing exercises, then clean up the kitchen while he finished. He would wolf down a plate of the day's pasta while he wrote, and tonight, nothing was left of his favorite dish, *spaghetti a cacio e pepe*, spaghetti with pecorino Romano cheese and pepper.

Elisabetta approached the table, and Marco's head was bent over his practice sheet. He had on a wool sweater with his slacks, and his dark, thick hair caught the light from the fixture above the table. He concentrated mightily, squeezing the pencil and holding his tongue to the side, like he used to when he was in school.

"How's it going?" Elisabetta asked, sitting opposite him.

"I just finished."

"Show me."

Marco turned his practice sheet around, so she could read it. The letters were oversized but legible:

## MARCO TERRIZZI

"*Bravo!*" Elisabetta said, delighted. "You did it!"

Marco smiled, with obvious pride. "I took too long, didn't I?"

"No, that doesn't matter. It's not a race."

Marco snorted. "No, a race is easy. Writing is torture. I did my other practice sheet, too."

"Already? Let me see."

"Hold on." Marco slid a piece of paper from his backpack, then set it down in front of her. In his oversized and imperfectly formed letters, he had written:

## MARRY ME, ELISABETTA

She gasped. "Marco, what's this?"

"Should I read it to you? I can. My mother helped me." Marco's expression grew serious, his dark eyes earnest. "Elisabetta, I love you and I always have. I know that Sandro was your first choice, and I loved him, too."

Elisabetta felt a wave of grief and guilt, as if she were betraying Sandro even to listen to Marco's proposal, but she didn't interrupt him.

"I admit, in the old days, I used to hate being second best to anyone, even him. But that's not true anymore. That was ego and pride, not love. None of that matters now. I don't mind being your second choice, if in the end, I get to be your husband."

Elisabetta felt so many emotions she couldn't sort them. Her heart responded to his words. So much had happened since the first time he had asked her to marry him, at the orange garden. She had chosen Sandro over him, and she was carrying Sandro's child, though she wasn't showing yet. She felt embarrassed, having no idea how to tell him about the baby.

Elisabetta braced herself. "Listen, there's something you don't know—"

"I know that you're pregnant."

"What, how?"

"I've been looking at you since you were little. I see the changes. Your dress is tight around the waist, and your face looks fuller, in the cheeks and chin." Marco reached for her hand, caressing her fingers. "You think I couldn't tell? I can tell. I've been looking at you your whole life."

Elisabetta didn't know what to say. She felt ashamed, but also seen, and understood. "It's Sandro's."

"Of course it is, *cara*. I remember you were with him that night. You told me." Marco smiled softly. "I know it won't be easy, so soon after losing him, but we can help each other. We both lost him, and we both loved him. That's what I've been thinking, and it's helping me. It gives me strength, and hope, and a future."

Elisabetta felt her heart fill with happiness. "But would it bother you to raise Sandro's baby?"

Marco squeezed her hand, meeting her gaze directly. "I *want* to raise Sandro's baby. There's nobody better than you and me to raise this baby."

Elisabetta felt speechless. Marco had always been that way, surprising her, and now he seemed more mature, even insightful.

"Elisabetta, isn't this what Sandro would have wanted? For you and me to get married, to love each other, and to raise his baby as our own?" Marco's eyes filmed, his expression soft, but urgent. "I promise you, I will love his child as I loved Sandro. I love the baby in his honor."

The emotion on Marco's face was raw, and Elisabetta felt as if he were opening his heart and soul to her.

"And you know what else I think, Elisabetta? In every relationship, there's one who waits. Once I told you that I would have waited forever for you, but I wouldn't have, back then. I was impatient. Proud. Cocky."

Elisabetta smiled, surprised that Marco could acknowledge as much.

"Well, I'm different now, and everything's different now. I feel different, inside. It broke me, all of it. I lost my brother, my father, my best friend— hell, Elisabetta, I lost a *war*. I was wrong about Mussolini, and about so many things. It humbled me." Marco rose, walked to her, and lowered himself to one knee. "Look. I wait now. I will wait for you, as long as it takes. I believe that someday, you'll love me the way I love you. Not yet, maybe not when the baby's born, but someday. And I can wait."

Elisabetta felt a wave of love for him, and Marco held her gaze, put his hand into his pocket, and produced the diamond ring he had offered her before. The gem caught the light, aglow.

"Please keep my ring this time. Please be my wife. I love you with all my heart." Marco met her eye. "Will you marry me?"

And Elisabetta answered, her heart soaring, "Yes."

CHAPTER ONE HUNDRED FORTY-ONE

# Maria
January 1944

Maria thought the wedding meal looked perfect, *rigatoni* with *pomodoro* sauce, then grilled lamb with roasted potatoes and fresh carrots, with fresh parsley, basil, and tomatoes from Elisabetta's garden. Only immediate family was present, and Maria had been pleased to host in the dining room at Bar GiroSport, which had been closed for the day, this time for a happy occasion.

Rosa wore a nice blue dress, sitting next to Emedio, who had performed the ceremony at the church, which had been beautiful. Emedio had blessed the meal and poured sparkling wine into the glasses, but no one was quite sure who was giving the toast, as Elisabetta had no parents and Beppe was gone.

"Excuse me." Maria rose, smoothing down her fancy dress. "I thought I should say something. Someone should, on this day. I'm not one for toasts and speeches. I never made one in my life. But I think someone should speak, from my generation." She paused, composing herself. "Beppe didn't like speeches, either. I know what he would have said today, but I won't say that. He would have kept it short. I can't keep it short, but I can keep it simple. I'll say what I think, and that's all I can say."

Everyone looked up at Maria, and their smiles were encouraging. She probably should have discussed this with them before, but she hadn't known if she would have the courage when the day of the wedding came. As it turned out, she didn't, but she stood up anyway.

"I look around the table on this happy occasion, the wedding of two wonderful young people, Marco and Elisabetta. They love each other. We're so happy for them. We love Marco and we welcome Elisabetta to our family."

Marco and Elisabetta smiled, perfect together. Marco was so handsome in his dark suit and tie. Elisabetta looked radiant in the wedding dress that Maria had given her, which she had worn when she married Beppe. Elisabetta had been proud to wear it, and Maria had been happy that her new daughter-in-law had felt that way. The past had been forgiven.

"The Mass was beautiful, Emedio. We are grateful for God's blessing on this marriage. We are happy today." Maria paused, mustering her confidence for what came next. "Yet, I look around the table and I see eyes with tears. Smiles that shake. Our hearts are broken, deep inside. We suffer. So many of the people we love are missing. Beppe. Aldo. Massimo. Gemma. Sandro. Nonna. Ludovico. Serafina. Friends and neighbors. People we loved very much. People we have lost. We are missing them. They are not here, but we are. We don't have to pretend this occasion isn't bittersweet."

Maria noticed Rosa look down, trying to stay in emotional control. Rosa was living in the Vatican, but Massimo had yet to return from the labor camp, and there had been no word of him.

Maria cleared her throat. "Not all of you know me well. I'm always in the kitchen. I'm in the kitchen at the restaurant or I'm in the kitchen at the apartment. I guess I never leave a kitchen, whether downstairs or upstairs."

Everyone chuckled, which Maria hadn't expected.

"I'm not a fancy chef or a pasta *professoressa* like our Elisabetta, my wonderful new daughter-in-law."

Elisabetta smiled up at her.

"And Bar GiroSport is a bar, not a restaurant. I was hired as a cook because I worked for free."

Everyone chuckled again, which made Maria happy. She realized that giving a speech was just talking to people and telling the truth, a notion that gave her the courage to continue.

"I mean to say, I'm only a normal cook, like every mother, every woman. And every day, before every meal, I open the refrigerator and I see what I have. I'm always missing ingredients I really need and really want. I'm missing them all the time. That's never been more true than now, with the war. So every day, before every meal, my question is the same. What can I make with what I have?" Maria nodded, feeling the truth of her words. "I ask myself that question, every time I start to cook. I always have, even when the boys were little. What can I make with what I have?"

Marco, Elisabetta, and Rosa were listening attentively. Emedio frowned, worried for her or perhaps wondering what her point was. Maria wasn't sure herself, since she was speaking from the heart. She didn't know if it would come out right.

"Anyway, every day, every meal, I put the ingredients I have together, whatever I have. Whatever scraps or leftovers, whatever bits and pieces. I make a meal of my scraps, and it always turns out better than I thought it would. It surprises me, every time. Every meal. Please don't think I'm boasting. We know the glory goes to God. He works through me, and every time, I end up with a meal I am proud to serve."

Maria clarified her thoughts, and her jitters ebbed away.

"Life in mourning is like that. We do not have everything we want. We do not have everything we need. We are missing so much. We are missing those we love. Our hearts ache all the time."

Maria's lips trembled. She wasn't sure she could continue. She forced herself, swallowing the lump in her throat.

"But I look around the table and I see some wonderful ingredients here." Maria shifted her loving gaze to Marco, Elisabetta, Emedio, and Rosa, each in turn. "I see ingredients that go very well with other ingredients. I know if we all come together, like we are now, that with God's help, we will make a beautiful, delicious meal that will sustain us all, with the love of one another."

Everyone smiled, and tears came to Maria's eyes, happy rather than sad. She had gotten her point out. She raised her glass.

"I propose a toast to my beloved son Marco and his new wife, Elisabetta. We love them and we respect their marriage and the family they make today. I think their future will be so delicious, it will surprise even them. To Marco and Elisabetta."

And everyone raised a glass.

## CHAPTER ONE HUNDRED FORTY-TWO

# Marco

#### 4 June 1944

Marco stood with Elisabetta at the glass window of the incubation nursery, in amazement. On the other side of the window was their tiny pink son, who had been born in the middle of the night, ahead of schedule. The infant slept under his white blanket, but his features remarkably resembled Elisabetta's, albeit in miniature. The baby's body was more like Sandro's, and Marco felt a deep pang of sadness that Sandro hadn't lived to see his baby born. Elisabetta felt the same way, he knew, for they had discussed it many times. The baby's birth had rekindled their shared grief, comingling now with their joy.

"A son." Marco placed a palm on the glass, as he gazed at the baby.

"A son," Elisabetta repeated, with a happy sigh. "You sure he's going to be okay? He's healthy? The doctor said so?"

"Yes, he's healthy. He's just impatient, like me."

"And you're happy, now that he's here?"

"I'm absolutely sure. I couldn't be happier, *cara*." Marco gave her a kiss, and Elisabetta nestled into his shoulder.

"Is it still okay if we name him Alessandro?"

"Of course," Marco said. "Alessandro Terrizzi. It's a wonderful name."

Elisabetta leaned in, and Marco held her closer. They were the only ones in the tiny hallway, which was windowless. Laughter and shouting came from the street, for Italy was celebrating all around them. The Allies had arrived in Rome this very day, and the city had erupted in jubilation. The war in Rome was finally over.

Marco chuckled. "He couldn't have a more special birthday, could he?"

"All of Rome celebrates his birth." Elisabetta burst into laughter. "I'm so grateful, Marco."

"So am I." Marco wrapped his arms around her, holding her tight.

Just then the bells of Saint Peter's Basilica pealed in the Vatican, and the crowd outside the hospital erupted into cheering, yelling, and singing amid the loud rumbling of cars, trucks, and tanks.

Elisabetta released him, with a smile. "They must be on the Lungotevere. Don't you want to go see? And tell the others about the baby?"

"Are you sure?" Marco asked, torn. "I can stay with you."

"Please, go, I need to rest." Elisabetta caressed his cheek. "I love you."

"I love you, too."

"Now, go celebrate for us, would you?"

Mamma, it's a boy!" Marco hugged his mother, amid a packed Bar GiroSport.

"I have a grandson, and Rome is free! Thanks to God!" His mother threw open her arms, hugged Marco, and smothered him with kisses. Customers cheered and applauded.

"Mamma, call Emedio and Rosa for me, would you? I have to go!"

His mother kissed him, and Marco hurried outside the bar, joined the delirious crowd spilling onto Tiber Island, and surrendered to the emotion, exulting, rejoicing, and feeling happiness flood his body. The war was over in Rome, and the bells of Saint Peter's kept pealing, a joyous sound. The sun poured gold on everyone, gilding the city, a blessing from heaven above.

Marco flowed across the Ponte Fabricio with the crowd, as they waved flags, flashed victory signs, sang, shouted, and kissed each other. Somebody sprayed *spumante*, and everybody laughed. They cheered as the Americans in Jeeps, trucks, and tanks filled the Lungotevere Sanzio and Lungotevere de' Cenci.

The crowd surged toward the Americans, but Marco found himself hurrying across the Lungotevere de' Cenci toward the Ghetto, drawn there by a deeper pull. He entered the Ghetto and walked down the Via del Portico d'Ottavia, where the happy, cheering celebration continued, but he didn't recognize any of the people. The kosher butcher, the baker, and all of the other shopkeepers he had known were gone, having been deported in the *rastrellamento*. Rosa and most of Rome's Jews still remained in hiding, in fear for their lives. Massimo hadn't been heard from, and neither had the other families deported that day. The Della Roccas. The Terracinas. The DiCavis. The Sermonettas. The Toscanos. No one knew if they would ever return, and everyone feared that the Nazis had done their worst.

Tears filled Marco's eyes, and his heart ached. He found his feet taking him where he had to go, and in time he found himself standing in Piazza Mattei with its beautiful Fontana delle Tartarughe. People thronged around the turtle fountain, singing, dancing, and cheering, but Marco was quiet, mourning anew.

He looked up at Sandro's house, and his gaze went to the window on the third floor, where his best friend's apartment used to be. The window was open and empty, but Marco didn't see it the way it was now. Instead he saw it the way it was then, when they were both boys, and he would ride his bicycle here and call—

"Sandro!" Marco called out, and tears spilled down his cheeks. In his mind's eye, he saw Sandro waving to him and calling back, and Marco realized why he had come here, for he had a vow to make. His gaze fixed on the window, he vowed in a whisper:

"Sandro, you have a son, and he is named for you. I promise I will love him as my own and I will raise him to know you and honor you. And I promise I will take care of Elisabetta as you would have, with all the love in my heart."

Marco wiped his eyes, but his gaze remained on the window, on the third floor of a building that had stood for centuries, in the middle of a city that had stood for millennia, by a river that had flowed since time immemorial and would flow into the future. Yet he had learned that Rome, as magnificent as she was, was merely a bystander to the glory and horror wrought by man, and that was the way of the world, now and forever.

War was eternal, but so was peace.

Death was eternal, but so was life.

Darkness was eternal, but so was light.

Hate was eternal, but above all, so was love.

### CHAPTER ONE HUNDRED FORTY-THREE

# Marco
June 1950

---

Marco stood in front of the bar, wearing an apron and a contented smile. The sun shone on a temperate morning, and customers had begun to make their way to the outside seating area for breakfast. He enjoyed running the bar, and he had already made a down payment on another location in Trastevere. He had changed the name of Bar GiroSport to Bar Terrizzi, and his dream was to own a string of Bar Terrizzis, which would cater to *tifosi* in his father's memory. He was a son not only of Lazio, but of Beppe Terrizzi.

Marco turned out to be an excellent businessman, and soon they would have enough money to move to an apartment of their own. A doctor had diagnosed his reading problems as "word-blindness," or dyslexia, a neurological condition that had nothing to do with innate intelligence. The diagnosis had made him feel better, and his reading skills were improving, as a result of exercises that the doctor had given him.

He glanced down at the riverbank below, where young Sandro and a group of his friends were playing on the bank of the Tiber. Sandro's light brown hair brightened in the summertime, some strands turning as gold as the sun, and the boy stood out as the tallest and leanest in his class, built like a sharpened pencil, as his father had been.

Marco's heart filled with peace, and his thoughts flowed freely. He had kept his vow to Sandro, loving Elisabetta with all his heart and little Sandro as his own. They were as close as any father and son, though he and

Elisabetta hadn't yet told Sandro about his paternity. They intended to do so, but Marco was leaving to her to decide when the time was right.

The war years had been devastating, and though those times were behind them, their memories were always with him. He thought every day of his father, of Aldo, of Sandro, of Massimo and Gemma, whose grave he had moved to the Jewish section. Rosa and David now lived in London with their two children, visiting Rome from time to time. His mother, who still worked in the kitchen, reveled in her grandchildren and kept alive the memory of those they had lost.

Massimo had never returned, and the horror of the Holocaust had been revealed to the world. The Ghetto Jews, who had been rounded up on the October 16, 1943 *rastrellamento*, had been sent to Auschwitz, and of the twelve hundred men, women, and children who had been deported that day, only sixteen had survived—fifteen men and one woman, Settimia Spizzichino. The Nazis had conducted subsequent roundups, but despite them, about ten thousand of Rome's twelve thousand Jews had survived by hiding in the Vatican, monasteries, convents, and homes.

It had always bothered Marco that no globally watched trials, like those at Nuremberg, had been held to obtain justice for the murders of the Ghetto Jews. A military tribunal did try Lieutenant Colonel Kappler in Rome, and he received fifteen years in prison for his extortionate demand of gold from the Ghetto Jews. He was also sentenced to life in prison for another massacre he had ordered at the Ardeatine Caves. Marco had been surprised to learn that a regular visitor of Kappler's in prison was Monsignor Hugh O'Flaherty, whom Kappler had tried so hard to murder. The monsignor and the Nazi came to know each other, and in time, Kappler converted to Roman Catholicism.

"Marco, you're letting him play down there, by the river?" Elisabetta appeared at his side with a wry smile.

"Why not? We did." Marco put an arm around her, holding her close. Today, she had on a dress he loved, one with yellow checks, and she was more beautiful than ever, since she was three months pregnant. They were both delighted that Sandro was going to have a little brother or sister, and Marco didn't prefer either gender, as long as the baby liked bicycles.

"But how can you reach him, if something should happen?"

"Nothing will happen. Anyway I've been waiting for you to come down. I have a surprise." Marco kissed her on the cheek, then turned to the brown bag beside him, retrieved the thick packet, and placed it on the stone wall. "I think this belongs to you."

"My old manuscript? How funny!" Elisabetta smiled, running a hand over the title page. "*A Talkative Girl*. Where did you find it?"

"In the cellar, in one of the boxes from your old place. You told me you had written a book, but you never showed it to me."

"It wasn't very good."

"I don't believe that, and you used to talk about wanting to be a writer."

"All young girls talk like that." Elisabetta shrugged, but Marco saw temptation flicker through her lovely eyes.

"Don't you think of writing, still?"

"No, I'm too busy, and the new baby will be here soon."

"But you're only at the restaurant in the mornings, and I'll help more. I know exactly what you need to start." Marco reached into the bag, retrieved her old typewriter, and placed it atop the stone wall, in its slim black case of covered cardboard.

"My Olivetti?" Elisabetta burst into astonished laughter.

"Yes, I just picked it up. I had it reconditioned." Marco opened the lid, and its black top gleamed in the sun. He smiled inwardly, thinking of the time that Sandro had urged him to buy her a notebook, way back when. Marco had thought of that advice when he had come up with this idea, so Sandro was still helping him, even now.

"Why did you get it reconditioned?"

"To make it like new. I got ribbons and paper, too. Don't you want to start writing again?"

"Don't be silly." Elisabetta waved him off, but Marco sensed that all she needed was encouragement.

"Why not?"

"I wouldn't know what to write about, anymore."

"You're just afraid, but don't be. Remember when you stood on the ledge at Palazzo Braschi? Or when you drove my boss's car? You were afraid then, too, but you always did well. Just take a chance." Marco gestured at the manuscript. "Besides, if you wrote one book, you can write another.

You read all the time, and you're always talking about that new author. What's her name, the one who won that prize?"

"Elsa Morante. She won the Viareggio."

"What does she write about?"

"Families, and love."

"And what about the other author, the older one who won the Nobel?"

"Grazia Deledda."

"What does she write about?"

"Families, and love."

Marco grinned, but said nothing.

Elisabetta smiled back. "You think I should write about families and love?"

"If that's what you like, yes." Marco put the lid back on the typewriter, placed the manuscript on top, and handed it to her. "Start now. I'll watch Sandro. You become the next great Italian female author."

"It's not that easy."

"You've done harder things. Go up to the rooftop to work. It's quiet up there." Marco had moved Elisabetta's garden to the rooftop of Bar Terrizzi. Their family, including Gnocchi and ancient Rico, enjoyed growing fresh herbs and flowers. "Just get started, and see what happens. I'll make sure the boy doesn't fall into the Tiber."

"Maybe I will." Elisabetta beamed. "I love you."

"I love you, too," Marco said, giving her another kiss. She walked off happily, and he watched her go, thinking to himself:

*Thanks for the advice, Sandro. This time, I listened.*

# Elisabetta

May 1957

E lisabetta finished telling her son the story, and Sandro had listened
with complete absorption, for he had inherited his father's characteristic powers of concentration. She had begun the story from its earliest, on
that afternoon by the Tiber when she had decided that Marco would be her
first kiss, then had been kissed by Sandro. It had taken her most of the
morning to tell the story, and she had ended it with the day that Marco had
presented her with the reconditioned Olivetti. Her son had heard some of
the stories before, but never in the context of finding out the truth about his
paternity.

His expression had changed only slightly throughout, except he had
burst into knowing laughter at the story of Marco climbing the pillar to
retrieve the Fascist flag during the party at Palazzo Braschi, and a troubled
frown had creased his young brow over the part about the gold of Rome
and the *rastrellamento* of the Ghetto. Tears had filmed his warm brown
eyes toward the end of the story, when Elisabetta had told him what had
happened at the Modena train station, where Sandro had been killed saving Marco's life, but he hadn't cried, nor had she, remaining in emotional
control for his benefit.

The sun streamed through the window of the dining room, filling it with
a golden warmth. She liked having a large apartment, which they could
afford thanks to Marco's success with his Bar Terrizzis. Gnocchi slept on
her chair at the table, though Rico had passed away, having lived a long
and admirable life.

Elisabetta exhaled, with finality. "Well, that's the whole story. I know it's a lot to hear all at once, and some parts are very sad, but I wanted you to know the truth, now that you're old enough. Do you understand?"

"Yes." Sandro nodded, moving a light brown curl from his forehead.

"And you understand that Sandro is your father, don't you?"

"Yes." Sandro nodded again, his lips set.

"I know you may feel strange, hearing that. Do you?"

"A little." Sandro shrugged uncomfortably. "You and Papa talk about him, but I didn't know that."

"I understand. Now that you know, it doesn't mean that Papa loves you any less. He loves you as his own son, and he always has, from when you were a baby. You understand that, don't you?"

"Yes, and I love Papa." Sandro smiled, brightening, which reassured Elisabetta, as she had been worried that the revelation would cause distance between him and Marco.

"Now, do you want to ask me anything?"

Sandro hesitated. "Does this mean I'm Jewish?"

Elisabetta was ready for the question. "It means you have Jewish blood, and if you want to attend synagogue and learn about Judaism, Papa and I will support you. He should be home any minute."

"Where is he?"

"At the market with Giuseppina. I needed greens for dinner."

"Mamma, is that your book?" Sandro gestured to the manuscript, which Elisabetta had set at the far end of the table, next to the Olivetti.

"Yes."

"Are you finished?"

"Yes," Elisabetta answered, although even she couldn't believe it was true. She had been working on the novel for seven years, writing in fits and starts after their daughter had been born.

"*Brava*, Mamma." Sandro broke into a grin. "Is it good?"

"I hope so."

"And the title is *Eternal*?"

"Yes."

"Now will you tell me what it's about? When I ask, all you ever say is it's about families and love."

"It is. It's the story I just told you."

"Can I read it?"

"Of course, I'd love for you to." Elisabetta smiled, gratified that Sandro had inherited her love of books. He even helped Marco with his reading exercises, which they got from a specialist.

"Are you going to try and get it published?"

"I don't know yet."

Sandro blinked. "Is that why you're telling me about my father now? Because you finished it?"

"Yes, I think so." Elisabetta had asked herself that very same question. "It sounds strange, but I didn't know the story in full until I told it to myself. You're the first one to hear it, and that's as it should be. I love you."

"I love you, too, Mamma." Sandro jumped up and threw his arms around her neck, clinging to her a moment longer.

Elisabetta released him when they heard the front door open and Marco and Giuseppina entering with the sound of a jingling bicycle chain, since Marco kept his father's Bianchi inside the apartment. Giuseppina was prattling on, an adorable little girl who had her father's smile and her mother's *bocca larga*, which had become more acceptable in modern times.

"Papa!" Sandro ran out of the dining room, and Elisabetta rose, too. She followed him into the living room to see her son throw himself into Marco's arms, with more feeling than usual. She felt surprised, as Sandro had been fine only a minute ago, but his emotions must have come to the fore at the sight of Marco.

"*Ciao*, Sandro." Marco hugged him back, catching Elisabetta's eye with bewilderment.

"Marco, I told him about what happened during the war."

Marco nodded, understanding. He released Sandro from their embrace, ruffling his hair. "So what do you think, son?"

"Papa, do you love me?" Sandro asked, then glanced at Giuseppina. "Even though, you know . . ."

"Of course, I do." Marco placed his hands on Sandro's shoulders and looked him directly in the eye. "Sandro, I love you, and that love makes me your father. I will always love you, and the man you're named for would have loved you, too. He saved my life, and I loved him like a brother. He was a hero."

"But you're a hero, too. You went to save him."

Marco managed a smile. "I don't think I am."

"I do," Sandro shot back, hugging Marco again.

Tears filled Elisabetta's eyes, and she understood how lucky she was to have been blessed with a wonderful marriage and a happy family. She realized in that moment that she never could have written about families and love, if she had not experienced the love of this very family. Her novel was their story, for every family has a story, and every family's story begins with love. And uniquely, her family story began with two loves.

Elisabetta imagined her family story joining so many others, layering atop one another over time, a palimpsest of stories encompassing the world entire, a veritable history of humankind told by one generation to the next, building upon each other.

And all of them everlasting, with love.

# AUTHOR'S NOTE

I have wanted to write this novel ever since my days as an English major at the University of Pennsylvania, where I took a year-long seminar taught by the late Philip Roth. The first semester of the seminar was titled "The Literature of the Holocaust," and Mr. Roth introduced us to the books of Primo Levi, an Italian Jewish chemist who was deported to Auschwitz but survived and wrote the seminal memoir *If This Is a Man,* published in the United States as *Survival in Auschwitz.* The subject haunted me for decades, and I knew I would return to it someday. Finally, after writing thirty-odd novels exploring themes of family, love, and justice, I decided to try. That effort is *Eternal.*

I have always loved reading historical fiction, and one of the questions I always have when I finish reading historical fiction is, how much of this novel is true? So allow me to differentiate the fiction of *Eternal* from historical fact.

First, the D'Orfeo, Simone, and Terrizzi families are products of my imagination, as are Elisabetta, Marco, and Sandro. Most of the novel's minor characters are also imagined, except as described below. However, I did the research to make their speech, dress, and other attributes consistent with their times.

But much of what transpires in these pages is true to the past.

Most importantly, the horrific *rastrellamento* of the Ghetto and other neighborhoods of Rome did actually happen on October 16, 1943, as described in the novel. Jewish men, women, and children were forced from their homes at gunpoint, then sent to the Collegio Militare and ultimately to Auschwitz. In fact, the families whom Sandro sees when he is taken away are the names of actual Jewish families who ended up on the Nazi transport from Rome to Auschwitz. Only sixteen people survived.

The events preceding the *rastrellamento* really did happen, as described in the novel. The Nazis did extort gold from the Jewish Community, and the Community met its demand despite impossible odds. President Ugo Foà and President Dante Almansi were real people, and their heroic efforts to save the Community and its priceless patrimony are shown herein. Chief Rabbi Zolli was a real person, as were goldsmith Angelo Anticoli, accountant Renzo Levi, and secretary Rosina Sorani.

Tullio Levi-Civita was a real mathematician, known as the "Einstein of Italy," and what happened to him as a result of the Race Laws, as well to many other brilliant Jewish professors, is described in the novel.

Dr. Giovanni Borromeo, the administrator of the Ospedale Fatebenefratelli, was a real physician and professor of medicine. Amazingly, he truly did devise the incredible ruse to fool the Nazis, fabricating the Syndrome K virus to save the hospital's Jewish patients.

Lieutenant Colonel Herbert Kappler was a real person who was the highest ranking officer of the Schutzstaffel, or the SS, in Rome. His words in his conversation with Massimo and Presidents Foà and Almansi at Villa Wolkonsky are taken from my historical research, notably from Robert Katz's nonfiction books. Monsignor Hugh O'Flaherty was a real monsignor at the Vatican during the relevant time period, and he was called the "Scarlet Pimpernel of the Vatican" because he donned disguises to evade the Nazis as he protected Italian Jews. It is also true that Monsignor Hugh O'Flaherty visited Kappler in prison, and that eventually Kappler converted to Roman Catholicism.

Baron Ernst von Weizsäcker was also a real person, an Italophile and the German Ambassador to the Holy See during the relevant time period. His conversations with Elisabetta are fictional, of course, but my research about him shows them to be consistent with his personality.

The transit camp at Fossoli existed, as did other transit and concentration camps in Italy. The Fossoli camp is outside the town of Carpi, near the city of Modena, as described herein. When I visited Italy to research this novel, I explored Carpi and what remains of the transit camp, and it was a deeply sobering experience. There is a memorial museum about the transit camp in Carpi, the Museo al Deportato, which contains exhibits that informed my research, as well as a memorial to those lost. I filmed videos of the camp and the museum, which can be seen on my website.

Most of the other locations in the novel are real places in Rome, with the exception of the exact location of Elisabetta's childhood home and Nonna's house in Trastevere. I fictionalized those streets, though Trastevere is a remarkably charming neighborhood in Rome and everything I described about it herein is true. Casa Servano is fictional, although anybody who visits Rome can tell you that the pasta is incredible, and carbohydrates are among the three billion reasons to go.

I also explored and filmed videos of the Ghetto, the synagogue, Tiber Island, the Tiber River, and Trastevere, as well as secondary locations like La Sapienza, Via Tasso, Collegio Militare, and the catacombs. You can find these videos on my website.

The pasta-making scenes I took from spending hours in the kitchen with my own beloved mother, Mary, who made "homemades" every Sunday morning. She was a feisty product of Chieti in the Abruzzo region, a background that I borrowed for Maria. Mother Mary was a true pasta *professoressa*, and I have written about her in my nonfiction memoirs, which I coauthor with my daughter Francesca Serritella. And like Nonna, Mother Mary always answered a question with a question.

After all, why not?

# ACKNOWLEDGMENTS

This is my chance to thank the experts who helped me with *Eternal*, but first, some background.

To write this novel, I had to research extensively the rise and eventual fall of Fascism in Italy, especially the barrage of Race Laws promulgated against Italian Jews. I read every book I could get my hands on and bought so many that I had to build new shelves. Booklovers will recognize this as a great problem to have.

After I had read as much as I could, I sought out one of the most preeminent historians on the subject, Stanislao Pugliese, a Fulbright scholar and professor of Modern European History and Queensboro UNICO distinguished professor of Italian and Italian-American Studies at Hofstra University. Despite Stan's busy schedule, he read *Eternal* many times for accuracy, making many terrific suggestions and corrections, for which I am forever grateful to him. Thank you so much, Stan.

For those interested in this subject matter, I strongly recommend Stan's books because they are superbly written and accessible. He is the author or editor of fifteen books on Fascism and Italian Jewish history, including *Fascism, Anti-Fascism, and the Resistance in Italy*; the collection *The Most Ancient of Minorities: The Jews of Italy*; *Bitter Spring: A Life of Ignazio Silone*; *Carlo Rosselli: Socialist Heretic and Antifascist Exile*; and many others.

Other standout books on the subject are Alexander Stille's *Benevolence and Betrayal: Five Italian Jewish Families Under Fascism*, Robert Katz's *Black Sabbath: A Journey Through a Crime Against Humanity*, and Susan Zuccotti's *Under His Very Windows: The Vatican and the Holocaust in Italy*. I give my thanks to those wonderful scholars, too, as their books informed my understanding of the subject. You can find a complete bibliography of similar books on my website, because they are too numerous to reproduce here.

Thank you to Ilaria Mazzaferro, the Italian translator of many of my previous books, as I am lucky enough to be published in Italy. I asked Ilaria for help because she has always gone the extra mile, often emailing me questions about a word or an idiom. I owe Ilaria a huge debt of gratitude for making everything in *Eternal* as authentic as possible. Ilaria made corrections and answered all my questions with her characteristic good cheer, and I thank her very much for all of her help.

Professor Andrea Dall'Aglio is an Associate Professor of Mathematics at the Department of Mathematics Guido Castelnuovo, University of Rome, known as La Sapienza. I met Andrea during my research into the real-life Italian mathematician Tullio Levi-Civita, who taught there. Professor Dall'Aglio was kind enough to take his time to discuss Levi-Civita with me and answer my questions, which informed the characterization of Levi-Civita and the fictional Sandro. Thank you so much, Andrea.

Thanks, too, to his colleague, Professor Enrico Rogora, also an Associate Professor of Mathematics at La Sapienza, who shared with me his lecture and research on Levi-Civita.

I love libraries and am their huge supporter, speaking at them and raising funds whenever I can. So when I needed to research these historical topics, I turned to one of the best academic libraries in the country, the Charles Patterson Van Pelt Library at the University of Pennsylvania. Thank you so much to librarian Matthew Pilecki, who helped me locate volumes of recently released Vatican archives, telegrams, and correspondence regarding the Italian Holocaust and related matters, which informed the background for this novel. Matthew was the most patient and perfect guide ever, and all librarians rock.

Special thanks to the Centro Primo Levi in New York City, a robust organization dedicated to educating the public about the legacy of Primo Levi and of Italian Jews. Deputy Director Alessandro Cassin and the Centro welcomed me into its community and at many of their programs and lectures, and its librarians helped me with my research, too. Thank you to the Centro and its terrific staff, especially Alessandro Cassin, Deputy Director, who answered my questions at lectures.

Thank you to the lovely Egidia Barbetta, daughter of the late Italian cycling great Giuseppe Pancera. Egidia took the time to meet and talk with me about Italian cycling of the 1920s and 1930s, which helped me with the characterization of the Terrizzi family. I also found helpful *The Story of the Giro d'Italia*, volume 1 (2011), by Bill and Carol McGann.

So much more is known now about dyslexia than in the time period of this novel, but to learn about dyslexia, I turned to expert Diane Reott, the then-executive director of the Pennsylvania Branch of the International Dyslexia Society. Diane helped me so much not only with the history of dyslexia, but with its emotional impact on young people. Thank you so much to Diane.

That said, any and all mistakes in the novel are mine.

Thanks so much to the incredible team at my publisher, G. P. Putnam's Sons, starting with Ivan Held and Christine Ball, who were so encouraging when I told them I wanted to write the historical novel that I had always dreamed of. I had known and admired Ivan for a long time, and he paired me with the great Mark Tavani, a brilliant editor and a wonderful guy to boot. Mark gave me pep talks during the writing process, since even allegedly professional writers need positive reinforcement. Mark also made an amazing edit to an early draft of the manuscript, which increased its emotional impact a thousandfold, and I am very grateful to him for that and everything else.

Thanks to the rest of the great gang, including Allison Dobson, Sally Kim, Ashley McClay, Alexis Welby, Laura Wilson, Katie Grinch, Emily Mlynek, Nishtha Patel, Anthony Ramondo, Danielle Dieterich, and designer Lorie Pagnozzi.

Thank you so much to my terrific agent, Robert Gottlieb of Trident Media Group, because he was the first person to whom I told this story. Other agents might have been wary of the risk, but not Robert. He was so excited that it made me feel as if I could do it, and what I love most about him is that he is completely positive. This novel would not have been written without his support. Thanks to his incredible team at Trident: Erica Silverman, Nicole Robson, Nora Rawn, Caitlin O'Beirne, and Sulamita Garbuz.

I am lucky enough to have besties/assistants, and I needed them for *Eternal*. Thanks so much to Laura Leonard, who not only encouraged me to write the novel but also accompanied me to Rome, where we investigated everything we could and knocked on doors to get our questions answered.

We even trespassed once, but we got our answer, which is pure Laura. She knows how much I love and adore her, so I won't get mushy here, but thanks so much to her, for everything.

Thank you so much to Nan Daley, who also had to run down so many questions I had, like which typewriter Elisabetta would use in 1930s Rome. I ended up buying the vintage typewriter, and you can see a video about its history on my website. Thank you to Katie Rinda, who held down the fort so that I could go into writing hibernation.

Thank you and all my love to my friends and family, like my bestie Franca, who was unfailingly encouraging to me while I was writing this book and throughout my entire life. God bless girlfriends.

All of my love goes to my amazing daughter, Francesca, who's been my co-author for ten years and is now a novelist in her own right. She speaks Italian, has been to Italy with me, and helped with the novel, making really terrific editorial suggestions. More than that, she's the best daughter and best friend that any mother could ever ask for. *Eternal* is dedicated to her because it wouldn't have happened without her, as the best encouragement for any of us mothers is the bravery of our daughters. Thank you, and I love you very much, Francesca.

I owe my ultimate acknowledgment to the memory of the Italian Jewish victims of the Holocaust and to their families. I hope I have honored them and their story, because that matters the most to me. Nowadays there is a plaque and a small museum in the Ghetto to honor them, which you may want to visit if you go to Rome. And throughout the Ghetto, you will see brass memorial bricks called *Stolpersteine,* which have been installed by artist Gunter Demnig in front of the homes of those who were murdered.

So for the victims and their families, I offer this moment of silence.

**Your family has been attacked, never again to be the same. Now you have to choose between law . . . or justice.**

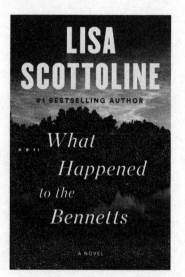

"Taut and tense from the first page to the last. In *What Happened to the Bennetts*, Lisa Scottoline thrusts the reader into one family's living nightmare—and their long, nail-biting battle to return to some sense of normalcy."

—**Riley Sager,** *New York Times* **bestselling author of** *Survive the Night*

"An emotion-packed thriller that stabs at the core of family, betrayal, and justice. Lisa Scottoline drives the plot at breakneck speed and keeps readers turning the pages. A must read."

—**Robert Dugoni, #1 Amazon bestselling author of the Tracy Crosswhite series**

Jason Bennett is a suburban dad, driving his family home one night after his daughter's field hockey game. Her team won, and they're enjoying the ride in their new car, a Mercedes. They enter a dark stretch of road, and a pickup truck begins tailgating them. Suddenly the pickup passes them and blocks their path—then the worst happens. Two men jump from the truck and pull guns on Jason, demanding the car. A horrific flash of violence changes his life forever.

Later that awful night, Jason and his family receive a visit from the FBI. The agents tell them that the carjackers were members of a dangerous drug-trafficking organization—and now Jason and his family are in their crosshairs. The agents advise the Bennetts to enter the witness protection program right away, and they have no choice but to agree. But WITSEC was designed to protect criminal informants, not law-abiding families. Taken from all they know, trapped in an unfamiliar life, the Bennetts begin to fall apart at the seams. Then Jason learns a shocking truth and realizes that he has to take matters into his own hands. There's only one way to save his family, even if it means sacrificing himself.

*Sometimes justice is a one-man show.*

I glanced in my rearview mirror at the pickup truck, which was riding my bumper. I hated tailgaters, especially with my family in the car, but nothing could ruin my good mood. My daughter's field hockey team had just beat Radnor, and Allison had scored a goal. She was texting in the back seat, one of a generation that makes better use of opposable thumbs than any prior.

My son Ethan turned around next to her, shielding his eyes against the pickup's headlights. "Dad, what's up with this guy?"

"God knows. Ignore him."

"Why don't you go faster?" Ethan shifted, waking up Moonie, our little white mutt, who started jumping around in the back seat. I love the dog but he has two speeds: Asleep and Annoying.

"Why should I? I'm going the limit."

"But we can *smoke* this guy now."

We had just gotten a new car, a Mercedes E-Class Sedan in a white enamel that gleamed like dental veneers. Ethan said the E stood for his name, but I said Exorbitant. My wife and kids had lobbied for the car, but I felt like a show-off behind the wheel. I missed my old Explorer, which I didn't need a tie to drive.

"Dad, when I get my license, I'm gonna *burn* guys like him."

I heard this once a week. My son counted the days until his learner's permit, even though he was only thirteen. I said, "No, you're not. You're gonna let him pass."

"Why?"

"We have a right to enjoy the drive."

"But it's boring."

"Not to me. I'm a scenic-route kind of guy." I moved over to let the pickup pass, since Coldstream Road was a single lane winding uphill through the woods. We were entering the Lagersen Tract, the last parcel of woodland preserved by Chester County, where Nature had to be zoned for her own protection.

I lowered the window and breathed in a lungful of fresh, piney air. Thick trees flanked the road, and scrub brush grew over the guardrails. Crickets and tree frogs croaked a chorus from my childhood. I grew up on a dairy farm in Hershey, home of the famous chocolate manufacturer. I loved living in a company town, where the air smelled of sweet cocoa and corporate largesse. Everyone worked toward the same goal, even if it was capitalism.

"He's not passing us," Ethan said, bringing me out of my reverie.

I checked the rearview mirror, squinting against the headlights. Moonie was facing backward, his front paws on the back seat and his ears silhouetted like wispy triangles.

"Come on, Dad. Show 'em who's boss."

"That's well-established," I said. "Mom."

Lucinda was in the passenger seat, the curve of her smile illuminated by the phone screen. She was a natural beauty, with gray-blue eyes, a small nose, and dark blond hair gathered into a loose ponytail at the nape of her neck. She had been on Facebook since we'd left the school, posting game photos and comments. **Great save by Arielle!!! Lady Patriots rock!!! Woohoo, Emily is MVP!!!** My wife never uses fewer than three exclamation marks on social. If you only get one, you've done something wrong. Or as my father would say, *You're in the doghouse.*

Lucinda looked over. "Jason, speed up, would you?"

"You, too? What's the hurry?"

"They have homework."

"On Friday night? Have you *met* our kids?"

Lucinda smiled, shaking her head. "Whatever, Scenic-Route Kind of Guy."

"Aw, I feel so *seen.*"

Lucinda laughed, which made me happy. I love my wife. We met at Bucknell, where she was an art major and I was a work-study jock slinging mac and cheese in the dining hall, wearing a hairnet, no less. She could've had her pick, but I made her laugh. Also she loves mac and cheese.

"Dad, listen to this." Allison looked up, her thumbs still flying. She could text without looking at the keyboard, which she called her superpower. "My friends just voted you Hottest Dad."

I smiled. "They're absolutely right. There's a reason I was Homecoming King."

"Dude, no. Never say that again." Allison snorted, texting. "We don't even have that anymore."

Lucinda rolled her eyes. "Allison, who came in second?"

I added, "Yeah, what troll came in second?"

Allison kept texting. "Brianna M's dad."

I scoffed. "Ron McKinney? Please, no contest. I got the bubble butt."

Allison smiled. "Stop it!"

"I bet I can twerk, Al. Show you when we get home."

"Nobody twerks anymore." Allison snorted again, texting away. "OMG, they're saying you look like Kyle Chandler."

"Who's that?"

"The dad from *Friday Night Lights*. We watched it together. You remember. Also the dad in *Bloodline*."

"What's that?"

"A show on Netflix."

"Never saw it."

"Anyway, you look like him, except he's way hotter."

I smiled. "Okay, but can he twerk?"

Allison burst into laughter, and I glanced in the rearview mirror to see her, but the headlights of the pickup truck were too bright. The outline of her head bent over her phone, then I saw the bump of a skinny headband, and the spray of shorter hairs coming from her double ponytail. Those ponytail holders were all over the house, and I fished them from the dog's mouth on a weekly basis.

Ethan kept twisting around. "Dad, if I were driving, I'd speed up."

Allison added, "Seriously."

"Me, too," Lucinda joined in, still on her phone.

"Okay, I'm convinced." I pressed the gas pedal, and the Mercedes responded instantly. We accelerated up the hill, hugging the sharp curve to the left.

Oddly the black pickup truck chose that moment to pass us, a dark and dusty blur roaring by with two men in the cab. It crammed us against the guardrail, and I veered to the right, barely fitting on the street.

Suddenly the pickup pulled in front of us and stopped abruptly, blocking our way.

I slammed on the brakes and we shuddered to a stop, inches from the truck. We lurched forward in our seat belts. Lucinda gasped. Moonie started barking.

"It's okay," I said, instinctively reversing to put distance between us and the truck. I scanned for an escape route, but there wasn't one. I couldn't fit around the truck. I couldn't reverse down the street because of the blind curve.

Two men emerged from the pickup, illuminated by our headlights. The driver was big, with shredded arms covered by tattooed sleeves. His eyes were slits under a prominent forehead and long, dark hair. His passenger wasn't as muscular, but had on a similar dark T-shirt and baggy jeans. The driver said something to him as they approached.

I inhaled to calm myself. If it was road rage, I could defuse the situation. I had a year of law school so I could bullshit with anybody. Otherwise I was six foot three, played middle linebacker in high school, and stayed in decent shape.

Lucinda groaned. "Should I call 911?"

"Not yet."

"Dad?" Allison sounded nervous.

"What do they want?" Ethan stuck his head between the seats, and Moonie barked, the harsh sound reverberating in the car.

"Don't worry. Lucinda, lock the doors."

"Okay, but be careful."

I climbed out of the car and closed the door behind me, hearing the reassuring *thunk* of the locks engage. The men reached me, and I straightened. "Gentlemen, is there a—"

"We're taking the car." The driver pulled a handgun and aimed it at my face. "Get everybody out."

"Okay, fine. Relax. Don't hurt anybody. This is my family." I turned to the car and spotted Lucinda's phone glowing through the windshield. She must have been calling 911. The carjackers saw her at the same time.

"Drop it!" The passenger pulled a gun and aimed it at her.

"No, don't shoot!" I moved in the way, raising my arms. "Honey, everybody, out of the car!"

Lucinda lowered the phone, the screen dropping in a blur of light.

Allison emerged from the back seat, her eyes wide. "Dad, they have *guns*."

"It's okay, honey. Come here." I put a hand on her shoulder and maneuvered her behind me. Lucinda was coming around the back of the car with Ethan, who held a barking Moonie, dragging his leash. They reached me, and I faced the men.

"Okay, take the car," I told them, my chest tight.

"Wait." The passenger eyed Allison, and a leering smile spread across his face. "What's your name, sweetheart?"

*No.* My mouth went dry. "Take the car and go."

Suddenly Moonie leapt from Ethan's arms and launched himself at the men. They jumped back, off-balance. The driver fired an earsplitting blast, just missing Moonie.

My ears rang. I whirled around.

Allison had been struck. Blood spurted from her neck in a gruesome fan. She was reeling.

*No!* I rushed to her just as she collapsed in my arms. I eased her down to the street. Her mouth gaped open. Her throat emitted gulping sounds. Blood poured from her neck. My hand flew there to stop the flow. The blood felt hideously wet and warm.

Allison's lips were moving. She was trying to talk, to breathe.

"Honey, you've been hit," I told her. "Stay calm." I tore off my shirt, breaking the buttons. I bunched it up and pressed it against her neck. I couldn't see the wound. It scared me to death. "Lucinda, call 911."

"My phone's in the car!" Lucinda grabbed Allison's hand, beginning to sob.

Suddenly the gun fired again behind us, another earsplitting blast.

We crouched in terror. Lucinda screamed. I didn't know who had been shot. I looked around wildly, shocked to find that one carjacker had shot the other. The driver stood over the passenger, who lay motionless on the street, blood pooling under his head. The driver dropped the gun and ran to the pickup. I spotted his license plate before he sped off. A sudden brightness told me another car was coming up Coldstream.

"Dad, there's Allison's phone!" Ethan thrust it at me. My bloody fingers smeared the screen, which came to life with a photo of Moonie in sunglasses.

I thumbed to the phone function and pressed 911. The call connected. I held the phone to my ear to hear over the dog's barking.

The 911 dispatcher asked, "What is your emergency?"

"My daughter's been shot in the neck. Two men tried to carjack us on Coldstream Road near the turnpike overpass." I struggled to think through my fear. Allison was making gulping sounds. She was losing blood fast, drenching my shirt. My hands were slick with my daughter's lifeblood, slipping warm through my fingers.

"Sir, is she awake and responsive?"

"Yes, send an ambulance! Hurry!"

"Apply direct pressure to the wound. Use a compress—"

"I am, please send—"

"An ambulance is on the way."

"Please! *Hurry!*"

Allison's eyelids fluttered. She coughed. Pinkish bubbles frothed at the corners of her mouth. "Daddy?"

My heart lurched. She hadn't called me that since she was little.

I told her what I wanted to believe: "You're going to be okay."

## CHAPTER TWO

The waiting room of the emergency department was harshly bright, and the mint-green walls were lined with idealized landscapes of foxhunts. Green-padded chairs had been arranged in two rectangles, forming rooms without walls. The front section held a handful of people, but we had the back to ourselves. Wrinkled magazines lay on end tables, ignored in favor of phones. There was a kids' playroom behind a plexiglass wall next to vending machines.

I had been in this waiting room so many times over the years, for so many reasons. Allison's broken arm. Ethan's random falls. Once, a moth flew into Lucinda's ear. Every parent knows the local emergency room, but not like this. Never before had I seen anyone look like us, right now.

The three of us huddled together, shocked and stricken. Allison had been taken to surgery. My undershirt was stiffening with drying blood, and Lucinda had spatters on her Lady Patriots sweatshirt and bloody patches on her jeans. She had stopped crying and rested her head on my right shoulder. Ethan's T-shirt was flecked with blood, though the fabric was black and it didn't show except for the white *N* in Nike. He slumped on my left, and I had an arm around each of them.

"She'll be okay, right?" Lucinda asked, hushed.

"Yes," I answered, but I was scared out of my mind. "How was she in the ambulance?"

"Okay. She didn't panic. You know her."

"Yes." I nodded. Allison had a high pain threshold. At lacrosse camp, she broke her arm in the morning and didn't tell her coach until lunch.

"The EMT was in the back, I had to sit in the front. He was nice. He talked to her. He called in her vital signs."

"How were they?"

"Her blood pressure was low." Lucinda started wringing her hands. I remembered her doing that when her sister Caitlin was dying of breast cancer, five years ago. I hugged her closer.

An older couple shuffled in together and took a seat in our section, glancing around. The husband had a walker with new tennis balls on the bottom, and he walked ahead with concentration. His wife noticed us, then plastered her gaze to the TV, showing the news on closed-captioning.

Lucinda wiped her nose with a balled-up Kleenex. "Jason, do you know what she said to me in the ambulance? She told me not to worry."

Tears stung my eyes. "What a kid."

"I know." Lucinda sniffled. "I wonder how long the surgery will be."

"They have to repair the vein. I think it was a vein, not an artery."

"How do you know?"

"If it were an artery, like the carotid, the blood would have pulsed out." I hoped I was right. Any medical information I had was from malpractice depositions, of which I'd done hundreds. I was a court reporter, which made me a font of information about completely random subjects. It wasn't always a good thing.

"We were supposed to look for a homecoming dress tomorrow. She found one she liked at the mall. She saw it with Courtney."

I remembered. Allison had shown me a picture on her phone. The dress was nice, white with skinny straps. She would have looked great in it. She had the wiry, lean build of an athlete. She worried it would make her butt look flat.

*Allison, your butt isn't flat.*

*Dad, you don't know. You just love me.*

I had so many nicknames for her. Al, Alsford, The Duchess of Alfordshire, and The Alimentary Canal because she ate like a horse. She called me Dad or Dude. I was an *involved* father, according to my wife. I was *present in my children's lives.* I sold raffle tickets and bought gigantic candy bars that I gave out at work. I taught both kids to pitch and saw that Allison was the better athlete.

Lucinda sniffled again. "I assume they'll keep her a few days, don't you?"

"Yes."

"I suppose I could pick it up for her."

"Pick what up?"

Ethan looked over, his eyes glistening. "The dress, Dad."

"Right." I was too upset to think, it just didn't show. I couldn't follow the conversation. My wife talked more when she was upset, but I talked less. I was lost in my own thoughts. I was *lost.*

Lucinda wiped her nose. "I hope she can still go to homecoming. She's so excited. I think she really likes Troy."

"I know." Troy was Allison's boyfriend of two months, already lasting longer than her last boyfriend. I liked Troy because he was as smart as she was, a true scholar athlete. He was on the quiet side, but I learned from having Ethan that there's more to introverts than meets the eye. My son had a circle of friends, but needed time to himself.

"I got her a hair appointment the same day as the dance. They all want to get in the morning of, but they don't want to miss the game. It was impossible, but I got her in." Lucinda's voice carried an unmistakable note of mom pride.

"Way to go."

"She wants beachy waves."

*Beachy waves.* I'd been hearing that a lot. I knew it was a thing. Allison had beautiful hair, but she thought it didn't have enough volume.

*Dad, I hate my hair, it's so flat.*

*Like your butt?*

Lucinda was saying, "Do you think they'll tell us something soon?"

"Yes, as soon as they can. They know what they're doing."

"Right, they do. It's a good hospital."

"It is." I squeezed her hand. We had often discussed the relative merits of Paoli Hospital, routinely rated among the top in the Philadelphia area. Lucinda had researched the hospitals before we moved here, and she became an expert on them and schools, comparing what the districts spent on instructional costs versus the state and national medians. My wife did the homework; we had that in common. Her mother had been the same way and her father had been a CEO of PennValue, a big insurance brokerage in Allentown. My father used to say she *came from money*, as if it were an actual place. Moneytown.

"Dad, do you think Moonie's okay?" Ethan looked over, his eyes pained. They were blue, a shade lighter than Allison's. I was the only brown-eyed one in the family. Well, me and Moonie.

"Yes," I told him. We had left the dog in the police cruiser, since the Mercedes was being impounded by the police.

"Don't be mad at him." Ethan hung his head, showing a gelled whorl of light brown hair, combed from a low side part. I supposed the style started with Justin Bieber, but Lucinda and I both hoped it would end soon.

"I'm not. Why would I be?"

"I thought you would say it was his fault, but it wasn't."

"No, it wasn't." I managed a smile to reassure him, but Ethan didn't smile back. His face was rounder than Allison's, his eyes were narrower set and his build skinnier. I tended to define him in relationship to his sister, which I knew wasn't a good thing, but as an only child, I found their differences fascinating. His skin tone was lighter, too. He had a sprinkling of small freckles on his upturned nose, since he got my thin Irish skin.

Ethan's face fell. "It was my fault."

Lucinda reached for his hand. "Ethan, no, it wasn't. Why would you say such a thing?"

"I should've held him tighter. If I had, Allison would be fine. I shouldn't have let him jump out."

Lucinda's gaze met mine, her expression agonized. We both knew our son could not bear this burden. He was the more sensitive of the two, carrying his hurts around like a backpack. Meanwhile he began looking down at his hands, where blood had dried within the lines in his palm.

"Ethan, listen." I squeezed his shoulder. "It's not your fault."

"Why not?" Ethan's troubled gaze lifted to me, and his lip caught on his braces, like it did when his mouth went dry. I knew he wanted an answer, since he was the kind of kid who needed to be reasoned with, not just told.

*Because I said so*, my father would have said, but that didn't work with my son.

"Ethan, you're saying Allison would be fine, but for your letting go of Moonie, right? But that's bad reasoning. Your letting go of Moonie is just the but-for cause." I was dredging up first-year torts class, from before I dropped out. "There's a bunch of other but-fors, and none of them is the real cause."

"What do you mean?"

"Well, think about it. How about, 'Allison would be fine, *but for* the fact that we won the game'? Or 'Allison would be fine, *but for* the fact we stayed late to celebrate'? Or 'Allison would be fine, *but for* the fact we have a new Mercedes'?" I spotted Lucinda wince, so I moved on. "But-for is the same trap as what-if. You drive yourself crazy with possibilities. There's only one cause, and it's the carjackers. *They* did it. It's *their* fault."

"But Moonie—"

"Not Moonie, not you. *Them*." My face went hot. I suddenly felt like I was raging inside, my emotions all over the lot. "The two of them, they're scum. Violent, stupid, evil men. They aren't worth one hair on your sister's head. They're the ones at fault, and I want them to *rot* in jail. I want them to suffer every damn day of their miserable lives and—"

"The one's already dead, Dad."

Lucinda's eyes flared. "Honey, we were talking about Ethan."

"I *am* talking about Ethan. I don't want Ethan to blame himself for what that *scum* did to Allison."

Ethan looked down. "I get it, Dad."

Lucinda looked shaky. "Your dad's just upset, is all."

I turned away, trying to calm down. I wished I knew how Allison was doing in surgery. I loved that child to the marrow. She was everything I could've asked for in a daughter. Strong, smart, funny, bold. More blunt than tactful. More sensitive than she looked. My father always said she was like a draft horse, that way. Big and strong, but not always rough and tumble. Growing up, we had a great brown draft, named Chocolate Soldier.

*He's a gentle giant, that one. Don't use the shank on him.*

Allison worried more than she should have, about everything. Hair, body,

GPA, extracurriculars, PSAT practice courses, and blackheads *in the T-zone*, whatever that was. She looked like Lucinda, but her blue eyes were narrower, and she had a long, straight nose and a big smile, now that her braces were off. She had brown hair that she wanted to highlight *and* lowlight. To her, nothing was as good as it should have been. I never understood. I wouldn't have changed a thing about her. *Good enough for government work*, my father said all the time.

I shifted in the chair. My mouth had gone dry. It was impossible that Allison was lying on an operating table, down the hall behind double doors. Every instinct told me to be at her side. Then I remembered I had been at her side on Coldstream Road. She had bled in the street with me right there.

The thought made me furious, and inside I boiled over with rage at the carjackers, at the world, and most of all, at myself.

*Daddy?*

I spotted two men in suits entering the waiting room, looking around in an official way. They had to be the county detectives, who were supposed to meet us here.

I jumped to my feet.

*Photograph of the author © Laura Leonard*

**Lisa Scottoline** is the *New York Times* bestselling and Edgar Award winning author of thirty-two novels. She has thirty million copies of her books in print in the United States and has been published in thirty-five countries. Scottoline also writes a weekly column with her daughter, Francesca Serritella, for *The Philadelphia Inquirer*, and those critically acclaimed stories have been adapted into a series of memoirs. She lives in the Philadelphia area.

Visit Lisa Scottoline Online
🐦 LisaScottoline